FALLING OUT

I0719632

LUCINDA BRANT BOOKS

— Falling Series —
FALLING IN
FALLING UP
FALLING OUT

— Roxton Foundation Series —
NOBLE SATYR
HIS DUCHESS
HER DUKE
THEIR GRACES

— Roxton Family Saga —
NOBLE SATYR
MIDNIGHT MARRIAGE
AUTUMN DUCHESS
DAIR DEVIL
PROUD MARY
SATYR'S SON
ETERNALLY YOURS
FOREVER REMAIN

— Alec Halsey Mysteries —
DEADLY ENGAGEMENT
DEADLY AFFAIR
DEADLY PERIL
DEADLY KIN
DEADLY DESIRE

— Salt Hendon Books —
SALT BRIDE
SALT REDUX

'Quizzing glass and quill, into my sedan chair and away —— the 1700s rock!'

A *New York Times*, *USA Today*, *Amazon*, and *Audible* bestselling author of award-winning Georgian historical romances and mysteries, Lucinda's books are renowned for their wit, heart-felt drama and a happily ever-after. She has degrees in history and political science from the Australian National University and a postgraduate degree in education from Bond University, where she was awarded the Frank Surman Medal. *Noble Satyr*, Lucinda's first novel, was awarded the $10,000 *Random House/Woman's Day* Romantic Fiction Prize, and she has twice been a finalist for the Romance Writers' of Australia Romantic Book of the Year. Her novels have garnered multiple awards and become worldwide genre best-sellers. Lucinda lives a stone's throw from the beach, in a writing hut with wall-to-wall books on all aspects of the Eighteenth Century, collected over 40 years—Heaven. She loves to hear from readers (and she'll write back!).

lucindabrant@gmail.com | lucindabrant.com
pinterest.com/lucindabrant | x.com/lucindabrant
facebook.com/lucindabrantbooks | youtube.com/lucindabrantauthor

FALLING OUT

An Enchanting Georgian Fairytale Romance...
of sorts...
Regarding Masquerades and Misunderstandings

Lucinda Brant

A Sprigleaf Book
Published by Sprigleaf Pty. Ltd.

This is a work of fiction; names, characters, places, and incidents
are the product of the author's imagination or are used fictitiously.
Resemblance to persons, businesses, companies, events,
or locales, past or present, is entirely coincidental.

*Falling OUT: An Enchanting Georgian Fairytale Romance...of sorts...
Regarding Masquerades and Misunderstandings.*

A YA retelling of *Midnight Marriage: A Georgian Historical Romance,*
available as Book 1 in the Roxton Family Saga.
*Back cover reviews are for the *Midnight Marriage* edition of this book.

Copyright © 2025 Lucinda Brant, all rights reserved.
Editing: Cathie Maud Cabot.
Art & design: Sprigleaf.
Deb's Viola fleuron design by Sprigleaf.

Georgian couple silhouette is a trademark belonging to Lucinda Brant.
Sprigleaf triple-leaf design is a trademark belonging to Sprigleaf Pty. Ltd.

Except for brief quotations embodied in articles and reviews,
no part of this book may be reproduced in any printed or
electronic form without prior permission from the publisher.

Typeset in EB Garamond.

ISBN 978-1-922985-33-0

10 9 8 7 6 5 4 3 2 1
Perfect Bound Paperback Edition. (i) I.

*For my nephews and nieces
Aarin, Amy, James, Matthew & Sarah*

PART I

THE ENGLAND OF GEORGE III

PROLOGUE

GLOUCESTERSHIRE, 1761

Deborah woke from a deep sleep to the sounds of a hasty late-night arrival in the cobbled courtyard below her bedchamber window. Commands were barked out at drowsy-eyed stable boys, and carriage wheels spun and slid to an abrupt halt.

At first she thought it all part of her dream, but the clip-clop of horses' hooves on uneven stone did not seem possible in the cool of a forest clearing. Her brother Otto was making beautiful music with his viola while she swung higher and higher on the rope swing, her silk petticoats billowing out between her long stockinged legs. She was sure if she swung higher her toes would touch the clouds. They both laughed and sang, and it was such a lovely sunny day. Then the sun went behind a cloud and Otto disappeared and she fell off the swing at its highest point.

Someone was shaking her awake.

Fervent whispering opened her eyes, and she blinked into the light of one taper held up by her nurse.

Before Deborah had time to fully wake, Nurse pulled back the warm coverlet and threw a dressing gown over her thin shoulders. Then with shaking hands the woman guided a tumbler to her lips, telling her to drink up. Deborah did as she was told. She grimaced. The medicine was the same foul-tasting brew she was given just before bedtime. It had put her into a deep, deep sleep. So why was she being woken if she was meant to fall asleep again?

Nurse evaded the question. She straightened the girl's lace-edged night cap, brought forward over one shoulder the long thick braid of dark red hair, needlessly straightening the white bow—all the while muttering for Miss Deb to be a good girl and do as she was told, and her prayers would be answered.

Drowsy and barefoot, Deborah was abandoned by her nurse at the door to Sir Gerald's book room. The passageway was dark and cold, and the book room was no better. At the farthest end of this masculine sanctuary blazed a fire in the grate, but it did not beckon her with the prospect of warmth and comfort. She went forward when ordered by her brother, Sir Gerald, a glance at the two strangers taking refreshment. They were divested of their greatcoats but the tall gentleman with the white hair and strong aquiline nose still wore his sword, the ornate hilt visible under the skirts of his rich black velvet frock coat with silver lacings.

Deborah could not help staring at this imperious ancient stranger, whose close-shaven cheeks were etched with the lines of time. His hair and eyebrows were as white as the soft lace ruffles which fell over his thin white hands. She had never seen an emerald as large as the one on the gold ring he wore on his left hand. She imagined he must be a hundred years old.

When he turned bright dark eyes upon her and beckoned her closer with the crook of one long finger, Deborah hesitated, swaying slightly. A sharp word from her brother moved her feet, and through a mental fog that threatened to overwhelm her, she remembered her manners at last and lowered her gaze to the floor. When she came to stand before this imperious stranger she shivered, not from fear because she did not know what or whom to fear, but from the cold night breeze coming in through the open window. She made a wobbly curtsy and placidly waited to be spoken to first, gaze obediently remaining on the Turkey rug.

The stranger's voice was surprisingly deep and strong for one so old.

"What is your age, child?"

"I turned twelve six days ago, sir."

The stranger frowned. He said something in French over his shoulder to his gray-haired companion. This gentleman answered the ancient stranger in kind, who nodded and addressed Sir Gerald in his own tongue.

"She is far too young."

"But—Your Grace, she is of age! The bishop raised no objection," Sir Gerald assured him with an eager, nervous smile. "Twelve is the age of consent for a female."

"That is true, Monseigneur," agreed the gray-haired companion. "But it is for Your Grace to decide... I do not know of an alternative."

"Surely Your Grace has not changed his mind?" whined Sir Gerald. "Bishop Ramsay was not pleased to be summoned here, and if the ceremony is not to go ahead..."

"Your sister is not fifteen as you led me to believe, Cavendish," enunciated the ancient stranger in an arctic voice.

Sir Gerald gave a snort that ended in a nervous laugh. "Your Grace! Twelve or fifteen—three years hardly matters."

Deborah glanced up in time to witness the look of disgust which crossed the lined face of the ancient gentleman, and she wondered what he found to fault in her. She knew she was only passably pretty. Sir Gerald despaired of her plain brown looks, but she was not disfigured, and her features were unremarkable. She was considered tall for her age but not so awkwardly big-boned that this stranger had the right to pull a face at her in her own home.

Why did her brother wear such a silly smile on his round fleshy face and stare expectantly at the arrogant ancient man as if his whole dependence rested on his will? He was acting as one of his own lackeys did before him. She had never seen her brother bow and scrape to anyone. It was strange indeed.

Deborah felt the black eyes regarding her from under heavy lids and she forced herself to look the ancient gentleman in the face without blinking. But she could not stop herself blushing when his gaze dropped to her stockinged feet and traveled slowly up the length of her nightgown to the brushed tip of her braid of dark red hair at her thigh, then up over her chest to rest on the lopsided bow tied under her chin that kept her nightcap in place. He then looked into her brown eyes again. She met his gaze openly through eyes that felt filled with oil, and thus she could not see clearly, because the medicine she had drunk was beginning to take effect. A small crooked smile played on the ancient gentleman's thin lips and Deborah wished she had the courage to tell him his manners were lacking in one so old. His question to her brother blanched her cheeks.

"Has she commenced menstruating?"

Sir Gerald was dumbstruck. "Your—Your Grace?"

"You heard the question well enough, Cavendish," prompted the gray-haired companion of the ancient one.

But even though Sir Gerald's mouth worked he could not speak.

Deborah, feeling as if her head were full of cotton wool, sluggishly answered for him. "Two—two months ago."

All three men turned and looked down at her then, as if finally acknowledging her mental as well as physical existence.

Sir Gerald frowned, but the ancient stranger and his friend smiled, the ancient one politely inclining his white head to her in thanks for her response. He seemed about to address her directly when a commotion in the passageway distracted them all. The gray-haired companion disappeared into the shadows and out of the room. He was gone for several minutes and in the interval, no one spoke. Sir Gerald brooded, once or twice looking at his sister with mute disapproval, while the ancient stranger calmly waited by the open window and fastidiously took snuff from a gold and enamel snuffbox.

Into the book room came a gentleman dressed in a cleric's robes, but these were no ordinary robes—they were edged in ermine and were of velvet and gold thread. He carried an ornately decorated Bible and wore a magnificent old-fashioned powdered wig with three curls above each fleshy ear. Deborah knew this to be Bishop Ramsay. He had arrived at the house earlier that day and set the servants on their ears with his imperious demands. Nurse said Cook was at her wits' end. The bishop took one look at Deborah in her nightclothes and put up his bushy brows. He ignored his host in favor of the ancient stranger over whose outstretched hand he bowed deeply. Deborah thought it odd that a bishop should bend to this old gentleman. He must be someone very illustrious indeed. Just then the little gray-haired man came out of the shadows looking worried.

"They've dragged him out of the carriage, Your Grace," he announced then hesitated.

"And—Martin?" asked the ancient gentleman with uncanny perceptibility.

"He's downed another bottle..." Martin apologized.

"Then he will endure the ceremony better than the rest of us," came the flat reply.

"The marriage is to go ahead as planned?" Sir Gerald asked eagerly.

The ancient stranger did not look at him. "I have no choice..."

He said this in such a weary tone that even Deborah, for all her youth and inexperience, heard the deep sadness in the mellow voice. She wondered what troubled him.

That these men were talking about a marriage ceremony barely registered with her. After all, no one had spoken to her of marriage. Everyone knew that when a girl was of marriageable age she left the schoolroom to be launched in society during the Season. She attended plenty of balls and routs and met many eligible gentlemen. She would fall in love with one of them and, hopefully, he would be the one who asked her brother for her hand in the usual manner.

Marriages did not happen in the dead of night between strangers. And they certainly did not happen in nightgowns after taking a measured dose of laudanum. There were formalities and mysterious things called settlements and a proper order to such a momentous step in a girl's life.

But Deborah was wrong and knew she was terribly wrong when her brother led her to the bishop, who called her a little sparrow of a bride and pinched her chin in a fatherly way. He said a great honor had been bestowed upon her and her family to be chosen as the wife of the Duke of Roxton's heir.

Her first thought was that she was asleep. The medicine Nurse had woken her to take had changed her beautiful dream with Otto in the forest to this nightmare, in which she appeared to be the central character of a Shakespearean tragedy. Perhaps if she tried hard enough to think about waking, it would happen, and Nurse would be there with a glass of milk and soothing words.

She closed her eyes, swaying and dry in the mouth. But she did not wake up from the nightmare. She was so bewildered she could not speak nor could she move. Panic welled up within her. She wished with all her heart Otto would come home and save her. She wanted to cry. There were hot tears behind her eyelids but for some reason she was incapable of crying. So why was she sobbing? She soon realized it was not her. The quiet sobbing came from the doorway and distracted her enough that she momentarily forgot this was her nightmare.

A tall, well-built youth with a head of thick black curls that fell into his eyes was being supported at each elbow by burly servants in livery. He was not so drunk that he could not walk, and so he told his captors in a growl. But the more he struggled to be free of them, kicking out his stockinged legs and balling his fists, the harder the grip on his elbows, and he soon gave up the fight to return to weeping into his chest.

An awkward silence followed as the boy was brought to stand beside Deborah. A languid movement of dismissal from the ancient gentleman and the burly servants retreated into the shadows.

Deborah stole a blinking glance at the weeping boy, but he had turned away from her to face the ancient gentleman. He addressed him in French, his voice breaking into sobs between sentences. He spoke faster than she could ever hope to understand, but he used the words *mon père*—Father, over and over. Deb could not believe this white-haired old man could possibly be this boy's father. Surely, he meant *grand-père*? And as she continued to stare at father and son, the boy suddenly broke into English. His words were so full of bitterness Deborah's face was not the only one to brighten with intense embarrassment.

"It's *all* your fault! *Your* fault," the boy growled at the ancient gentleman, fists clenching and unclenching with rage. "Why should *I* be banished for *your* sins? Does my presence make you uncomfortable, *Monseigneur*, now I know the sordid truth? Poor Maman. To think she's had to live with your—your *disgusting* secrets all these years—"

"Alston! That will do," cut in the gray-haired companion. "You're drunk. In the morning you will regret—"

The boy tore his tearful gaze from his father to stare at the man at his side.

"*Regret*? Regret knowing the truth about *him*? *Never!*" he spat out, lip trembling uncontrollably. "You've known all along, haven't you, Martin? Why didn't you tell *me*? I'm his *heir*. I have a right to know. A-a *right*." He began to sob again and dashed a silken sleeve across his wet face. "*Mon Dieu*, I'm cursed. *Cursed.*"

"It's all in your head, my son," the ancient gentleman said quietly.

This made the youth give a bark of hysterical laughter.

"In my head? Then it's a-a *lie*? It's a lie His Grace the most noble Duke of Roxton—*my father*—has littered the land with ill-gotten *bastards*—"

The slap across his face knocked the boy off his feet and left the Duke nursing a smarting hand.

Deborah watched the Duke turn his back and walk into the shadows, while at her feet the boy picked himself up to his silken knees, a hand to his stinging cheek. The gray-haired gentleman known as Martin put an arm about the boy's shaking shoulders, and with a glance at Deborah said in a soothing voice,

"If you ever want to see your mother again, marry this girl. Then we can be on our way to France."

The youth gripped Martin's arm convulsively, his tear-stained face close to his. "If I do as he wants, may I see Maman before we sail? May I, Martin? *Please*. I must see her before we go. I *must*. *Please*."

Martin shook his head sadly. "The early birth of your baby brother has left her very weak, my boy. She needs time to recover. The rest is up to God."

The youth broke into fresh sobs. "He'll never let me see her again! I know it, Martin. *Never*."

Deborah's brown eyes widened, and she held her breath, awaiting the gray-haired man's response. When he looked over the youth's bowed head and smiled at her kindly, she felt a great relief. Though why she should be anything but panicked at the prospect that lay before her she could not explain. Perhaps it was because she did not believe any of this was real. It was a laudanum-induced dream and soon she would wake up. If only she could shake her head free of cotton wool.

"After the ceremony, I am taking my godson to France and then on to Rome and Greece," Martin told her in a confiding tone, adding for good measure, as if living up to the promise in his smile, "We will be away for many years. Do you understand, *ma chérie*?"

Deborah nodded. There was something oddly reassuring in the gray-haired man's smile, as if he would protect her from this strange, sad boy and the consequences of this hasty midnight marriage. France was over the water. And Greece and Rome were so far away that it took months and months of traveling to reach such exotic countries. Otto had told her so. Suddenly she felt safe. This boy was going away for many years. She would never see him again after tonight. The sooner the bishop performed the ceremony, the sooner this bad dream would end. All she had to do was lie still and wait for Nurse to wake her with the breakfast tray.

Martin's words of reassurance had an effect on the boy, too, for he pulled out of the man's embrace and dashed the hair from his eyes.

The bishop quickly came to stand before these two children, his Bible open, and proceedings began in a rush. It was as if there were no assurance the boy's capitulation would last long enough for the exchange of vows, or that the girl, who swayed on her feet and had a gaze that seemed incapable of blinking, would be able to stand upright for very much longer. The bishop's fears seemed justified when all of a sudden the boy began to chuckle under his breath, disconcerting the bishop enough for him to pause on two occasions.

Deborah blinked uncomprehendingly at the boy to see what he found so amusing. Finally, the boy had to share his amusement with his ancient parent who stood behind him like a sentry made of marble.

"*Monseigneur*? Is this plain, awkward *bird-witted* creature the best you could find to marry your heir?" he threw over his shoulder in arrogant bitterness. "Surely my lineage begs better?"

"Her pedigree is as good as yours, my son."

The youth sniggered. "What an illustrious union to be sure! Something of which you all must be very proud. *Pshaw*."

He snatched up Deborah's hand when requested by the bishop, and obediently repeated the words that would make them husband and wife.

Deborah, too, repeated the words after the bishop, but she said them without comprehending. She had no idea what this boy's Christian names were, despite there being a string of them, because she could not take her eyes from his face. Her nightmare had unexpectedly turned into a wondrous dream. Her youthful husband was the handsomest boy she had ever seen. His eyes held her mesmerized. They were green, but not just any green. They were a deep emerald green. They were the same color as the large square-cut emerald on the thin white hand of the ancient stranger Deborah was convinced had to be a hundred years old.

ONE

THE SPA TOWN OF BATH AND ITS ENVIRONS
NINE YEARS LATER...

JULIAN HESHAM thought he had died and gone to Heaven. But angels did not punctuate their harp playing with "*damns*" and "*blasts*". He supposed the music in Heaven to be a gentle plucking of the strings, the melody more *largo* than *allegro*. He was not musically inclined, but the cacophony that assaulted his ears was a frenzied piece of playing, irritating to the nerves. If he was to slowly bleed to death, much better to do so in the peace and quiet of a spring morning, with only the attendant sounds of an awakening forest.

He wished the musician a hundred miles away.

That the fiddler might prove his salvation did not cross his mind.

He was slumped under a birch tree. To the casual observer, he had the appearance of a gentleman sleeping off an evening of heavy drinking: Long muscular legs sprawled out before him, boots muddy, neckcloth and silk embroidered waistcoat disorderly. His square chin rested on his chest, and a lock of black hair, having escaped its ribbon, fell forward into his eyes. His right arm was limp in the leaf litter, beside his discarded rapier. His left hand was shoved inside his flowered waistcoat, and pressed a folded handkerchief to a place just under his ribs where a thrust from his opponent's blade had sliced the muscle.

Suddenly the music stopped. The wood was again at peace.

Julian sighed his relief.

In the silence there was the unmistakable click of a pistol being cocked, and this slowly brought his chin up. Standing only a few feet away, at the edge of the clearing, was a youth in a blue velvet riding frock, not holding a pistol but a viola. Julian guessed he was about eight years of age—the same age as his much younger brother.

When the boy-musician wedged the viola under his chin and set bow to strings again, Julian grimaced and shook his head, bringing the recital to a halt before it began. He was not about to be a willing audience to more screeching, however curious he was to know the musician's next move.

"I'm certain you'll be very good on the night, but couldn't you rehearse elsewhere?" he asked conversationally. When the boy-musician spun about on a heel, almost dropping his bow, he added, "At your feet." And smiled weakly when the boy took an involuntary step backward. "Do me the favor of fetching my frock coat. It's behind you... There's a flask... right-hand pocket..."

The boy-musician removed the viola from under his chin.

"What do you want with a flask? You look as if you're drunk already."

"What deplorable manners you have," Julian complained, adding when the boy-musician continued to hesitate, "I mean you no harm. Even if I were a footpad, I'm too knocked about to attempt to do you a mischief."

This speech was an effort and Julian's breathing became labored.

The boy-musician watched a spasm of pain cross the handsome features and wondered what he should do. The man's face was too pale, the strong mouth too blue, and the breathing now short and quick. It was then that the boy-musician saw the dark spreading stain seeping out from under the soiled waistcoat.

"Good God! He's injured!"

The exclamation did not belong to the boy-musician, forcing Julian, through a supreme effort of will, to look up. A pair of damp brown eyes framed by long dark lashes regarded him with concern, and then a cool feminine hand touched his forehead and stayed there.

Julian grinned and promptly fainted.

"Fool!" muttered the young woman—she of the damp brown eyes. She laid aside her pistol and hurriedly unscrewed the lid of a monogrammed silver flask handed to her by the boy-musician. She glanced up at her nephew. "Jack. Take Bannock and fetch Dr. Medlow. Tell him a man's been injured. Don't mention it's a sword wound."

The boy-musician hesitated.

"Will you be all right left alone with him, Aunt Deb?"

She smiled reassuringly.

"Yes, I'll be fine, Jack. I have my pistol, remember?"

She watched her nephew scurry off to find their horse, before turning her attention once more to the injured duelist. Gently, she tilted his head and slowly dribbled the contents of the silver flask between his cold, parched lips.

"It won't be my fault if you die," she admonished him as one does a naughty child. "But it would serve you to rights for being foolish enough to fight a duel!"

"No. It won't be your fault," the injured duelist murmured

at last. "Thank you. Another sip, if you please." He let his head fall back into the circle of her arm and looked up into a flushed face framed by an overabundance of dark red hair. "Does he always play his fiddle punctuated with oaths? It adds color but it would offend Herr Bach."

"It's not a fiddle, it's a viola. And not Bach but Herr Telemann. The oaths were mine, not Jack's."

"And the—er—pistol?"

"Mine," Deb admitted truthfully, and promptly changed the subject. "What did you think of the composition we were rehearsing?"

"I didn't like it at all."

She laughed good-naturedly, showing lovely pearly-white teeth.

"Perhaps in another setting, after a few more days of practice, and..." He paused, distracted by the faint feminine scent at her throat. "That's very pleasant," he announced with surprise. "As a rule, females wear far too much scent. Is it lavender or something else? Rosewater, perhaps?"

"You're a lunatic!" When he chuckled, she added, "How can you talk pleasantries while you're bleeding all over me?" Gently setting him upright against the tree trunk, she then brushed down her petticoats as she got to her feet. "Don't laugh. It will only make your suffering worse. If I don't do something to staunch the bleeding you'll die, and I've enough to worry me without a corpse adding to my difficulties."

"My dear girl, don't put yourself to any trouble. I'm sure I'll last until the physician arrives."

Deb wasn't listening. She was thinking. The last thing she wanted was for this gentleman to die on her. Besides, she would be in enough trouble explaining away to her stiff-necked brother what she and Jack were doing in the Avon forest, alone and with their violas. Sir Gerald loathed their music-making nearly as much as he loathed Jack's very existence. What could she use to make bandages? She groaned. She supposed she'd have to sacrifice her shirt (it was one of Otto's and quite worn thin anyway). To cover her nakedness, she'd borrow the gentleman's frock coat.

"I'll have to use his cravat, too," she muttered aloud as she unbuttoned the mannish shirt at her throat and promptly pulled it up over her head. She scooped up the gentleman's discarded frock coat and disappeared behind a tree.

"H-how old did you say you were?" he asked conversationally, an appreciative audience to her undressing, disappointed he was only permitted a view of her narrow back in the thin cotton chemise.

"I didn't. You may detest my viola playing," she called out, "but I am considered good in a crisis."

"What are you doing back there? Please don't go to any trouble..."

"I assure you; I won't do more than is necessary until Dr. Medlow arrives."

Deb stepped out from behind the tree, the frock coat buttoned up but hanging loose about her shoulders and arms and with the narrow lapels turned up and tickling her ears. She knelt beside Julian and went to work ripping up her shirt to make bandages.

"I'm going to have to remove your waistcoat and shirt," she said, addressing the torn strips of fabric. "I'll do my best to be gentle."

"I'm sure you shall," came the murmured reply.

He submitted with good grace to having his silk cravat pulled this way and that, the diamond pin extracted with care and put aside, but it took great presence of mind for him to sit up, straighten his leg and remove the hand that was pressed to the wound. At the latter he fainted with the pain but made a swift recovery, gaze riveted to the girl's face—on the expressive brown eyes, the straight indifferent nose and the full bottom lip that quivered ever so slightly. Several curls had escaped from their pins and fell across her flushed cheek. Were they a dark strawberry-blonde or a more autumnal red? He was certain he had never seen such rich red hair before, or such shine. He would have remembered such a particular color. The question consumed all his thoughts as he was stripped out of a richly embroidered waistcoat to reveal a shirt wet and heavy with his blood.

Removing the shirt presented a problem for Deb. She knew her patient did not have the strength to raise his arms above his shoulders to slip the shirt over his head, so it would have to be torn from his back. Yet that was no easy thing. The cloth about the wound was wet with blood and had adhered to the slit like glued paper to a wall. But Deb did not dwell on the pain she was about to inflict. It only had to be endured for the briefest of moments.

Decided, she took hold of the opened shirtfront and ripped it left and right off the broad shoulders. It took three tugs to rend the fine fabric. The third tore the cloth to his waist, exposing a wide expanse of chest. For an instant her eyes registered surprise. The silk cravat, the richness of the exquisite fabric of waistcoat and frock coat, and his patrician features, all concealed the measure of the man's muscle. It gave her hope for a full recovery. Such a well-exercised physique would stand him in good stead, but only if the bleeding could be staunched, and at once.

When she carefully peeled away the sodden shirt from the wound, exposing a deep gash under the rib cage, the gentleman expelled a great guttural oath from deep within his throat, and his whole being convulsed with an unbearable pain.

"I don't think he meant to kill you," she commented, examining the wound. "Or your opponent has no notion of anatomy. The slice is deep, but if he'd wanted to kill you, he'd have pinked you on the left..."

Without warning, she pressed a wad of folded cloth over the wound, and so firmly that to Julian it was as if her whole fist had been thrust through the wound to mingle with his entrails and meet up with his spine. Disorientated with pain, he fought to remain conscious. His limp hand was placed over the dressing. He was told in a strident voice to keep it there with a firm pressure until the makeshift bandage was securely about his chest to hold the padding in place.

It was no easy task to bind up the wound.

Deb managed to slip the bandage once around her patient's middle but having achieved this much, his eyelids fluttered, and he promptly fainted. Quickly she scrambled up, roughly pulled aside the layers of her petticoats to free her long stockinged legs to straddle his inert thighs, and in time to catch the full weight of his upper body against her shoulder as he pitched forward.

She was almost knocked off her knees but managed to put her shoulder into his upper chest, and at such an angle that it permitted her arms to remain free. This enabled her to pass the bandage freely across the width of his bare back. She did this several times, each time pulling the binding a little tighter so that the wound was sealed and the padding secure under the wrappings.

Certain her shoulder was bruised and her back about to buckle under her patient's weight, she quickly groped about the tangled tree roots for the diamond-headed stickpin she had set aside. With the pin secured through the top layers of her makeshift bandage, she used her remaining strength to set her patient upright.

She gently leaned him up against the birch tree. But he did not look at all comfortable, so without a thought to modesty she stripped off his frock coat, folded the embroidered silk garment up into a bundle and successfully placed this makeshift soft pillow behind his neck, thus avoiding his raven head banging back against the tree trunk with a thud.

Exhausted and in need of catching her breath, Deb then sat there in her thin cotton chemise—straddled atop her patient's lap, feeling bruised, battered and on the verge of tears.

"How dare you do this to me!" she demanded of the unconscious gentleman. She picked up the flask, uncertain whether to force the rest of its contents down his throat or dash the liquid in his face. "You're probably a notorious criminal and well served to be left to bleed to death! My misfortune to stumble across you."

She leaned forward and poured a drop of brandy between the parted lips.

"I'm a fool," she muttered, scanning his angular face. "I don't think you can be a criminal. Your eyes are too honest... You are far too swooningly handsome to be—Oh! You ungrateful brute! Unhand me!" she yelped, for her patient had her hard about the wrist and the flask fell into the grass. "That hurts!"

Julian regarded the flushed face close up to his and blinked.

"Promise me you won't run off."

Deb gave a twisted smile.

"Afraid I mean to leave you to the footpads?" she goaded, plying at the strong fingers about her wrist.

"No. I want—I want to talk to you."

"Save your strength for the physician. Oh, do let me go! You'll bruise my flesh."

He released her and she sat up.

"I haven't the strength to make you stay. But I'm apt to decline into a blue melancholy without you." He swallowed and closed his eyes, and spent a few moments regaining his breath. "That would wound my pride far greater than any wound to my body."

Deb was suddenly curious. "Who did this to you?"

"Men of little consequence." He sighed his annoyance. "They weren't particularly good swordsmen. Uncle Lucian will be disgusted with me."

"Uncle Lucian...?"

"Premier swordsman in France and England in his day. He thinks I lack grace in my movements. He's right."

"You should have shot 'em!" Deb said savagely.

Julian smiled. "Uncle Lucian? I know he thinks me a sad trial on my parents and never has a good word to say on my behalf, but—"

"Silly! Not Uncle Lucian, the cowardly curs who did this to you. Why didn't you use pistols? Much quicker result and you need not break a sweat."

"Precisely. Uncle Lucian deplores the methods of chivalry employed by the modern youth."

"But you're not exactly—Sorry!"

"I'm hardly in my dotage, dear girl," Julian drawled. "And to a man in his sixties, four-and-twenty is barely of an age to be out of leading strings."

"Oh! Well, that's not old at all," Deb agreed. "Actually, I thought you were older—Oh dear! I have the most wretched tongue. I am forever saying the first thing that comes to mind."

"Don't let it bother you," he said dryly, gaze flickering across her bare shoulders and slim arms. "I expect you thought me older because I'm graying at the temples?"

Deb met his gaze. "How—how many swordsmen were there?"

"Three."

"*Three*? That's unfair and dishonorable."

"Yes. Tell me your name."

"Name?" she repeated with eyes downcast, suddenly self-conscious. "My name is unimportant."

"I'm sorry you had to ruin your shirt," he apologized after a short silence. When she looked away, out to the forest, unable to meet his steady gaze, he said gently, "Won't you tell me why you and—Jack? Yes, Jack—are fiddling in the forest at this hour? Wouldn't the schoolroom be a more appropriate place to practice your music playing?"

"I-I—must go…"

"My name is Julian," he continued. "I can't thank you if I don't know your name."

"I told you. It's not important. I'd have done the same for-for—Oh! *Anyone*."

"I see. Is it necessary for you to carry a pistol?"

Deb threw him a sullen look. "You're very busy."

"Are you in trouble?"

"That's none of your concern."

"If you are, I'd like to offer my assistance."

"Is that so?" she said with another twisted smile. "When do you think you will be in a position to offer your services? A month—two months from now?"

"I'm not about to beg," he replied mildly.

"I didn't mean to sound ungrateful," she apologized, face a mask of hard indifference. "It's just that you can't help. So, please forget you ever saw us or that I have a pistol. If Gerry ever found out… I'll go and meet up with Dr. Medlow—show him the way through the forest."

"Must you carry a pistol?" he persisted in the same gentle tone.

Deb regarded him steadily then made up her mind that there could be little harm in confiding just a little bit about herself, especially to such a willing ear. Besides, it might just take his mind off the pain in his side.

"My brother Gerry—*Gerald*—doesn't know about the pistol. It belonged to Otto, who gave it to me just before he died, and said that I must keep it on me always when I am out alone. Otto was my other brother and my best friend, and Jack's father. He was a splendid musician and Jack has his talent. If Jack is to go to Paris to be tutored under Evelyn Ffolkes, then he must practice. But as Gerry has forbidden us to play our violas, Jack and I come out here to be alone, and so the servants won't report back to him. So, you see, that's why I carry a pistol."

"Gerry has no ear for music?"

Deb's brown eyes lit up. "Gerry is tone deaf."

"Hence he has no appreciation of Jack's talent."

"Precisely!"

Julian's breathing became labored again and he closed his eyes.

"I dare say Gerry has the same lack of appreciation for beauty," he said in a contrived tone of disinterest. "If you were *my* sister, I'd take better care of you. I certainly wouldn't allow you out of the schoolroom, dressed in a man's shirt and without your stays."

"You obviously have no idea what it's like to be spied upon!" she said indignantly. "I can't be expected to sneak out of the house with Jack if I must first wake my maid to lace me into my stays. Brigitte would have the whole house up within five minutes of my departure."

"Well then, that certainly excuses you."

"And you are a bad judge of age. I will be one-and-twenty *very* soon."

"Accept my apologies. You look younger. Perhaps because you aren't wearing your stays...?"

Deb gaped at him. "Because I'm not wearing my stays?" she repeated incredulously. "Your manners are appalling. If you weren't wounded, I'd—I'd—"

"Yes?" he asked expectantly, and opened one eye, shoulders shaking with silent laughter. "You would...?"

A crimson flush washed over her shoulders and up her throat. She bravely looked him in the eyes, no doubt to tell him what she thought of his insolence, when something caught her attention. It was a spot of fresh blood on the bandage, and that he was trembling.

"You're shivering!" she announced, all embarrassment forgotten.

"Yes. I'm cold and can't move my legs. No matter, the physician will be here shortly."

She suddenly realized that as well as being practically naked from the waist up, she was straddled atop his lap and had been settled there for quite some time.

"You should've said something instead of letting me rattle on at you!" she threw at him angrily as she scrambled to her feet and brushed down the layers of her crushed petticoats.

"What? And cut short our *tête-à-tête*?" he replied with a frown. "Now *that* would've been bad-mannered."

"You must be a lunatic!"

"Yes, I must be," Julian answered with a private smile and closed his eyes.

TWO

WHEN NEXT Julian Hesham, Marquis of Alston, looked out on the world, three pairs of eyes were peering down at him in anxious silence. He thought himself still in the forest and looked about for a pair of damp brown eyes belonging to the boy-musician's aunt. But his head nestled amongst soft down pillows and he was lying in a big bed. He closed his eyes again. Looking. Thinking. Both were too much for him. His head seemed too large for his weak body. He tried to raise an arm and found he was too feeble to perform even this simple task.

"He opened his eyes. That's a good sign," said an unfamiliar, well-satisfied voice. "The fever's broken, thanks be to God. I will call again on the morrow. If he has a restless night, give him the tincture of opium—"

"No! No opium," Julian interrupted in a sluggish voice. "Frew? Tell M'sieur Physician I won't—"

"Yes, my lord. No opium, my lord," agreed the hovering valet. "Just a teaspoon if absolutely—"

"No!" growled his master, fixing a stare on the stranger in the room. "When can I get up?"

"In a sennight, my lord."

"*Sennight*? How many nights have I been here?"

"Three, my lord."

"Three? Good God!"

"Yes," answered the physician with a smile. "And you're making excellent progress, thanks to Mr. Ellicott's—"

"Martin?" Julian interrupted, and turned his head on the pillow to look down the foot of the bed at an elderly gentleman with grizzled hair. "Have I been a sad trial, *mon parrain*?"

Martin Ellicott smiled and shook his head. He showed the physician to the door and then returned to pull up a chair beside the bed, motioning away his lordship's hovering valet.

"How do you feel?"

They spoke in French.

"Passable," Julian replied. "I have a thumping headache. Have I really been tossing about in bed for three nights?"

"Yes. You contracted a chill which turned into a fever. That is not important now. You must rest and regain your strength."

"Always in and out of some scrape, aye, Martin?" Julian grinned self-consciously. "But this time it was not of my making. If you can believe me."

"I never doubt you, M'sieur."

"*M'sieur*? When has my godfather ever called me anything but Julian when we are private?" He frowned. "Ah. Your expression, or should I say—*lack of one*—gives you away. You look remarkably like *mon père* when you put on that face. Did you learn from Father, or vice versa? Never mind. You are about to lecture me on my folly."

"No. Not now. Could you eat something?"

"I don't know. Mayhap something other than that pap I seem to recall being pushed down my throat." He watched the old man stand. "Martin," he said abruptly, "was I ever lucid during those days?"

"Occasionally." He gave a rare smile. "Always in French."

Julian sighed. "Thank God for that." He looked past his

godfather. "Did I make mention of any particular circumstance...?"

Martin Ellicott was silent a moment and it brought the younger man's eyes back to his face.

"You asked that your parents not be told. I did not tell them. You know I would not distress Their Graces for the world. I need not add that *Monseigneur*—"

"I am well aware of the Duke of Roxton's uncanny ability to know my every move. He'll be as mad as hellfire, but I'll deal with that when the time comes. Anything else?"

"No."

"Oh... Then I must have dreamed... I seem to recall asking you—"

"—about a young lady with brown eyes?"

"Yes. She patched me up."

"Is that so?" mused Martin Ellicott, a twinkle in his eye.

"I didn't conjure up this female in some opium-induced dream. She is flesh and blood."

"If she is the one who bandaged you up, then you do indeed owe her a debt of gratitude." Martin Ellicott executed a neat bow. "Now you must rest, and I will send Frew in with a tray of something palatable. Tomorrow we will discuss what is to be done to find your savior."

The Marquis gave a grunt of laughter that made him grimace.

"Well, I'd hate for you to think me as weak-brained as Uncle Lucian—"

The old man gave an involuntary shudder. "No one could be as weak-brained as that."

"—but you shouldn't have difficulty finding her. She sneaks out to the Avon forest to play her viola because Gerry don't like it one bit. Then again, he's tone deaf, so he wouldn't, would he?"

Martin Ellicott refrained from commenting and went out of the room. Opium, he thought. It had to be the opium.

THE YOUNG WOMAN with the brown eyes who occupied the Marquis of Alston's thoughts in his sickbed waking hours was Miss Deborah Cavendish.

Miss Cavendish lived in a tall, narrow-fronted house on the east side of Milsom Street, two doors up from the Octagon Proprietary Chapel. It was a respectable address, close to all the amenities of town and only a short walk to the newly opened Upper Assembly Rooms. Yet it was not considered a fashionable place to reside by the first families. The street housed chapels and trade, and the great rumble of traffic during the Season was considered unpleasant. The buildings lacked the style and elegance and aspect to be found in Queen Square, the Circus or Gay Street. Such an address might do for the seasonal lodger but could not be considered a comfortable or respectable address for a Cavendish.

Yet the house and its situation suited Deb. So much the better to be crammed in amongst seasonal lodgers, faceless chapelgoers and industrious merchants, who had more to do with their time and energy than to squander it in idle conversation, as did the Quality. The Quality spent their time at the Pump Room sweating out their ills in the hot water of the King's Bath, ingested scandal with their morning glasses of mineral water, and later in the day, sipped tea laced with the latest gossip in the Assembly Rooms.

Not that Deb was out to shun Bath society or its jostle of habitués. She was often to be seen at the offered entertainments. Promenading in the Pump Room. Dancing at the Assembly Room Balls. Taking breakfast with a party across the river Avon at Sydney Gardens. She had become a well-known favorite of the year-round inhabitants. Indeed, she was sought after to play at cards with the old infirm gentlemen whose membership boasted three retired Colonels, a General and a sprinkling of knighted self-made men. And there were the widows, titled, genteel and mercantile, all hypochondriacs of one form or another, who confided their ills to dear Miss Cavendish.

Yet, she was politely overlooked by the most intimate of circles, made up exclusively of the sons and daughters and cousins of the first families in the land. These illustrious personages readily rubbed shoulders with all degrees of society at the public entertainments, but were highly selective as to who could enter their drawing rooms or put their feet under the dining room table. It was not that Deb's lineage was to be sneered at, after all she was a Cavendish and cousin to the fifth Duke of Devonshire, and a considerable heiress.

Deb's social consequence and respectability were severely tarnished by her volatility of character. When she was just eighteen years old, she had left the sanctuary of her brother's house against his wishes and run away to the Continent to look after her ill brother, a musician who was the black sheep of the family. Her months spent on the Continent might have been overlooked—after all her disobedience to her brother Sir Gerald was due to her devotion to her brother Otto, who sadly, but thankfully for the family's good name, died in Paris before he could disgrace the family further.

Deb had resurfaced in Bath, fresh-faced and looking for all the world as if scandal had never touched her lovely form. But she returned with her orphaned nephew in tow, and a Mr. Joseph Jones, Otto's major domo, acting as family watch dog.

The nephew was the product of Otto's extraordinary marriage to the daughter of wandering gypsies. That Miss Cavendish chose to give the boy a roof over his head, when her elder brother Sir Gerald had at first refused to acknowledge such base offspring, scandalized society. And to such a degree that speculation was rife about the sort of life Miss Cavendish had led on the Continent, providing the tea table gossips with a plethora of conjecture.

Deb had heard the whisperings, saw the lascivious glances of disreputable men, and the hostile looks of upright matrons.

It would have been too simple to say she did not care in the least what was thought of her. She did. But she also knew there was nothing she could do to change society's opinion of her. That was carved in stone. As long as society kept its distance—and with the hovering presence of Mr. Joseph Jones, they certainly did—she was quite content to be left alone to pick and choose whom she associated with, and on her terms.

And so, it was with head held high that she stepped out of a sedan chair and paid off the chairmen, green velvet riding skirts over one arm, to enter Bath's noisy and crowded Pump Room in search of her sister-in-law, Lady Mary Cavendish.

She had been about to ride out for a breakfast engagement with her French tutor—an elderly gentleman who had settled in a quaint Queen Anne House on the outskirts of town after a lifetime's service in the employ of some illustrious but nameless French aristocrat. Lady Mary's hastily scrawled note arrived as she was dressing and requested her immediate presence in the Pump Room.

It surprised Deb that Mary had come to town so early in the Season. Not to have forewarned her of such plans made Deb suspicious. It would be too much of a coincidence for Mary to be in Bath the precise week Deb was about to quit the declining waterhole for Paris. She suspected her odious brother had once again sent his wife in his place. Deb had no proof, but she believed he kept abreast of her every move by paying a member of her household to spy.

Deb found Lady Mary seated at a window overlooking the King's Bath and caught in conversation with a stiff-necked society matron, who rose immediately as Deb came through the crowd towards them.

"Don't get up, Lady Reigate," Deb said cheerfully. "I came only to say good morning to Lady Mary."

"Deb! How good of you to come," said Lady Mary, fluttering her fan in agitation, a sidelong glance at her conversationalist. "Will you take a glass of water with us?"

Deb leaned over to kiss Lady Mary's cheek. "No, thank you. I hate the taste and it's quite fouled, you know."

"Good day, Lady Mary," Lady Reigate said with an outstretched hand and a curt nod in Deb's direction. "It's reassuring to see a familiar face so early in the season. You will come to my *soirée*? I want to hear all about how your cousin the Duchess is holding up, what with her son embroiled in another seduction scandal. Not that I blame Alston. So handsome and so virile, is it any wonder silly French girls swoon at the sight of him? But such a trial on his poor dear Mamma. Do come on Tuesday, won't you?"

"Thank you for the invitation," said Lady Mary. With Lady Reigate's back turned, she pulled Deb down beside her. "Thank goodness you came when you did. I've heard enough about Alston's degrading behavior not to want to be subjected to a moral monologue of his ills by that creature!" She noticed Deb's riding skirts. "I haven't upset your morning plans, have I?"

Deb was staring down at the waders in the King's Bath, smiling at the bobbing figures in their ridiculous brown gowns and small bars of soap on floating plates. She turned her head.

"Not at all, dearest. I intend to ride out to keep my engagement. But your note expressed some urgency. I hope little Theodora isn't ill?"

"Theodora? Oh, no. Your little niece is very well indeed. I hated to leave her with Nurse at such a time. She is teething y'know. But Sir Gerald is tied up with tenant matters and cannot get away to see you himself for at least a sennight, so he thought it best I come to Bath in his stead."

Deb couldn't help a crooked smile.

"If Gerry is tied up with estate matters for a sennight, then I do see the urgency for your visit." When Lady Mary appeared suitably blank-faced, Deb shook her head. "I'm sorry you came all this way for little return, Mary. I won't alter my travel plans."

"So, it is true." Lady Mary moaned. "I wanted to call on you in Milsom Street, but I feared finding a hallway stacked with trunks, and so thought it best to talk with you here, in a public place where we could be private."

"Dearest Mary, how like you to think it more private in a crowded Pump Room than within my four walls. Yet how true. Yes, my hallway is piled high with luggage. I intend on taking Jack to Paris as soon as I receive word from Mr. Ffolkes. Colonel Thistlewaite! How do you do?"

Gloved hand outstretched, Deb acknowledged a middle-aged gentleman who had broken away from his own party to bow before Deb with a flourish.

"Permit me to present my sister Lady Mary Cavendish." To which the portly gentleman in purple silken knee breeches and saffron yellow frock coat with black lacings bowed over Lady Mary's plump little hand, a twinkle in his jaundiced watery eye. "You mustn't mind the Colonel," Deb continued with a bright smile. "He admires all the pretty females with the eye of a connoisseur."

"Have you been out riding, my dear Miss Cavendish?" he asked, his whole attention returning to Deb—the strawberry-blonde sister thought pretty but not animated enough for this military man. "For shame that you did not spare a thought for Colonel Thistlewaite."

"You cannot join me upon this occasion, Colonel, for I go to my French lesson as usual. Lady Mary, Colonel Thistlewaite and I are Hazard partners, are we not, Colonel?"

"And fleece all comers!" laughed the Colonel. "You haven't forgotten our engagement this afternoon?"

"With the Brownlowes? Not I."

When the Colonel politely took his leave to join his cronies at the far end of the room, Lady Mary said in a thin voice of disapproval, "You don't sit down with him to cards, Deb?"

"I do, Mary."

"Can't you guess what he is?"

"Why of course."

"I wish you wouldn't," complained Lady Mary. "The way

he looked at you, and those others over there with him. I don't know who they are, of course because—"

"Then you must not judge them. They're old and quite harmless, I assure you."

"But what would Sir Gerald think if he knew you—"

"—played cards with a retired regiment? What do I care for Gerry's censure?"

Deb said this with a careless shrug, but there was an edge to her voice that should have warned Lady Mary to beware. The latter was not very quick on the uptake where her sister-in-law was concerned and rushed headlong into a defense of her husband, and thus disaster.

"I'm sure you think them harmless enough, and mayhap they are," Lady Mary lectured. "You were never one to worry your head over gossip, but it really does matter what people think of you, if you are to marry well. Particularly after your foolhardy behavior in running off to care for Otto. As I am older, and married, I can speak with some authority—"

Deb stood and shook out her petticoats.

"Mary, you're wasting your time to try and persuade me not to go to Paris. I must, for Jack. He has progressed far beyond what I can teach him. He needs an experienced tutor such as Mr. Ffolkes. I only await his letter of reply to leave this watering hole. You should return to Theodora, who needs you. It was quite selfish of Gerry to make you come."

"I hate to remind you of what happened in Paris when Sir Gerald had to drag you home before you eloped with Mr. Ffolkes—"

"Then don't!" Deb said through gritted teeth.

"How do we—*you*—know you won't fall in love with him all over again when you see him?" Lady Mary asked in a small voice. "It's been years, but I know Evelyn still holds a candle for you. He never married and says he never shall. Sir Gerald thinks—"

"Oh, for God's sake, Mary! You are being ridiculous! Would

it be such a bad thing if Mr. Ffolkes offered for me again? After all, he is the nephew of a duke and will one day be a viscount. Gerry should be pleased, not worried. I could do worse."

Much worse, thought Lady Mary, if the rumors about a certain Mr. Robert Thesiger pursuing her sister-in-law proved true. She wrung her gloved hands. The interview was not going as planned—how she and her husband had discussed it should progress if she were to convince Deb to remain in Bath. And the Pump Room was not the place to continue such a conversation.

"You'll be late for your ride, Deborah," Lady Mary said quietly. "And you're quite right. I do not understand Sir Gerald's opposition to Evelyn's proposal."

Deb put up her brows. She couldn't remember the last time her sister-in-law had openly admitted to disagreeing with her husband. Something must truly be bothering Mary for her to call her "Deborah" in such a formal manner.

"Come for morning tea tomorrow. Jack is home from Eton and would welcome a visit from his aunt. Now I must leave you for I can't keep Joseph walking the horses forever. Oh, dear. Here comes Mrs. Overton with her toothy son. The Overtons are exceedingly well-connected and Sir Henry left a plum, so I am told. *Au revoir.*"

With a sinking feeling, Lady Mary watched Deb escape across the hall only to be waylaid by the one person whom she had come to Bath to warn Deb against.

THREE

MR. ROBERT THESIGER was a broad-shouldered gentleman of average height and good looks, who made the most of what God had given him with an exquisite sense of dress and exceptionally polished manners. He was resplendent in an Italian silk frock adorned with sprays of silk-threaded flowers on the close, upturned cuffs and hem of the short skirts. His midnight blue cashmere breeches fit him like a glove and a short waistcoat, from which dangled many gold fob chains and seals, was sure to start a trend. His highly polished black leather shoes with their enormous tongues carried a higher-than-average heel that was said to be all the rage in Paris. To romantically minded ladies of all ages, the mysterious dueling scar which cut the length of his left cheek elevated his masculinity to that of the swooningly handsome.

Yet, despite his charming good looks and prospects of inheriting an ancient title, Mr. Thesiger's marriageability was severely compromised by his shoddy parentage. He was the acknowledged heir to the baronetcy of his father, a man of papist inclinations and Jacobite tendencies, who had danced attendance on the Young Pretender in Rome and retired a semi-invalid to

Bath. Yet, it was his mother's scandalous reputation which had brought Robert's pedigree into question.

A French Comtesse, at the time of her separation from Baron Thesiger, Therese Duras-Valfons had publicly declared her only child not to be the son of her husband, but the bastard offspring of an English duke, whose mistress she had been at that time. She had gone so far as to proclaim her son was fathered by this notorious duke while on a Hunt with the King of France. Not many moons after impregnating his mistress, the English duke up and married a girl much younger than he.

Robert Thesiger did himself no favors by his devotion to his mother, a woman whose sordid reputation sank even further when she became the mistress of a French tax collector for mere pecuniary gain. Yet Mr. Thesiger's frequent visits to his father's bedside here in Bath went a long way to redeeming him in the eyes of Society's matrons, who looked upon him as a potential son-in-law for their daughters. That he was courting an Englishwoman, and none other than Deborah Cavendish, who was worth fifty thousand pounds, was proof positive to all but Society's sticklers that Baron Thesiger must indeed be the gentleman's sire.

He had been watching Deb out of the corner of an eye while she spoke with Lady Mary Cavendish and merely awaited the opportunity to waylay her. He strolled about the Great Pump Room with the two Miss Reigates—the pretty, freckled twins of an impoverished viscount. Their mother, Lady Reigate, was just being complimented on their deportment when Robert Thesiger suddenly took his leave of the girls and presented himself to Miss Cavendish. Envious friends sympathized with Lady Reigate. After all, Deb Cavendish was always in her best looks in a riding habit. Perhaps a little too masculine in cut, but how well it suited the young woman with the Amazonian stature and unusually dark red hair. What was Lady Reigate's opinion?

"Miss Cavendish! One moment, if you please," Mr. Thesiger commanded softly, touching her arm.

Startled into dropping her hat, he promptly restored it to her, pleased to have momentarily put her off guard.

"Oh! It's you," she said bluntly. "I thought for a moment... No. How foolish of me. How are you, Mr. Thesiger?"

He smiled and bowed over her gloved hand.

"My feelings are sadly bruised. Who did you wish me to be?"

"I can't stay. Joseph is walking the horses."

"A pity I'm not dressed to accompany you. Did you come looking for me?"

"I came to see my sister. She's just arrived."

"Ah. The lovely Lady Mary. She didn't drag the very correct Sir Gerald with her, I hope?"

Deb chuckled, and slowing her stride to a walk, allowed him to slip her arm through his.

"Gerry leave his pigs and cows? Not likely!"

"Then I shall pay Lady Mary a morning call," said Mr. Thesiger with a quick smile. "I still maintain you came to find me. I can tell by the look in your eyes you are annoyed with me for not being at the recital."

"How extraordinary you should say so," she said conversationally. "It is a talent you need to perfect. I am not so foolish or so shallow."

"You are piqued because business kept me in Paris longer than I anticipated."

"Business with blue or green eyes?"

This made him laugh softly. "Blue," he confessed. "The adorable Dominique is more beautiful than you, my dear, but she has none of your wit or fire. Jealous?"

"No. That requires an effort I do not feel inclined to exert on your behalf."

He was not fooled by her light tone. That she kept her gaze straight ahead, never once looking at him, told him what he wanted to know. He smiled and bowed to a passing couple seeking his attention, before saying to Deb,

"These verbal sparring matches you and I indulge in are amusing, but it is time we progressed, Miss Cavendish."

"What a fantasy you have woven," Deb answered lightly, and withdrew her hand from his silk sleeve as they had come full circle and stood to one side of the front doors. "I am sorry to disappoint you, Mr. Thesiger, but I cannot give you the answer you seek."

"You won't disappoint me," he said in an under-voice.

"Paris must have been dull indeed," she commented, allowing her gaze to wander out the front doors onto the street.

"I am a patient man, but I am no saint, my dear."

"You had my answer before you left for Paris. I own to being a fickle creature, but I have not changed my mind."

Mr. Thesiger followed her into the morning sunshine, side-stepping an elderly couple being wheeled about by their attendants, and grabbed her arm before she could go to her groom, a short stocky man of Italian extraction, who now took a step forward at this cavalier treatment of his mistress.

"It is not an answer I am willing to accept."

"Do you imagine this is the way to go about getting what you want? What fine manners you have, sir!"

Mr. Thesiger recovered himself almost at once and dropped his hand, but not before raising it in a gesture of annoyance.

"Forgive me," he stated woodenly, and retreated with a curt bow, saying as he straightened himself, "I am determined to win you, Miss Cavendish."

"I admire such single-minded purpose, Mr. Thesiger. It does you credit. I only wish I knew my own heart half as well," she apologized as she put on her hat, running a gloved hand down the length of the plume. "You may think it a female whim, Mr. Thesiger, but I cannot entertain any marriage proposal that does not—not engage my—my—*feelings*."

"And if I were to tell you that you and only you have engaged my feelings, Miss Cavendish?"

Deb regarded him with a lopsided smile. He was quite dashing, and she should have been flattered, but his words embarrassed her because she could not return his regard. She expected more, indeed *knew* there had to be more than mere fondness for the man with whom she would spend the rest of her life. She wanted a certain sort of unexplainable something to happen to her when a gentleman proposed marriage. Perhaps she was being stupidly romantic...? Still, it was the way she felt, and she could not change.

"No doubt you have these same feelings for blue or green eyes, Mr. Thesiger," she quipped, and left him standing on the footpath.

FOUR

Deb and Mr. Joseph Jones were some distance from the town center when she slowed her pace to enjoy the open fields and morning air, free of the bustle and noise of town. She was thinking about what Lady Mary had said regarding Evelyn Ffolkes still holding a candle for her, and how she might feel when she saw him again. Almost three years had passed since those heady months spent in Paris with Otto and his musician friends, and although she and Evelyn corresponded erratically, she had not once thought more of him than as a dear friend—Otto's closest friend. Then Joseph cantered up and rudely disturbed her peace.

"Been pressin' you again, has he?"

"Who?"

"That prosy dandy."

"Mr. Thesiger? He doesn't press," she answered mildly. "He merely persists."

"What charmin' manners he's got," Joseph said with a snort.

That Joseph Jones spoke to his mistress with all the familiarity of a gruff uncle was due to the fact he had known her from the cradle. After her brother Otto's untimely death, he had taken it upon himself to act as Deb's major domo, and thus felt entitled to be as plain-spoken as he thought necessary.

"Why do you dislike Mr. Thesiger?"

Joseph looked between his horse's ears.

"Beggin' your pardon, ma'am, but he pretends to be more French than he is English, despite his papa being English to the core, and that's enough for me!"

"That's not reason enough to dislike him. He may make Paris his principal place of residence, after all his mamma is French, yet he goes to considerable effort to regularly visit his ailing father—"

"Eager to get his hands on that ancient Baronetcy, is my guess."

"You judge him too harshly," Deb answered stridently, "as does the rest of society."

Joseph decided to keep his opinions about Mr. Thesiger to himself, and they rode on in silence until turning into a laneway with a set of high gates proclaiming the entrance to a small estate, set well back off the main road and surrounded on three sides by forest. Mature oak trees lined either side of a drive that led up to a Queen Anne red brick house set in twenty acres of parkland. At the bottom of the well-cared-for gardens flowed the river Avon.

Joseph jumped down to swing the gates wide.

The house was in sight when Deb next spoke, a determined look on her face as she struggled to overcome a desire to ask after the injured duelist. To her annoyance, she often found her thoughts wandering in his direction and speaking about him never failed to heighten her color.

"Joseph... You did—you did inquire after my injured duelist with Dr. Medlow?"

Back astride his mount, Joseph cast her a sly glance and kept his features perfectly composed.

"No sooner had Medlow tended him than along comes a

carriage to take your duelist away, to who-knows-where. The painmerchant didn't recognize the arms on the door, and none of the servants did either. Vanished, that's what he's done."

"The carriage must have stopped at one of the respectable inns. He couldn't have traveled far in that condition."

"I inquired at the less respectable inns, too. I know you said he's a gentleman, but just 'cause he's dressed in a duke's garments don't make him one." He glanced at Deb again and said to goad her, "He could've won the fineries from some poor sot of an impoverished lord. Seen that done before. You'd be surprised how many coves go about dressed as if they've got two or three titles to their name! I remember in Turin—"

"Nonsense! He is a gentleman. He—His features are such—"

"Plenty of 'em come out on the wrong side of the blanket these days. If rumor is to be believed, so did Mr. Robert Thesiger. Shocking it is how the nobility have littered the countryside with their by-blows."

Unconsciously Deb stiffened in the saddle.

"The rumors about Mr. Thesiger's shoddy parentage are hardly his fault. It can't be easy for him, having a mother who is a notorious courtesan. But as the Baron owns him, I think we can safely ignore the rumors." She glanced slyly at Joseph. "As for my injured duelist, you did give my description of him to the landlords?"

"To the word. And none have seen him. Though, if they had, I've no doubt about 'em rememberin' your man. Now let me see... Tall with raven hair and the greenest of green eyes. And he's got muscle and a very charming smile. Not to mention a great gaping hole in his side. No. I don't think a landlord or his servants would miss a man like that, d'you?"

Deb felt she had to say something in her defense.

"You needn't think I've lost my heart to some nameless duelist! The notion is absurd. I'm merely curious to know how he got on. There is nothing unusual in that, given my exertions on his behalf. What a wasted effort if later he were to die of his wounds."

Joseph helped her dismount and bowed, saying in a low voice, for their host had come out onto the gravel drive to greet them,

"A damn shame, ma'am, as you say…"

Deb cast him a dark look and then turned to her host with gloved hand outstretched.

"Ah, M'sieur, forgive my lateness. I trust I've not kept you awaiting your breakfast? *Ma belle-sœur* has newly arrived in town and I spent a little time with her in the Pump Room. It is not an easy place to escape."

They spoke in French.

"*J'ai regret*, it is as you say, mademoiselle," the old gentleman answered, patting her gloved hand.

Soberly dressed and elderly, he nonetheless had alert, bright eyes and an upright gait. Deb did not know much about his background, only that he had been in the service of some magnificent personage, whom from time to time he mentioned as *Monseigneur*. Deb concluded his employer had been a French duc.

She had met him in the Pump Room when she had first come to Bath and found they had a similar taste in music and painting. He spoke impeccable French, and once when she had lamented her inability to find a suitable native speaker of that tongue, he had offered his services. She had been coming to his house once a week ever since. She had not seen him in three weeks; he had sent a note to say he would be out of town. Now, as they stood on the gravel drive, she asked him about his stay away, and after looking at her blankly for a moment, recovered enough to smile but change the subject.

"Today we will sit outside," he said, escorting her through the hall to the back of the house where there was a broad terrace overlooking the lawn and river beyond. "My godson is staying with me and I have asked that he join us. I hope you don't object? He, too, is a native French speaker. I should like for the two of you to meet."

"Your godson? How delightful!" Deb dropped her gloves into the crown of her hat and set it aside on the low terrace wall. "I only hope he can bear with my conversation. It is weeks since I saw you last. As you know, my cook is a poor substitute and hardly fit to converse with. She teaches me many idiomatic sentences that would turn your ears very red, M'sieur."

"That," he said, handing her a glass of wine, "I can readily believe."

He excused himself and disappeared into the house, leaving Deb to contemplate the summer garden and the inviting coolness of the river. She wondered if anybody swam down by the little pier or went out in the skiff moored to one of the pylons—possibly the old man's godson. She wondered at the godson's age. He might be just a schoolboy. Someone Jack might like to have as a friend now that he was home from school. The thought had barely time to register when she was startled into dropping her wine glass. It smashed on the stones of the terrace, the last drops of wine splashing the hem of her petticoats. She spun about, flustered, eyes wide in astonished disbelief.

A voice, masculine and pleasantly drawling, had spoken to her back.

"*Excusez-moi, mademoiselle*. My godfather—No, that won't do at all," he continued in English. "You may speak excellent French, but I prefer introductions to be conducted in English."

The words were hardly out of his mouth when Deb spun about to find herself confronted with her injured duelist of the wood and had her little disaster with the wine glass. He was seemingly fully recovered, more handsome than her remembrance of him, and at least three inches taller than her previous estimation.

"Good God!" she blurted out. "What are *you* doing here?"

FIVE

Two hours before Deb was due to arrive at Martin Ellicott's Queen Anne house, the Marquis of Alston and his godfather were seated on the terrace, immersed in reading the London newssheets, drinking strong black coffee and keeping their own counsel.

The old man had been up and dressed since dawn. A lifetime of habit could not be easily broken, as hard as he tried to enjoy a leisurely morning in bed. He walked about the gardens, sat on the pier awhile, and came back to the house to speak to his housekeeper about the arrangements for a late breakfast. He had then ordered a pot of coffee and settled himself on the terrace to reread a letter received the day before. There was a similar billet awaiting the Marquis, the messenger arriving after his lordship had retired for the evening.

The Marquis was still in the dressing stage when he joined his godfather on the terrace. He had suffered Frew's ministrations to be shaved and his natural hair combed off his face and secured in a silk bag with a large velvet ribbon tied at the nape. He put on a white linen shirt and velvet breeches and had even permitted the fastidious valet to adjust the silk cravat about his throat, but he refused to be shrugged into an embroidered waistcoat until he had consumed his morning coffee. In horror did Frew watch his master negligently throw a brocade banyan over his meticulous dressing and go downstairs with this bedchamber article left hanging loose.

Martin Ellicott looked up from the printed page and eyed his godson with the critical eye of a man who had valeted a duke for two decades. The son would never match the father for sartorial elegance, but the boy was more handsome, except when he frowned. He was frowning now, hands thrust deep in the pockets of his dressing gown, shoulders slightly hunched. The frown caused Martin to put up the newssheet to hide a smile. When the Marquis pulled such a face, he was his ancient parent. Such an observation would hardly have pleased either nobleman.

"How did you sleep?" he asked conversationally.

"I had the most appalling thought this morning," said Julian, looking out across the manicured lawn. "It was while Frew was fussing at me to put on a waistcoat. Did you ever fuss at my father? I dare say not." He sighed. "Martin... What if she has left Bath? I've assumed all along she resides in town. But she might very well live in London, or Wales or-or—*Northumberland*, for all we know about her. And we don't know the first thing, do we? Playing a viola isn't much to go on. And you can't make polite inquiries after a girl who carries a pistol and escapes to the forest to play her viola in peace. I distinctly remember her brown eyes because they are lovely. As for the rest of her face, I'm rather vague." He looked at the newssheet concealing his godfather. "Are you certain you've exhausted all possible avenues of inquiry? I thought Bath the sort of place crawling with poets and would-be artists and musicians."

"Sit down and have a dish of coffee," said the old man and set the sugar bowl in front of the Marquis. "The London papers arrived last night, as did letters from His Grace. One is addressed to you."

"Ah," said the Marquis absently and sipped at his coffee.

He seemed not to have heard, so intent was he to pursue his thoughts, with little regard for his listener, who was tiring of the monologue on the mysterious lady fiddler.

"There must be a hundred musicians in Bath. And not all of them play a viola. She might give lessons or take lessons. She has to get her music from someone. Then again, she might just have been passing through. There are always the inns. What do you think?"

He addressed the raised newssheet and as it did not answer him, he said with a laugh, as if reading Martin Ellicott's thoughts,

"My convalescence has turned me into a great bore! If you hadn't found me bound up with makeshift bandages I dare say you'd think I'd seen an apparition, to be forever boring on about my fiddler."

"Whether this young lady exists or not, my lord, I am grateful to her for aiding your quick recovery," Martin answered diplomatically. "Your determination to solve the mystery has got you out of bed quicker than any medicinal." He put the newssheet aside. "However, a week of sitting about the house with only my humble self for company, and the lack of physical exercise, has magnified your little mystery into—forgive me—an obsession."

"Thank you for being frank," Julian muttered.

"As for pursuing every avenue of inquiry," continued the old man. "I am confident all the usual channels have been exhausted. That is, only persons relied upon to remain discreet were approached. You told me once, you believe this female to be in some sort of trouble. Carrying a loaded pistol would indicate she may be in more trouble than is worth your while. Playing a viola in the forest at dawn with only her young nephew for chaperone and a loaded pistol for protection is hardly ladylike behavior."

Julian's eyes danced.

"Martin, just because you spent a lifetime steeped in my father's vice doesn't mean that every female who crosses the path of the son is fit only to grace his bed. I am hardly worthy of the Duke's reputation. After all, he did not meet Maman until well into his fourth decade. And it must have been a most shocking reputation at that, because, even after all these years, it's stuck."

"The Duke has been devoted to your mother since the day they met!"

"All right. All right," the Marquis grumbled good-naturedly. "Don't get nettled. Why shouldn't he be devoted? Her loveliness is matched by her sweet temperament. Sometimes I wish—No, don't build up steam under your cravat—just because I was going to wish her a little bit of age and ugliness. I know you're as besotted as my father."

Martin Ellicott's face changed color. Julian had never seen the old man blush and it embarrassed him as much as it did the blusher. He picked up the letter and fumbled with the seal, giving his godfather an excuse to once again retreat behind the pages of his newssheet. Although the letter's direction was written in his father's elegant hand, the contents belonged to his mother. As always with her it was written in French, with only a sprinkling of English. He read the two pages of closely written script, saying without looking up,

"They are staying in London until the end of the month and then taking Harry down to Treat for the holidays. It seems *Tante* Estée is unwell yet again. When isn't my aunt coming down with something? Poor old *Oncle* Lucian! Maman has persuaded them to spend a few weeks at Treat; says the country air will do *Tante* good. She tells me she wrote to you in *mon père's* letter. She ends by hoping I am well and to see me at Treat on the sixth." He folded the parchment and slipped it into his banyan pocket. "No hint she knows of my latest folly. And your missive from my esteemed pater? Well! You needn't pretend he doesn't know because I am persuaded he must, just by the look on your face."

Martin refilled their dishes. He looked pensive as he liberally sugared his coffee, and he did no more than glance at the Marquis.

"When your fever broke, the first question you asked was if your parents knew if you were injured and the circumstance of your injury."

"And you assured me you did not tell them."

"I did not. Yet, your father knew—"

"Damn!"

"—and was here—"

"*Parbleu*. No."

"—for one night," continued the old man. "He would have stayed another but I persuaded him, with the physician's help, that you were out of danger. If not for the fact Mme la Duchesse knew you were coming to Bath, M'sieur le Duc's presence here would have made Her Grace decidedly suspicious."

"Now do I ever feel the jack-pudding," Julian remarked, wiping a hand over his mouth. "I'm sorry, Martin. I hope he wasn't too difficult. His arctic tempers can freeze over a room. This means I will have to tell him everything, of course," he said more to himself and took out his snuffbox. "He may already know..."

"A word of advice, Julian. You will never keep anything from Monseigneur. Not where his family, his name, Her Grace —especially your mother—are concerned. I don't pretend to know all his methods, but if he desires to involve himself, he will, and count no cost. You are best to tell him everything."

"His letter to you, did it confide anything?"

"M'sieur le Duc confides in no one. He merely inquired after your health. He did say I may tell you your unworthy adversaries are now returned to Paris. He did not mention them by name, and I do not care to know."

Julian took snuff and shut the gold box with a snap, a hard glint in his green eyes.

"Interesting. Exceedingly interesting."

A lackey came out to clear away the tray and dishes and to inquire if the table should be set for breakfast. The nod was given, an eye on the Marquis who was looking particularly grim about the mouth. Before Martin could suggest he change into a waistcoat in anticipation of the imminent arrival of their morning guest, Julian was halfway across the terrace and saying,

"I must be mended enough to ride into town. Have one of the horses saddled, would you? I won't be home for dinner."

"May I suggest the carriage, rather than a saddle, my lord? The physician did say—"

"He can go to the devil! I've wasted enough time poking about here."

"As you say, my lord," the old man answered calmly, following the Marquis through to the back parlor and into the expanse of hallway. "If I may remind your lordship that the wearing of swords is not permitted in town."

"Eh? Not permitted? By whose order? But thank you for the advice. I won't need my sword. I'll carry a pistol." He stopped at the bottom of the staircase to put a hand on the old man's shoulder. "I'm not about to be foolish. I merely want to make a few inquiries of my own about my lady fiddler. Ah, did you think I had other plans? No. Not yet. That matter can wait. The charming scar below my ribs will serve as a reminder of that unfinished business." He caught the butler hovering in the doorway and called out to him. "What is it, Fibber?"

"Miss Cavendish has arrived, my lord."

"Miss Cavendish? Here?" Julian scowled. "*Now*?"

"Very well, Fibber," said Martin, dismissing the butler. "We spoke yesterday of the best method of approaching this delicate situation, my lord," he said to the still scowling Marquis.

"Did we?"

"Yes. It was decided, given your mishap and the fact you do

not immediately want your identity made known to your wife, it would be for the best if you were to meet her here under unexceptional circumstances. This is Miss Cavendish's usual visiting day, so her suspicions are unlikely to be aroused by the presence of my godson."

"A chance to look over the filly before purchase, aye, Martin?" Julian teased, an edge to his voice.

"I need not remind your lordship that the—um—purchase was made a long time ago," he gently apologized.

"Are you certain she has no recollection of the night we were married off?"

Martin Ellicott bravely looked his godson in the eye.

"On the direction of your father I made it my business to befriend the Marchioness—or Miss Cavendish as she is still known to the world—and it is my considered opinion that the young woman has no recollection whatsoever of that unfortunate evening. Her family and yours permitted her to remain ignorant of her marriage and thus her elevated station, until such time as you came to claim her. Thus we have arrived at a highly delicate situation that requires, I am sorry to say, extreme care on your part."

Julian heard the note of censure in the old man's voice and his smile was bitter.

"Every man has his Achilles heel, Martin, even His Grace of Roxton. Surely you can't blame the Duke for marrying his heir in haste? Eight years banished to roam the Continent gave me ample time and opportunity to make an imprudent match just to spite him."

When his godfather looked unconvinced, he leaned his wide shoulders against the polished mahogany balustrade and said flatly,

"So my wife has no recollection of our midnight marriage. So she's turned out to be a social misfit who made a bolt for Paris. That doesn't greatly concern me either. Her prig of a brother has repeatedly assured the Duke that my wife's virtue remains intact, and that's the main thing, isn't it? But if I don't rein her in *now* and for long enough to get her with child, you tell me there's every likelihood she'll repeat the Paris fiasco, and this time elope with Cousin Evelyn if that piece of vermin, Robert Thesiger, doesn't get to her first? Now *that* I won't allow."

He grinned.

"Once she's met me, and not my title, she'll soon forget the existence of my rivals."

Martin Ellicott regarded his godson impassively. It was easy to understand why the young man was so arrogantly self-assured. He had looks, breeding and was destined to inherit an ancient and exceedingly wealthy title. He came from a long line of arrogant noblemen who knew their own worth and counted no cost in achieving their wants and desires. Arranged marriages were commonplace and considered the only way of ensuring lineage, land and wealth remained within the confines of the aristocracy. Still, Martin was left with a nagging doubt as to the infallibility of such arrangements, and so he calmly voiced his concern.

"Your parents have a very different marriage from the one your father arranged for you, Julian."

The Marquis was dismissive.

"Ha! An aberration. Anyone will tell you so."

He went up the stairs two at a time and on the second landing looked down at his godfather with a sly grin.

"I always suspected you of harboring romantic notions. Now it is confirmed."

"When you speak in that manner you remind me of Lord Vallentine!" Martin Ellicott said stiffly.

"Good God! Do I? How distressing for you. I hope she is halfway to being pretty."

"I leave that decision entirely in your hands, my lord," the old man threw over his shoulder as he hurried out of doors.

SIX

WHEN JULIAN descended the stairs some ten minutes later, he was shrugged into a close-bodied embroidered waistcoat of Venetian silk, and diamond buckles glittered on his shoes. He was absurdly nervous at the prospect of meeting the female his father had forcibly married him to when he was on the cusp of his sixteenth birthday. He hardly remembered the events of that fateful night. He'd been blind drunk and what details he did remember were so painful that he'd conveniently blocked them from his memory. Thus, he had not the slightest idea what his wife looked like, only the impression of a small brown-haired girl with a frown. Nor had he given her a single thought since.

That he was wedded for better or worse, the choice of bride taken wholly away from him, did not bother him. Marriages for people of his station in life were arranged and for the sole purpose of ensuring continuance of the line. But then Julian had the most appalling thought: What if his wife were cross-eyed or pock-fretten with bad teeth or worse still, resembled her brother, that mealy-mouthed, egg-headed bore, Sir Gerald

Cavendish? God forbid! How was he to beget an heir under such appallingly difficult conditions? Drunk? Drugged?

He hurried out onto the terrace with the frightening image of a female version of Sir Gerald Cavendish lurking in the back of his mind and found his wife alone on the terrace. She was admiring the gardens and sipping wine from a crystal glass. She had her back to him, and had he stopped to really look at her he would have noticed the deep autumn tones to her upswept hair. But he was not in the habit of summing up females on the straightness of their backs and height alone. He did not mean to startle her, but he did, and in the confusion that followed, he stared not at her but at the smashed glass and the damage done to the hem of her petticoats. It was her exclamation that instantly brought his green-eyed gaze up to her face.

If Deb was startled into uttering an impudent sentence, Julian was momentarily struck speechless. He could not believe his luck. Standing before him was his beautiful fiddler of the forest. Her majestic figure was perfection itself in a deep green velvet riding habit with wide lapels and square low-cut neckline that complemented her deep red hair. Horrid images of a female Sir Gerald burst like a soap bubble as he stepped forward and, without a second thought, firmly took hold of her gloved hands.

"Forgive me," she was saying, her brown eyes searching his handsome smiling face. "I did not mean to be so horridly ill-mannered. You gave me quite a shock. Oh, but it is *such* a relief to see you looking so well. You can't know." She gave a nervous laugh at his widening smile. "I had visions—horrible ones—that my clumsy attempt—"

"Never clumsy."

"If not clumsy, then unskilled. Allow me that," she said, returning the pressure of his fingers, oblivious to her surroundings and the fact the butler, agog with curiosity, had twice stepped out onto the terrace. "Oh, but you *do* look well," she sighed with satisfaction.

A lackey came out from behind the butler with pan and

brush and quickly set to sweeping up the shards of broken glass from Deb's smashed wine glass.

This broke the spell for Deb, and she quickly pulled her hands free and crossed to the table, feeling the heat in her cheeks. The Marquis followed; one sharp soft word directed at the crouching servant. The moment of intimacy between them was over. Julian saw it in the tilt of her chin and the determined set to her full lips.

"If you think I've given away your forest forays," he said softly at her ear as he pulled her out a chair, "you are sadly mistaken in my character."

"Thank you. I never thought you would."

"Miss Cavendish," he began and smiled crookedly at her quick frowning glance. He took his place at the table directly opposite her. "Now you are being foolish. It is only reasonable I should know your name if you came to visit Martin."

Deb looked down at her lap where her hands were pressed firmly together.

"Yes, of course. Damn. What a muddle."

He smiled and privately wondered if their meeting had not been fated all along.

"Does Martin know you play your viola in the wood—?"

"*No.*"

"No, I don't suppose he can," he agreed, thinking that if his godfather had known about his wife's penchant for playing a fiddle in the forest he would have set it all down in one of his regular missives to the Duke. "Poor Martin. I put him to the unnecessary trouble of trying to find you."

This did bring her gaze up to his face. She gasped.

"You made inquiries about me?"

"Discreet inquiries, Miss Cavendish."

"Thank you very much! No doubt whomever you asked thought you fit for Bedlam. I just hope it doesn't reach the ears of—"

"—tone-deaf Gerry perhaps?"

This made her laugh.

"Ah! You remember that, do you?" She put out her dish. "May I please have some coffee?"

"Certainly. Where are my manners? I don't know where Martin has disappeared. Problems in the kitchen, I suspect. He has a temperamental French housekeeper."

"I sympathize. I have a temperamental French cook who regularly sullies my ears with the most unladylike of idiomatic sentences."

"Most lamentable," he mocked. "Martin tells me your French is very good indeed—and that you spent some time on the Continent...?"

"This coffee is very good."

"Yes, it is. But I'm not interested in the coffee. I'm interested in you, Miss Cavendish. *Comment vous appelez-vous?*"

Deb stared into her dish.

"My name? Claudia Deborah Georgiana Cavendish. Dreadful mouthful, isn't it? I prefer my second name."

"I knew I would have it from you eventually!" he said with a smile. "Deborah or Deb? I like both. And the—er—Cavendish?" he asked, although he knew well enough her family's long illustrious history.

"Deb. And if you must know, my great-grandfather was the younger brother of the first Duke of Devonshire. I am cousin to the present Duke through both sides of my family. Quite a lineage, isn't it?" she said nonchalantly. "If you count such social intangibles as important."

"I see that you don't."

"Why should I? Oh, it is all very awe-inspiring on paper. The name Cavendish gets one in the door at important social occasions. It doesn't matter to the toadeaters and trencherflies that, like my father, I too am a Black Cavendish. He had three wives, y'know."

"Your father had *three* wives?" Julian commented encouragingly.

"The second was positively unsuitable—an Opera singer. He did redeem himself by marrying my mother, a Boscawen. Her family is on the roll of Norman nobles."

"The Norman rolls? Now *that* is impressive."

Deb peeped up at him, wondering if he was laughing at her. But as he sat with his chin cupped in his hand and gaze riveted to her face, all interested inquiry, she rattled on for want of something to mask the sensation that he made her feel as if she were sitting too close to an open fire.

"I suppose if one wanted to, one could throw one's relatives about, especially now as the name of Cavendish is connected to practically everyone who is politically and socially important," she commented with a shrug. "My brother, Sir Gerald, lives for all that sort of nonsense. He's very good at lacing his conversation with his titled relatives. It adds to his self-consequence, and that he has in abundance."

The Marquis pulled a face.

"Sir Gerald is a positive bore."

Deb laughed.

"Yes, he is, isn't he? But he married a sweet creature who'd been left on the shelf. Unrequited love for a rakish cousin, so my brother Otto said. That must redeem Gerry somewhat." She leaned forward, as if fearing to be overheard and said confidentially, "I secretly suspect my brother was aware of Mary's lineage well before he ever realized she was pretty."

"The cad!"

"Mary's cousin is a duchess. I won't bother you with the name. Suffice that the Duke's family is on the roll of Norman nobles and, Mary tells me, is the largest landowner in the kingdom."

"Dear me! An ancient name, a title, *and* half of England! You see me all agog."

"Well you needn't feel humbled. Gerry toad-eats them enough for all of us."

"Does your brother have anything to recommend him?"

"I'm sure, given time, I shall think of something," she said simply, her brown eyes alight with mischief. She dimpled delightfully when he put up his brows in expectation of her suggesting at least one redeeming feature that Sir Gerald might possess. "He is forever plagued with having me for a sister. Although he does enjoy the sympathy this elicits. You needn't appear so interested. I'm not about to tell you why I'm a Black Cavendish. But you really should feel for Gerry's position."

"I certainly will not!" he said and sat up. "The fellow is not only a bore but devoid of sentiment. I hope you won't expect me to receive him once our marriage is made public, regardless of his sweet wife and her connections."

"I avoid him at all costs, so I don't see why you should—" She blinked, and the breath caught in her throat. "You're absurd! You don't know the first thing about me. My name and face aren't sufficient reason to marry me—oh! You're as impertinent as ever!"

Julian grinned. He was enjoying himself hugely.

"You're adorable."

"Mad," she said with conviction, showing him her profile, chin tilted in affront. "I-I wish I'd never set eyes on you!"

"That's a shame because I'm very glad I set eyes on *you*."

He was playing with the sugar in the ornate silver sugar bowl, eyes seemingly on the spilling grains as he tipped over the spoon, yet his whole concentration was on her.

"Naturally you have my word that your—um—lack of stays will not be disclosed to anyone, particularly odious Gerry."

When her jaw swung open and the color reignited in her cheeks, he couldn't help a lopsided grin,

"Of course, as your husband," he added matter-of-factly, "I would counsel the wearing of stays in public."

Now Deb was angry.

"You may think it a great piece of funning to-to *flirt* with me but—"

"And I thought you'd taken a fancy to me...?"

"Did you indeed?" she answered with arched brows. "I'd say you were feverish at the time."

Julian gave a bark of laughter.

"Please! Don't make me laugh or Dr. Medlow will have to put his needle and thread into me again."

When she said nothing, lips pressed firmly together, he put out his hand across the table and said in quite a different voice, "I am in earnest."

She ignored the hand, saying in a small voice, "If you knew the first thing about me, about my family, you wouldn't use me in this way. Besides, what do I know of you or your connections? My groom thinks you're an adventurer."

"An adventurer? He could think worse. Are you in the habit of discussing gentlemen with your groom?"

"Joseph Jones was my brother Otto's major domo. After Otto's death, he took it upon himself to look after me. But that has nothing to do with anything!"

"It does. That I'm considered a worthy topic of discussion with the estimable Joseph Jones gives me hope. More coffee, Miss Cavendish?"

"No! Yes! Oh, where is M'sieur Ellicott?"

"Gone to Paris to fetch our breakfast, the time he's taking about it. Fibber!?" Julian called out over his shoulder. "Find out what's happened to our breakfast. Miss Cavendish and I are ravenously hungry. A roll, an egg, whatever you can scavenge. And while you're about it, find out what's happened to your master." He called out to the retreating butler's stiff back, "And more coffee!" then turned a smile on Deb to catch her staring at him in a penetrating manner. "My name isn't branded on the back of my scalp, y'know. That's better. I do so like your smile. And you have the loveliest eyes, and your hair... I've been trying to decide if it is red or brown. It is unusual. Sort of an autumn-leaf red, isn't it?"

"This is all very gallant, but it's getting you nowhere," she said crushingly. "No doubt I ought to be flattered. I'm sure your charm is irresistible to the vast majority of females."

"That's hard to say," he said with a thoughtful frown. "It depends on what sort of female you mean. If you mean the sort you are unlikely ever to meet, I don't waste a lot of words on them. And if you mean females of your quality, I am inclined to believe they hear none of it because they don't know the real me. They are only interested in what they will get by marrying me."

For one moment Deb thought him in jest, but when she realized he was being serious she giggled.

"You are the most extraordinary man I've ever met. I should think you only have to enter a room to set all female hearts aflutter. And five minutes in your company would put the seal on your worth as a gentleman."

The Marquis nodded absently, looked unconvinced and sighed in feigned resignation. Her frown of embarrassment at speaking so candidly made him smile to himself and say resolutely, "If you feel I must acknowledge your boring brother then I suppose we will have to invite him to dinner upon occasion. But I put my foot down at having Odious Gerry to stay over a weekend. I loathe trencherflies as much as you do."

"Will you be serious?" she demanded.

"I've never been more so. Drink your coffee, or do you want a fresh dish? That one you've let go cold."

Deb decided it was impossible to talk to a lunatic. She put his silly mood down to the effects of the medicinal drugs he'd been given to dull the pain of his injury. He was obviously an outrageous flirt whose thoughts and opinions were not in earnest. She suspected that he was being familiar with her because she had come to his rescue and thus was deserving of his attentions for the moment. Yet there was no denying that, for the briefest of seconds, the prospect of accepting his outlandish offer of marriage was exhilarating. Of course, she banished the thought as soon as she had conjured it up, then mentally upbraided herself for allowing this handsome stranger to so easily put her off-balance.

Why couldn't she control the heat in her face?

MARTIN ELLICOTT saw at once the heightened color in Deb's cheeks as he stepped out to the terrace from the French windows. He had been hovering in the back parlor, awaiting his opportunity to join the Marquis and his guest. As he sat at the table, he wondered what his godson had said to make the young woman blush and look coy. But he kept his thoughts to himself and his features suitably blank and signaled to Fibber and two lackeys to bring out the breakfast things.

"Back from Paris so soon, *mon parrain*?" asked his godson.

"A minor disaster in the kitchen," the old man lied. "*Excusez-moi, mademoiselle*. I hope my godson has kept you suitably entertained in my absence. Try one of these excellent rolls."

"Thank you, M'sieur. *Entertained*, yes," Deb answered, an eye on the Marquis who was plying his plate with roast beef, eggs, slices of bread and a sliver of pie. "A roll and perhaps a little butter. *Merci*."

Julian glanced up from inspecting the contents of a covered dish.

"Fussy appetite, eh?"

"Not at all! I usually eat a good breakfast. It's just that I—I seem to be drowning in coffee." His sad shake of the head goaded her into retorting, "I see you possess a bottomless pit for a stomach!"

"Yes," he answered with a laugh and devoured a slice of roast beef.

Martin Ellicott listened to these exchanges, saw the looks that passed between his godson and Miss Cavendish, and felt a stranger at his own table. The two young people spoke with a familiarity of long standing, which pleased him more than he cared to admit. Miss Cavendish might maintain a semblance of decorum in her demeanour, but her replies to his lordship's playful banter stripped away her façade of indifference. As for his godson, he was enjoying himself hugely, no doubt because he had the upper hand in this meeting. The old man was of the opinion that Miss Cavendish's exceptional beauty was the reason his godson had the appearance of a well-satisfied cat who has discovered that the bowl of water put before it is in fact a dish of fresh rich cream.

"Martin will vouch that *mon père* refuses to sit down with me at the breakfast table. He positively shudders to watch me tuck into a hearty meal such as this at so early an hour. Is that not so, *mon parrain*?"

"Your father must be a gentleman of infinite sensibility," Deb teased.

"M'sieur le du—" Martin began, stumbled on the name and immediately corrected himself. A sharp, open look from the Marquis warned him to be on his guard. "M-My godson has an appetite beyond his father's comprehension."

Julian finished off the pie with the last of the coffee, an appreciative wink at his godfather that did not go unnoticed by Deborah.

"Maman blames herself. She has a sparrow's appetite, yet when she was pregnant with me she craved all this. Rather an omen. Poor *mon père*," he laughed, "how he must have suffered."

Martin Ellicott thought such intimate conversation unfit for the ears of a young lady and his whole being stiffened. Yet he needn't have concerned himself Miss Cavendish would take offense. She barely heard a word Julian had said for she had fixed on her host's quickly corrected slip of the tongue and the wink of secret understanding that had passed between the two men. Her gaze flew across the table to the Marquis, who was looking at her intently, before she lowered it to the contents of her coffee dish.

"Ah. Apologies," he said as he pushed back his chair to stand. "Martin will be appalled at my lack of manners." He made her a short bow. "Allow me to introduce myself: Julian Hesham Esquire." He glanced at the old man. "Miss Cavendish and I have been discussing our marriage—"

Deb's eyes immediately lifted from her coffee dish as a ready blush of embarrassment seized her throat and cheeks. It was one thing to jest of marriage with her in private conversation, quite another to continue the jest in front of her host. One swift glance in his direction told Deb the old man was in utter disbelief at his godson's pronouncement.

"You must stop this nonsense at once," she demanded in a low voice, up on her feet.

"—and how I put my foot down at inviting her brother Sir Gerald to stay overnight," the Marquis finished off.

"It wouldn't have mattered to me one jot had you been an adventurer," Deb continued, napkin cast aside. "But to tease a girl you have only met once and in-in *trying* circumstances, a girl you know not the first particular about and who knows nothing about you, with an offer of marriage, an obligation you have no intention of fulfilling, is beyond *forgiveness*."

Julian appealed to Martin Ellicott.

"Tell her I am in earnest, *mon parrain*."

"I do not know what circles you mix in, Mr. Hesham—if that is in truth your name—but in the society to which I belong, your actions would not only be considered heartless but unconscionable! And—and those of a-a *lunatic*."

"Please, Miss Cavendish, if you would—"

"Why do you smile? Do you think it amusing? Do you see me as an object of fun, sir? To a gentleman of your address, adventurer or no, I suppose a spinster nearing her twenty-first birthday must amuse someone used to the attentions of—oh! a dozen females at every ball and rout. Well, I assure you, yours is not the only marriage proposal I've ever received! In fact, the ones I have received were in earnest, not made as a cruel jest! Indeed, I had one this morning. And from a gentleman who would never make me such an offer unless he truly meant it!"

"I repeat *I am* in earnest."

"To think I went to the trouble of bandaging you up!"

"And a very good job of bandaging you did, too. May I know the fellow's name who proposed to you?"

"No. You may not!" she breathed indignantly, and then opened wide her brown eyes at his look of amusement. "Oh, I see. You don't believe me, is that it?"

"Of course I believe you, Miss Cavendish," he assured her, following Deb to the low wall, his handkerchief at the ready. "It's just that I wonder why you have not accepted one of these proposals before now...?"

Deb rounded on him then and he found it hard to keep a straight face because she was scowling at him, and it brought back a flash of vivid memory, of a thin-shouldered barefoot girl in an over-large nightgown. It amazed him to think he had not recalled her before now.

"I will not take offense at that remark because you do not know my history," she said in a low voice, the scowl deepening on spying the handkerchief in his hand. "If you must know, Black Cavendishs do not receive many marriage proposals. Certainly not from respectable gentlemen! I dare say you are not respectable, or I wouldn't have found you bleeding to death from a sword wound and you certainly would not have offered me marriage."

He quickly put away the handkerchief.

"I assure you; it was not my object to offend you, Miss Cavendish. I am merely curious to know of any potential rivals for your hand."

"Is that so?" she said, tongue-in-cheek. "As my hand is not engaged there is little point in divulging the names of my suitors to you. Now you must excuse me, M'sieur," she said politely, addressing the old man who stood woodenly by the table trans-fixed by the conversation between the couple, "I have packing to do. Thank you for the breakfast. I hope to see you in the Pump Room before I leave for Paris. *Au revoir.*"

"Leaving for Paris soon, Miss Cavendish?" Julian persisted, following Deb down the terrace steps to the pebbled path that led to the stables.

Deb stopped and turned on him, the scowl returning. "If you must know, I am taking my nephew to Paris within the next few days, where undoubtedly I will receive more marriage proposals from dashing adventurers. Good day, sir!"

"Not if I can help it," Julian muttered, returning to the terrace.

He propped one leg on the low wall and took snuff, main-taining a face of polite indifference under his godfather's steady gaze.

"Cousin Mary is in town," he said conversationally. "I hope dull Gerry isn't. I must pay her my respects. I'll drive the char-iot. Do you have any errands for Frew?"

"Julian..." the old man said and faltered, trying to collect his thoughts. "Miss Cavendish isn't the—She couldn't possibly be... *Mon Dieu.* What a coincidence! It is quite a shock. I had no idea she ventured into the woods to play her viola. As for a loaded pistol... I cannot believe I did not discover these things before now."

The Marquis snapped shut his snuffbox, a hard brilliance to his emerald green eyes.

"Don't let it worry you, Martin." He dared to smile to himself as the image of the thin-shouldered girl in the overlarge nightgown faded, bringing into sharp relief a young woman in a thin cotton chemise straddled across his lap. "You may leave the discovering to me..."

SEVEN

"COME TO KEEP an old lady company, Deb?" asked Harriet, Dowager Marchioness of Cleveland, shifting her heavy satin petticoats and her bulk to the end of the settee to allow Deb to sit beside her. "You won't see much from back here. That Reigate creature, with her turban and plumes enough for a whole bird, is blocking everyone's view of the floor. I've a mind to have Waverley shoot the thing to put it out of its misery!"

General Waverley leaned across from the next settee and inquired calmly, "Bird or beast, my dear?"

"Ha! Ha! I believe you'd do it, too, if you had your pistol," laughed Lady Cleveland and gave his lace-covered knuckles a playful rap with her fan. "Say hello to Deb, you rogue."

"How are you, Miss Cavendish?" asked the General, kissing the gloved hand extended to him.

"Better for escaping to the back of the room. I left Lady Mary talking to Lord Orminster. He pounced on us as soon as we entered the vestibule and insisted on finding us seats in the front row." Deb peered over her fan, out across the sea of powdered heads. "Poor lamb. He's still with her."

"Fred is a bore," said Lady Cleveland. "I don't suppose little Mary Cavendish will think so."

"Because she is married to one, my lady?" Deb inquired.

Lady Cleveland looked about in alarm. "She didn't bring him with her, did she?"

"No."

"Sir Gerald knows a thing or two about horses," opined the General with a firm nod.

Lady Cleveland and Deb exchanged a significant look, the ancient Marchioness rolling her eyes heavenward, causing Deb to laugh. "We missed you at cards this afternoon, my dear. I hope it wasn't on account of Thistlewaite's win on Wednesday last?"

Deb shook her head and leaned toward the Marchioness so as not to be overheard, their shoulders touching and Deb's fan up to hide her words.

"If Gerry comes to hear of it, poor Mary will carry the burden of my lost guineas. He sent her to keep an eye on me. As if he doesn't get a surfeit of gossip from Saunders already!"

Lady Cleveland's eyes bulged. "Your butler spies for your brother?"

Deb nodded.

"Good God! That's monstrous. Get rid of him at once!"

"For Gerry to set another in his place? No, I thank you. The thing is, Saunders doesn't know that I know what he's up to. And he is good at his job."

"How did you learn of his treachery?" asked the Marchioness, her fan waving in agitated movements across her bejeweled bosom; all interest in her surroundings momentarily forgotten. "You didn't catch him spying through a keyhole or-or scribbling notes on his cuff? Horrid man."

"Nothing quite so exciting. Joseph always suspected Saunders was less than loyal. I hate to think what methods he employed but he found a sheet of paper, part of a letter addressed to my brother. Joseph says it was a discarded copy. Somehow I don't believe him."

"Who cares where or how he got it. He did. But why must you be spied upon?"

Deb lowered her fan and shrugged. "All that comes to mind is that Gerry's life is so dull that reading Saunders' accounts of my paltry existence in Bath is an improvement on his own. Poor Mary."

"P-poor M-Mary indeed!" blustered Lady Cleveland, her double chins bouncing with laughter. "Don't the gal amuse him?"

"Can one amuse the dead, my lady?"

This sent the old lady into such whoops of laughter that several heads turned in her direction. That Deb Cavendish sat between Lady Cleveland and General Waverley surprised no one. That she was the cause of the old Marchioness's coughing fit was taken for granted. Wherever Deb Cavendish was there was sure to be some scene or other. She never disappointed the disapprovers.

"I said it would be Deb Cavendish," breathed Mrs. Dawkins-Smythe. "I said, if there is a disturbance, trust her to be at the center of it. Sitting up there with the likes of Harriet Cleveland, who should be at home in bed at her age. Flaunting those diamonds. Do you think they are real, Sarah?"

"Harriet Cleveland wear paste?" exclaimed Lady Reigate, craning her squat neck to better view Deb Cavendish. "The woman is merchant-born and -bred. She knows the value of a good investment. And she made certain her third and last husband had a title into the bargain. Vulgar creature." She turned away, annoyed at herself for staring too long at Deb Cavendish's flawless complexion.

Mrs. Dawkins-Smythe saw the envy and smiled smugly.

"She is lovely, isn't she?" And to twist the knife further, "Is it a wonder Mr. Thesiger seeks her out? She always dresses splendidly, to the envy of us all. That sapphire blue gown is divine and shows off her statuesque figure to perfection."

"Vulgar!"

Mrs. Dawkins-Smythe smiled sweetly. "Not a match for your two beauties, to be sure, Sarah. But no one can deny Deb is a diamond of the first—"

"Flawed! Remember her flight to France, to her brother's sickbed, so it was put about. But it is generally acknowledged that she attempted to elope with a musician. A *musician*. No wonder she remains unmarried. No parent wants a bolter for a daughter-in-law," retorted Lady Reigate and presented her friend with a view of her profile, her daughter Sophia having completed the minuet with Mr. Thesiger.

She expected him to ask Rachel for the final minuet and was all smiles as he deposited Sophia into her care once again. But he did not ask. Nor did he hover to make light conversation. He took his leave, and mother and daughters watched him saunter off and disappear to the back of the room. His choice for the second minuet froze their smiles.

Deb, who had been fanning Lady Cleveland while General Waverley fed her sips of iced lemon water to take away the cough, glanced over her shoulder, wondering why there was a sudden hush to the crowd. She had not intended to dance— that was why she had chosen to sit at the back of the room. But she knew she could not refuse to dance the minuet with Robert Thesiger. So it was with a fixed smile that she took his hand and went out onto the dance floor—one couple in the middle of the vast ballroom, scrutinized by an audience of upwards of five hundred people.

It was not a dislike of dancing which gave her a dread of being Mr. Thesiger's dance partner. She enjoyed the country-dances very much. But the minuet was the most public of all dances at the Assemblies, and she knew that those mammas with eligible daughters must be willing her to trip, to make a wrong step, to appear awkward and stilted, if just to show their own daughters to better advantage. She might smile and look as if she were enjoying herself in the company of her partner, but underneath she was trembling and praying she would not make a fool of herself in front of all Bath society.

As they turned and touched hands, Robert Thesiger came near enough to say, "You suppose that by turning me away at your door this afternoon I would magically disappear?"

"Can you? I did not know you for a conjurer, Mr. Thesiger," she quipped, and gave him her hand again as they danced toward the orchestra.

"You could do worse than I, my dear Miss Cavendish."

Deb's thoughts went immediately to her injured duelist. Yes, she could do worse indeed! She mentally castigated herself for even thinking about him at all. She had promised herself that she would not spend one thought on him the entire Assembly. She felt a fool. She had been consumed for weeks by fears for her injured duelist's well-being, but after his cavalier treatment of her that very morning, she was now furious with him for teasingly pretending to want to marry her. The gall of the man!

"Miss Cavendish...?"

Deb blinked at her dancing partner. "Mr. Thesiger?" She came to a sense of her surroundings and said kindly, "You seem to have forgotten that when I marry I must have Sir Gerald's approval."

"Ah. Yes. And yet, it is my belief you use Sir Gerald as one does a shield. You bring him out to hide behind, hoping he will protect you from all manner of declarations from prospective suitors, only to throw dull Gerry in a corner, forgotten, when your suitors are in retreat."

Deb could not deny this because it was true. Whenever she felt the need to put a stop to the verbose compliments of overeager gentlemen callers, she routinely trotted out her brother's name, which produced an immediate effect—not unlike dousing the hopeful gentlemen with the contents of a pail of cold water. Yet, Mr. Thesiger remained persistent and she really had no wish to hurt his feelings. After all, unlike a certain other gentleman, Robert Thesiger was nothing if not sincere in his wish to marry her. She made no comment and they continued along the dance floor, Mr. Thesiger squeezing her hand before releasing her and saying with a sad smile,

"I have been mistaken in you, Miss Cavendish. I had taken you for an independent thinker." The quick angry knot between Deb's brows was evidence enough that he had made a direct hit, and he added in a voice full of resignation, "I had no idea you held to medieval principles."

It was impossible for her to answer him, such was the sequence of their dance steps, but as they came together again, he circling her sweeping petticoats, she was angered enough by his comment to retort, "I am not at liberty until my twenty-first birthday. Then I may do and say and marry whom I please."

He smiled, the scar on his left cheek puckering up, and made her a bow, the white lace at his wrists sweeping the polished floorboards.

"It warms my heart to hear you say so. And to know that in less than a month you will be freed from your brother's shackles."

"Is that so, Mr. Thesiger?" Deb said with some surprise, intrigued he should be so blunt in his opinions about matters that were none of his business. "You and I are the only ones who hold to the belief that I am shackled."

He gave her a sidelong glance. "I have heard a rumor, of course it is absurd, but I will mention it any way, that Sir Gerald has plans to marry you off to the Marquis of Alston."

"I beg your pardon? Gerry betrothe me to the Duke of Roxton's rakehell heir?"

Deb stopped dead in the middle of the floor, forgetting where she was and that a hundred pair of envious eyes watched her every move. Robert Thesiger's idea was so absurd, laughter bubbled up in her throat.

"No one has seen Lord Alston on English soil since he was a youth. Sir Gerald certainly hasn't had the pleasure of his company or he would be lacing his correspondence with *his lordship this* and *his lordship that*." She was skeptically amused. "What an absurd and quite fanciful notion, Mr. Thesiger."

Robert Thesiger smiled weakly and made her his final bow, the lace ruffles at his wrists again sweeping the floor.

"That you are to marry Lord Alston, or that he is debauched beyond redemption?"

Deb frowned and remembered to curtsy.

"I can assure you that my brother has never put to me such a ridiculous proposal, nor have I any desire, despite my brother's slavish devotion to the Roxtons, to ally myself with that family. As for the latter?" She shrugged. "Everyone has heard the whispers about Lord Alston's many dalliances, his Parisian parties, and his total disregard for his good name. That does not mean there is any truth in the rumors, of course." Without expecting an answer, she teased him, "Perhaps you have attended one of his lordship's bacchanalian affairs and can make comment?"

Robert Thesiger's smile did not waver, yet there was no laughter in his blue eyes. The music had ceased, and the crowd began to shift in their seats, restless for the country-dances to commence. He did not take her flippant remark as intended.

"You will excuse me if I do not give an account of our history here and now, Miss Cavendish. Suffice for me to say that Lord Alston and I were once intimately acquainted. Indeed, when we were boys we were enough alike to be taken for brothers. But now, sadly, I have no wish to be associated with a nobleman who lives such a depraved existence. So depraved, in fact, that unlike other noblemen's sons, Alston chooses to live outside the unwritten rules of his kind. He preys on the innocent daughters of the Parisian middle-class, girls who are ignorant of the ways of the aristocracy and thus are easily taken in by the debonair Marquis. Alston offers them marriage like one offers a pretty girl compliments, and when he has gained their confidence with this lie, he seduces them, then moves on to pick the next budding rose."

Deb put up her gloved hand, nauseous at the prospect of ever coming into contact with such a predatory creature.

"Please, Mr. Thesiger, I have heard quite enough. If what you say is true, and I have no reason to doubt you, then he is certainly beyond redemption." She rested her fingers in the crook of the silken sleeve he offered her and allowed him to escort her from the dance floor. "You may rest easy, sir. When I marry, it will be to a gentleman of *my* choosing. Sir Gerald has as much reason to hope of his sister agreeing to an arranged marriage with the Marquis as a leper has of being cured!"

Robert Thesiger smiled with relief, the tension easing in the dueling scar that indented his left cheek.

"Thank you, Miss Cavendish. I always knew you for a female of independent mind. Thus I will continue to hope."

"I have already told you..." Deb began and faltered, angry for becoming flustered in a public place and before this gentleman who had never been anything but open and patient about his intentions. "Please, you must excuse me. I need refreshment."

"Allow me to accompany you—"

"No! No, there really is no need. Thank you."

Deb picked up her satin petticoats and made a hasty exit for the refreshments, shouldering her way through the laughing groups forming for the country-dances, looking neither left nor right. She was about to follow two couples through to the Octagon room when the lace flounce at her elbow was ruthlessly tugged, and a voice from behind a column whispered near her ear,

"Come outside."

She stood quite still, a shiver passing across her bare neck and the oddest sensation knotting inside her chest. She wondered if the voice had been conjured up in her mind, but she did not hesitate to hurry out of doors.

WITH AN INDULGENT eye, Lady Cleveland watched Deb Cavendish and Robert Thesiger part and go their separate ways at the end of the minuet. Her gaze followed Deb as she crossed the room. The girl then disappeared, not into the refreshment rooms, but out the entrance doors and into the night. A gentleman who had been lingering on the fringes of the dance floor, seemingly content to hover by a pillar to scan the room with his gold quizzing glass, lifted his shoulder off the marble support and sauntered out into the night air not two steps behind Miss Cavendish. He was tall, broad-shouldered and it was his patrician profile that alerted Lady Cleveland as to his identity.

"Waverley! Look!" she breathed, sitting forward on the settee, a hand gripping hard the General's large silken knee. "I'd know that nose anywhere. There's no mistaking it. He's more handsome than his father, though Roxton has more presence. Ah, but the son, he has so much charm. I wonder..."

General Waverley put up his quizzing glass but missed his chance at a view of Lord Alston.

"Who's that you say, Harriet?" he asked, a magnified eye turned on her ladyship. "Not the satyr's son? Here? No doubt you've heard 'bout the latest mischief he's caught up in?"

"Mischief?"

"Rumor has it he was run out of Paris by a M'sieur Farmer-General for seducing his unmarried daughter."

Lady Cleveland gaped at him. The General continued.

"M'sieur Farmer-General followed him across the Channel with two of his cronies and demanded satisfaction. Imagine! A common little Frenchy demanding satisfaction of an English duke's son. It don't bear thinking about. Trumped-up little peasant." He lowered his voice. "Just between you and me, Harriet: Do you think there's any truth to the rumor the boy's a card short of a deck? Y'know, *touched*?"

Lady Cleveland's bosom swelled. "Touched? Roxton's son, *touched*? For shame, Henry! And the Duke one of your Newmarket cronies."

General Waverley shrugged, embarrassed at having voiced the doubt that he knew many privately held about the Marquis of Alston.

"You can't deny that Alston's had a dark cloud hanging over him since that disgraceful episode in his youth. Why, it stands to reason we are left to wonder at the strength of his brain when one considers his unforgivable behavior toward his dear mamma. Such a divine beauty..."

"He was a mere boy, Henry."

"A boy, mayhap, but that don't excuse such insane behavior, does it?" continued the General, made confident by Lady Cleveland's slump of the shoulders. "He and that cousin of his, Ffolkes, were hell-raisers at school. Expelled on two occasions and only taken back because old Roxton is a Duke."

"My dear Henry, have you never considered that Alston was led astray by his cousin and not the other way 'round, as is common report?"

"Aye. That's a possibility," conceded the General. "But that don't excuse Alston's unconscionable conduct toward his mother, now does it?"

The Dowager Marchioness shifted uncomfortably on her seat, painted mouth puckered up with annoyance.

"No, it does not, Henry, but... The Roxton marriage is not in the common way, and to a sensitive youth such a circumstance is rather difficult to explain." She unfurled her fan with a snap and rallied. "Besides, we will never know the absolute truth of that night. And as the boy's brain seems perfectly recovered, it is better we not dwell on it."

General Waverley could offer no argument, but added, "But

what do you make of the persistent rumor that the Roxtons' other son is also weak-brained? Complications at birth, it's said. A physician's been his shadow since he could walk because he has fits—what's it called—the *falling sickness*, that's it! Now if that affliction don't point to a weak brain in that family—"

Lady Cleveland stopped such speculation with a dismissive snort. "Idiotic rot!"

EIGHT

Despite a full moon bathing the cobbles in an eerie light, linkboys lounged about under the portico, ready to light tapers for a small fee and accompany those who chose to walk home. Chairmen waited by their sedan chairs, exchanging gossip and ribald anecdotes. A carriage stood in the road with its steps folded down and the door wide, a footman in livery patiently waiting the arrival of its owner.

Deb took all this in as she stepped out into the cool night air and looked about her, feeling rather foolish when approached by a linkboy. She did not have her cloak and was rightly at a loss, standing in the street unaccompanied.

"May I compliment you on your dancing, Miss Cavendish. Or was it the skill of your partner which showed you to best advantage?" drawled a pleasing masculine voice, its owner coming out of the deep shadow of the building.

Deb waved away the linkboy.

"Why am I not surprised to find you lurking in darkness, Mr. Hesham?" she asked conversationally, although she was annoyed at being oddly elated that her injured duelist had sought her out despite her angry rebuff earlier that day. "Is it that adventurers prefer the exciting company to be found in laneways to that to be had under the bright lights of a dance floor?"

Julian grinned.

"You find me living up to a reputation I neither want nor deserve. Come closer. I don't bite, my dear."

"Why did I not spy you on the dance floor?" she asked, in a voice she hoped sounded disinterested. "Do you dislike dances, sir?"

"I dislike being the center of attention."

"Indeed! I hope you are worthy of your own high opinion."

"It is *your* opinion of me that matters," he said calmly as he guided her into the laneway.

When she tried to withdraw her gloved hand, he would not let her go.

Deb dared to look up at him. It was a mistake. The light in his green eyes was all gentleness, and she quickly looked away.

"Forgive me. My remark was exceedingly stupid and uncalled for."

"I've come to take my leave of you, Miss Cavendish."

Deb gave a start.

"You—you are going away?"

He smiled at her quick look of dismay.

"For a few days. To reassure my parents I am alive and well."

"I see," she said, keeping the disappointment from her voice. She drew a little away, suddenly cold, and shivered. "Of course you must go to them. They will be anxious after your health." She caught his smile and added defiantly, "Not that you need justify your absence to me—"

"May I call on you when I return?"

"—as we are the merest of acquaintances."

"Mere acquaintances, Miss Cavendish?" he inquired lightly. "You, who have seen me stripped of this decorative façade?" He drew her up against him. "I meant every word I said to you this morning. No. Don't bite my head off. I am *not* an adventurer and I am *not* in jest. I am in earnest."

"If you care anything for me, you will have done with this taunting!"

"I assure you my intentions are wholly honorable," he whispered near her ear.

Deb's throat constricted. Why was she emotionally vulnerable with this man when others had tried and failed? She wanted to be angry with him. At the very least, to coolly rebuff him as she had Robert Thesiger. She had never permitted emotion to rule good sense and yet here she was going weak at the knees with a complete stranger! What lunacy had come over her? Not since she had run away to be with Otto in Paris had she felt like scattering caution to the four winds. She had let her heart rule her head upon that occasion and never regretted her decision. Otto had needed her and she had loved him dearly. But Otto was her brother, and there was never any doubt that her sisterly devotion would be returned with brotherly love. But this was different. This gentleman was not her brother.

Indeed, he was so unlike a brother that the sensible course of action was to demand that he unhand her at once and flee back inside to the light and crowds within the Assembly Rooms. And yet she stayed within the circle of his embrace. His sheer physicality, the warmth of him, the faint smell of his masculine cologne, stirred in her feelings and sensations that threatened to overwhelm her. She tried to rally herself before she said or did something that could not be undone.

"If you are an honorable gentleman, you would do well to keep your distance. I... I have a checkered past! I ran away from home when I was eighteen," she blurted out, speaking to the complicated knot in his cravat. "I'm considered by good society an *eccentric*." When he remained silent, she peeped up at him, adding, "Just like my cousin Henry, the scientist, and my brother Otto, who was a great musician. You cannot seriously want—"

"You?" he said, smiling into her eyes. "Most certainly I do."

"—a female who plays a viola with her nephew in the forest—"

He chuckled in his throat. "—without her stays!"

"—against the wishes of her brother Gerry."

"Ah, the one snag in my eagerness for us to be man and wife without delay."

Deb blinked. "Not wearing my stays?"

Julian smiled to himself catching the apprehension in her voice, yet he made himself look very grave.

"No, not your stays," he said levelly, and pinched her chin. "Although, as your husband, I will demand you wear them in public. Yet, in private..." He stooped to kiss her mouth, and momentarily unable to master his self-restraint, pulled her up against his chest. "Damn these layered petticoats..."

"Please! No!" she demanded and pushed back, though she had instinctively returned his kiss. "I've never—You mustn't think that just because I want you to-to—*kiss* me, I am—I'm the sort of female who wants to be taken advantage of!"

He instantly let her go, his tone calm and reassuring.

"I've no intention of taking advantage of you, my dear girl. I am here to make certain that circumstance does not befall you." When she continued to regard him with uncertainty he added flippantly, "The snag isn't your stays, or put more correctly, lack of one, my doubting beauty, but *Gerald*. He may be your brother and a Cavendish, but he is a bore and a toady and his French tongue grates on the ear. I will not have him to stay with us over a weekend. Dinner, yes, but not to sleep under my roof. Never."

Deb relaxed and tried not to giggle. "Gerry? A snag? Are you ever serious?"

He tilted her chin with one finger. "I have never been more so."

Deb colored painfully. "And what of the loaded pistol?"

"Ah. Two snags then. No loaded pistols. If you've a taste for shooting, by all means take to my pheasants, but no pistols."

She swallowed and made one last half-hearted attempt to turn him away by admitting, "I am under my brother's guardianship until my twenty-first birthday. He would never agree to-to—"

"Have I been mistaken in you, Miss Cavendish?" he murmured, as he brought her back into the circle of his embrace and this time kissed her very gently. His mouth barely brushed against her slightly parted lips. "I thought you and I were like-minded souls. That you, too, believed in love at first sight…"

His words registered somewhere at the back of her mind as she craved another kiss, a proper kiss. The promise in the light, feathery touch of his salty mouth on hers was so deliciously wicked she felt strangely exhilarated, as if he had heightened all her senses at once. But it was the warm tingling from somewhere deep within her that was the real surprise. That, and the knot in her chest that threatened to stop her breathing.

"Damn your conceit, sir," she murmured, as her arms went up about his neck and her mouth hungrily met his…

THE SHADOWS CAST in the moonlight were no protection against the inquisitive patrons taking their leave of the Assembly Rooms. Half a dozen pairs of eyes had riveted themselves to the stooped broad back of the Marquis of Alston. To enable a better view of the embracing couple, a gentleman dressed in puce velvet waved his Malacca stick about at two linkboys and ordered them to shine light upon that side of the building. Movement and sound ceased under the portico. Shocked and outraged to find an embracing couple kissing in the shadows, several matrons put up their fans at the sight. Such licentious behavior was not to be tolerated at an Assembly Ball. One titled lady, a Methodist with two eligible daughters in tow, went so far as to loudly voice her opinion so that even those standing in the street could hear her venomous tongue.

"Yes, you may blush, Rachel, as every female in Bath must blush at such wantonness! I thought we were at the Upper Assembly Rooms, but it is obvious we have strayed into a bordello!"

There was a snort of laughter from a nondescript gentleman closest to the doors and a nervous giggle from one of the ladies. Then all at once farewells were picked up where they had left off because the Marquis had turned a broad shoulder, careful to keep Deb shielded from curious glances, and glared at the onlookers in speechless fury. He fixed a disdainful gaze on the titled Methodist lady.

Lady Reigate noticed that the group on the portico had fallen silent and that all veiled eyes were turned in her direction. She wondered why and glanced back at the couple half in shadow. She received a momentous shock. She was sure it had to be a trick of the light, for the gentleman's angular features and tall wide frame so reminded her of the Marquis of Alston that this gentleman could very well be his twin. But everyone knew the Marquis lived in Paris... Or did he?

Lady Reigate had another look at the immobile gentleman. He was regarding her with such an expression of haughty contempt that instinctively she dropped into a respectful curtsy, not willing to chance that he wasn't the Duke of Roxton's heir. When she straightened, his back was to her. Outrageous expectations of her eldest daughter one day becoming a duchess crumbled to dust.

DEB WAS FUSSING with her mussed hair and pinning up a few stray curls, and although she had heard Lady Reigate's spiteful remarks, she missed the woman's curtsy to rank because the Marquis's tall frame had shielded her from the curious onlookers spilling out onto the portico. With her hair pinned again, she stepped out from behind him, grateful the crowd was dispersing, and in time to see Lady Reigate's carriage set to.

"You mustn't mind our resident Methodist," she said conversationally. "She barely acknowledges my existence, yet her pride won't allow her to ignore me because I am a Cavendish. And Cavendishs do not lurk in shadows with men of unknown social consequence." She frowned. "I hope she won't mention this to Mary…"

"I think you will find Lady Reigate has a pressing London engagement and must quit Bath immediately."

Deb put up her brows. "How do you know her ladyship by name? I did not tell you."

All the coldness went out of Julian's voice. He grinned and chucked Deb under the chin.

"You may have found me in the forest but I am not a mushroom."

"Oh! Yes, how silly of me!" Deb said, flustered. She lowered her long dark lashes, saying hesitantly, "I expect you know Lady Reigate from London and she—"

"—has two daughters of marriageable age," he interrupted, and smiled to himself when she nodded and looked anywhere but up at him. He drew her closer. "But I have no desire to kiss them."

This pleased Deb more than she cared to acknowledge. Still, doubt lingered. "Tomorrow you will regret—"

"Never. When I return I am going to take you for a carriage ride."

"And after that?"

"Ah, that depends on how you conduct yourself."

She plucked a stray hair from the lapel of his embroidered waistcoat.

"And if I fail to conduct myself...?"

He chuckled and lightly kissed her forehead.

"Then we shall dispense with the formalities and ride straight into our future." He made her a bow, slightly stiff in its execution. "Now, Miss Cavendish, if you would permit me to propose—No, that sounds stuffy. Deb, will you—will you do me the honor of being my wife?"

"Ah! There you are, Miss Cavendish," hailed a voice from the portico.

Mr. Thesiger came lightly down the steps carrying Deb's cloak over one arm.

Immediately, Deb stepped into the light without giving her injured duelist a response and met Robert Thesiger half-way, eager that he should not find her conversing with a stranger in the shadows. She had no wish to answer questions, nor did she want to deal with Robert Thesiger's disappointment and censure at what would be seen by all, even the most free-thinking residents of Bath, as most unladylike behavior. She was so flustered at such an awkward circumstance that she sighed her relief when Lady Mary followed Robert Thesiger out under the portico and hailed her with a wave of her fan.

"There's Lady Mary. I must go to her."

Robert Thesiger placed the cloak about her shoulders, while he continued to peer into the darkness of the narrow lane. He was certain he had detected a large shape move off, and knew his eyes had not deceived him when there was the sound of footfall on the uneven cobbles disappearing down the laneway.

"My dear Miss Cavendish, you're shivering," he purred, making a mental note to question the linkboys for a description of the stranger in Miss Cavendish's company. "I'd never forgive myself if you were to catch cold. Allow me to escort you to Lady Mary's carriage."

Before she had gathered her wits Deb found herself beside Lady Mary, with Robert Thesiger ushering from behind. A fleeting glance over her shoulder confirmed that her injured duelist had indeed vanished into the night, just as magically as he had appeared at her side in the Octagon room. With a sinking feeling, she wondered what tomorrow would bring—if indeed Mr. Julian Hesham would ever return to Bath to take her for the promised carriage ride.

NINE

THE DUKE OF ROXTON signed his name to the document and handed it to his secretary to fix the ink with a sprinkle of pounce. That being the last order of business, the Duke put the quill in the silver standish and waved away the hovering secretary. Yet he lingered a little longer by his wide mahogany desk, a glance down the length of the library to where his son and heir was patiently waiting to speak with him. The Duke had kept him waiting until he had decided how best to approach the subject uppermost in his mind. Yet, his son did not seem to mind the wait. In fact, the boy had taken a bundle of day-old newssheets to the far end of the library and was casually reading through them, stretched out on a sofa, a hand behind the tapestry cushions under his head.

Finally, the Duke walked slowly to the far end of the long room to warm his white hands at the second fireplace. When he turned about, it was to find his son on his feet awaiting his pleasure.

A tug of the tapestry bellpull and the butler came soft-footed to his master's side. A word spoken, and the servant retreated to return with a footman carrying a tray laden with breakfast items, and a silver coffee urn that the butler placed on its pedestal on the low table between the two sofas. Neither nobleman had said a word to the other, and kept their own counsel while the butler was in the room. When they were finally alone, the Duke returned to the fireplace. His son poured out the coffee into two porcelain mugs, which he then set on the table. A wave from his father and he helped himself to the hot rolls, slices of ham and wedge of pie.

"Your mother said you would not stop to eat your breakfast at the Bull and Feather," the Duke remarked, taking up his mug and setting it on the mantel. "That establishment's fare must be lamentably lacking or you have a higher—er—*regard* for my opinion than I had supposed?"

Julian cocked an eye at his father but said nothing, finishing off a second roll before pushing aside the plate. He drank down his coffee and poured a second dish.

"The fare at the Bull and Feather is rather good, sir; the venison pie is particularly excellent."

The Duke smiled thinly and took out his snuffbox.

"I am glad to hear it. I must increase my head of deer so that you can continue to enjoy such excellent venison pie. I trust I did not tear you away from—er—*unfinished* business?"

"Your letter stated that I present myself at my earliest convenience, and so I have, convenient or otherwise. I'm glad I find you well, sir."

"You can dispense with the niceties, Alston," the Duke replied bluntly. "I am no better and no worse than when I last saw you in Paris. I see that your appetite has returned, therefore I take it that you are fully recovered from your *mishap*?"

"Yes, sir. I only wish that you had not been inconvenienced—"

"You should have thought of that before you crossed swords!" the Duke enunciated coldly before turning to the fire, angry for letting emotion get the better of him, and the interview just begun. He took a moment to collect himself before continuing. "Those fools were beneath your touch. You had no right to engage them in a bloody struggle."

Julian regarded his father's rigid back and snow-white mane with a private smile—he knew him better than he knew himself. Anger masked parental concern.

"The fight was thrust upon me, sir," he explained calmly. "Lefebvre and his sons followed me from Dover. I had no idea I was being pursued until ambushed in the Avon forest. The old fool was determined to have satisfaction, whatever my arguments to the contrary. A determined man, a man who believes himself grossly abused, does not listen to reason. How was I to tell him he was beneath my consideration?"

The Duke pushed an errant log back into the grate with the toe of his black leather shoe, the large diamond-encrusted shoe buckle glinting in the firelight.

"I realize that the pistol is fast becoming the preferred dueling weapon of the modern youth. In my opinion, it is a rather—er—*crude* and inaccurate method of dealing with one's opponent. A rapier thrust to a precise point on the body is the much neater, cleaner and gentlemanly way of ridding oneself of an annoyance. Did M'sieur's determination make you forget all your years of training?"

"No, sir. Those years of training allowed me to fend off Lefebvre's two sons. They quickly gave up the attempt on orders of their father, but it was no easy matter getting myself into a position where I could be pinked without killing the old man. I could have disposed of Lefebvre on no fewer than four occasions during our encounter. My object was to give him the satisfaction of spilling my blood without slicing up my entrails."

The Duke regarded his son with considerable surprise.

"Then I am all admiration for your skill. But you find me momentarily stunned as to why you thought it necessary to carry out such an elaborate deception. Why didn't you—er—*finish* them off?"

"As you say, those thugs were beneath my touch. As for

M'sieur Farmer-General..." The Marquis held his father's steady gaze. "He is an old man. Old men should die in their beds."

There was a moment's pause before the Duke inclined his white head. He took snuff and turned back to the fire. And although he continued to stand with his back ramrod straight, Julian could tell it was an effort for his father because his breathing had become laboured. He decided there was no point in delaying the inevitable.

"Sir. Killing M'sieur Lefebvre would only have strengthened the case against me. Think what his lawyers would have made of that? Isn't it enough that I stand accused of a crime I did not commit, without being branded a coward? How convenient for a nobleman to use his prerogative to settle a dispute with a duel. My opponent would be silenced, the threatened lawsuit dropped, but it would not wipe away the doubt of my guilt."

"Enlighten me, if you will," the Duke drawled, "how you come to be threatened with a French lawsuit for breach of promise?"

"If you know about the threat, then I need hardly elaborate further."

"Indeed?" said the Duke with a sneer. "Then am I to presume there is substance to M'sieur's claims?"

"Yeast alone does not make bread, sir."

"Undoubtedly. Yet, it is the yeast which defines the substance."

Julian pushed a hand through his thick black hair and walked away from the fireplace before turning on a heel to come back and stand before his father.

"It was never my intention to involve you."

"You are my son; thus I am involved. Why does Lefebvre hold to the stubborn belief you offered his daughter marriage?"

"I have no idea, sir. The notion is absurd."

"Quite absurd," Roxton agreed, regarding his son with the dispassionate eye of a nobleman with half a century's experience of the fairer sex. "You did not perhaps offer mademoiselle the inducement of your name in the—er—*heat* of the moment?"

The son's lip curled as he looked his father in the eyes. "That question is rather academic, is it not, given that I am already married?"

"You have relieved me of an anxiety I never thought warranted."

"Then it must please you that I went to Bath for the express purpose of meeting my wife. It is time my marriage is more than a marriage in name only."

The Duke was pleased. Pleased that his son's hastily arranged marriage years earlier would finally be consummated, and thus legalized beyond doubt. It was about time his son took on the responsibility of husband and, hopefully, in the not too distant future, that of father. The physician's depressing prognosis had made the Duke eager to see his line secured beyond his immediate family.

"Am I to congratulate Martin on his descriptive powers?" the Duke asked, a rare smile amid a twinkle in his black eyes.

"If you are asking if Martin's prose leans to flowery exaggeration," Julian responded with a shrug, "then the answer is no. Deborah is beautiful but no more beautiful than the beauties trotted out on the marriage mart season after season. She's a bit of an Amazon, with the temperament to match. She speaks her mind and knows what she wants. But that's not such a bad thing and preferable to a doe-eyed creature with cotton between her ears."

A muscle quivered at the corner of the Duke's thin mouth.

"Indeed. But does she want *you*, Julian?"

The Marquis shrugged again.

"When I left her, she was half-way to falling in love with Julian Hesham. After an absence of a fortnight, I believe she'll marry me out of hand when I return to Bath."

"You feel it is necessary to go through with this elaborate deception rather than tell her the truth?"

"Sir, she has no recollection of the night we were married off as children. The shock of the truth could turn her against me, whatever her feelings. Then where would that leave me? I won't bed a reluctant female, even if she is my wife." He smiled crookedly. "Thus I thought it prudent to allow her to believe me a common man."

The Duke was intrigued.

"Such consideration humbles me. Your morals are indeed far better than mine."

"You misplace my consideration, sir," the Marquis stated flatly. "You, like I, do not desire to see my wife seduced into bigamous wedlock, be it with Cousin Evelyn, some unnamed suitor, or the son of Mme Duras-Valfons."

"Yet, we are not rid of the problem of M'sieur Farmer-General and the alleged ruin of his daughter," the Duke said smoothly, to turn the conversation from a topic he found distasteful and beneath his notice. He was not about to discuss Mme Duras-Valfons' lurid claims with his son and heir. Still, the boy's remarks smarted and more than he cared to admit. "Mademoiselle Lefebvre's statement to the Lieutenant of Police names the Marquis of Alston as her seducer."

Julian gave a huff of embarrassed laughter. "That document of high drama? It's fit only for the stage."

The Duke regarded him with an unblinking stare. "I think I've lived enough of life not to be shocked by anything you may care to tell me."

"As I said, sir, I don't bed reluctant females."

"Lefebvre's lawyers say they have evidence that supports the girl's claim she was seduced with the promise of marriage."

"They may say what they please. It is a lie."

The Duke inclined his head.

"I believe you. You should know this matter has come to the attention of the French Ambassador here at the Court of St. James's. The Duc de Guînes is sympathetic to your cause." The Duke sighed his annoyance. "Unfortunately, he and his contacts in Paris can do little to shut up the girl's father. As a tax collector, Lefebvre has more power in Paris than any noble, and as a man who believes he has been grossly wronged, he will stop at nothing to see his honor avenged." The Duke sneered. "He is so eaten up with his own self-consequence that he had the audacity and self-conceit to force a duel on you!"

The Marquis made his father a low bow. "I am determined to clear our name, sir. If it comes to a trial, so be it."

"I applaud your sentiments, Julian, but you are under no obligation to give satisfaction. Although, had your adversary been one of us, your impromptu duel would have seen an end to the matter, honor satisfied. You are of the English aristocracy. You cannot be brought before a French court of law unless application is made to our sovereign by His French Majesty's representative at the Court of St. James's. The French Ambassador has given me his word he will not make such an application. M'sieur Farmer-General may puff out his consequence until he—er—*pops*, but he will soon come to his senses and realize it is pointless to pursue such untouchable prey. I am reasonably confident that when this fact is made clear to him, he will—er—*crawl* back under the floorboards where he belongs."

Julian grinned. "I envy you your supreme indifference to your fellows, sir. And I wish I had but a thimbleful of your sangfroid—your arrogance is rightly justified. But I cannot sit about waiting for the dust to settle on this matter." He added seriously, "It is my belief that the accusation brought against me is a deliberate attempt to bring discredit upon our family. The girl is merely the excuse. Nor am I ignorant of Lefebvre's connections and his motivations. I am sorry if my decision to push the matter to a just conclusion disappoints you, Father."

The Duke was not surprised by his son's declaration. After all, he is his mother's son, he told himself, and with her clear emerald-green eyes.

"You do not disappoint me, Julian," he answered quietly.

He, too, harbored a nagging suspicion there was an undercurrent to this imbroglio that had little to do with a girl's ruin, and was surprised his son was of the same opinion, but he did not care to discuss these thoughts for the present.

"I am still regarded as somebody at Versailles, but Paris is of an altogether different political complexion. Even His French Majesty has difficulty controlling the *parlements*. Whatever action your lawyers deem necessary, I will have delayed until after your honeymoon. I will do what I can. Or perhaps I—er—*interfere*?"

"No, sir. Thank you," Julian answered sincerely, and kissed the long white hand extended to him.

TEN

Lady Mary entered Deb's Milsom Street townhouse to discover a state of domestic chaos. The front hallway was stacked with traveling trunks, narrowing the passageway, causing her to pick up her voluminous hooped petticoats and walk crab-like behind the long-suffering butler. The melodic sound of a violin somewhere above Lady Mary's head, a scream and a string of abusive French from the back of the house, and an animal, possibly a dog—she hoped it wasn't a large rat—slipped along the polished wooden floor of the passageway and collided with a portmanteau before bounding up the staircase out of sight. It was pursued by a stout woman in an apron whose floured fist was raised above her head.

Saunders gave an audible sigh of long-suffering as he ushered Lady Mary into the front parlor, apologized for keeping her ladyship waiting on the doorstep—he had been indisposed and Philip the footman was nowhere to be found—then bowed himself out of the room and closed the door.

Not many minutes later the door was flung wide, and a boy with long legs and a head of dark copper curls falling into his eyes bounded into the room, with a large rat on a lead. On closer inspection, the rat turned out to be a puppy. Mary knew nothing of dogs so had little idea as to its breed or disposition. But she did know something of their habits, and she shrunk back into the sofa cushions, a hand to her voluminous petticoats.

"Down, Nero! *Down!*" Jack commanded and gave a tug on the puppy's lead. He went on a knee and received a lick across his face. "Good boy! Good boy! Hello, Aunt Mary! Saunders told me you'd come to call." He made her a bow. "Aunt Deb's upstairs. We've been busy on a composition I wrote. This is Nero. My best friend Harry made a present of him. He won't bite but he does jump. Aunt Deb says I must keep him on a lead when there are visitors, and because Alice doesn't like dogs. But Aunt Deb likes him, and Joseph promised to keep him while I'm away. Do you like dogs, my lady? Would you care to give Nero a pat?"

"Oh, no! That's very kind of you, but no, I won't, Jack. Thank you," Lady Mary said, with a smile that made Jack smile despite her refusal to touch Nero.

"He won't bite or drool on your petticoats like Sir Gerald's beagles. He's a whippet and very well-behaved."

"There you are!" declared a voice from the doorway. It was Joseph. He took a step into the room, saw Lady Mary, and remembered his bow when Nero trotted up and nuzzled his hand. "Beggin' your pardon, m'lady. Out with you and that brute, Master Jack."

"Nero isn't a brute. He isn't even a dog yet."

"He'll be mincemeat for pies if Alice gets her hands on him. Cook is blaming your friend for the disappearance of a good chop. And by the looks of the wag on that tail, he swallowed it all right! Sorry to be of bother to your ladyship."

"We weren't bothering you, were we, Aunt Mary?"

"No. Not at all, Jack," Lady Mary responded with a smile, yet she was relieved to have the dog on the other side of the room.

"If you want to come along with me, we'd best be on our way," Joseph told Jack. "And before Miss Deb changes her mind." He bowed to Lady Mary. "Beggin' your ladyship's pardon for the state of things around here, but it's on account of our impending journey."

"I've been invited to stay with Harry. Joe's taking me there. Harry lives in a palace in Hampshire," Jack explained excitedly, adding, "You mustn't mind Aunt Deb. She hasn't been very friendly to anybody in days. We're hoping a letter from Paris will arrive to improve her mood. Aren't we, Joe?"

"Now that ain't for anyone's ears but ours, Master Jack," Joseph was heard to say as he closed the door.

Saunders appeared with the tea tray and informed her lady-ship that his mistress would join her directly. Hardly had he shut the door when there was another commotion in the passageway. It seemed to travel out onto the street, then there was silence once again. Lady Mary sighed her relief only to sit bolt upright when the door was flung back and Deb sailed into the room.

"Well! Who'd have thought one little puppy would cause such a fuss!" she said with annoyance. She shut the door on the butler and rolled down the sleeves of a mannish white shirt that looked as if it belonged to a footman and which covered her bodice. "Did Jack show you his puppy? Friendly little thing. A gift from his school friend Harry, who has invited him to stay for a couple of weeks," she rattled on as she poured out the tea into two porcelain dishes. She put the teapot back on its stand and set the milk jug and sugar bowl in front of Lady Mary but did not sit, preferring to stand by the window with its view of the busy street. "I couldn't say no, could I? So our journey to Paris is put back yet again. Oh well, it can't be helped. That should please you, Mary—that I remain in Bath...?"

"I came to tell you Sir Gerald arrived in town last night," Lady Mary said quietly, a keen eye on her sister-in-law who was preoccupied. The fact she did not react to the news of her brother's arrival was evidence enough she was more than usually distracted. "Is anything the matter, dearest?"

Deb did not answer because there was a curious lump in her throat. She merely shrugged and looked out of the window, braiding and unbraiding a handful of the long deep-red curls that fell forward over one shoulder. Her thoughts were a complete muddle and she hadn't slept well in days. It was all the fault of her injured duelist and that kiss in the shadows of the Assembly Rooms. She was apprehensive and knew she had no good reason to be. He said he would return to Bath to take her for a drive in the park and it had only been a little over a sennight since their kiss in the shadows, so why should she worry he didn't mean to keep his word? Eight days wasn't very long at all. His parents might live on the other side of England, for all she knew...

But with every day that passed her conviction grew that he had merely amused himself with her. Perhaps he was an adventurer out for her fortune? Her brother Gerry had spent years drumming it into her that men were interested in her for one reason and one reason only: She was an heiress. In every other respect that mattered she could not be considered pretty—she was too tall, her walk too mannish, and her eyes were the wrong color. She certainly wasn't violet-eyed and petite like Mary.

She should have known better than to lose her heart to a handsome stranger found in the Avon forest bleeding from a sword wound! Where had her wits been wandering? And Mary was looking at her in a forlorn way that suggested she felt sorry for her, and that made Deb angrier than anything.

"I really must see to the rest of Jack's packing," said Deb, tugging at the bell-pull, "if there is going to be any food to put on the table for dinner after this morning's tantrums by Cook. So I'm sorry to cut short your visit. I expect you need to get home to Gerry—Good God! What has happened *now*?"

As she spoke there was a series of thuds overhead accompanied by a scuffle of boots and the familiar bark of Nero, and lastly a shout of laughter. Lady Mary was on her feet the moment the butler stepped into the room with his usual look of long-suffering on his marble countenance.

"Well, Saunders?" Deb asked, trying to glimpse into the passageway, but the commotion had moved on to another part of the house. "If you're going to tell me Cook has taken a cleaver to Nero, or is chasing Jack about the pantry mouthing Gallic obscenities, I don't want to know. Or are you about to give notice?"

"Not at all, ma'am."

"It is a brave man indeed who can weather one grubby schoolboy and his faithful hound."

Saunders ignored the sarcasm, saying, "There is a gentleman come to call, ma'am. He put his boot in the door and followed Master Jack and Mr. Joseph—"

Before Deb could answer Lady Mary interrupted.

"You can't possibly admit a gentleman to your parlor dressed-dress—"

"Mary, I don't see why Bath should be denied a look at my olive-green petticoats. Don't pretend to be shocked for Saunders' sake," Deb said with a sly glance at her butler. "If the visitor came into the house with Jack and Joseph it is probably Fotheringhay or General Waverley. And as neither of those two elderly campaigners can walk without the aid of a Bath chair, they are hardly likely to ravish me in these fetching garments."

"Deb! Please—"

"Call Lady Mary's chairmen, Saunders."

Lady Mary sat down again.

"I am staying. It's what Sir Gerald would want me to do."

"Well, Saunders? Don't gape at me."

The butler hovered in indecision and looked from one stubborn face to the other. He was prepared to wait out the argument until he was startled into moving away from the doorway by a soft word from the visitor, who had slipped into the room unannounced.

"It is most inappropriate of you to receive a gentleman dressed like a-a *gypsy*," Lady Mary lectured with a sniff of disapproval. "You've not even put a comb through your curls. And *that* is a-a *man's* shirt!"

"Can you guess to whom it belongs?" Deb teased.

"When you say such provoking things, is it any wonder people are willing to believe the worst about you? Yesterday I had a visit from Mrs. Dawkins-Smythe—"

"My dear Mary, you really must learn to be politely rude. Toad-eating you again, was she?"

"Toad-eating?" Lady Mary gasped. "No. She was not toad-eating me! She came, she said, on a mission of mercy. She had the information from Lady Reigate, and thus thought it best I know that there is indeed truth in the rumor doing the rounds of Bath's drawing rooms, so that I could prepare Sir Gerald for the worst."

"Mary? I have no idea what you are talking about. Why do you have your handkerchief at the ready?"

Lady Mary sat up straight, the white handkerchief crushed in a gloved hand. "Deb, is there any truth to the rumor you were seen in the shadows of the Assembly Rooms last week with—with a—"

"—an apparition?"

"You know perfectly well what Lady Reigate witnessed!"

"No, I do not." Deb smiled wickedly. "I was rather preoccupied at the time to take notice; be it vision or no."

"So it *is* true," Lady Mary announced in tragic accents. "You allowed a-a—*lothario* to kiss you! How-how—*common*."

Deb laughed, but her eyes were very hard.

"Common? No. There is nothing common about him."

"You think it amusing to have people ogle you, talk about you, think you *improper*?"

"Damn and blast what people think of me!" Deb growled, though this masked a genuine hurt that her sister-in-law was prepared to think the worst of her.

"Oh, Deb, when you talk like that I lose all hope of you making a good match. Is it any wonder Sir Gerald despairs of you—Oh! What—*You*?" Lady Mary stuttered and stared straight ahead as one who had seen a ghost, completely losing her train of thought.

Deb slowly turned from the window and came face-to-face with her injured duelist, dressed for riding in thigh-tight buff breeches, dark blue riding frock coat with embroidered cuffs and highly-polished jockey boots. His wide shoulders were up against the closed door, arms folded across his chest. There was an appreciable twinkle in his eye, and although he bowed to both ladies, his eyes were all for Deb.

ELEVEN

"YOU DID KEEP your promise!" Deb declared with a smile and took a step forward. Then she checked herself, blushing to the roots of her auburn hair, for her spontaneity surely gave away her feelings.

"Yes. I'm here to take you for a ride about the park as promised," Julian said conversationally, as if it were only yesterday he had kissed her in the shadows of the Assembly Rooms. "There is a chill in the breeze, so you will need to fetch a wrap and your bonnet."

Lady Mary gaped at both of them and rallied herself enough to say, "Deb can't go riding dressed—"

"Yes, I would like that," Deb interrupted, not looking at Julian, for he was smiling at her in that way that made her ridiculously happy. "Don't wait for me, Mary."

He opened the door for her to pass into the corridor then closed it and turned to Lady Mary, who was on her feet, blushing furiously and looking out of sorts.

"You can't allow Deb to—" she began, and was cut off.

"Has it never occurred to you that every time you say *no* to Deb she will instantly defy you?" he interrupted calmly. "Got a devil of a temper, too, I'll warrant. Born with it, by the color of her hair. And she is very young, for all her worldly façade."

"I suppose you gleaned all of this from one kiss at the Assembly Ball?" Lady Mary asked indignantly.

"No, dearest Cousin," Julian said simply. "It comes from having many years' experience of your sex."

"Well!" breathed Lady Mary. "You needn't brag about your conquests to me!"

He shrugged.

"Think what a dull dog I'd be if at four-and-twenty I hadn't notched up a few conquests."

"I don't care to know how many females you've ruined!"

He smiled and said softly, "Only those wanting to be ruined, Mary."

"You may think it vastly amusing, my lord, to seduce Deb in the shadows of the Assembly Room—"

Julian sighed.

"Mary. Don't get yourself in a passion over matters which you can neither influence nor alter."

Lady Mary lifted her chin defiantly.

"You may have ruined the daughter of a French tax collector, but I won't allow you to ruin Deborah's chances of marrying well. It has taken Sir Gerald and me years and considerable effort to bring Deb back from the brink of social disaster after she bolted to Paris." When her cousin put up his brows in interest she became flustered. "Not that *that* is any of your concern." Adding in an about-face that would have surprised her husband, "When Robert Thesiger asks her, I know she will accept him, despite his-his *unfortunate* parentage."

"Robert has asked her," Julian said flatly. "She has refused him on no less than three occasions."

"How-how do you know this?"

"I have made it my business to know," he drawled. "One must protect one's investment."

"Investment?"

The Marquis came to stand beside her.

"Listen to me, Mary. Why do you think Thesiger is pursuing Deb? Why is he so keen for her to accept his offer of marriage when he is at liberty to pursue any female of his choosing?" When his cousin continued to blink uncomprehendingly up at him, he sighed. "By enticing Deb into wedlock and bedding her he will have his revenge on a family name he can never call his own."

Lady Mary's eyes widened. So the sordid rumors were true. She had heard the whispers about Robert Thesiger's parentage but she had never had confirmation that the man was indeed her cousin's half-brother and thus the Duke of Roxton's bastard son. Still, that did not adequately explain why the Marquis was also pursuing Deborah, unless he and Robert Thesiger were locked in some bizarre battle with Deb's virtue as the prize. Knowing a little of their history at Eton, she could well believe it.

"You are at the same liberty as Mr. Thesiger to choose any female," she said as she manoeuvred her wide hooped petticoats between the furniture to stand by the window, because her cousin was too close for comfort. "Why Deborah?"

Julian frowned down at his intricately-engraved initials on the polished lid of his gold snuffbox.

"Because Deborah Cavendish is my wife."

"Your—*wife*?"

"Yes."

"How? When? It can't be true!"

"We were married off as children, just before I was sent to the Continent. Deb has no recollection of that night, and it was thought in our best interests that she and the rest of society remain ignorant of the match until my return. I ask that you not say anything to her." He smiled crookedly. "She knows me only as Julian Hesham, and I would prefer her to go on thinking me a gentleman of no particular family for the time being. If she were to discover the circumstances behind our union before I've had a chance to make her my wife in more than name only—"

"You intend to bed her without telling her who you really are?" Lady Mary was outraged. "You think it preferable that she be deceived into your bed than be married honestly and willingly to Robert Thesiger?" She gave a hysterical laugh. "You think she will accept with equanimity a husband capable of turning on his own mother—"

Quick as lightning Julian lashed out and grabbed Lady Mary about the wrist and pulled her hard up against his chest, his red face stuck in hers.

"You know nothing—*nothing*!" he snarled, green eyes ablaze with fury.

He pushed her away and turned to regain his composure, angry with himself for letting his cousin's words get the better of him.

"Don't interfere in this, Madam," he added coldly, squaring his shoulders and adjusting his cuffs just as the door was flung wide. "Well, Jack, where is your Aunt Deborah?" he asked, forcing a smile.

Lady Mary threw her cousin a resentful look and rushed out into the hall. Her head thudded and her heart pounded. She had the beginnings of a terrible megrim. She needed to return home as quickly as possible to tell her husband. She really couldn't believe Sir Gerald would be party to such a horrid scheme of deceit against his own sister. He must do something to save Deborah from her unconscionable cousin.

"Mary? I thought you'd gone," said Deb, descending the stairs.

She was dressed in a many-petticoated gown of pale blue silk, embroidered in the Chinese manner on the tight bodice and its hem with flowers and singing birds. The low, square-cut décolletage was made respectable by the expert arrangement of a thin silk-tasseled shawl draped across her bare shoulders and tucked in at the bosom. She peered into the large gilt looking glass in the hall and patted into place her upswept hair, several curls allowed to spring out over one shoulder. She frowned, catching her sister-in-law's reflection.

"Are you perfectly well, Mary?"

"I have the headache!" Lady Mary announced, suddenly wretched—more so because Deborah looked positively radiant in her ignorance—and scrambled into her waiting sedan chair.

Deb followed her.

"I hope it wasn't Nero's antics that brought on your headache, dearest," Deb said cheerfully at the window of the sedan chair, a suspicious glance at Jack, the wayward puppy, and Julian Hesham, all of whom stood in the hallway. The latter shrugged his shoulders, denying all implication in Lady Mary's failing health. "If we see Mrs. Dawkins-Smythe in the park, shall I tell her to visit you with one of her restorative jellies?"

"No! I couldn't bear it! Not now!" Lady Mary exclaimed in a shattered voice, and with a sob banged on the side of the door with the closed sticks of her fan, eager for the two burly chairmen to lift her chair up on its long poles. She then threw herself against the damask upholstery and was unceremoniously bounced away out into the street.

"Poor Mary," Deb said with a concerned frown, twirling her straw bonnet by its ribands. "Gerry has come to town and now she won't have a moment's peace."

"Aunt Mary is always complaining of a headache," Jack commented.

"I don't recall asking for your opinion, you rude boy," Deborah said sternly, but with such laughter in her eyes that Jack grinned. She turned to Julian, saying, "I didn't mean to keep you waiting above a minute, but Brigitte threatened to throw herself from the second landing if I stepped outside without first changing into this fetching gown and allowing her to put up my hair." She glanced at her nephew. "Well, Jack, I thought you'd promised to help Joseph?"

Her nephew looked expectantly at the Marquis.

"I have consented to allow Master Cavendish to ride with us about the park," Julian said, taking Deb's arm and leading her a little way up the street to where his open carriage-and-four awaited. "His reward for getting your butler off my back." He looked over his shoulder to make sure the boy was behind them. "Yes, you may bring that black brute with you. But you and he must sit up front with Thomas and behave. Which means leaving your aunt and me in peace. Agreed?"

"Thank you, sir! I won't be a nuisance. Promise!"

Deb sat back against the plush red velvet upholstery and tied on her bonnet, a sideways glance at Julian as he settled himself beside her.

"I don't pretend to understand how you came to take Jack into your confidence, but it is clear he is firmly in your camp already."

"Why, Miss Cavendish, I do believe you think me capable of underhandedness, and for the sole purpose of gaining your undying devotion. That bow will never do! Come here," he said, and proceeded to retie the silk ribands of her bonnet. "Head up! Good girl."

With a nod to his driver, they set off up Milsom Street at a leisurely trot.

They had not gone very far when a gentleman on horseback reined in alongside and proceeded to accompany the carriage on its journey.

It was Robert Thesiger.

"Miss Cavendish! What a delight to see you out-of-doors!" he called out from astride a magnificent black stallion.

He carried a pearl-handled riding crop which he used to bring his mount beside the open carriage. He inclined his head to both occupants, but whereas Deb returned the salutation, Julian stared straight ahead, as if the man were not there at all.

The carriage stopped at a congested intersection, where a wagon and a traveling coach were vying for space.

"It required only the right inducement, Mr. Thesiger," Deb called out teasingly.

Robert Thesiger's smile was tight. "I must speak with you, Miss Cavendish," he demanded, a glance at the Marquis. "It is a matter of the utmost urgency."

Deb stared at him keenly and noted the sheen of perspiration on his forehead.

"Has something happened? Is Lady Mary truly ill? Did you see her just now in her chair?"

"No, Miss Cavendish, I have not seen Lady Mary!" Robert Thesiger snapped, a note of desperation creeping into the normally cool voice. "This matter concerns you and me!"

Deb breathed easier knowing Mary was all right, and settled herself against the velvet upholstery.

"I am most happy for you to call on me this afternoon, Mr. Thesiger," she called out to him with a smile. "But I have quite made up my mind to take a turn about the park before nuncheon."

When Julian put an arm over the back of the seat and let his fingers toy with one of Deb's curls, she glanced up at Robert Thesiger, who still rode beside the carriage, and was surprised by his thunderous expression. She was unsure what angered him more—being ignored by her traveling companion, who continued to stare out at the opposite side of the road, thus affording them a view of the back of his head, or the fact that her traveling companion signaled his possession by playing with her hair.

"Miss Cavendish! I must insist!" Robert Thesiger demanded, pressing his mount into action, an eye on the road and eager to keep up with the Marquis's horses as the carriage moved off to merge with the flow of traffic. Receiving no response from her, he appealed to the driver, shouting to be heard over the carriage wheels on the cobbles. "Master Cavendish! I say, Master Cavendish, order the driver to pull over!" he called out to Jack, up on the box beside Thomas.

"Your aunt must return home this instant! Master Cavendish? Do you hear?"

Jack turned to take direction, not from Robert Thesiger but from the Marquis. Julian shook his head slightly, and Jack nodded. He put up his shoulders at Robert Thesiger, as if there was nothing he could do, and faced forward again.

Robert Thesiger was so incensed that he swung his mount violently to the left and galloped around the back of the carriage to rein in beside where sat the Marquis.

"Enjoy your hour of triumph," he snarled in French. "It'll be your last! Lawyers from Paris carry a warrant for your arrest." When Julian continued to stare straight ahead as if not spoken to, crossing his legs in a leisurely fashion, Robert Thesiger leaned so far forward in the saddle that the brim of his hat almost tickled his lordship's ear. "M'sieur Lefebvre is intent on French justice, exposing you for a despicable cad. *Our father* can't protect you this time."

This did make Julian turn. He stared Robert Thesiger full in the face, as if he'd spoken a language he did not understand, but then he winked and broke into a wide grin saying in French, "Better despicable cad than bastard. *Foutre le camp.*"

A thump to the boards with his boot, and Julian's driver gave the horses their heads. The carriage took off, swerved around two gentlemen officers on horseback, narrowly passed between a wagon laden with kegs and an open barouche carrying three elderly ladies, and was half-way up the street before Robert Thesiger had completely righted himself in the saddle. Julian finally acknowledged him without turning around with a cavalier wave of one gloved hand high above his head.

TWELVE

D EB SAT IN thoughtful silence a long time after Robert
Thesiger was left by the curb, but it was not until the
town was behind them and the carriage rattling along the Wells
Road that she came to a sense of her surroundings. She sat bolt
upright.

"Where are you taking me?"

"I've kidnapped you, Miss Cavendish." When this quip fell
flat, Julian smiled ruefully. "That is—only if you *wish* to be
kidnapped."

"Well! It was very unromantic of you to invite Jack along,
not to mention that black fiend with four legs." She looked sideways at him. "Or are you about to off-load them at the nearest
inn with the ransom note?"

He laughed and the tension eased in his shoulders.

"How is it you know me so well? And of course, you never
wavered in your conviction that I would return to Bath for you,
did you, Miss Cavendish?"

"May I know why you gave Mr. Thesiger the brush-off just
now?" she asked, ignoring his question. "You seemed determined to ignore his existence."

Julian gave a ghost of a laugh.

"I've been trying to do that since Eton, Miss Cavendish, but the fellow refuses to go away."

Deb tried to sound disinterested. "You were at Eton together? How intriguing."

"No. It was a dead bore," he answered flatly, and abruptly changed the subject and the language with a question of his own in French.

"How long have you had the care of your nephew?"

"Since Jack was six years old," she answered in kind, following his lead. "Gerry turned his back on him—the poor little chap. You see, Jack's mamma, Rosa, was a gypsy... Well, that's all ancient history now. I brought Jack back from Paris and we set up house in Bath."

"You must have been very young to take charge of a small boy."

"I was eighteen," she answered, and in a more rallying tone, "And I had the help of Joseph Jones, my brother Otto's major domo... That was almost three years ago, and I would rather—"

"May I know why you were living with Jack's family in Paris," he interrupted, "and not under Sir Gerald's protection here in England?"

Deb bit her lip. The conversation had taken a dangerous turn, and she was unsure how best to steer it clear of a topic she would rather not discuss. Yet, it was far better to have the story from her than hear a distorted version from a stranger. She took a moment to consider her words, all the while conscious of Julian's gaze upon her. A mile down the road she glanced up at him and spoke in a measured tone.

"When I was eighteen I ran away to Paris to care for my brother Otto, who was very ill. Otto went off on the Grand Tour just after my tenth birthday and never came home. He preferred a bohemian existence as a musician, and as he had married totally inappropriately, he couldn't return home even if he wanted to. Not that he did want to, because he and Rosa had a wonderful life together amongst the musical community in Paris. Rosa was heavy with child and could not care for a sick husband, a small boy and herself all on her own. She-she and the babe died in childbed just after I reached Paris."

"And after Otto's death, you and Jack and Mr. Jones returned home without incident?" Julian asked gently, knowing full well that this was not the case but hoping she would refute the statement without his prompting.

Deb took a deep breath and stared out at the blur of fields. "I wish it had been uneventful..." She met his gaze openly and smiled ruefully. "Otto's best friend Evelyn, who is also a splendid musician, wanted to marry me, but he needed the permission of his father and of his uncle the Duke of Roxton, as that old roué is head of his family. They refused him."

"Understandable. You were both too young to be contemplating marriage."

"Too young?" Deb looked thoughtful. "No, I don't believe that was the reason at all. Plenty of children are married off by their parents at a far earlier age."

"Perhaps the Duke and Evelyn's father felt your feelings weren't entirely fixed?"

"Not *fixed*? It is obvious you have no idea how this business is conducted. Character and disposition are irrelevant, as are the opinions of the prospective bride and groom. What matters to noblemen such as the Duke of Roxton is the legal union: The transfer of money and property; the connection of one family to another; the consolidation of power and prestige. Feelings have no role to play in such contractual arrangements."

Julian stared at the toe of his polished boot, a private smile hovering about his curved mouth.

"But as you and Evelyn were not *cold-bloodedly* contracted to one another, perhaps Evelyn's family were not persuaded you would make him a suitable wife?"

Deb turned her head and gaped at him.

"Not suitable? A Cavendish heiress not *suitable* to marry the son of a viscount?"

Julian shook his head sadly.

"Ah, my dear Miss Cavendish, despite your protests to the contrary, I see that wealth and title do matter to you."

Deb turned away, mortified at being so conceited as to throw her name and fortune in his face. Taking a peek at him, she soon realized that despite his grave look he was laughing at her. She stared at the box where Jack sat holding the reins, Nero licking his face. Yet she saw none of it. Evelyn had offered to marry her and she had refused him. He had protested that he loved her and had not merely offered her his name out of loyalty to Otto. But Deb had rejected him because she had not loved him enough to elope with him.

As it turned out, the Duke of Roxton had discovered Evelyn's plans and had forbidden his nephew to marry her. She had been relieved, but ashamed to think the Duke and Evelyn's father had rejected her despite her being a considerable heiress. She had had to conclude her unsuitability was because she was thought volatile of character—running away to Paris and her involvement with Otto, the black sheep of her family, and his gypsy wife, was surely proof of that. Yet she believed she had done nothing wrong—indeed, had responded to her heart and in the only way she knew how. So why was she ashamed every time she thought of the consequences of her flight to Paris?

"There is no need for you to involve yourself with me," she said sullenly. "Nothing came of Evelyn's offer of marriage. That is an end to the matter."

He shifted to sit opposite her and possessed himself of her gloved hands, but she could not look at him. He frowned.

"You allow me to kiss you and yet you say I am not to involve myself with you...?"

"I wanted you to kiss me," Deb answered truthfully, gaze on her hands in his. "But I don't want you to involve yourself with me. There is a difference in the two."

"Are you in the habit of allowing gentlemen of the merest acquaintance to kiss you?"

Deb gaped at him, heat burning in her cheeks.

"Just because I won't unburden myself on you, and yet permitted you to kiss me, that I am—that I have—Why! Yes!" she said, changing her tune at his spreading smile. "Dozens! Not dozens, but too many to count. And in public. So you can banish that smug smile!"

"More and more do I sympathize with dull Gerry," he said with a sad shake of his handsome head. "And Evelyn doesn't know how fortunate he is. Better he concentrates on his music than have to wife a female who is in the habit of kissing dozens of gentlemen in public. You saved him from a marriage that could only have ended in disaster."

Deb tried to pull her hands free, but he would not let go.

"You know not the first thing about me or him, for that matter, to pass judgment on either of us! That you have the audacity to tell me to my face... Stop this carriage at once!" When he grinned and ignored her plea to have the carriage pull over, she said, "You are a fiend and a brute! After such an appalling roasting I've no intention of telling you anything!"

"No? I can wait it out. Thomas has his orders. He will keep on driving until the horses give out, if need be, or I give the order to pull up. And I wouldn't be concerned with Jack's welfare. There's a basket of foodstuffs under the box. He, at least, won't go hungry."

"You won't coerce me in this way," she stated, but did not sound particularly convincing because she was trying very hard not to laugh. "There is nothing to tell. I say and do the most shocking things to relieve a natural boredom—nothing more."

Julian folded his arms, black curls back against the velvet upholstery, and closed his eyes.

"You may wake me when you are ready for confidences..."

Five minutes passed.

Deb pretended to enjoy the countryside and Julian kept his

word, only once opening an eye to take a peek at his hostage, quick to close it when she glanced his way. The road was beginning to climb and the horses slowed, but there was no sign of an inn or a farmhouse and Jack was happily chomping into an apple.

"Why should I unburden myself on you when I am certain you must have as many secrets to tell?" Deb demanded. "I don't know the first thing about you."

When this was greeted with continued silence, she let out a great breath of exasperation, shifted on the seat, and turned to view the deep woods that now lined both sides of the winding road. She could see he was going to be stubborn so she had to offer him something if only to get him to be pleasant enough to take her home again.

She was surprised when he broke the long silence between them.

"Have you fallen in love, Miss Cavendish?"

At this, Deb's throat constricted and again her cheeks burned. Her gaze flew up to his face and then she looked away just as swiftly, wanting to refute the question, yet unable to do so because it was true. She had fallen in love, inexplicably and without good reason, with him, but she could not bring herself to say so. She felt foolish, not knowing how he felt, whether he returned her regard, and if he cared enough for her to flout convention and disregard Sir Gerald's opposition and society's censure to elope with her.

"Miss Cavendish," he said firmly, "are you in love with Robert Thesiger?"

"*Robert Thesiger*?" Deb was so taken aback that her color deepened at such a blunt suggestion. "Why would you think me in love with Mr. Thesiger?"

"I saw you together at the Assembly Ball."

Deb put up her chin.

"I hardly think that dancing the minuet with a gentleman constitutes a love match, do you, sir?"

"Yet, his display just now on horseback... He was most insistent you speak with him..."

At this, Deb looked down at her gloved hands, embarrassed.

"I cannot return Mr. Thesiger's regard. And he is a most persistent gentleman... But you asked if I am in love with him, and the answer is no, I am not."

"I am relieved to hear you say so. I have no wish to come between a love match."

"Just because I am not in love with him does not mean I do not champion his friendship. I refuse to be prejudiced by his questionable parentage."

"My dear girl," Julian drawled, "let me assure you his motives are far more questionable than his parentage."

He sprung down from the carriage, for it had come to stand in a wooded lane. He assisted Deb to firm ground, then turned away before she could respond, Jack running off up the path that led into the wood, Nero at his boot heels. A word to his driver, and he escorted Deb along the same path, a basket in one hand, and in the other, of all things to bring on a carriage ride, a cricket bat.

THIRTEEN

DEB SOON KNEW why. Up ahead, through a break in the forest, was a clearing. Beyond the clearing, the river, and across the water, undulating farming land. Over the first rise, a curl of smoke drifted up into the darkening clouds.

Jack was busy collecting sticks for the stumps of a wicket he had marked out, while Nero devoted himself to ferreting out possible rabbit holes on the edge of the clearing. A blanket spread out, the basket deposited, the cricket ball found in amongst the foodstuffs, and Julian turned to Deb with a small bow.

"If you will be so kind as to do the honors with the contents of the basket, I shall endeavor to entertain your nephew—part of the bargain, I'm afraid."

Deb frowned as she took off her bonnet. "You're not going to play at cricket in your condition, surely? It cannot be many weeks since you were stitched up."

"It has been three weeks, five days and several hours since we first met," he said, and was pleased when she was instantly flustered and looked anywhere but at him. "I am better mended than you realize and am quite capable of bowling a ball. But I won't. I shall leave that treat for Jack. I will merely bat and let Jack bowl me out. Excuse me. You will find a bottle of excellent burgundy and two goblets in the basket."

Jack proved a tireless competitor and would not give up the game until he had bowled Julian out for a third time. On one occasion he caught and bowled him, which sent Jack into such spasms of delight that it had Nero barking loud and long, thinking his young master in danger of losing his life. It took Deb much coaxing with a succulent slice of lamb before Nero forgot the danger and thought of his stomach. He trotted over to Deb, ears down, and obeyed her command to be a good dog and eat his dinner without a fuss. For his obedience he received a pat. Julian and Jack soon followed, bat and ball let fall into the leaf litter beside the feast laid out on the blanket.

"Well done, Jack. That was a splendid catch," said Deb with a smile. "Your father would've been proud. Otto played at school," she explained to Julian, handing him a goblet of burgundy, the intervening interval of cricket serving to make her at ease again. "And before he went to the Continent, I spent Saturday afternoons at the village green watching him play at cricket with the local farmers' sons."

"Your aunt is beyond price, Jack. Plays a viola, tells me she is a crack shot with a pistol, and not only does she like the game of cricket, but she also understands it." Julian bit into a slice of pie, a wink at his young friend. "Will you mind sharing her?"

Jack grinned.

"I've seen Aunt Deb take the corner off a playing card at ten paces. Joseph made her as mad as hellfire once and she had him hold up the King of Diamonds in the back parlor and—"

"Jack! That will do!"

"And what, Jack?" Julian asked, passing the boy a wedge of venison and mushroom pie.

Jack ate hungrily of the pie, hesitating to give Julian an

answer. Yet he received such an encouraging look from him that he couldn't help a little family disloyalty.

"The shot hit its mark all right, but it shattered the big looking glass over the fireplace. Alice was still picking up the shards two weeks later."

"Thank you very much, John George Cavendish," Deb said without heat. "You failed to add that the said looking glass had the most hideous frame imaginable. No one was sorry to see it go, except Sir Gerald."

"Only because every time he visits, Uncle Gerald sneaks into the back parlor to peer into that glass," Jack confessed, adding for Julian's benefit, "He's always fixing his wig. But no amount of fixing is going to make a difference. He still looks like an egg fitted with a cozy!"

Deb opened her mouth to upbraid her nephew for such lack of respect, but instead she giggled behind her hand.

"He does look like an egg, doesn't he? Oh dear! I shall never be able to view him the same way again! P-poor M-Mary."

"Well, I don't want to look like an egg," Jack confided, falling back onto the blanket and staring up into a sky gathering clouds. "I'm going to wear my own hair—always. My friend Harry says his brother *and* his papa both wear their own hair." He looked across at Deb. "Harry—well his name isn't really Harry, it's a mouthful—Lord Henri-Antoine—but he likes his chums to call him Harry. And he don't like it to be known he speaks French better than he does Shakespeare's English. Harry says his papa has always worn his own hair and he's *ancient*. Harry says his papa wore his coronet in the processional at the coronation of King George *the Second*. I wouldn't have believed it had any other fellow told me, but Harry never lies."

"Perhaps Harry meant to say his *grand* papa?" Deb suggested.

Jack sat up on an elbow. He selected a chunk of cheese from the platter put before him.

"No, Aunt Deb. But he does look like a *grand* papa. He was

dressed all in black velvet with silver lacings, and his hair is white like fresh snow, and he wears the largest emerald ring I've ever seen—"

"Snow-white hair and a large emerald ring..." Deb repeated, a sudden vivid remembrance in her mind's eye of a dream she'd had as a child—of an ancient gentleman with bright black eyes, white hair, and on a long white finger a large square-cut emerald that glinted in the firelight. He was someone very important, and he was very sad. "He looked a hundred years old..." she murmured to herself.

"He came to school in the most magnificent coach-and-six," Jack was saying, hardly drawing breath, such was his excitement to tell his aunt about Harry's papa. "The horses were all black high-steppers and the coach was of black lacquer with gold leaf *everywhere*. There were *six* outriders in scarlet and silver livery! It had us fellows at the windows when we should've been at our Latin, but who could think of grammar?"

"Who indeed," Julian commented, and in a tone that did not encourage Jack to continue. He rummaged in the basket for a fruit knife to cut up an apple, slices of which he offered to Deb. "It will rain in the next hour..."

"Are you certain it was an emerald, Jack?" Deb asked quietly, unconsciously taking the apple slices Julian offered her from the knife's edge.

The boy nodded. "It was a green stone. As green as your eyes, sir. Pardon, sir. That's an emerald, isn't it, Aunt Deb?"

Deb nodded, distracted, as she turned to look into Julian's eyes. She knew they were green but she had not realized just how emerald-green they truly were. They were beautiful eyes—eyes that reminded her of a sad boy in one of her dreams. She was on a swing and Otto was there with her. And then the boy was there, sobbing uncontrollably, and Otto was not. Nurse had told her it was just a bad dream brought on by the medicine she had been given for some minor ailment she now could not remember. She was told to forget all about it...

"Are you certain this ancient gentleman came to collect Harry? That he wasn't just visiting the school for some other purpose?" Deb persisted.

"Why this sudden fascination with white-haired old men, Miss Cavendish?" Julian asked lightly. "Some men do wear their own hair, be it white, brown or black. Or perhaps we are confusing white hair with powdered hair or a wig?"

Jack shook his head and answered before his aunt could speak.

"No, sir. It was his own hair. Harry told me his papa wears his own hair. And Harry's papa came to the school because Harry had taken one of his turns."

"Turns?" Deb asked gently, an eye on Julian who was frowning, paused in mid-slice with knife and apple.

Jack was uncomfortable talking about his best friend's malady, only because Harry hated having it discussed. But he wanted to explain himself to his aunt and this gentleman who had been so kind to them.

"Harry suffers with the falling sickness. He never knows when it's going to happen. Sometimes he'll get a terrible headache and then he just faints dead away. Just like that! He says he was born with it. And that's why his papa came to school—to take him home after one of his attacks. He has his own physician and his mamma—"

"Dear me, Master Jack! Are you Lord Henri-Antoine's self-appointed confessor?" Julian interrupted coldly, getting up off the blanket and roughly brushing down his breeches. "What gives you the right to share such intimate details with us when they were obviously told to you in the strictest confidence?"

"No, sir," Jack answered quietly, coloring up as he scrambled to his feet. "I mean, yes, sir, he did tell me in confidence. It's just that Harry is my best friend in the whole world."

When Julian turned to pick up the empty burgundy bottle, Jack looked to his aunt, wondering what he had said to offend the gentleman.

Deb smiled kindly at her nephew.

"Why don't you take Nero for a run before we head back?" she suggested, and as soon as he was out of earshot rounded on Julian full of angry embarrassment for her nephew. "That was uncalled for, sir! Jack is a sensitive, caring boy. He wasn't pouring scorn on Harry's malady. Anyone with eyes could see poor Harry's affliction affects him deeply. Why you should see it differently—"

"Your nephew has no right to speak on matters he knows nothing about! Nor should they concern you!"

"Is that so?" she enunciated, shaking out her silk petticoats and snatching up her bonnet. "I know not the first thing about you, your family, your connections—indeed what you do with your time, apart from getting yourself involved in duels with the odds stacked against you! Yet I am expected to allow you to concern yourself in my affairs? Indeed, you expect me to give you a full and open account of my history, without the same courtesy being offered me in return—"

"If you loved me—"

"Loved you?" Deb stared at him. "*Loved* you?" she repeated in a whisper, the color draining from her cheeks. "How dare you presume!"

He smiled sheepishly. "Ah. I have overstepped the mark." He bowed. "Forgive me for such overbearing presumption."

"God, I wish I'd never set eyes on you!" she said savagely, the straw bonnet crushed in her hand. "Life was so much the simpler before I bandaged you up. I wish you'd never returned to Bath. Damn you! Don't think I've spent my days pining. I haven't. No! I won't allow you to hold me," she said, trying to push him off. "You presume that I have fallen in love with you just because—Oh! I can't believe you had the effrontery to—to—"

He caught her to him and held her until she stopped struggling and fell against his chest.

"I want you, Deborah," he murmured, lifting her chin so he

could gently kiss her mouth. "I want you as my wife in every sense. Do you understand me? *Do you*?"

She nodded, staring up into his handsome face and the deep green of his lovely eyes. He was the handsomest man she had ever set eyes on, so like the boy in her dream that it made her shiver, and she was in his arms and he wanted her. *Her*. And as his wife. She knew she loved him. She'd known that from the moment she'd set eyes on him in the Avon forest. It was love at first sight for her.

Until she'd come across her injured duelist in the forest she wasn't at all sure she believed it possible to fall in love with someone within a blink of an eye. Otto and Rosa had. Rosa confided that when she and Otto had first met, each knew instantly that they wanted to be with the other and no one else for the rest of their lives. But she had always presumed her brother and his wife to be a special case...

So if she loved him and he wanted her to be his wife, why did she hesitate at the thought of giving herself to him body and soul? It was true that she knew not the first thing about him. He looked and spoke and had the air of a gentleman of means and position, yet he had avoided telling her anything more than his name. But did his wealth and social standing really matter to her? It certainly hadn't mattered to Otto, and he and Rosa had been blissfully happy. Why then did this feeling that he was withholding something fundamental to their future happiness niggle at her so? But surely, if she loved him and he loved her, they could overcome any obstacles put in their path...?

She made a movement and he let her go and stepped back, awaiting her response. For want of something to do, because he felt awkward and clumsy standing in the middle of a blanket, his embraces rejected, Julian set to packing away the picnic things.

She knelt to help him, saying over the basket, "You are under no obligation to me because I saved your life in the forest."

"I am eternally grateful for your assistance, but that episode has nothing to do with us being husband and wife."

Deb looked him in the face.

"You want me even though I ran away from home—that I almost eloped with a musician—that I play a viola, *and* can handle a pistol as good as the next man?"

He smiled. "I am determined, Miss Cavendish."

She sat forward on her knees. "And if I accept? Perhaps it is I who am entering into a bad bargain?"

He gave a bark of laughter. "That depends on whether you want the man or his consequence."

At this she gave a tinkle of laughter and relaxed. "Oh, give me the man!"

He grinned self-consciously and together they folded the blanket.

Deb glanced at him.

"You are determined to have me?"

"Quite determined."

"And if Gerald objects?"

He took the folded blanket from her and dropped it across the basket, saying lightly, "If you marry the man and not his consequence, then Gerry's opposition should hardly weigh with you, should it?"

"It doesn't."

"I've given Jack's situation some thought," he stated, changing the subject, an eye on the boy who stood at the edge of the clearing playing at fetch with Nero. "Naturally he must live with us when he is not in school. And Evelyn should tutor him, if he can be induced to return to England. Then again, Jack may prefer to spend part of the year with Har—Come along before we are soaked to the skin!" he said, grabbing at her hand as large drops of rain began to fall. "Jack! The bat and ball, if you please!"

They ran back to the carriage, Thomas with the forethought to put up the top and secure the windows. It did not stop them receiving a soaking, or Nero putting muddy paws over his young master's buckskin breeches. To Deb it seemed as if they had just settled themselves comfortably when the carriage swept through a set of iron gates and on up a gravel drive. It stopped in front of a Queen Anne house: Martin Ellicott's residence.

FOURTEEN

BEFORE DEB COULD ask the question, Julian apologized. "I must confess to a slight deception. Our picnic was not half a mile from here. I had Thomas drive about the countryside in circles."

"I thought you would have discovered that, Aunt Deb!" Jack said, exchanging a grin with Julian.

"Traitor," Deb said lovingly. "As for you," she said to Julian, who was peering out at the constant rain, "I'm not at all certain I should allow Jack to spend time with such a corruptive influence."

"Aunt Deb!"

"I shouldn't take your aunt's words too seriously. Her actions speak volumes," Julian commented as he opened the carriage door. "The rain is easing," he added and stepped down and offered Deb his hand. "Jack, be sure and change out of those wet clothes when you get home." He handed the boy a sealed packet from his frock coat pocket. "Give this to Mr. Jones. He'll know what to do."

Deb stood in the rain, wondering what she should do. A footman came dashing out of the house and took delivery of two portmanteaux from the driver. She recognized them as hers. She was speechless. Julian was issuing last minute instructions to Jack and had solicited his utmost secrecy, which the boy readily gave. With a last pat for Nero, he said the word and Thomas sprung the horses, and the carriage left without her.

Deb pointed to the portmanteaux as the footman disappeared with them into the house. "Those-those are my—*my* bags!"

Julian looked up from studying the face of his gold pocket watch, then slipped it back into his flowered waistcoat pocket.

"Yes. How convenient they were packed and awaiting me in your hallway. And we are getting wet," he said and unceremoniously pulled her toward the house. "No doubt they contain everything you'll need."

"Everything I need? For what?" she demanded, oblivious to the rain and the droop of her bonnet. "But they are packed for my trip to—"

"You can't go on your honeymoon without luggage. Now come along!"

Deb ignored the butler's bow of welcome.

"*Honeymoon?*"

"You'll be pleased Brigitte was in total agreement and wished me luck."

Deb looked about her wildly. "Agreement to what?"

"We have already kept the vicar waiting twenty minutes."

"Vicar?" Deb almost screeched.

She brought herself up short. Julian held wide the drawing room door. Deep in the room there was hushed conversation and the tinkle of glasses. Somebody laughed. Deb kept her feet firmly planted in the hallway. She looked inquiringly at the doorway, then at Julian but said nothing.

He smiled in understanding.

"No one who bites," he assured her. "The vicar, his good wife, her sister to stand as matron of honor, and Frew, of course. Sadly, no Martin, who always spends this time of year with my parents. I have a special license and the vicar is willing to forgo a church service as a favor to my deep-seated need for absolute privacy. Shall we...?"

Deb shivered and pulled the damp shawl closer about her shoulders. She felt ill.

"I—I—What about Gerry and Mary and your family and—"

Julian laughed. "My father had begun to despair of ever becoming a grandparent, and as I have your brother's blessing to our marriage that's all that matters really, isn't it?"

"How did you get Gerry to—"

"Let's not spoil the moment by talking about your groveling brother." He smiled reassuringly and kissed her hand. "Shall we go in? The vicar is waiting—"

"But our clothes," Deb argued, "are wet and—and—Oh! A hundred other objections I'm sure I could think of if I weren't in a state of utter nervous collapse! You can't be serious?" When he did not answer, just stood there expectantly, fingers about the door handle, her shoulders slumped. "Must it be now?" she asked in a tiny voice.

"If it will make you feel better able to struggle through the ceremony, I am just as nervous."

Deb wrung her gloved hands. "I'm not dressed! We're wet through! My hair..."

"The sooner we set off on our honeymoon the sooner we can get on with our lives."

Slowly, Deb stripped off her soaked gloves, removed her drenched bonnet and dropped these and the wet shawl onto a chair in the hallway. She did not bother to take a step back to glance at her reflection in the looking glass. She knew her hair was untidy and that her lips needed color. Her boots were muddy, too, and her bodice damp, as were her pale blue silk petticoats, which had acquired a large grass stain about the knees.

Such petty details, and the vicar kept waiting...

FIFTEEN

DEB WOKE TO the muted sounds of dawn—of waterfowl in the tangle of tall reeds shrouded in mist at the river's edge, and beyond that the breeze rustling the tops of the beech trees in the awakening forest. It was still dark enough for the light of a full moon to shine through the open curtains and across the heavy coverlet on the four-poster bed. She lay amongst the tumble of feather-filled pillows listening sleepily to the distant noises outside her window, reveling in the warmth under the covers and supremely happy. Married three days and yet she felt so comfortable and unselfconscious in her new role as wife that it was almost as if she had been married to Julian for years and years.

The marriage ceremony seemed a lifetime ago. The vicar and the attendants looked as nervous as she herself had been. Julian held her hand so tightly it was as if he feared she would flee. And in their nervousness neither bride nor groom looked left or right, nor did they glance at each other until their vows had been exchanged. It was only with the ink dry in the Parish Register and the couple toasted with a glass of Martin Ellicott's finest champagne that tension eased enough for there to be light conversation.

Deb had been too overwhelmed by the progress of events from picnic to wedding service to finding herself married that she had been oblivious to the finer details of that wet afternoon. She could not recall the inconsequential chatter over champagne and cake, only that there was an atmosphere of uncomfortable self-restraint. The vicar, his good wife and the attendants never once initiated conversation nor looked at their ease, and barely sipped the bubbles in their crystal glasses. Yet, when her husband spoke, they became animated and hung on his every word, answering him in monosyllables. It reminded Deb of a king surrounded by his courtiers who, acutely aware of their lowly station in life, knew they were not worthy of engaging their liege lord in proper conversation. If Julian were aware of this, he did not show it. In fact, he went out of his way to put everyone at their ease, even her, for when the vicar announced it was time to leave the young couple to themselves, Deb knew she had blushed rosily. Julian had winked at her with a kind smile and quickly ushered everyone from the room to farewell them on the portico.

She wished Rosa and Otto had been there on her wedding day to share in her happiness, and Rosa had been right about the marriage bed. Deb had followed her advice, given long ago and not understood at the time. Love must be on equal terms, she had said: Honesty, mutual respect, pleasure, all must be given and received in equal measure and from the first night alone together as man and wife. And so, on her wedding night, in this very bed, Deb had followed Rosa's advice.

Alone together that first night, she forgot her own embarrassment as soon as she saw her husband. She had stared at Julian, momentarily taken aback when he appeared shy by her open look of admiration. It made her wonder if he had ever been regarded with such candor. His shy smile made her appreciate that for all his experience, at that moment, alone with her, he was just as nervous as she. It made her forget about her own inexperience and realize that if she were true to herself, the first night with her husband would be the beginning of a wonderfully joyous union. And so she had joined him in the big four-poster bed unafraid and on equal terms.

She turned her head on the pillow, smiling at the remembrance, wanting the touch and warmth of his body, only to discover she was alone. She immediately sat up and brushed the tangle of long hair from her face, frowning at the light coming from under the door that led into the next room. She threw on an embroidered silk dressing gown, buttoning it up carelessly, and in bare feet silently went through to the warmth and light of the small dressing room.

Julian sat at the gilt writing desk by the window adjacent to the warmth of the fire in the marble grate. He was dressed in an elaborately embroidered silk banyan that gaped at the throat. With one hand he held back the mop of shoulder-length black curls from his forehead while his quill moved quickly across a sheet of parchment, totally absorbed in his writing. When the page was filled with his elegant sloping script it was put to one side to be dried with a sprinkle of pounce, and another sheet of parchment was selected to continue the correspondence.

Standing to one side of the cluttered desk was his valet, Frew. Sleepy-eyed, yet immaculately dressed for such an early hour, he waited patiently to offer assistance with affixing the wax seals to the parchments. A small stack of answered correspondence had been placed on a silver salver by the valet's left hand, and only one letter remained unanswered.

Deb watched from the doorway, unnoticed, waiting for her husband to finish this letter before going forward. Yet he took his time and when he had come to the end of the second page his eyes wandered to the flames amongst the burning logs in the grate. One of their number suddenly popped, cracked, and fell amongst the ash, sending a snow of grey-white flakes up into the chimney. On to this fallen burning log Julian tossed the remaining page of an opened letter and watched it curl in on itself, the look on his face so intense that in the flickering light he appeared a stranger. It occurred to her then, as it had on numerous occasions over the previous couple of weeks, that she had learnt very little about her husband since that fateful day in the Avon forest.

The thought stayed with her as Julian turned away from the fireplace and ordered Frew to fetch a pot of coffee and some rolls to sustain him while he wrote a reply to this last letter—a letter that was to be sent at once by separate dispatch to His Grace in Paris. When the valet saw Deb and hesitated, causing his master to coldly inquire without looking up why he stood as a statue in the middle of the carpet, she announced herself.

It brought Julian's head round with a snap. Such was his scowl of preoccupation that Deb faltered in surprise to receive such a cold reception. Yet in the next moment he was out of his chair with a warm smile, pulling the banyan tighter about his shoulders and dismissing the valet with a sharp word that brought the servant to a sense of his social lapse.

Deb glanced at the cluttered surface of the writing desk with its scatter of parchments, silver standish holding quills and ink, melted sealing wax and a heavy gold seal on a length of gold chain, all bathed in the glow from the guttering candles of a six-stemmed candelabra.

"You've been awake for some time," she commented with a shy smile, and took the hand he held out to her.

"Letters that can't wait," he answered as he softly kissed the palm of her right hand. "I have one more to write—to Martin."

"Who is staying with your parents?" she asked in a tone she hoped sounded disinterested.

"Yes."

"You and he are close," she stated, and moved to the fireplace to spread cold hands to its warmth. "Closer than what is usual for godparent and godchild. I've never met my godparents. They used to send a gift on my birthday, until I fled to Paris to be with Otto. I guess I fell from favor."

Julian followed her, scooping up his gold seal and slipping it into a pocket of his banyan before placing himself between Deb and the writing desk.

"Frew is brewing Turkish coffee—"

"Turkish?"

"Yes. I acquired a taste for the filthy stuff when Martin and I lived in Constantinople."

"Constantinople? How fascinating," she said, wondering what had taken him to such an exotic city. The Grand Tour perhaps? "For how long were you and Martin in that city?"

"Three years," he answered, remaining fixed in front of the desk. "Long enough to enjoy the wondrous architecture of the Infidel, the unique smells, and explore the burying fields that are surprisingly far larger than the city itself. You're shivering, my dear. A hot chocolate would warm you."

Deb shook her head, fingers playing with a long strand of autumn-colored hair, determined to pursue a line of thought he continually avoided.

"Strange, you and M'sieur Ellicott lived in such a far-away city. I dare say you shared many an interesting adventure, and yet in all my visits here, he never once mentioned his godson."

He smiled and shrugged self-consciously.

"Martin is a very discreet and loyal creature. Accompanying a wayward youth on the Grand Tour was not his idea of restful retirement, yet he never complained. And I dare say the antics of his godson were not what Martin would've thought an appropriate topic for French conversation with a young lady." He lifted an eyebrow. "You have a measure of my godfather's upright character. You never once mentioned your penchant for playing a viola in the forest."

"Ah! But I was at pains to ensure he didn't know, for fear he would ask me to play, which would've necessitated being impolite and refusing him," she answered in a rallying tone. "I am competent, and I enjoy playing for my own pleasure, but I have a morbid fear of public performance."

Julian grinned. "That makes two of us. I told you once how I hate being the center of attention. I, too, dislike being on display. You would never know it to see me in society." He took her in his arms and kissed the top of her head. "Now that, my darling wife," he whispered at her ear, "is to be kept between us and no other."

"Do you go into society very often?" she persisted, snuggling into his warm embrace by the fireside.

"When required—"

"—by your family?" she asked too quickly, and wished she had held her tongue for he let her go and moved to the sofa.

At that awkward moment Frew came through the servant door carrying a tray holding the coffee things. The valet placed this on the table and quietly departed.

Deb watched Julian arrange the coffee things, items that were richly patterned and lacquered and Oriental in design—a souvenir from his stay in Constantinople he told her. The pear-shaped coffee pot of fine porcelain patterned with gold rested on an elaborate silver stand that had at its base a candle warmer to keep the pot's contents at drinking temperature. There were two fine porcelain dishes, into one of which Julian poured out a liquid so thick and black it was the consistency of treacle. He stirred a precise amount of sugar into the coffee with a long-handled silver spoon and this he set aside on a lacquered spoon rest before picking up the dish and sipping the Turkish brew to test for the correct proportion of bitterness to sweetness.

"The wine of Islam," he commented, savoring the taste. He held out the dish. "Would you like to try it?"

Deb did not immediately answer. She had been watching him intently, how his long fingers curled about the curved handle of the coffee pot, the way he sprinkled sugar into the little dish and stirred it gently before bringing it up to his lovely mouth to take the smallest of sips. Such fastidious movements were in marked contrast to his want of dress and the black hair that fell unbrushed about his shoulders. She found herself wondering for the hundredth time how she had come to be married to such a man—a man who reminded her of a boy she had once dreamed about. It was a foolish and absurd thought and she wished it would leave her alone, and yet it continued to haunt her.

When he repeated his offer she took the dish, feeling the heat in her face for being distracted by absurd thoughts. Gingerly, she sipped at the dark liquid and such was the bitterness on her tongue that she screwed up her mouth and quickly thrust the dish back at him. He laughed at her expression of disgust and drank up, chucking her under the chin for her bravery. She in turn playfully grabbed at his hand. Then suddenly they both felt awkward in each other's company and fell silent.

DEB RETURNED to the fireplace to warm her hands, while over the rim of the porcelain dish Julian watched her. His green-eyed gaze traveled from her bare toes up to the swell of her bosom under the silk dressing gown, and he knew that if he did not immediately return to the writing desk to complete his correspondence, he would give in to an intense ache and make love to her there and then.

Since deciding to claim his wife, he had presumed that the consummation of their marriage would bring him a sense of closure and release: The marriage in name only would finally be legally binding, and God willing, his wife would soon be pregnant and provide the Duke with a grandson—tangible evidence of the continuance of his line. And once she was pregnant, his intention was to return to Paris, to his life there, and to the unfinished business of dealing with an overly ambitious Farmer-General, who had plotted to entrap him into marriage with his very beautiful but scheming daughter.

What he had not counted on was returning to England to discover that the girl to whom he was married had blossomed into a beautiful, desirable woman. There was no denying he was instantly attracted to her. He'd wanted her from the moment she'd straddled his lap in the forest. And so he had eagerly anticipated the consummation of his marriage. But their first night together as man and wife had turned out very differently from what he had imagined. Far from providing closure and release, he found himself intoxicated—the ache of wanting her growing more acute rather than abating. He felt as an alcoholic must who tastes wine for the first time and is instantly addicted.

She surprised and delighted him with her candid enjoyment of the marriage bed. The efforts of the most skilled courtesan now seemed tawdry by comparison to his inexperienced wife's honesty. In making love with Deb he discovered that honesty mattered a great deal, and that her physical honesty was the most potent aphrodisiac of all.

He forced himself to look away from her and returned to the writing desk. Putting aside the empty coffee dish, he needlessly shuffled through a few pages of correspondence.

"This letter cannot wait," he apologized. "It must reach its destination with all speed or two Parisian lawyers will be on our doorstep."

Deb took a step toward him. "Parisian lawyers, *here?*"

"Not if my letter reaches them first," he said, keeping his gaze on the page. "But I won't be able to put them off indefinitely. I have unfinished business in Paris."

Deb would have crossed to him, but he looked up then, sensing her nearness, and steered her away from the desk. She frowned, wondering what he did not wish her to see. Yet mention of Paris was uppermost in her mind.

"Paris? You are going to Paris?"

"Yes. To clear up a tiresome legal matter that need not concern you."

"To do with your duel in the forest?" When he nodded, she said, "I will come with you."

"No! I won't have you subjected to such an absurd ordeal."

She put a hand on his broad chest and stared up into his frowning countenance. "Ordeal? Will Paris be an ordeal for you, Julian?"

He smiled reassuringly but could not bring himself to reply with a lie. The warmth radiating from her, the pleasing scent in her hair, the touch of her hand on his stubbled cheek, all combined to melt what little resolve he had secured by going to the desk. He brushed aside the tumble of heavy, dark red curls that fell forward over her shoulder to kiss the base of her throat.

"Paris is the last place I wish to go," he murmured. "I want you to myself a little longer... Three days is not enough time..." He kissed her mouth. "Go back to bed. I'll be there shortly. Today we set off on a proper bridal trip."

Her arms went up about his neck as she sought another kiss. "Where are you taking me?"

He kissed her again, this time passionately, saying finally, a little breathlessly, "Where they won't find us."

"Will you be writing many letters while we are on our bridal trip?" she teased as she slid the banyan off his shoulders and down his bare arms.

"This letter—this letter is the last for a month, that I promise you."

She smiled under her lashes, enjoying the feel of him brushing against her, knowing that the writing of this last letter would be put off until they had made love.

"Are letters to be my solace while you're in Paris without me?"

"Every night separated from you will be wretchedly cold and lonely."

"I'm glad to hear it, for I'm not above protecting what is now mine alone. Must I remind my husband that I am a deadly shot?"

He chuckled as he carried her effortlessly through to the bedchamber and fell with her amongst the tumble of bedclothes.

"You deserve a good thrashing for such uncharitable thoughts, madam wife!"

She stared up through the gray morning light, into his lovely green eyes and wondered not for the first time if it was all a wonderful dream from which she would awaken at any moment to find Nurse smiling down at her, holding a little silver tray with a porcelain mug of sweetened hot chocolate upon it. But this wasn't a dream. This man was her husband, and he was muscle and bone, and she was his wife, and they now shared a bed. Those facts were indisputable.

"Make love to me, Julian," she whispered, seeking his mouth, fingers at the buttons of his breeches.

"*Sweet Jesu, Deb*," he uttered thickly. "You've utterly ruined me."

SIXTEEN

Julian's valet Frew had been polishing the same pairs of shoes for over fortnight. He had little else to occupy his time. Once a day he rode into Bath, to kick his heels at one of the taverns, to take a stroll to the Pump Room to see if there were any new faces in town, and then he visited the Barr Hotel in Trim Street to collect his master's redirected mail. After a bite of lunch and another stroll, he then returned to Martin Ellicott's Queen Anne House. If he had collected any letters and cards of invitation, these he placed with the rest accumulating in a pile on the sideboard in the book room. That was the extent of his day.

He had returned to Bath from the Lake District with the news the Marquis of Alston and his bride were only a day's ride behind him. That had been fourteen days ago. Frew had expected the old gentleman to question him about his seven-week stay at the Elizabethan manor house by the shores of Lake Windermere. Martin Ellicott did not once inquire about his godson's honeymoon, thus denying Frew the opportunity to confide in him the goings on during his stay. One episode in particular still made him grin from ear to ear...

THE MARQUIS and his bride had taken a basket nuncheon down to the lake, where they spent the afternoon swimming and fishing. They came back up to the house, dripping wet and in such animated conversation about the merits of the pistol over the sword as a preferred dueling weapon that the house-keeper and Frew were left to stare at one another open-mouthed as they were passed on the stair. Water had pooled at the doorway and the carpet made wet on the stair. And as if this weren't enough to make Frew's jaw swing, the bride was wearing a shirt that belonged to his master. This blatant disrespect for his master's wardrobe scandalized the valet more than anything, and he was in such a state of shock to think she had dared to don male attire that the subsequent noises above his head, of unrestrained laughter, of running about and of the slamming of doors, went entirely unheard. The loud, almost deafening report of a pistol did not.

Frew had burst into the paneled bedchamber unannounced. What he saw horrified him. He thought he would faint. He wanted to lean up against something to steady his legs, but his feet would not move. His hands were shaking so much that he drove them deep into his coat pockets, and clenched hard his fists. His eyes would not blink.

The Marchioness was standing in the middle of the room, side-on to the window, her bare feet slightly apart, the weight of her long wet curls clinging to the damp shirt, making the whole transparent. Her right arm was outstretched, pointing toward the open doorway that led into the dressing room and beyond that to the closet. In her hand was a smoking pistol. Frew recognized the pistol by its silver handle inlaid with pearl. It belonged to his master.

"Damn!" she said with a frown and dropped her pistol arm. "I didn't do that at all well."

Frew's brain pulsated with possibilities. She's found him

out! Had he finally told her the truth? Or had one of the servants… But no, none of the household servants knew the Marquis's true identity—that's why they'd come north. To them, as to his bride, he was simply Julian Hesham Esq. But she must have found out somehow and she'd taken her revenge for being duped. And now, she's shot him! screamed in Frew's brain. But he could not work his mouth to say it out loud.

Then the mundane intruded into his disordered thoughts and he felt uncannily calm. By the large carved mantel, a pile of discarded clothes lay sodden on the hearth—they would need laundering. He glanced quickly about the room, carefully avoiding the tumble of bed linen occupying the massive four-poster bed. Nothing was amiss with the heavy Elizabethan furniture. No signs of a scuffle. In the next breath he was suffering from an acute attack of embarrassment, far worse than any feelings of faintness or panic.

The Marquis bounded barefoot into the bedchamber from the dressing room, clad only in his breeches, damp hair falling into his eyes. Laughingly, he grabbed his wife's hand and dragged her after him, through the dressing room into the closet. Without realizing it, Frew followed them.

"Not at all well?" the Marquis declared. "You're much too harsh on yourself, darling! I told you it would pull to the right and you compensated for that splendidly. Look! Not a mark on the canvas and only the slightest of shaves to the frame. No one would be the wiser save for the dent in the paneling."

There was a small hole in the closet wall; it had split the heavy walnut paneling. The gilt wood picture frame had fared less well, the bullet shearing off a long sliver of wood before impacting the wall. The painting of the Elizabethan manor house's topiary garden was unharmed. The damage to the wall was forgotten in Frew's admiration for the Marchioness's accuracy of eye with a pistol. She'd be deadly in a duel.

But Deb continued to frown.

"I meant to miss the canvas and I certainly didn't intend to hit the frame." Then she smiled saucily, saying from under her lashes as she inspected the pistol, "Perhaps if I were to have a second try...?"

"No you don't, vixen!" The Marquis grinned and took the pistol from her. "A dent in the paneling can be patched up. A second shot would require an explanation to the Dunnes I don't care to give."

He then swept his wife off to the bed, both of them laughing.

Frew stood in the doorway until it was almost too late for him to depart with his self-respect intact. Finally, he closed the door behind him and slowly went downstairs, shaking his head, a spreading smirk still in evidence when the cook handed him a mug of ale.

AND NOW HE was back in Bath, sent on ahead with the luggage to ready the Queen Anne House for the couple's arrival. The valet waited and so did the pile of correspondence —one letter in particular. It was from the Duke. It had come by liveried courier three days earlier. Martin Ellicott had sent a response without knowing the letter's contents.

Also awaiting the Marquis were two lawyers who had landed on the doorstep and also sent by the Duke.

Frew met them as he crossed from the stables, having just returned from Bath with the day's mail. He presumed them to be travelers who had lost their way on the Bath road, but the taller and elder of the two men dismounted and divested himself of his traveling cloak, revealing a richly embroidered frock coat with a froth of fine white lace at his throat. He dumped the traveling cloak on Frew and stripped off his riding gloves to show hands that had never done a day's manual labor, and which were covered in rings studded with precious stones. He then turned to his companion and remarked in French about the quaintness of the English architecture. His companion, who had the look of a lawyer's flunkey with his ill-fitting brown bagwig and nondescript suit of worsted wool, was preoccupied with the unpacking of the saddlebags. He replied that the English fascination for quaintness was exceeded only by their generous helpings of bland food. He prayed a good drop of wine was to be had within doors, unlike their lodgings in Marlborough, where the food had been unpalatable and the wine insipid, to which the elder man snorted his pessimism.

"M'sieur Muraire, he is here to see M'sieur le Marquis de Alston," the soberly dressed Frenchman announced, juggling an armful of documentation tied up with ribbon. "You will tell him at once: We have arrived."

Frew pushed the heavy cloaks onto Fibber, who had appeared at the front door, and acknowledged the two Frenchmen with a curt bow. He began to explain that his lordship was not in residence but was cut off by the lawyer, who gave a haughty sniff.

"Me he will see!" He accompanied this command with a wave of his heavily scented, lace bordered handkerchief. "It is most necessary."

After which pronouncement the two men minced past the butler to be greeted by Martin Ellicott, who spoke to them in their own tongue and showed them into the book room. Here they remained for the entire day, filling every space with mountains of documents, paper, quills and ink, and demanding that their nuncheon be brought to them on trays. They could not possibly interrupt their work by taking food in the dining room. Martin Ellicott took this in his stride, as he did everything else, and Frew could only marvel at the old man's calm, putting it down to his absolute and unquestioning loyalty to the Duke of Roxton and his son the Marquis of Alston.

MARTIN ELLICOTT'S butler was clearing away the remnants of dinner from the parlor late one night when he heard carriage wheels on the crushed stone drive. Such was his haste to be the first in the tiled entrance vestibule that he collided with his master, who had come downstairs in his embroidered night robe and matching night cap with tassel, taper in hand.

The old man gave the taper to his butler, as a footman unbolted the front door, and sent Fibber out into the night air to greet a dusty and mud-spattered coach, the horses worn and thirsty from the speed of travel rather than the extent of their journey. The carriage door was thrown open and out jumped the Marquis of Alston dressed in a many-caped greatcoat and boots. He put up a gloved hand to Martin in greeting, who waited under the lighted portico, then turned to assist his wife to firm ground.

The old man bowed to both of them, eyes keen and bright, yet features schooled to show polite interest.

"I am very pleased to finally have you both here safe and well, if a little overdue...?"

"Are we overdue?" Julian asked rhetorically, gripping the old man's hand and smiling broadly. "I hope Frew hasn't been under your feet this past fortnight?" he asked, a glance at his sleepy-eyed valet who had just stumbled out into the night air, half-dressed, to see what all the commotion was about.

"Not at all," came the bland reply as the old man bowed over Deb's outstretched hand. "Welcome back to Moranhall, my dear. You must be tired and hungry after your journey."

Deborah smiled shyly, a little awkward at this first meeting with the old man since her marriage to his godson, but she rallied herself enough to say, "Thank you, sir. Tired, yes, but not the least hungry. I should be grateful for a warm bath. We have been on the road all day."

"Fussy appetite," Julian said cheerfully.

"Fussy? *Fussy!*" Deb said with a gasp and laughed. "Just because I didn't feel like sitting down to a banquet when we stopped for dinner after bumping about for miles and miles on end."

Julian grinned. "You did look quite green when the beef was put before me."

Deb giggled and gripped Julian's arm affectionately. "Did I? How awful for you."

The Marquis linked arms with his wife and godfather and walked them into the house.

"After the green episode," he explained to Martin, "we traveled the rest of the day at a more sedate pace."

"Reason we are here in the moonlight," Deb added, "for which I apologize." She glanced at the bowing valet, who had stepped out of the way to allow the three persons to enter the house. "Poor Frew. Has he been twiddling his thumbs in our absence? We sent him on ahead with most of the luggage, expecting to be only a day or two behind him." She looked up at her husband with a shy smile, "But the day stretched into a fortnight..."

"He has been kept busy, my la—"

"Come to think on it, I am quite ravenous," Julian interrupted, cutting the old man off as he thrust his traveling cloak and gloves on his sleepy valet. "You must eat something," he said in an under-voice to Deb, but with a quick look at Martin who had turned to give Fibber directions for the disposal of the bags and trunks and to see that a bath was drawn for the Marchioness. "You've not eaten all day," he added, looking down at her with concern.

"I did. A piece of bread at the Duckpond Inn," she whispered back with a smile. She stripped off her gloves and put a hand to her disheveled hair. "I really do want a bath, so you go ahead and I shall say good night to M'sieur Ellicott."

He kissed her hand and left her to Martin, while Fibber followed him to the dining room, Martin taking the Marchioness up to the suite of rooms she had occupied the first night of her marriage, and with apologies for not being able to provide her with a female attendant. But as Deb pointed out, she had not had the benefit of her maid for over two months now, save for a girl from the local village coming daily to help her with her hair and her dress, that she was quite used to doing most things for herself.

When Martin finally entered the dining room, he found his godson staring out of the window into the shadows of a moonlit night, a deep scowl of preoccupation on his handsome face, and the food on the table of no interest. Fibber came and went with covered dishes and wine glasses and a bottle of burgundy, and still Julian remained at the window, oblivious to the activity at his back and the fact his godfather stood watching him intently.

Martin closed over the door.

"You haven't told her, have you, Julian?"

The Marquis took a few moments to answer him. He did not turn around.

"No."

"Do you think she has any idea?" When his godson merely shrugged, the old man sat with a sigh and poured wine into two crystal glasses. "My boy, was there not a single moment in the time you were away to confide the truth of your consequence?"

"Have you been to the estate in Cumbria?" Julian asked the windowpane, as if Martin had not spoken. "The house is an Elizabethan monolith that needs modernizing. But the Dunnes —they're the present tenants—have made a reasonable job of maintaining the rooms and grounds. In fact, the topiary garden is coming along splendidly, given it was planted by James the Second's gardener. I've given the Dunnes permission to restore the south wing. And I want a jetty built. Harry and Jack will enjoy the fishing."

"Prolonging the revelation has only made it that much more difficult for you. Especially," Martin added with a kind smile, "when your wife is so very much in love with you."

At that, Julian turned and stared at the old man, face white and throat tinder dry. He felt ill.

"Curse it, Martin, I don't need you to tell me that!" He returned to looking at the night sky, pressing his forehead on the silken arm that rested across the window frame.

"It wasn't supposed to turn out this way. I never anticipated I would—she would—I imagined how it would be hundreds of times, but it—*she*—is unlike any female—Damn..." He swallowed hard and blurted out, "It's impossible for me to explain!"

Martin came over to stand beside him, a frown between his white brows.

"The time away did not go at all—well?" he asked gently, handing over a wine glass.

To Martin Ellicott's amazement, Julian gave a ghost of a laugh.

"Are you inquiring if I enjoyed the fishing and the wilds of the Cumbrian landscape, or if I was able to perform my conjugal duty with mutual and satisfactory regularity? To which I must answer *yes* to all three. If she's not with child by now, the Duke had best look to Harry to supply an heir!" The startled expression of embarrassment on his godfather's face that accompanied this blunt speech made him immediately recant. "*Excusez-moi, mon parrain*. That was uncalled for," he murmured in French. "You, more than any other, understand my morbid morality. Why I forced myself to-to—*wait*. Why I am so eager that she now give me a son, and soon."

"Yes, *mon filleul*," the old man muttered, face still flushed with heat from his godson's frank confession.

The Marquis nodded self-consciously, and for want of something to cover an awkward embarrassment at voicing what his godfather had always privately known about him, he pretended to notice for the first time the neat stack of correspondence on the sideboard.

"Any letters needing my immediate attention?" he asked and

picked up the top packet and broke the seal. "When did this arrive from His Grace?"

"Three days ago."

Julian scanned the elegantly sloping handwriting, then folded the page and laid it aside to flick through several other letters.

"I've been summoned to Paris," he said conversationally, and held up an unopened letter drenched in scent and sniffed at it tentatively before tossing it aside with a frown.

"The Duke is not—*pleased*—you chose to ignore his earlier summons," Martin told him. "You were to be in Paris six weeks ago."

"Put bluntly, he's as mad as Hades with me," said Julian, continuing a casual perusal through the cards and letters, picking up an invitation here, a letter there, aware his godfather watched him with a critical eye.

"Two Parisian lawyers, sent by His Grace, arrived this morning," Martin stated. "They spent the day in the book room consulting their papers, and tomorrow morning will brief you on matters in Paris. I should warn you; the Lieutenant of Police for Paris has issued a warrant for your arrest. M'sieur Lefebvre has brought a charge of breach of promise against you on behalf of his daughter."

When Julian shrugged and looked unconcerned, it put up the old man's hackles. It angered him his godson could be so nonchalant about so serious a charge. He expected the Marquis to at least be concerned how M'sieur Lefebvre's publicly declared accusation was affecting his parents, particularly his mother. The Duchess might show the world a beautiful face of disinterest that her eldest son was being vilified and lampooned by French newssheets as the embodiment of the worst sort of English nobleman. In private, however, she was so worried about the effect this charge was having on the ageing Duke's deteriorating health that it broke Martin's heart. It made the old man forget decades of trained restraint to say curtly,

"Will you alert the Marchioness as to why two French lawyers have invaded the book room, or shall I?"

"My wife is not your concern," came the flat reply from behind the pages of a closely scripted letter.

"I beg to remind his lordship of the considerable part I played in watching over your wife these past few years," Martin Ellicott replied in a steady voice. "My letters to the Duke concerning her welfare have placed me in a most awkward position. My loyalty is and always will be to the House of Roxton, but I cannot but feel a responsibility for her well-being and—*happiness*."

Julian tossed the letter aside and met the old man's gaze with an unblinking stare.

"That you are Father's most trusted and devoted confidant gives you a certain latitude, but it does not give you leave to lecture the son on his duty as a husband. I repeat: My wife is not your concern."

The two men stared at one another. The old man was the first to look away. He inclined his gray head with extreme politeness. Yet he could not help voicing his thoughts.

"Duty to one's name and rank is indeed a heavy burden, Julian, but it should never be endured for its own sake, or to the arrogant exclusion of everything and everybody else. The Duke your father learnt this lesson when he fell in love with your mother. Good night, M'sieur."

He bowed and left the room, and as he closed the door, he heard Julian swear loud and long in vernacular French, fist coming down hard upon the table, rattling the china and the silver domed dishes and toppling the wine glasses.

SEVENTEEN

EARLY NEXT MORNING, Fibber directed Deb to the terrace, where Martin sat with his morning coffee perusing a London newssheet. When he saw Deb hovering by the table in shy expectation of being noticed, he quickly folded the paper and got to his feet. He thought she looked far lovelier than his remembrances of her from her weekly visits to his house. She was dressed very simply in a day gown of yellow cream silk and wore matching mules. A single ribbon pulled the weight of her deep red curls across the back of her slender neck and over one shoulder. But it was not only her choice of gown that complemented her natural beauty, there was a radiance about her person of good health and happiness, that served to further depress the old man. He noted her one piece of jewelry, a three-strand choker of exquisite milky pearls, from which dangled a long single strand, looped up into three and affixed with a sapphire and diamond brooch. He knew it well. They were the Alston pearls, passed down through the generations and presented by the heir to the Roxton dukedom to his bride on their wedding day.

"Did you sleep well, my dear?" Martin asked, managing a bright smile.

She took the hand he held out to her, and he offered her the seat opposite with the warmth of the sun on her back, and sent Fibber away to fetch her breakfast.

"Very well," she replied brightly. "So well, in fact, that I may even be able to eat something this morning."

"Good. I am glad to hear it. There are fresh fruits of the season and newly-baked brioche."

"Do you know, I don't recall, in all the times I rode out here for French conversation, that we ever spoke in English," she said with surprise. "And here we are! Not one word of the French tongue! You have no accent at all. I had assumed you to be a Frenchman."

"My mother was a Frenchwoman. And in my other life, before I retired here to Bath, my master and I conversed almost entirely in French. His mother, too, was French, as is his wife. But no," said Martin with a warm smile, "my English is not accented. Although the same cannot be said of Julian's mother who has not spoken two words of English in my presence in over twenty years."

Deb took the mug of chocolate offered her. "Julian's mother is a Frenchwoman?"

Martin cursed himself for not guarding his tongue better. "Yes."

"Will she approve of me, do you think?"

The old man saw the apprehension in her brown eyes and smiled kindly. "Very much."

Deborah was not so certain, yet there was a twinkle in her eye. "Perhaps upon first introduction I should not mention that I play a viola or that I am a better marksman than I am an embroiderer?"

"Not at all, my dear. I think it is you who will be pleasantly surprised by her—Julian's mother. She is, to say the least, a most *fascinating* lady."

"And his father?"

Martin put down his coffee dish. "Ah. Now Monseigneur, he is an acquired taste."

"M'sieur Ellicott," Deb said, with a heightened color, "you may find this strange and almost unbelievable, but I have been married to your godson for almost ten weeks now and still I know so little about his family. Oh, he has spoken of them in a general sense, but I know no specifics, and while we were in Cumbria I did not feel the necessity to question him. Indeed my happiness made me not want to ask for fear of discovering some awful impediment to our marriage. It was as if by the very act of asking I would somehow shatter my hopes for the future." She gave a tinkle of laughter. "Oh dear, you are looking at me as if I *am* the silly goose I feel I am!"

She took a brioche from the plate Fibber placed in the middle of the table and gently teased apart the sweet buttery bread, yet the thought of eating it made her inexplicably nauseous. She had suffered the same unpleasant sensation at the Duckpond Inn, and before that in the last days of her stay in Cumbria. She pushed the plate a little away from her.

"Forgive me if I have made you uncomfortable by my confidences. I am being one of those missish females I so despise, and I can't account for it."

The old man lightly touched her hand but could not bring himself to look into her eyes.

"My dear, if at any time you need—*support*... What I am trying to say," he stumbled on, "is that we have known each other for a number of years now, and I have come to regard you as one would a granddaughter. You must know that I care for you, and that your happiness is important to me. I want you to know that I—I am here if ever you should need me."

Deb stared at his thin white hand and then at his clear blue eyes and frowned. Her heart thudded against her chest.

"Thank you. Your support means a great deal to me,

M'sieur," she said gratefully, and then voiced in a whisper her innermost dread, "Am I truly married to Julian?"

The old man's smile was reassuring.

"Very much so. And before you ask it, yes, Julian truly is my godson—an honor bestowed upon me by his parents. Those two facts are not in dispute." He squeezed her hand before sitting back in his chair. "And as you are married to my godson, I would like you to call me Martin."

"I should like that very much. Thank you." She nervously toyed with the curls that fell into her lap. "It would be naive of me to think Julian hadn't discussed me with you, so perhaps you offer your support because you are worried lest his parents object to his choice of bride. After all, I did defy my brother to live in Paris, and did not come home again until forced to by him. Well-bred young ladies do not behave that way." Her face flooded with color. "Nor do they elope."

"My dear girl, Julian's parents cannot but love you as I have come to love you. I do indeed know a little about that episode in Paris and it does you credit that you felt compelled to defy Sir Gerald to be at the bedside of your very ill brother. You, a young girl, nursed him and took care of his wife and young son when other family members, more obligated than you, failed him. You are to be commended not condemned, and I am sure this must be the view of Julian's family."

Martin refilled his coffee dish, wondering how best to explain his innermost and most pressing concern without being disloyal to his godson.

"His father can be overwhelming. Indeed, Julian was over-whelmed by him when a youth, so much so that he found it almost impossible to live under the long shadow cast by his father's consequence. I would not be exaggerating if I told you my godson's boyhood was stormy and somewhat notorious." He glanced up at Deb. "In the coming months you will, I have no doubt, hear many conflicting reports. Some may be true; others are the fabrication of those who seek to damage Julian in retribution for what they believe are past wrongs. I make no excuses for his behavior, nor do I judge him. All I ask is that you remember that he is shaped by what he is destined to become. I have every faith in you being able to come to terms with these unalterable facts. If you cannot..." He stopped himself and forced a smile, and changed the topic completely before Deb could utter a word. "I have not been to Crewehall, but I am told its situation on the foreshores of Lake Windermere is something to behold..."

Deb was still digesting his advice, so his diverting question about her honeymoon destination did not immediately register. She wanted to probe the old man further about Julian's background, but they were distracted by a horse and rider galloping across the lawns between the terrace and the river, and heading for the stables. It was her husband.

The Marquis reappeared on the terrace, in a lather of perspiration and dust. His thick black hair was damp, as were his white shirt and buff breeches. He looked as if he had ridden himself and his horse to the breaking point, and as if he hadn't slept at all the night before. Deborah and the old man slowly rose to their feet. They waited for him to speak.

Wiping the hair out of his tired eyes, he focused on the broken but uneaten brioche on Deb's plate.

"You need to eat, and more than that," he stated, then turned to Martin, adding in French, "I've put a stack of correspondence on the table in the hall. Would you see it is taken into Bath today?"

"Certainly," Martin answered without a blink.

"Has M'sieur Muraire risen?"

"Yes, M'sieur."

"I won't keep him waiting. I need only bathe and change."

"I shall have Fibber inform M'sieur Muraire that you will see him in—say—an hour's time?" the old man said politely, as if nothing were amiss.

Deborah glanced from Martin to Julian, unable to fathom

the formality in the tone of their French tongue, nor the fact that both men were at pains to avoid stating the obvious. It was too much for her.

"Good God, Julian, you're exhausted!" she blurted out in English. "You've been up all night. You need sleep."

The Marquis bowed to her but did not make eye contact.

"Thank you for your concern, my dear," he answered. "Now you both must excuse me," and he went into the house, Deb watching him go, biting her bottom lip, and she hadn't done that in months.

EIGHTEEN

"DOES MONSEIGNEUR understand that if we are unable to persuade Mademoiselle Lefebvre to change her outrageous claim, then it will be necessary for him to be interrogated by M'sieur Sartine, the Lieutenant of Police for Paris?" M'sieur Muraire, the celebrated French lawyer, explained patiently. "I tell you, her father he is determined to have you up before a judge. If we cannot convince Sartine that the girl she is a liar, then our efforts they are wasted. I am sorry for it, Monseigneur, but Sartine he will have no choice but to charge you with breach of promise."

"Lefebvre's threat hardly strikes me with dread," Julian drawled, refilling his glass with claret. "Once I state my case to Sartine, this preposterous charge will be dropped."

M'sieur Muraire eyed his client warily.

"There is a way perhaps that might be considered worth pursuing with the girl's father. M'sieur Lefebvre he is very proud and very rich. This breach of promise nonsense it can be overcome if Monseigneur were to—to—" The lawyer fortified his nerves with a luxuriant sniff of his scented handkerchief. "—if Monseigneur were to agree to *marry* Mademoiselle Lefebvre."

The proposition hung in a heavy silence.

"Marry? Marry a *putain*?" Julian growled in angry incredulity. "Have you taken leave of your senses? That is precisely why that whore has accused me of seducing her, you imbecile! I'd rather take my chances with a hanging judge!"

"Of course! Of course!" muttered Muraire. "An imbecile! Pothier you are an imbecile for suggesting such a thing!" he admonished Auguste Pothier, his flunkey, with a vigorous wave of his handkerchief. "Why do I listen to you? It is preposterous to suggest Monseigneur he would ever contemplate marriage with a bourgeoisie whore!"

"With all due respect to Monseigneur, the girl she has given an intimate description of his—er—*equipage* to the Lieutenant of Police," Auguste Pothier said with a nervous snort, addressing himself exclusively to his esteemed colleague, not daring to look in the direction of the nobleman. "I realize that this is not proof in itself that Monseigneur offered the girl marriage so that she would allow him to share her couch but it is a damning piece of evidence nonetheless."

"Do not be an ass, Pothier!" M'sieur Muraire threw at the flunkey contemptuously, another luxuriant sniff at his heavily-scented handkerchief. "Again you are acting the idiot! So this silly wench, this Mademoiselle Lefebvre, she has given an intimate description of her lover to Sartine. What does that prove, eh? That she is a calculating little *putain*. And that is all it proves. *Enfin*."

"And what of the rumor, unsubstantiated of course, that Monseigneur has impregnated Mademoiselle Lefebvre?" Pothier the flunkey asked. "Leaving aside her claim of breach of promise, a pregnant Mademoiselle Lefebvre would surely win the sympathy of a judge." He burst out with one of his annoying nervous snorts. "That too, then, is a problem worth considering, is it not, M'sieur Muraire?"

The lawyer exchanged a meaningful look with his noble client before the Marquis turned to face the window. Muraire bent and whispered in Auguste Pothier's large florid ear a piece of intimate information the Marquis had shared with him, but which had so far been denied the flunkey. It sent Pothier into a spasm of embarrassed choking.

"Poor Auguste! His rudimentary skills at being pleasured by a whore do not run to the imaginative." M'sieur Muraire sniggered with a shake of his powdered head. "Perhaps if Monseigneur would be so kind as to write him out an introduction to Mme Celeste's cathouse in Saint-Germain, one of her sweet-mouthed sapphists would be only too willing to broaden his education?"

No sooner had the lawyer said this than he instantly regretted such free and easy speech, for it was immediately apparent by the rigidity in the tall nobleman's back that such unguarded remarks had crossed the deep social divide that separated them. But before the lawyer could rectify his social solecism, he caught sight of a vision of loveliness framed in the doorway. That Auguste Pothier saw her too, and had stopped his choking fit, convinced Muraire that he was not witness to an ethereal apparition.

DEB HESITATED on the threshold in uncertainty, on whether to enter or retreat. Without the services of a maid and not in expectation of receiving visitors, she had dressed for comfort, her dark red hair tumbled unrestrained down her back, a silk ribbon tied in a bow under her left ear keeping it off her face.

She appeared to the two French lawyers as if a statue of a Greek goddess had come to life, and they could not help but openly admire her, and wrongly conclude that such a beauty must be the latest in the English nobleman's long line of beautiful mistresses.

Ill at ease and embarrassed at being so openly and carnally admired by these strangers, Deb's usual self-assurance deserted her, and she blushed. Yet it was the look on her husband's ashen face that completely unnerved her. For although he had bathed and shaved after his exhausting morning ride and was dressed immaculately, as he always was when in company, his green eyes were dull and hollow, circled by the deep shadows of a sleepless night. With his mouth set in a hard line, gone was the friendly smile, so that there was something altogether cold and aloof about him. To Deb he could very well have been a stranger...

JULIAN'S ANGER at these Frenchmen for daring to openly appraise his bride as if she were a common harlot was so intense that it inflamed a jealous and covetous anger that was new to him and not at all welcome. Yet it never occurred to him to correct the Frenchmen's presumption, and his pride would not allow him to offer up an explanation he did not think they deserved. His one thought was to remove Deb as quickly as possible from an embarrassing situation.

To this purpose, he strode forward, pushing both men aside. But before he could act, Deb came further into the room, speaking French in her clear strong voice, long fingers plucking at the strings of heavy pearls about her neck—the only sign of her nervous embarrassment.

"Monseigneur," she said, taking her lead from the way the Frenchmen addressed her husband, "I thought perhaps you would care to introduce me to our guests before we are called to nuncheon?"

She might be embarrassed, but Julian was quick to see the spark of defiance in her brown eyes, and knew at once she must have been standing in the doorway for a considerable time, and thus overheard much of the conversation. He addressed her in English.

"I am sorry, my dear. This tiresome legal matter is taking longer than anticipated."

"Oh?" she replied, reverting to her native tongue. "Perhaps I may be of some assistance?"

He frowned. "There is no need. I don't want you bothered by it in the slightest."

"Need it not?" Deborah replied, fighting to keep the tremble out of her voice. She shot the Marquis an angry look as she went over to the window and out of earshot of the two lawyers, despite the fact she was very sure they did not understand the English tongue. "Need it not bother me that my husband and his lawyers see fit to discuss the finer points of his —of your—Discussing you as if you're a prize bull put out to stud!" She gave a half-hearted laugh of unconcern but inside she was falling apart. "To think that the most intimate of personal details are the stuff of a written deposition taken from a French whore. Is that what you call a tiresome legal matter that should not concern your wife? Perhaps they would care to take *my* statement, or do they wish to inspect for themselves *Monseigneur's offending implement?*"

"Madame has no right to speak on matters she knows nothing about!"

Deb gave a practiced sigh and lowered her gaze in a gesture of mock humility, her interest seemingly on the long strands of pearls.

"That is very true, sir. After all, I am only your bride, and my experience is sadly limited. I have only enjoyed the carnal delights of the bedchamber with my husband, and as such I am unable to make the necessary comparisons. No doubt the whores of Saint-Germain would be only too willing to give the Lieutenant of the Parisian police a glowing report of your—your—"

"Enough," Julian growled, closing the small gap between them.

Deb took a step away, a hand about her burning throat, and made herself look him full in the face, saying with a huff of incredulous laughter, "Oh? I had no idea it was perfectly acceptable to discuss such intimate details with flunkeys, but not with your wife, who has enjoyed you in all your glory."

Julian's face turned livid with acute embarrassment, but before he could reply, she turned to the two Frenchmen, put out a hand in greeting, and said to her husband in French,

"Will you not introduce me to these charming gentlemen, Monseigneur?"

The Marquis turned to the two bright-eyed lawyers, thankful they were ignorant of the English language, and said in an arctic voice that wiped the appreciative and lewd grins from their swarthy faces, "M'sieurs Muraire and Pothier, I give you my wife—Mme la Marquise de Alston."

Muraire was so overwhelmed he wondered if he had heard right. Then he staggered back and dropped his perfumed handkerchief, quickly readjusting his features into a look of respect as he executed a bow fit for a royal audience at Versailles. Pothier was just as shocked, and to think he had dared to openly appraise the girl's beauty in front of her noble husband! He bowed until he fell to his knees to pick up the dropped documents littering the carpet, for want of something to cover his state of agitated embarrassment. Both men respectfully averted their gaze.

"Mme la Marquise de Alston?" Muraire repeated in shocked surprise as he bent over the long white hand extended to him. "Indeed! Of course! How delightful! How enchanting!"

"Delightful! Enchanting!" Auguste Pothier mimicked, his bulbous nose amongst an armful of creased parchments.

The lawyer looked expectantly at his noble client as if he were entitled to further explanation, but Julian ignored him. He was staring fixedly at Deb, who had snatched back her hand and turned to glare at him as if he were an apparition. Her shock far outstripped anything the two Frenchmen felt at their social *faux pas*. The mixture of disgust and angry incredulity on her face did not surprise him.

"I see that you are not best pleased to discover you are Marchioness of Alston."

Deb was so paralyzed with disbelief, she could not move or speak for several moments. She was numb from her toes to her ears.

"This is a cruel jest!" she finally blurted out, looking at her husband in frantic expectation that he was merely play acting for the benefit of the Frenchmen, or that she had misheard his pronouncement that she was the Marchioness of Alston, wife of the heir to the Roxton dukedom.

But he did not look down at her and wink away her worst fears. He nodded to the two French lawyers as he pocketed his gold snuffbox then inclined his head to his wife and said near her ear as he took hold of her upper arm, "I suggest we continue our *tête-à-tête* without an audience," and propelled her towards the door.

She tried to shake him off as she fought to keep a grip on her dignity, as the full force of her predicament hit her in a wave of denial and angry disbelief.

No. Her husband could not possibly be the Marquis of Alston! Her husband was Julian Hesham. It was utterly absurd to think she had eloped with a conscienceless libertine. But the sordid details she had overheard in this very room merely confirmed the rumors about the Marquis's disreputable reputation. Why had she put her faith in such intangibles as instinct and intuition? Why had he eloped with her? It set her brain reeling with the hideous new knowledge that he had married her for any number of reasons known to himself, but that love was certainly not one of them. Ruminating on this, she realized with startling clarity that made her sick to her stomach: Not once, at any stage in their time together, be it at the height of passion or in the quietest of moments, had he ever declared his love for her.

Her married life collapsed in on itself and turned to dust.

She tried to remain upright, to not let the two Frenchmen,

who watched from under hooded eyes, and this nobleman she now did not know in the least and who jostled her to the door, know that she was ill and empty and panic-stricken. Her bones felt as brittle as burnt paper, and her heart was bruised, as if it had been stomped under foot. And then the enormity of her situation became all too much. Her knees buckled and the carpet rushed up to meet her.

NINETEEN

W HEN DEB OPENED her eyes and tried to sit up a wave
of nausea forced her to lie still a little longer amongst
the cushions. She was on the sofa by the fireplace. The lawyers
were gone from the book room, and Martin Ellicott was peering
down at her with concern. She turned her head away, a sob
catching in her aching throat, and there, staring into the fire
with his hands clasped behind his broad back, was the tall
brooding figure of the Marquis of Alston: Her husband.

The Marquis of Alston was *her husband*.

Part of her still did not believe that the gentleman she had
married, with whom she had shared the most intimate of
moments, was the notorious heir to the Roxton dukedom.

How could she have been so stupidly naive and trusting?
How could she have followed her heart? Had her wits been
sleeping? Why had her head not cautioned her heart? What
madness had possessed her to marry him out-of-hand? Was it
the same impetuousness that had seen her run off to care for
Otto? But Otto was her brother and their love for one another
was unquestioning. She had thought her love for this man and
his love for her was of the same unquestioning kind. Love must

truly be blind. Not only blind, she thought, but completely witless!

She despised herself for fainting dead away. She had no idea what had come over her to react in such an absurdly weak-willed way. She had not been herself lately, and although she had her suspicions, she had not voiced them because she wanted to be certain before giving her husband the wonderful news. Now, her news was not so wonderful—it terrified her.

She would not faint again. She must be strong. She needed to make sense of this shocking situation in which she now found herself. Not since she had boarded the ship for the Channel crossing to France to be with Otto had she felt so alone in the world.

"I've never fainted before in my life," she said aloud in disbelief as she slowly righted herself and put her slippered feet to the carpet.

"Not surprising," Julian said dully, addressing the flames. "You haven't eaten a proper meal in three days."

Deb stared at his back, illness giving way to a heaviness of heart and mind. She addressed herself to Martin. "I would be grateful for a glass of cordial."

The old man brought her the cordial with a stricken look. "I meant what I said to you this morning, my lady," he murmured in a rush. "Had I realized the shock would... I—I am so very sorry."

The Marquis looked over his shoulder. "Martin, I need to speak with my wife alone—"

"No!" Deb shot to her feet and swayed.

In one stride, Julian had her by the upper arm, but she shrugged him off, not wanting the touch of him, and steadied herself with a hand to the sofa arm.

"I need someone—someone other than you—to help me make sense of this—this *nightmare* in which I find myself. Please, M'sieur Ellicott, tell me: Is this man in truth the Marquis of Alston?"

"Yes, my lady."

"And are we truly man and wife?"

"Yes, my lady."

Deb took a few moments to collect herself, breathing deeply as she fought off panic. It did not help that Martin's short responses were followed by a heavy silence. Neither man spoke and she knew they were watching her and waiting. She let out a small hysterical sob but stifled the urge to burst into tears, a shaking hand to her trembling mouth.

"How ironic! It wouldn't have mattered in the least had my husband been the bastard son of some illustrious nobleman," she confessed. "Yet finding myself married to the heir to the premier dukedom in the kingdom fills me with sickening dread." She addressed Julian. "London must be overflowing with bird-witted heiresses willing to marry you despite your sordid reputation. Why me?"

"Dozens," Julian answered bitterly. "But none so bird-witted as to dare insult my lineage!"

"What was I to think when you never once spoke of your family? In fact, you were at pains not to divulge their identity," Deb argued. "Yet M'sieur Ellicott is your godfather, a man who has been valet to an old aristocrat, whom I now realize is the Duke of Roxton. How many noblemen of your acquaintance have made godfathers of their valets to their legitimate children?"

"My lady, that great honor was bestowed upon me because—"

"Martin! You need not justify yourself!" Julian cut in angrily.

"Yet, her ladyship has a point," the old man answered calmly, adding with a smile at his godson, "Your wife was left to draw her own conclusions about your parentage, and still she married you."

Julian threw up a hand, a dull red glow of embarrassment to his lean cheeks. "And that is supposed to appease me? That my wife thought me of bastard blood—the debased product of a—of a—*lustful* mount?"

"Your pride is insufferable!" Deb exclaimed angrily. "It's a wonder it permitted you to lower yourself to take to wife a female who puts more store in a man's character than she does his impeccable pedigree. A noble title does not make a gentleman! Nor does it give a nobleman the right to look down his aristocratic nose at those who shouldn't be blamed for the sins of their fathers!"

"My bride was chosen for me when I was *fifteen* years old," Julian stated without preamble, her blink of incomprehension making him add coldly, "The last thing I wanted to do on this earth was to go through a wedding ceremony in the middle of the night with a skinny chit still in the nursery. But my father, in his infinite wisdom, considered it the wisest course for a wayward heir about to venture off on the Grand Tour, and who would reach his majority on foreign shores. Who knows what might have happened in those years in exile? I may have returned home with a wholly unsuitable bride."

Deb blinked at him and swallowed, mind turning over his words with a crease between her brows.

"In the middle of the night? *Fifteen...*?"

Julian smiled crookedly.

"You were a drab brown thing when you were twelve years old," he drawled. "Luckily for me," he added, gaze raking over her with a crooked smile, "you blossomed into a rose of rare sensual beauty. It makes our marriage that much more—*palatable*."

Deb's eyes opened wide with a dawning realization, a swift glance across at Martin, before fixing tearfully on Julian.

"But—Oh! No. No. No. *No.* That was a dream. A vivid opium-induced *dream*. Nurse gave me a teaspoonful before bedtime. I don't remember what for. And when the next day I told her about my dream, she told me to forget all about it. *She said* it was the laudanum. I dreamt I was on a swing and Otto was playing his viola, and we were in the forest, and the very next moment I was standing before a-a fat bishop and there were these two old men and a sad boy with green eyes. Indeed, everyone seemed sad, and that made me sad. It was all too fantastical to be real. It had to be a dream. It made *perfect sense* to me that it was a dream."

She shook her head, hands shakily to her face, telling herself there could be no other plausible explanation. But one look up at the Marquis, at his emerald-green eyes, and she knew he was telling her the truth. She put a cold hand to the pearl choker about her constricted throat and slowly sank onto the edge of a wingback chair.

"I was half-asleep... It was midnight. I—I don't remember the half of what was said to me. To be married off in the middle of the night in such a barbaric way... It's positively *feudal*."

She turned to Martin.

"You were there," she stated in wonderment. "You and the —*Duke*? Yes, the Duke... *His* father and Gerry and the bishop. Otto wasn't there at all was he? That part was a dream..." She shut her eyes to blink away tears. "Gerry never said a word. He must've ordered Nurse to give me the opium to guarantee my complicity. Much easier to marry me off *drugged*. And then to tell me it was all a dream? My God, what a despicable *coward*." Disbelief soon gave way to anger, and her fingers convulsed in the silk of her petticoats as large tears fell into her lap and stained the fabric. "How *dare* he marry me off in such a deceitful, underhanded way. I was a child, his *sister*. Not a farm animal to be led to market and auctioned off to the highest bidder!"

"My dear girl, you know as well as I that in our circle, females aren't entitled to decide for themselves," Julian stated flatly. "It matters not if you be twelve or twenty." He gave a lopsided grin. "Yet, my insufferable pride aside, given the choice, you married me anyway. You certainly didn't think twice about eloping with a stranger you found bleeding from a sword wound in the forest. What's the difference? Best make the most of it."

Deb gaped at such sublime arrogance.

"You deceived me into thinking I had a-a—*choice* because you allowed me to fall in love with a false being: A gentleman of fine feelings and elevated thought who loved me for myself. All the things you are not! All you truly cared about was getting me into your bed!"

The Marquis took snuff, a sidelong glance at his godfather who had politely retreated to the far corner of the room. He had been dreading the coming of this day for months, and managed to convince himself that after spending almost every hour of every day of the past two and a half months together on their honeymoon, she would know the difference between the public persona conjured up by the gossips of Society, and the very private man with whom she had fallen in love, and that it would not now matter to her that Julian Hesham and the Marquis of Alston were one and the same gentleman. But he could see by the horror writ large across her beautiful face that she had not been able to reconcile the two, and that it mattered to her a very great deal. His own acute discomfort and bitter disappointment made him angrily supercilious.

"Of course I needed to get you into bed, you foolish girl. You are my wife. I couldn't have you seduced into a bigamous union with the likes of Robert Thesiger. You belong to me, body and soul, and to no one else."

"So you think?" she threw at him, up on her feet again. "I may be female, but I have a mind and a will. I won't be party to a cold-blooded marriage contracted for *your* dynastic self-preservation! And I won't be paraded about society as your wife, an attachment to your consequence. That is a hollow, *shallow* existence. You may legally own me for the present, but you will never have me!"

The Marquis shut his snuffbox with a snap, his smile

hovering between lewdness and embarrassment. He glanced her over and put up his brows.

"But I have had you, my dear. Two, often three times a day."

"How dare you degrade our most intimate—"

"Oh, I'm not complaining. Far from it. I was delightfully surprised to discover our physical appetites are well matched. Although..." He affected puzzlement. "Such carnal enthusiasm is not what one expects from a virgin—"

She slapped his face, a hard stinging blow that made him reel back in shock.

"You *disgust* me. Did the stallion hope to put the mare in foal? Was that the purpose of those ten weeks away? What a tiresome business for you! Oh? Does the bald truth make you wince? I just thank God I discovered the truth before the *hideous* prospect of conceiving your child befell me. I will *never* have your children!"

Her words pierced his conceit, and with the sting of her slap still smarting in his reddened cheek, he allowed anger to get the better of him. He caught her wrist and yanked her hard up against his chest, forcing her arm into the small of her back and holding her fast so that she could not move.

"For better or worse, *my love*, you are my wife," he whispered viciously in her face. "And bedding you is my right as your husband. And as my wife, you have a duty to give me children. And, by God, when I come to your bed, you will accommodate me willingly. Do you understand?"

Deb stared up into his face contorted with rage and shivered with loathing.

"I can readily believe a-a *monster* capable of cold-blooded deceit, is capable of forcing himself on his wife. If you hope to get me with child, you will have to *rape* me."

Julian pushed her away with a huff of furious disgust and turned to the window.

"Take comfort in the fact that the sooner you give me a son, the sooner our relations are at an end. You can then go your own road, for all I care."

Such a prospect froze Deb to her marrow, and she slumped on the sofa with head bowed, tears of anger, frustration and disbelief now sliding freely down her hot cheeks. She mustered what reserves of dignity were left to her and took a deep breath. She had to make him see reason, for both their sakes.

"If you have no thought for me, then spare a thought for a child conceived of such a hateful union," she said quietly. "Surely you would not want your son to grow up to one day discover his father is a libertine who begets bastards by French whores and then abandons them to their fate? What if one day a half-brother or -sister confronted your heir with the truth about his libertine father's whoring ways? What would your son think of you, the father he was taught to look up to, to emulate one day, how you treated with contempt and disrespect the marriage bed shared with his long-suffering mother? Whatever your feelings for me, could you, in good conscience, be such a monster to your son and heir?"

The audible intake of breath came from the old man, and he crossed the room in a few quick steps and put a hand on Deb's shoulder, his eyes wide in warning, a finger to his lips, and a worried, nervous glance at his godson. But Deb would not be silenced.

"Never mind that as your wife I am supposed to hold my head high and ignore your whores and your ill-gotten off-spring because as Marchioness of Alston they are but dirt beneath my feet." She put up her chin. "You are grossly mistaken if you think I will meekly submit to a cold-blooded marriage of the sort entered into by your parents—"

"*Enough*. I've heard *enough*," Julian growled, suddenly coming to life and turning on Deb with a face flushed with absolute fury. "Ten. *Ten* weeks—No!—Seventy-eight days to be precise—Seventy-eight days in my company and you've learned nothing—*nothing*—about *me*?" he spat out incredulously and took a few moments to master his emotions, bright green eyes fixed on Deb's flushed face. "Never mind you have insulted me, but to insult my esteemed parents who you do not know in the least? That is more than is humanly possible for me to forgive. Know this madam," he continued with icy formality. "You are my wife for better or worse and as my wife you are also the Marchioness of Alston. You will learn restraint and the manners befitting your elevation. You have a month to have your belongings in order before I send for you to join me in Paris. And you will come to Paris when I bid, even if I have to return to carry you across the Channel myself. Is that understood?"

Deb bravely looked him in the eyes, determined to be in control of her emotions, but she could not keep the deep note of sadness from her voice.

"And you, my lord, have so cruelly used me and abused my trust and love that I will do *everything* in my power to ensure we remain forever parted."

Because my heart is irreparably torn asunder, she wanted to add but was too emotionally drained and listless of mind to continue. Her life—the life she had so looked forward to sharing with Julian—was now so turned inside-out that her head ached to think about it. Through a haze of disbelief and unbelievable sadness she watched this stranger, this nobleman to whom she was irrevocably wedded, turn away from her without another word and speak in rapid French to the old man. He then strode from the room and slammed the door so hard it reverberated on its hinges.

"My lady, I have been charged with the care of you until—"

"Please, Martin. I cannot think any more today."

The old man was regarding her with such sadness and pity in his troubled eyes that Deb wanted to burst into fresh tears and run from the room. Instead she walked quietly to the door, only stopping when he called to her. She looked over her shoulder, hoping her features did not betray her disordered emotions.

"My lady, these revelations today have been a great shock,"

Martin said quietly. "I wish matters had been handled differently. I make no apologies for my godson, only that he has the unrestrained temper of youth. More I am not at liberty to say. I trust that in time—when you know the truth behind the rumors about the Marquis of Alston, and finally meet his illustrious parents—you will gain a deeper understanding of the man to whom you are wedded... Perhaps then you will be able to find it in your heart to forgive him."

"I have no heart, Martin," she answered dully. "Your godson just tore it from me."

PART II

THE FRANCE OF LOUIS XV

TWENTY

FRENCH HOME OF THE DUKES OF ROXTON
THE RUE SAINT-HONORÉ, PARIS

SIR GERALD and Lady Mary Cavendish were hosting a select *soirée* for relatives and friends newly-arrived in Paris for the celebration of the Dauphin's marriage to the young Austrian princess, Marie-Antoinette. The royal wedding was taking place in the French capital, and to mark such an auspicious and historic event, all of Paris was rejoicing. Balls, routs, open-air concerts, plays, operas, fireworks and a hundred free entertainments had been organized for Parisian society high and low. The whole city was in a festive mood. Cards of invitation crossed back and forth to society's gilded salons. Every invitation was accepted, to show off a painted face and the latest powdered hairstyle, if only for half an hour in a crowded salon before being whisked away in a sedan chair into the heady perfumed atmosphere of the next *soirée*.

Yet, despite the typically French surroundings of gold leaf

furniture, polished parquetry flooring and white and blue paneled walls, the Cavendish *soirée* was quite markedly an English affair. The guests were either from the English Embassy or young Englishmen staying briefly in Paris at the start of the Grand Tour, people with whom Sir Gerald, who did not have an ear for languages and thus knew little French, could have a decent conversation. Unlike twittering, effeminate painted French nobles, the guests at Sir Gerald's little gathering knew his worth as a favored relative of the Duke and Duchess of Roxton—Englishmen with whom he had a natural superiority.

He congratulated himself on how well the evening was progressing as he looked out across the large square courtyard with its avenue of chestnut trees, gravel walks, fountains, and shrubbery illuminated by flickering flambeaux. And at the southern end, the imposing black and gold iron gates kept out the world as it traveled up and down the Rue Saint-Honoré.

His wife had been the perfect hostess and the guests were suitably impressed by his noble connections and surroundings. After all, not every relative of the Duke and Duchess was given use of one of the large apartments within the compound of the Hôtel Roxton: a collection of four-storey seventeenth-century buildings with mansard roofs, awe-inspiring in size and aspect even by Parisian standards.

But as Sir Gerald drank the Duke's excellent claret and surveyed the aristocratic landscape with his usual pompous self-consequence, his thoughts were niggled by the specter of his recalcitrant sister and her lunatic demands.

Every morning he awoke with the expectation that Deborah had come to her senses and accepted her arranged marriage. But every day he was disappointed. He had hardly believed his eyes when reading her letter damning him for marrying her off to the Marquis of Alston. He had expected, at the very least, gratitude, and for his troubles he had received words dripping with reproach and ungratefulness. And when she had demanded he contact his lawyers to discover an impediment to her marriage so that it could be annulled forthwith, his bowels had opened of their own accord.

He did not understand her. One day she would be a duchess. And not just any duchess, but the Duchess of Roxton, wife of the most powerful and wealthy nobleman in England. What better incentive did she need to remain married to Lord Alston than that? The nobleman's nefarious lifestyle, the fact he was being sued for breach of promise by a Farmer-General and was being daily lampooned in Parisian newssheets, was of small consequence—a mere trifle that his sister, if she had her wits about her would, like any good and obedient wife, dismiss as beneath her notice.

Fortunately, he had avoided any unpleasant face-to-face confrontation because she had refused to join her husband in Paris. This had the added advantage that her esteemed parents-in-law were still none the wiser about her lunatic whim to seek an annulment, and in so doing, discover that he had given in to her demands to contact his lawyers. After all, he had to hedge his bets, as it were.

Let Deborah believe he was obliging her for as long as it took for him to sufficiently ingratiate himself with the Duke, so that when the thunderstorm of his sister's annulment plans poured a cold torrent on any Parisian nuptial announcement, he could cut his connection with her without fear of being socially ostracized by the distinguished family into which she had been married.

And then the moment he had been dreading sneaked up on him.

A footman whispered in his ear that a visitor awaited him in the adjoining small reception room. The visitor was his sister. A frisson of unease tingled his spine and his shaved head under its snug powdered wig began to sweat as he excused himself to his guests.

DEB WAS LOOKING out on the same view as her brother, admiring the avenue of chestnut trees. Disheveled by travel, tendrils of her red hair had escaped from under the small peaked velvet-trimmed bonnet and fell about her face. Despite a warm evening, she wore a silk-lined woolen cloak over her traveling gown. She was tired and in need of a good night's sleep in a decent bed after a three-day journey from Dover. Yet she was determined to speak with her brother before reluctantly presenting herself at the main entrance to the Hôtel Roxton.

When he came into the room and closed over the door, she barely had time to turn from the window before he was across the parquetry and had taken possession of her gloved hands. He guided her to sit with him on a hard-backed red velvet settee, his face flushed from too much wine and wearing an embarrassed smile that put Deb on her guard.

"What a delightful surprise, my dear! Yet I cannot help but wonder if it was quite the right thing to make such an arduous journey when at last report you were still in your sick bed being attended by Dr. Medlow. A most distressing episode. I had hoped you would heed my wise counsel and remain in Bath. Such a long journey can only have taxed your reserves of strength."

"Medlow assures me I am now in no danger whatsoever," she interrupted, her brother's pompous speeches never failing to grate. "In fact, Gerry, I'm so much better that I'm plumper beyond even Medlow's expectations."

Sir Gerald screwed up his mouth at this, unconvinced.

"Yet, I don't understand, despite Medlow's assurances, why you felt you had to come, when I quite specifically stated in my last letter that you remain in Bath to receive Bishop Ramsay."

Deb let out an involuntary laugh. "Gerry, Ramsay can't help me out of my predicament. Nor should I think he would want to. After all, he was the one who performed the original marriage ceremony."

Sir Gerald shook his powdered head sadly.

"This is a most distressing business. Naturally I blame myself—"

"Oh, it is only right and proper you blame yourself! That you can sit there inquiring after my health when I know you don't give a button for me... But I didn't come all this way to go over old ground. My letter to you was blunt enough, and if it weren't for the despicable situation I now find myself in I would gladly be anywhere than here with you!"

"Deborah? How can you abuse me when I have only your best interests at heart?" he answered, casting her a wounded look. "Naturally, your offensive and unladylike letter did not please me, and the accusations and plain language directed toward your eldest brother were such that I did seriously wonder at your mental state." He sniffed and stretched his neck in its tightly-bound silk cravat. "Yet when it was made known to me that you were ill and had taken to your bed, I was more forgiving and of the belief that you wrote that letter under the duress of illness. You have never been ill a day in your life, so for you to take to your bed meant—"

"Did you do as I requested and write to your lawyers?" Deb asked bluntly, the only sign of her frustration showing itself in her tightly-clenched gloved hands.

"Of course. My lawyers thought it prudent to brief Bishop Ramsay on this most distressing business, to garner his support, if possible, for an annulment. The bishop was willing, despite his age and infirmities, to undertake the journey to Bath. I thought perhaps you would appreciate the comforting words of a man of God."

"You have a very odd sense of comfort!"

"I fail to see why you must treat this very serious and quite shocking matter with levity!" Sir Gerald lectured through a tight mouth. "I admit I had hopes that a match between our family and the Roxtons would be a great success and set you, my only sister, up for great things in life. Yet, I should have known it would come to this. You and Otto both have been a sad disappointment, but I have strived to do my utmost for you as your guardian and as a Cavendish, and what is my reward? Otto's total disobedience and stupidity and your ungratefulness! Deborah, I have bowed to your wishes for an annulment, because I want what is best for you. Do you think it is an easy thing to hold one's head up high when Otto saw fit to contract a marriage with a gypsy, and now my only sister's marriage to a future duke is to be annulled on the grounds of her husband's lunacy?"

Deborah listened to her brother's impassioned speech with suspicion. She had been wary of his eagerness to help her since his letter of reply to her request for a dissolution of her marriage. She had expected a downright refusal and was prepared to seek assistance from lawyers recommended to her by Lady Cleveland. After all, Sir Gerald did not exert himself for others unless there was something to be gained for him. Yet when he had jumped at the chance to engage the family lawyers in a case of litigation that was sure to create a major public scandal of the sort Sir Gerald deplored, she had been so surprised she was certain he was up to something underhanded. Reason enough for her to travel to Paris, but it wasn't the reason she had done so.

She caught on the word *lunacy* and raised her arched brows.

"You think Lord Alston mad, Gerry? Is this a new thought, or did you know him to be of unstable mind when you married me to him?"

"My lawyers inform me that there are only two possible avenues for a marriage to be annulled," Sir Gerald said, ignoring his sister's sarcastic question but acutely discomforted under her cool gaze.

He was not a perceptive man, but there was something different about his sister that he could not put his finger on. He had expected her circumstances to have turned her into a weeping pot, instead she might have been fashioned from stone, such was her frosty manner. She unnerved him, and more than usual.

"One is non-consummation of the marriage," he muttered, clearing his throat and avoiding her widening smile. "In the event the husband is—the husband is—er—incapable of the—um—the um—*act,* the bride's guardian has every right to seek an annulment on her behalf."

"Incapable of the act? Ha! As any Parisian whore will tell you, Alston is more than capable of satisfying a female between the sheets."

"Deborah! Indeed! For you to talk of such matters is—is..."

She shrugged indifferently, Sir Gerald oblivious to the film of tears across her soft brown eyes that belied her cold tone.

"Do stop this pretence of offended sensibilities, Gerry. I am a married lady and as such have learnt a thing or two about the marriage bed. What is the second circumstance for annulment?"

Sir Gerald wiped a sweaty hand across his glistening brow at such blunt speech and stumbled on.

"That is complicated and more difficult to prove. An act passed in '42 makes provision for the annulment of a marriage on the grounds that the husband was of unsound mind at the time vows were taken. If this can be proved, then the marriage is void."

"And was Lord Alston mad the night we were wed?"

Sir Gerald wandered to the window. Suddenly the majestic view of illuminated chestnut trees and fountains lost its appeal.

"You may not recall the night you were married, but I can, vividly. I was most uncomfortable with the way the marriage was conducted. There had been a long understanding between our families, since almost from your cradle, that you and Alston would wed, but I could hardly credit it when His Grace demanded a most hurried affair. And when one saw the boy's unstable condition, I was most reluctant to proceed."

"Not enough for you to call the whole thing off!" Deb scoffed, joining her brother by the full-length windows. "And I remember aspects of that night, *vividly*, despite being drugged. Oh, you can look the stunned trout, Gerry, but you can't deny that you had Nurse give me a dose of laudanum to keep me biddable. No wonder I thought I was dreaming! I could barely put two thoughts together. As I recall, Alston was extremely distressed, and there was an ancient gentleman with white hair who looked very sad."

"The Duke." Sir Gerald nodded and swallowed. "Yes, a very sad business indeed. If the rumors be true, it was also a very shocking business."

Deb regarded her brother's look of contrition with the suspicion it deserved.

"Gerry, why are you so eager to have my marriage annulled when it will surely mean disfavor with the Roxtons?"

"Isn't it enough that I want to see my sister parted from a man who is of unsound mind?"

"No. I don't believe you. But tell me why you believe Lord Alston was of unsound mind the night we were wed."

"You had best sit down, my dear, for it is a most appalling business."

Deb bit her lip and stared out at the deserted courtyard, the flambeaux flickering in the breeze of a balmy evening.

"No. I will stand. Tell me."

"A few days before you were wed, Alston had attacked his mother."

"When you say *attacked*, what do you mean?"

Sir Gerald threw up a hand and blustered. Where were his sister's feminine sensibilities? If he had been telling Mary, she would have been satisfied with the word, no details necessary. Why did his sister always have to be so annoyingly quick-witted?

"Well, Gerry? Please don't feel you need to go all big-brotherish on me now and shield me from any unpleasantness. That ended the night you married me off!"

He let out a sigh of defeat and told her.

"Attacked, as in he dragged the Duchess out into the middle of Hanover Square in full view of the world and denounced her as a whore, a slut, and a witch."

Deb decided she did need to sit after all and sank onto a nearby spindle-legged chair, a hand hard about the ornately-curved arm. She took a deep breath and nodded for her brother to continue.

"That in itself is shocking enough, but the Duchess at the time was heavy with child. She and the unborn babe came close to death. Alston's insane actions brought on his brother's premature birth. It is the opinion of learned medical men that the boy suffers to this day with the falling sickness because his mother went into an early labor."

Deb looked up at Sir Gerald, a tightness in her chest, realizing he lacked the imagination to invent such a tale.

"Does Harry suffer badly with the falling sickness?"

"Yes. A physician is his shadow."

"Poor little fellow..."

She recalled what Jack had said that day in the forest, and Alston's anger, incomprehensible at the time, at Jack's confidences about his best friend Harry. No wonder the Marquis had been uncomfortable at the mention of his brother's affliction. She took a few moments to collect herself then asked,

"How did you come by such information? Surely Mary didn't—"

"Good God, no!"

"If not Mary, then who?"

"Does it matter where I heard—"

"It matters a great deal! A *very* great deal, especially if I hope to convince a judge as to Alston's state of mind at the time of our marriage."

"I am certain you will take the tale as fact when I tell you it was confided in me by someone who was witness to the whole sordid episode, and who cares deeply for your welfare. In fact, he has asked for your hand in marriage."

"Hand in marriage? But I am already married."

"Can you have forgotten in what deep regard Robert Thesiger holds you?"

"Robert Thesiger?"

Deb was not only surprised, but again her suspicions were aroused.

"You put store in the word of Robert Thesiger, a gentleman you have long held in aversion because of his shoddy parentage, at the expense of your illustrious connections by marriage? Gerry, for shame on you! When have you not condescended to birth over all other considerations?"

"I should wash my hands of you! Stay married to a lunatic!" Sir Gerald growled in frustration, all semblance of understanding and patience evaporating. "I've done everything in my power to assist you, and you repay my loyalty and duty with sarcasm and ungratefulness. And there is Robert Thesiger, a gentleman of wealth and polished address, who still wishes to have you as his wife, would elope with you now, before the annulment came through, if you let him."

Deborah slowly got to her feet and stared at her brother through narrowed eyes.

"Let me understand you: You are in favor of Robert Thesiger eloping with me *before* my marriage is annulled?"

Sir Gerald's quickly averted gaze was evidence enough for Deb that there was an ulterior motive lurking somewhere in the recesses of his mind. Under her silent penetrating stare, he finally blurted out in annoyance,

"If you had any common decency left, you would do the noble thing!"

"The *noble* thing? I beg your pardon? What are you drivelling on about?"

"You must see that any judge in his right mind would grant

you the annulment you seek, given the evil Alston perpetrated against his own mother. But do you truly want such scandalous and shameful revelations to be aired in a court of law for all the world to hear? Do you sincerely wish to break the health of the old Duke, see the Duchess heartbroken, her youngest son wise to his brother's mad folly? Can you truly be so cold-hearted and calculating?"

"Am I to understand that you want me to run off with Robert Thesiger in preference to going through the proper legal channels and seeking an annulment to a marriage that was forced, yes *forced*, upon me?" When hope sparked in her brother's eyes, Deb looked away, sickened. "How much better that would look for you, that a sister's scandalous actions caused her own downfall, than the truth caused yours." She peered at him hard. "And that is what you consider is the noble thing? For me? *Your sister*?"

Sir Gerald took a step toward her, hopeful.

"Then you will consider Thesiger's offer?"

"Get away from me, you snivelling coward!"

He struck her, an instinctive swipe across the left cheek with the back of his hand. She was so stunned that she dropped back on the spindle-legged chair, a hand to her smarting flesh. He immediately repented and fell to his knees to clutch at her hands, but she pushed him off.

"You made me strike you! You did!" he blubbered in a gasping voice. "You shouldn't have called me a-a coward! Don't you see that if you go ahead with this annulment, if you air the Roxtons' dirty linen in public, I will be *utterly* ruined. I will be struck off the register at White's. I will never again be able to set foot in this house. Alston will turn his back on me. If not for me, then for my wife! Think of Mary!"

"You are pathetic, Gerry! Get up before Mary comes in and knows you for what you truly are! Mary? Mary! How lovely to see you again!"

Mention of his wife sent Sir Gerald diving into the pocket of his frock coat to find a kerchief to wipe dry his florid face. He dropped his snuffbox close by his silken knee, as if he were down on the floor to retrieve it, scooped it up and scrambled to his feet, all the while keeping his back to his wife.

But Lady Mary had eyes only for her sister-in-law who, despite being travel-weary, looked in glowing good health, so much so that she appeared radiant. Instead of returning Deb's warm embrace she sank into a respectful curtsy, acutely aware that Deb was now Marchioness of Alston, and as such outranked her.

Deb frowned and pulled her up.

"I was so certain you would be pleased to see me, Mary," Deb said with a nervous smile, the mantle of hard indifference she had cultivated since discovering she was married to the Marquis of Alston slipping ever so slightly. Mary's formal reception hurt her more than she cared to acknowledge. God help her to keep herself in check when she was reunited with Jack!

"I am pleased to see you, Deborah," Lady Mary replied, and kissed her sister-in-law's cheek. "*Very* pleased. I was just—*surprised*—to find you here unannounced. We thought you fixed in Bath. Did we not, Sir Gerald?"

When Sir Gerald made an unintelligible reply and took snuff, Deb ignored him and spoke exclusively to her sister-in-law.

"Forgive me for disturbing your little gathering," she apologized. "Perhaps, when I am well rested from my journey, you will come and see me tomorrow? But for now, I do believe I need to eat something, or I shall be ill again, and that would never do. Dr. Medlow insists I take nourishment every few hours for the sake of the baby. Excuse me. Mr. Ffolkes is expecting me."

Without waiting for a response to her momentous news, Deb left her mouth-gaping brother and his equally speechless wife, and had herself and her portmanteaux shown upstairs to the spacious apartment occupied by the Honorable Evelyn Gaius Ffolkes, musician and composer, nephew of the Duke of Roxton, and closest friend and cousin of the Marquis of Alston.

TWENTY-ONE

T HE COMPOSER Evelyn Gaius Ffolkes sat at his gilded clavichord with a viola balanced on his silken knees, and a parchment spread across the ivory keys. He was busily making notations, the music running on in his head faster than he could scrawl it down, the fine white lace ruffles at his wrist trailing across the parchment as he wrote. At his back, through the open double doors of his grace-and-favor apartment, a rowdy dinner continued unabated in the dining room.

There was laughter and belching, and the three musicians at his table continued to eat and drink as if they had no idea where they would find their next meal. Between mouthfuls of roasted pheasant, pâté-stuffed fowl, seasonal vegetables swimming in creamy sauces, and all washed down with the best wines his uncle the Duke's cellar had to offer, they shouted out for their host and fellow musician to join them.

It was the very early hours of the morning, and a cursory glance at the ornate mantel clock told Evelyn what his drooping eyelids already knew: The sun would soon rise, and he and his musicians had worked through the night.

He picked up his wine glass and returned to his seat at the dining table.

"May the Marquis of Alston's amorous adventures continue to provide entertainment for the Parisian masses and choke our salons with inconsequential babble!" declared Georgio, a barrel-chested baritone in a threadbare frock coat that had once belonged to the valet of the Duc d'Orleans. When his two fellow musicians glanced knowingly at Evelyn and then looked down at their dirty plates, the baritone gave a grunt of annoyance. "What? It is better I toast Evelyn's noble cousin behind his back and not to his face? This scandal involving the Marquis, it continues to rage through Parisian salons faster than a fire through Saint-Germain, and you think I should not speak of it? I for one would like to know the truth of it from the mouth of the horse's cousin!"

"To be honest, I've not picked up a newssheet in three years," Evelyn confessed, reaching for an uncorked bottle of champagne.

"Then what do you make of this!" Georgio continued and slapped down one of a number of crumpled pamphlets scattered amongst the dinner things. "These are being distributed everywhere. Funded by the Farmer-General Lefebvre, so it is said, though he denies all knowledge of their very existence."

Evelyn picked up the dog-eared and wine-stained piece of parchment and gave it a cursory glance. The caption under a lewd cartoon read: *An English nobleman's Grand Tour: pillaging foreign works of art and the virtue of middle-class French maidens.*

Evelyn screwed up his mouth and put the pamphlet aside as if it was something unclean. He realized well enough that the cartoon depicted the Marquis of Alston and Mademoiselle Lefebvre, and he was shaken by the extent to which the Parisians were vilifying his cousin.

"Casimir," he said quietly to a consumptive musician with a

bad complexion, "be good enough to collect up all this waste of paper and ink and put it to the flames."

"I have heard there is a trial brief with M'sieur le Marquis's name upon it," offered Casimir as he did as he was requested.

Georgio turned a bloodshot gaze on a man of middling years and faded good looks who wore a mouche at the corner of his painted lips.

"Sasha! There! If Casimir he has heard of a trial brief then this rumor is no longer rumor, it is a situation most serious for M'sieur le Marquis!"

"I'd hardly call his name on a factum serious, Georgio," Sasha drawled. "Three-quarters of what is set in ink is inflammatory and the other quarter? It isn't to be believed. This trial brief it is a piece of high drama, it too is wasted paper. It is fit for the stage, not a court of law."

"And you would know this, Sasha, aye?" Georgio scoffed, sticking out his fat bottom lip and looking about at his friends to support him. No one offered it.

Before Sasha could answer, Casimir spoke.

"And so he should. Sasha, he gave up the law to follow his passion: Music. Is that not so, Sasha? His father and grandfather before him they were barristers and members of the prestigious *Ordre des Avocats*. Sasha—"

"Enough, Casimir," Sasha ordered, although he smiled approvingly at such praise and ignored Georgio's gaping mouth. "I, too, was a great lawyer but..." He shrugged. "Music! Ah now that is much the purer form of entertainment, yes?" He sipped from his crystal glass, a satisfied look at the rapt faces of his friends, and added solemnly, "The Farmer-General Lefebvre used his beautiful and guileless but quite stupid daughter to try and entrap M'sieur le Marquis into marrying her. But what he failed to understand is the nobility's great arrogance for marrying within the confines of its own class. It mattered not that she enticed him to her couch, and he took liberties with her person, he would never have married her, had he offered her that inducement or not."

Georgio plunged the conversation back into the scandal-monger's gutter by saying with a punctuated belch, "That's all well and good, Sasha, but what I am more interested in knowing is if there is truth to the rumor that M'sieur le Marquis has refrained from taking his love making to its satisfying conclusion for fear of fathering bastards?"

This outrageous question went unanswered, for the outer door opened with a squeak and a bleary-eyed footman appeared in the doorway, then did an about-face and scurried away, leaving the door ajar. The three musicians looked at one another, seeing this as sign for them to depart, yet reluctant to do so, for their meager lodgings on the Left Bank. They hoped Evelyn's generosity would extend to allowing them to catch a few hours' sleep on the sofas and chairs in his study, a regular occurrence when they rehearsed for an upcoming performance.

But Evelyn wasn't paying attention. He was thoroughly bored with the incessant and mindless speculations regarding his cousin's amorous adventures, real or imagined. He sipped from his champagne glass, blue-eyed gaze wandering to the row of undraped French windows with their view of the hôtel's large rectangular courtyard of manicured lawn, cobblestoned walks and trickling fountains. His thoughts were not on his cousin, but on his cousin's beautiful young wife and how she must be dealing with the strain of an arranged marriage to a nobleman accused of breach of promise. At least Deborah had the good sense to remain in faraway Bath.

She had not only defied her husband by remaining on the other side of the Channel, but she had also openly flaunted her total disregard for the Duke of Roxton's authority by turning away at her door the Duke's secretary and a six-man escort sent to bring her to Paris. He smiled to himself at such audacity. No one ever challenged his uncle's authority—*ever*.

Evelyn yearned to see Deborah again. But why were her eyes

so bright? Had she been crying? And surely he hadn't seen her in that particular velvet traveling cloak with its collar and cuffs trimmed in fox fur. And why was his valet, Philippe, hopping about on the balls of his feet babbling something about instant dismissal if his master was disturbed for any reason except the hôtel burning to the ground.

Philippe? Why was his valet intruding in one of his daydreams? Evelyn decided he must be more tired than he imagined. Drinking champagne on an empty stomach didn't help...

He put aside the glass and rubbed his eyes. Good God! She was still there. Deborah was standing in his apartment, in his very dining room and smiling at him, while his valet continued to spew inanities at her. He glanced swiftly at his three dinner guests. They had risen as one and were bowing to the unexpected visitor.

Evelyn shot up off the padded chair, offsetting his wig and sprinkling powder down his high forehead.

"Deborah?" he whispered with mouth-gaping awe, as if speaking to an apparition, and took a tentative step forward. "*Deborah*."

"It's wonderful to see you again, Eve," she replied in English, a nod at the three bedraggled men who shuffled their feet and smiled sheepishly, not least because she had scooped up off the turned arm of a silk-covered chair one of the Lefebvre pamphlets, accidentally dropped by the consumptive musician on his way to the fireplace. "Eve... I need—I need *your* help."

The composer smiled sympathetically and kissed her forehead, gently removing the crushed pamphlet from her fist as he did so. He tossed the offending paper onto the crackling fire behind him.

"Yes, *ma chérie*, I rather think that you do."

TWENTY-TWO

MUCH LATER that same morning, Evelyn was sitting at the breakfast table by the long windows with their view of the rectangular courtyard when Deb appeared from his bedchamber dressed in a pretty day gown of muslin, her hair in a single plait down her back. She was very much better for a good night's sleep. He had insisted she take his bed. He slept as best he could on the daybed in his dressing room. They had exchanged not more than half a dozen sentences in the early morning light, leaving what was most important to be said at breakfast.

Deb knew Evelyn's gaze never wavered from her profile as she sipped *café au lait*, but she pretended an interest in the cobblestone walk lined with chestnut trees and the team of gardeners working in the flowerbeds. She picked up a warm bread roll, relieved that she no longer felt nauseous at the prospect of eating, with her maid one step behind holding a basin. And that had been on the good days when she was well enough to take a little fresh air in the back garden of her house in Bath. Then one day, after four months of morning sickness, and as Dr. Medlow had continually assured her on his frequent visits, the nausea had disappeared as instantly as it had begun.

She had so much to say and discuss with Evelyn that she did not know where to begin. That she had not seen the composer for three years made conversation all the more awkward. Particularly when he must know by now about her arranged marriage to his cousin. She wondered how much he knew and what he knew. Her marriage and the consequences of its consummation had consumed her every waking moment since that hateful day at Martin Ellicott's Queen Anne house, and were still so painfully raw she avoided talk of it altogether. Instead, she asked after her nephew, whom she had missed dreadfully and who had been living with the Roxtons since their eldest son had orchestrated the mock elopement.

"Have you seen much of Jack?" she asked lightly, then added in a rush, meeting Evelyn's unwavering gaze, "Is he well? Is he happy? Do they make him welcome? Does he ever ask after his aunt?"

"Yes, *ma chérie*. He is well and he is happy and yes, he is made very welcome by the Duke and Duchess," Evelyn replied with a smile, reading the apprehension in her brown eyes. "Henri-Antoine likes him, which says a great deal about Jack, for my haughty young cousin does not like many people. And yes, he has asked after you on many occasions, particularly the question of your arrival. But of course, he is a boy who wants to appear a man, so he does not reveal to anyone that he misses you terribly. The Duchess she sees this and does her best to make him comfortable."

"Her Grace is very good," Deb murmured, eyes downcast.

"Yes, my aunt is, and is always, very good."

"My house—my house was very empty without Jack," Deb admitted quietly. "But an aunt with morning sickness is no company for a boy in his ninth year... You say he has played for you? Tell me honestly your opinion of his playing. Does he live up to his aunt's high praise?"

Evelyn put up his brows at her open pronouncement of her condition but ignored it for the time being, saying evenly, "When he plays, he reminds me of Otto."

Deb heard the note of sadness and put out her hand across the table.

"Did I not tell you in my letters? There is the same natural grace in his style, and he feels the music as I never can and—"

"Deb, dearest. He has his father's ability to be sure, but not his passion," Evelyn told her seriously. "Jack enjoys playing for its own sake, but he is first and foremost like other boys his age. And that is no bad thing."

Deb bit her lip. "I see. I've pushed him too hard."

"Not at all, *ma chérie*. I think you miss Otto. I do, very much. And when Jack plays, it is as if Otto is with us again. Jack is his father's son and he has talent, but you must permit him to decide if composing and playing music will be his way of life. One may have a love of music and the love of playing a musical instrument without making it their sole purpose for existence as Otto did. Look at me. I pretend to be a composer—"

"—but you are!"

Evelyn laughed.

"I compose music, but I am not the composer or even the great musician that Otto was. He lived for his music. He sacrificed his comforts and his wants, his good name and even his family—yes, even Rosa and Jack came second to Otto's compositions. I, on the other hand, could never sacrifice my all for music."

He held Deb's hand across the cluttered breakfast table.

"To put it bluntly, *ma chérie*, music is my escape from the suffocation of being related to a ducal house. Every move is watched by a thousand pairs of eyes. Most of us have little to do but parade about in fine silks from one social function to the next with our social equals, for the entertainment of our inferiors. If we are unlucky enough to be an eldest son, life is spent in limbo waiting to inherit title, estate and the seat in the House of Lords.

"I escaped such an existence by immersing myself in music. Alston spent several years wandering Italy, Greece and the Ottoman Empire and thus he, too, managed for a time to avoid such social suffocation. However, he can no longer do so, nor delay the inevitable. His father, the grand old Duke of Roxton, is ill. It is whispered he is dying from a complaint of the lung."

"Dying?" Deb repeated softly. "How dreadful..." She stood, a hand to her aching lower back, and stared out of the window, down at the velvet green lawns where a huddle of lackeys was creating a commotion struggling to erect a striped marquee. "Do the physicians know how much time is left to him?"

"We have heard widely differing opinions from numerous physicians. The more morose say it is only a matter of months. Those who wish to remain in their noble client's pay tell him confidently he has many more years of earthly pleasure. Then there are those who see the sorrow in my aunt's lovely eyes and lie, predicting M'sieur le Duc will live to see three score years and ten."

"Then I see why Lord Alston felt some urgency in getting me with child," Deb said bitterly.

Evelyn went to her, took hold of her hands and met her sad gaze squarely.

"I do not excuse my cousin's conduct any more than you do, *ma chérie*. But perhaps I understand it a little better knowing my uncle the Duke and the arrogant shadow he casts over his family and retainers. Tell me honestly: Do you love your husband?"

"I cannot answer that," she said, meeting his steady gaze. "Because I do not know to whom I am married."

Evelyn was more attuned to her confused feelings than she realized, for his response startled her.

"You may not know the Marquis of Alston, indeed your feelings for him must be quite repellent after such a deception, but what of the man you willingly eloped with and married—the man you know as Julian Hesham? What are your feelings for him?"

Deb stared at Evelyn through a blindness of tears, overcome with such sadness as her mind's eye flooded with memories of her honeymoon with the man she loved and had known only as Julian Hesham. The hard emotional shell she had cultivated and shown her brother cracked down its center and fell away.

"You are right," she answered quietly. "I do not know the Marquis of Alston at all, except to say he is detestable and arrogant and everything hateful and despised that is written in that disgusting pamphlet."

She took the lace handkerchief he offered her and smiled a watery smile as she dabbed dry her eyes.

"Eve, it's as if I married two men. One is caring and solicitous, and he enjoys the simple pleasures of life. I care about him deeply. I love him. The other, this Marquis, he is an insufferably arrogant creature. Banished by his father for some unspeakable behavior, it is whispered he is depraved beyond redemption. That one I hate."

"I sometimes wonder if he himself knows which one he is," Evelyn said on a sigh.

At Deb's sudden intake of breath, he was quick to reassure her.

"But no, I don't think him beyond saving. Rumor has become mingled with historical fact. My mother spoke once of a most shocking incident that occurred soon after the Duke and Duchess married. A mad young nobleman, the Duke's natural son, attacked and tried to abduct the Duchess. She was with child, carrying Alston in fact, and came close to having her throat cut."

Evelyn pressed Deb's hands and smiled ruefully.

"When my cousin was seen to repeat, in a different way, the folly of this mad half-brother, there were those who were quick to magnify the hideous error of judgment of a wayward youth into something far more sinister. History repeating itself, you might say."

"Then my brother did not lie... But for Julian to attack his own mother... It is too hideous to contemplate... Eve—*why*?"

"You can blame my cousin's reckless and most shocking outburst on Robert Thesiger, who knew very well the sad story of the mad young nobleman and used it to advantage—"

Deb was mystified. "Robert Thesiger? What has Mr. Thesiger to do with Julian?"

"Everything, *ma chérie*," Evelyn replied with a tight smile. "Robert was at Eton with us. He made a point of informing my cousin of their connection by blood—that the Duke was also his father, something of which Alston was unaware. It truly shocked him. He had no idea about his father's nefarious past, nor that such a debauched existence had produced rotten fruit. Suffice for me to say Robert used his connection by blood to sinister effect."

Deb's mind was awhirl with new knowledge.

"But what could Robert Thesiger possibly say to make Julian condemn his own mother as a whore and a-a witch?"

Evelyn looked down at the lace ruffles covering his long hands and took a moment to answer her. He was in two minds as to what to tell her, so he said with a sigh of resignation and a lift of a hand,

"It is not my place to tell you. I have said too much already, *ma chérie*. You must ask Alston. Let me just add that Robert's motives have always been transparent. He is eaten up with bitter envy—envy that, but for the Grace of God, *he* would be heir to the Roxton Dukedom, not Alston. His mother, who had expectations of marrying the Duke and was rebuffed, taught her son from a young age to loathe the Duchess." He touched Deb's cheek. "What is important is that Alston can be forgiven his one act of youthful folly."

"I can readily forgive the disordered emotional *drunken* outbursts of a naïve and misguided fifteen-year-old boy," Deb said with a wry smile. "But the impetuous naivety of youth cannot explain away the actions of the gentleman who is not only accused of breach of promise, but who went to great lengths to deceive his own wife about his identity and intentions!"

Evelyn held Deb by the shoulders and looked into her eyes.

"If there is one sure thing I know about my cousin, it is that he would never offer Lisette Lefebvre, or any other female for that matter, marriage merely to get her into his bed! Believe me, Deborah, I know. *I know*. You are not to believe the inflammatory writings in a filthy pamphlet. They are putrid *nothings*. They are written to inflame a starving populace! Written by uninformed hacks that don't know the real circumstances or motives behind the accusations against my cousin. Do you understand me?"

"I understand what you are saying, Eve," Deb answered levelly. "But how am I to believe you when Lefebvre's lawyers have instituted proceedings against my husband?"

She pulled free and stepped back.

"Eve, Lefebvre and my husband fought a duel! A man does not follow another over water and into a foreign land to cross swords, not unless he believes his daughter was grossly wronged, and as a father he has the right to defend her honor."

Evelyn threw up a lace-ruffled wrist.

"Of course Lefebvre believes his daughter was grossly wronged but—but there are always two sides to any imbroglio!"

"Oh? Don't tell me the girl *ensnared* Alston with her charms, and he was powerless to resist her, because that is a very lame excuse and not one I am willing to entertain!"

"Alston is a stiff-necked bloody fool!" he blurted out savagely. "I warned him how it would be when he returned from exile. But no, he follows his own path and won't live by society's dictates! That's what has landed him at the center of this absurd scandal."

He put an arm about Deb's shoulders, seeing her hurt and

confusion, and led her through to the blue and white gilded salon, saying in a much calmer tone,

"Forgive me, *ma chérie*. Alston and I are the best of friends but we do not see eye-to-eye on this matter. You and I, we must help him be more Julian Hesham and less the Marquis of Alston, yes?"

Deb wished in her heart of hearts for nothing truer. But Evelyn's confidences were far from reassuring. After all, he had made no excuses for the Marquis's deceiving her into consummating their marriage, nor had he adequately explained the sordid business with Lisette Lefebvre. It was all very well for Evelyn to assure her his cousin had not seduced the girl with the promise of marriage, but where was the proof? And until she had the same assurances from her husband she could not believe Evelyn out-of-hand.

"Seeing you, knowing your mind, has decided me, *ma chérie*," Evelyn announced, as he tucked his viola under his square chin. He handed Deb a sheaf of musical notations and then began to play a pretty piece he had composed. "Follow the notations. Give me your opinion of this piece of froth I've written for Dominique. It is a betrothal gift I will play for her at tomorrow afternoon's concert in the Tuileries gardens. Jack has consented to be part of my small string ensemble. Having the boy will add a certain tender piquancy to the occasion, don't you think?"

Deb indulged his whim and reclined on the striped silk chaise longue by the clavichord with the sheets of musical composition, while Evelyn pranced about the room in his high-heeled shoes, seemingly lost in his playing, but acting the clown for her benefit—anything to take her mind off her present troubles. She couldn't help a giggle at such antics.

"It is a pretty piece," she admitted with a laugh as the composer pirouetted in front of her, the silk skirts of his waistcoat flaring out around him. "But how can you expect me to concentrate on your music when you talk of betrothal pieces, a girl called Dominique, and Jack performing with you at the Tuileries, all in the same breath? Is he truly playing in your ensemble?"

Evelyn finished playing his composition with a flourish and bowed to her.

"Yes, *ma chérie*. And his aunt must be there to applaud his efforts and help me persuade the boy to perform before an audience. His talent must not remain in a cupboard, and so I told him."

Deb's brown eyes lit up and she clapped her hands.

"I knew you would see my Jack's talent! And Dominique...?" she asked, head to one side.

"Ah, Dominique! I will tell you a secret, *ma chérie*. I am about to incur the wrath of the Duke and my parents. My mother will naturally take to her bed, declaring never to rise again from the shame I inflict on her and my illustrious ancestors. But I beg you to wish me happy. I am about to elope!"

"Elope? *Elope* with this Dominique? But, Eve, you've never once mentioned this girl in any of your letters. Who is she? Why must you elope? Why won't your parents approve of her?" Deb's arched brows contracted sharply when Evelyn smiled ruefully. "Why of course I wish you happy but... Are you *truly* happy, Eve?"

He put aside his viola, flicked out the embroidered skirts of his Italian waistcoat and sat on the striped silk footstool beside the chaise longue.

"Ha! You were ever the perceptive one. Yes, I am *determined* to be happy."

"But you do not love her?" Deb said gently and felt his fingers convulse in hers, which said more than his words of explanation thus far.

"It is not a *grande passion*. But perhaps that is for the best," he confessed with a smile of resignation. "I have a distracted and obsessed musician's disposition, and she, for all her youth, has a firm grasp on reality. Unable to catch the prize, she magnanimously settled for a dilution in the noble blood and a connection by marriage."

Deb touched his close-shaven cheek with the back of her hand.

"Oh, Eve, but if she is marrying you merely because of your noble connections, why elope with her?"

"*Ma chérie*, I assure you, the sooner I am married, the sooner this hideous entanglement we all find ourselves in will be resolved and we can return to a semblance of normality. Although, I fear the Duke will send me into exile, if only to keep Alston's fingers from choking the life out of me. Poor Maman, she will not recover from the shame of having Dominique for a daughter-in-law."

"You've not told me more than her name."

"Soon all will reveal itself. For now, she is simply Dominique. I was her pianoforte teacher."

"Teacher? When did the son of a viscount, nephew of a duke, ever need to descend to earning a living from his talent?"

Evelyn's blue eyes were alight with mischief, and he grinned.

"Didn't Otto ever tell you that passing oneself off as a musical genius who must needs earn his keep as a teacher makes for easy *entrée* into the best houses, and the best houses have the prettiest daughters!"

Deb playfully pinched his cleft chin.

"You are execrable. What will my husband think—"

"If you cared anything for my opinion, Madam wife, you'd have thought twice about sleeping in my cousin's bed!"

TWENTY-THREE

A N HOUR EARLIER Deb's major domo Joseph Jones had been kicking his heels at the Roxton stables, waiting for the Marquis of Alston to return from Versailles. He did not have to loiter long when a carriage-and-four turned into the courtyard, sending an army of lackeys into a frenzy of activity. It came to a halt close to where Joseph was propped on a low, ivy-covered stone wall, smoking a Turkish cheroot.

The first noble to alight from the carriage was the Marquis. He lingered on the portable steps two liveried footmen had rushed to place on the cobbles under the carriage door.

From the chatter and squeals of laughter, Joseph reckoned there were at least half a dozen aristocrats deep within the velvet-upholstered interior. A pretty painted female, her powdered hair swept up in a confection of dyed plumes, satin ribbons and strings of pearls, managed to stick her head and an arm out of the curtained window and demanded Alston kiss her fingertips. He did so with a flourish, and she disappeared inside with a giggle, to be replaced by another female with an equally complicated and absurd headdress. The Marquis was required to kiss her plump wrist, too, just above the string of pearls. He obediently complied and then descended the steps, three bewigged noblemen emerging from the dark interior to follow him out onto the cobbles. That the carriage door remained wide told Joseph the Marquis's friends were not staying.

"Perhaps another time, Bertrand," said the Marquis. He bowed. "Give my regards to Mme D'Aprano, and thank her for the invitation."

"You can't refuse Madame's invitation so brutally, Julian! It is most unfair of you. You must come to Chaillot for a few days. It is expected, no?" asked the Vicomte de Chaillot, looking to his two companions for support. "Henriette and Marguerite, they are expecting you. Their disappointment, it will be unbearable." He indicated the carriage window. "You saw just now how they miss you already."

"Alas, Sebastian, your dear sisters must be denied my company upon this occasion."

The Vicomte frowned. "This absurd trial, it is bothering you more than it should, my friend."

"Sebastian he is right in this," agreed the Vicomte's younger brother Bertrand. "This stinking fishmonger does not bear a moment of your thoughts. He is absurd. This business, it is absurd. Ugh! I do not know why you do not turn your back on it all. Then it is done with. *Voilà!*"

"That you do not turn your back, that is what feeds the rumors. But what of that, I say? It is not the truth that is important. It is that this tax collector had the effrontery—"

"*Excusez-moi*, Frederic," interrupted the Marquis with an embarrassed half-smile, turning to the third nobleman, one Chevalier du Charmond, "I beg to differ. The truth it is very important to me."

"M'sieur le Duc your father, he will arrange everything, I am certain of it," the Vicomte put in hurriedly, hoping to avoid offending his English friend. "This middle-class *putain* and her ridiculous father, they will be paid off. Then all will return to normality."

"Yes! Yes. Sebastian, he is in the right," Bertrand nodded, offering the others snuff. "All Farmers-General, they are open to bribery. Is that not how they gathered up their great wealth in the first place? Is it not criminal that they should be so wealthy?"

"M'sieur, as I am innocent of the charge, I do not see the need to resort to bribery," Julian said flatly, ignoring the commotion in the carriage. "And were I to do so, what would that say about my innocence?"

The three noblemen pondered this as if the idea were new to them, the Chevalier adding good-naturedly after he had snorted a goodly quantity of snuff up one fine nostril,

"But—Alston! That is being too stiff-necked about a trifle of a thing. This bribery of which you speak, it is a commonplace thing. It is done at the highest levels. It is expedient, no?"

There were calls from within the carriage for the noblemen to hurry along or they would be late for the recital. Henriette had to change her gown, and Marguerite, her hair needed more powder. Why were their brothers so unthinking? Bertrand? Sebastian? *Frederic*? The three noblemen exchanged comments and gestures of hopelessness and forgiveness about the excessive needs of sisters, bowed to their friend with a flourish, and piled back inside the carriage to be off.

Julian waved them away with a smile, the Vicomte de Chaillot calling out from the window that he and his brothers would next see their friend when they came to collect him for the Opera.

But when he set off across the courtyard, Joseph saw that the nobleman's face was devoid of laughter. He pulled at his cravat as if eager to be rid of it and walked as fast as he could in red-heeled court shoes that were meant for mincing about, not striding at pace.

Julian had not gone far when he was bluntly commanded to wait up. The shock of being so rudely addressed caused him to turn about with a thunderous expression that scattered the stable hands to all corners of the stable yard.

Joseph stood his ground and waited for the Marquis to come to him. Now was not the time to show nervousness. He had genuine concerns to raise with his lordship about Deb, and it was for her he must remain resolute. Yet, when Julian came over to him, a liveried flunky in pursuit, Joseph quickly stubbed out the cheroot under the toe of his boot and was momentarily lost for words under the lofty, angry, yet nonplussed gaze of a pair of emerald green eyes.

"Joseph? Why are you in Paris? I thought you had returned to England?"

"I've been to Bath and back, my lord," Joseph answered levelly and in English, a glance at the steward who had come part-way across the cobbles in anticipation of Joseph receiving a whipping for his insolence. "I went to see Miss Deb for myself."

Julian flinched, and sensing the steward at his back, turned on the astonished lackey, who couldn't believe his master was conversing socially with this inferior oaf, and growled at him to go away. He turned to Joseph with a scowl.

"Favored retainer to both our families you may be," he enunciated in English, "but you will address my wife as is her due. Is that understood, Mr. Jones?"

"Aye," Joseph answered demurely. "Beggin' your lordship's pardon, but it's her health and happiness which concerns me, not her elevation."

Julian took a step forward. "Damn your impertinence—"

"'cause I care about her, my lord!" Joseph argued, taking a nervous step away. "She's never been ill a day in her life, and when I'm told she's taken to her bed and is so weak she can't eat, that worries me. That ain't like her. So I decides I have to see her for myself. I don't care to take the word of a painmerchant and leave it at that! Beggin' your lordship's pardon, but— neither should you."

"I cannot leave Paris at this time," Julian muttered, a heightened color in his cheeks. "The trial…"

"Well I can and I did!"

"And is my wife as ill as Medlow makes out?"

Joseph heard the note of sneering disbelief.

"It ain't like her to feign illness, my lord. And Medlow ain't the sort of man who exaggerates. He ain't one of them quacks who panders to a man's imaginary ills."

"So satisfy my curiosity. What illness does her ladyship suffer that has made it impossible for her to join me?"

"Medlow wouldn't say. Said it was against his hypocritic oath."

"Hippo*cratic* oath," Alston corrected. "Very convenient. Now you will excuse me. I need to get out of these Court clothes."

He turned away and strode toward the imposing archway that proclaimed the entrance to the inner courtyard, and the main building of the hôtel, and where only soft-footed household livered servants were permitted.

"I do know what's kept her bedridden, my lord!" Joseph announced, scrambling across the cobbles to keep up with the big man's strides. When the Marquis did not stop, he added, "And I know where she is!"

That stopped Julian in his tracks. He turned from the stairwell.

"So tell me. What has kept her ladyship bedridden?"

Joseph swallowed under the mutinous gaze.

"I don't think it's my place to tell you, my lord."

"*For the love of God*! Out with it or leave me in peace!"

"I know Miss Deb—*her ladyship*—would prefer to tell you herself."

Julian looked out across the inner courtyard and then down at his large feet in their ridiculous court shoes before meeting the old retainer's gaze openly.

"Joseph, believe me when I tell you that had it been in my power to do so, I would gladly have gone to Bath to fetch her ladyship myself. But I cannot leave France. Lefebvre's lawyers have seen to that."

Joseph nodded and couldn't help a smile.

"I thought that was how it was, so when she was well enough to travel I went and fetched her for you, my lord."

Julian grabbed his elbow.

"She's here? Here in Paris? Tell me. Where?"

Joseph pointed to the clouds. "Upstairs. M'sieur Ffolkes' apartment."

The words were hardly out of his mouth when Julian turned on a heel and took the stairs two at a time.

JULIAN ENTERED his cousin's apartment on a soft scratch to the panelled double doors, and made his way toward the melodic sound of the viola, ignoring the goggle-eyed valet who hopped about on the balls of his feet screeching in a whisper that there was no female in his master's apartment and if there were, she was a lady, despite owning a pistol which she kept in a holster sewn into her boot. He Philippe had seen it while tidying the bedchamber, where the lady had most definitely *not* slept and not had a bath. So would his lordship kindly leave before the young lady splattered their brains across the wallpaper.

The valet then retreated, a quick glance into the salon in time to see his master kiss the beautiful young lady's fingers and say something that made her laugh. She playfully pinched his chin in response. Philippe glanced swiftly up at the dark look on the impassive handsome face of the Marquis, and ran back through the rooms of the apartment and down the servant stairs as fast as his fat little legs would take him. He wasn't going to be the one to wipe his master's blood off the chaise.

Stopping in mid-stride just inside the door, Julian saw his bride reclining on a chaise longue with her stockinged toes to the warmth of the fire. She was more beautiful than his remembrance of her, with liquid brown eyes full of laughter, luminescent skin, and a thick braid of hair that he knew shone wine-red in the sun—hair he had once caressed and brushed and liked best when it cascaded freely about her bare shoulders. She also glowed with vitality.

In fact, she was such an epitome of bountiful good health that his happiness at seeing her turned to anger. He had been duped by the physician Medlow's written assurances that his wife was too ill to travel. He had worried himself needlessly about her welfare. And he had spent every night wanting her, needing the touch and the warmth of her, and seeking solace in excessive exercise to take away the constant ache of not having her, and all the while she was feigning illness, to bide her time so her lawyers could find her an escape from their marriage.

Annulment be damned!

He had been without her for twelve long weeks. They had been apart longer than they had shared a marriage bed and it felt like a lifetime.

Thus his first words to her were cold and mean, fuelled by jealousy, and thoroughly unwarranted. They served to startle apart the couple by the fire.

Evelyn scrambled to his heels and Deborah sat up, tucking her stockinged feet under the froth of her pretty muslin petticoats, and in so doing, scattered the sheets of musical composition across the Turkey rug.

Julian ignored his cousin, a smoldering eye on his furiously blushing bride.

"Well, Lady Bountiful, how gratifying to find you in good health. I can now look forward to an immediate resumption of my conjugal rights." He glanced fleetingly at his cousin before fixing his gaze on his wife once again. "Of course, I need hardly remind you that your paramount wifely duty is to remain chaste until you've given me a son. I want no by-blows, however closely related."

And with that blunt speech he turned on a heel and was across the room before Deborah's retort made him return to the chaise longue.

"What—did—you—say?" he rasped, voice barely above a whisper, hoping his hearing had not deceived him.

JULIAN HAD BEEN in the room a full thirty seconds before it registered with Deb that the nobleman in Court dress was her husband. His face was powdered and patched, his shoes had stacked red heels with enormous diamond encrusted shoe buckles, and his black unruly hair was plastered to his scalp with pomade and wax. It was only his deep mellow voice that alerted her to the fact that somewhere beneath all that grease paint and gold thread was Julian Hesham, the man she had fallen in love with. But as he appeared first and foremost the epitome of a French courtier, it was easy for her to appear just as cold and unsentimental as he.

Her chin had tilted up in defiance with his first sneering words, and she clasped her hands behind her back, effectively bunching up the yards of light muslin so that her petticoats were taut across her stomach, exposing the growing roundness of her belly and leaving her noble husband in no doubt she was pregnant.

"I assure you, my lord, I pray daily to be delivered of a son," she repeated as he came back to stand before her, adding with an icy calm she did not in the least feel, "Because *nothing* will induce me to share your bed again!"

For what seemed an eternity of minutes, Julian stared at her and such was the change in his expression, the softness that came over his handsome features, that for one heart-stopping moment he was again Julian Hesham. His gaze finally met hers, and there was a look in his eye, hard to read, as he gingerly put out a hand to her.

But Deb stepped away from him, releasing the bunched up yards of muslin so that they draped naturally from her bodice.

"So that's why you could not come to Paris? Why you were ill?" he asked in a voice filled with wonderment. When she nodded without looking at him, he added gently, "When—when did you know?"

"On—on our return from Cumbria."

"Back then?" He was surprised. He smiled softly. "How far along is the babe?"

She bit her lip and focused on his intricately-tied lace cravat with its single large diamond-headed pin. But she could not help smiling when giving him the news.

"Five—five and a half months."

"*Five and a half months*?" he repeated in the same tone of wonderment. He smiled broadly and gave a huff of laughter. "Then you conceived almost from our first night together..."

Deb hesitated, confused. This nobleman in all his silken and powdered finery certainly appeared the arrogant Marquis of Alston, but the deep, gentle tenor of his voice and the soft light in his green eyes was pure Julian Hesham. She wondered which man she should answer. But it was his conceited grin, and the movement out of the corner of her eye that decided her.

Evelyn had stooped to pick up the sheets of musical notation from the Turkey rug, and Deb caught the grin exchanged between the cousins. It caused her to blanch white with embarrassment that Julian would openly and arrogantly discuss intimate details that were the private preserve of husband and wife.

"Impregnating a bride on the wedding night must be a feat worth bragging about to your male compatriots," she said bitterly. "Eve certainly shares in your conceit. What a shame your lordship wasted two tiresome months in Cumbria. Had I realized my condition earlier, you could've returned to France and your whoring."

"I beg your pardon?"

He looked so shocked and affronted Deb was incredulous he could stand there pretending moral outrage. They stood facing one another, mute, neither willing to give an inch, and yet both acutely aware of the other. Both secretly hoped the other would say or do something to end this nightmare and return them to Cumbria, where they had been so happy and so in love.

It was only when Evelyn spoke, that time moved on, and not in a good way.

"Deborah, *ma chérie*. Julian, *mon cousin*—Is it not possible, with this momentous news, for you both to—"

That broke the spell. Before the musician had uttered another syllable, Deb turned away from her husband on a shattering sob and fell into his cousin's embrace, burying her face in his silk waistcoat.

"Deborah, *ma chérie*," Evelyn murmured soothingly, and on a heavy sigh looked imploringly to his cousin. "Julian, you must understand—her condition—"

"I understand all too well, *Cousin*!" Julian enunciated bitterly, a significant look at the composer's hand that stroked his wife's back. "When you've done *comforting* my pregnant bride, be so good as to send her to the library. The Duke will be home on the hour."

And with that icy pronouncement, he turned on a heel and strode from the room.

Evelyn called him back, but Julian was gone.

Without looking left or right he marched along corridor after corridor, passing countless blank-faced liveried footmen standing to attention, and he did not stop until he was at the stairwell that led to his spacious apartment on the second floor. A hand to the ornate balustrade, he hesitated to ascend the stairs, head bent and back stooped. It was as if all the emotional fight had suddenly drained from him. He let go of the balustrade and slumped sideways, shoulder against the wall, and slowly slid downwards until he was sprawled on the bottom step. Only then did he give way to his inner turmoil.

Covering his face with his hands, he wept.

TWENTY-FOUR

Sir Gerald Cavendish stumbled upon the Marquis ten minutes later. He made a bumbling speech full of verbose compliments and inane observations about the weather because he was nervous at having a private word with his noble brother-in-law. But what made his delivery even more blundering was the fact he had not expected to find his lordship slouched on the floor, long legs sprawled out before him, head back up against the wall, eyes closed and chin skywards, particularly when he was dressed in powder, gold thread and diamonds.

He just didn't understand it. He did not know how to proceed. He wondered if the Marquis were drunk, or having an attack of some kind. The nobleman's face was flushed and his cheeks damp, as if he'd been blubbering like a girl. It certainly wasn't the sort of behavior Sir Gerald deemed usual for the son of a Duke...

When Julian opened his eyes on Sir Gerald's greeting, he wiped his hands over his damp, flushed face and got to his feet.

He straightened his frockcoat and brushed down his silken breeches, and then, with a heavy sigh of resignation, he invited his wife's brother up to his sitting room.

Here, Frew kept a good fire burning. The valet momentarily emerged from the closet off the bedchamber, but as his master appeared distracted and was not alone he retreated, leaving the connecting door ajar, affording Sir Gerald a glimpse within his lordship's inner sanctum. He watched the valet quietly go about his duties. With him were two lackeys. One was pouring steaming scented water from a copper pail into an enormous hipbath central to the room, while the other was arranging a richly embroidered banyan of red silk over an ornately carved arm of a gilded chair.

That these preparations for the nobleman's bath continued unabated made Sir Gerald realize the timing of his visit was ill-judged. He felt most unwelcome. This deepened into acute discomfort, knowing the Marquis was newly returned from Versailles and obviously wished to change out of full Court dress.

When Julian silently stood his ground by the fireplace and did not offer Sir Gerald to sit on any of the chairs in the room, Sir Gerald coughed to clear the nervousness from his throat.

"I must tell you how grateful I am to your esteemed parents and to you, my lord, for permitting my nephew the honor of spending time in the company of Lord Henri-Antoine."

Sir Gerald ended this rehearsed speech with a smile, but the Marquis remained unmoved. It was as if he stared straight through him, with emerald-green eyes so piercingly clear Sir Gerald's palms began to sweat. He continued on regardless.

"No one was more surprised than I to learn Jack had such an esteemed school friend. He has always been an impetuous youth, somewhat wayward at times, and often given to speaking his mind—"

"A circumstance of residing with his aunt perhaps?"

"Yes. Yes. Not the most ideal of circumstances for my nephew."

"Yet, the only option open to him...?"

"Um—er—Well, I am confident that time spent in the elevated company of your brother, who is a most worthy young nobleman, will be most beneficial to my nephew's uneven temperament."

"Are you? I'm hoping Jack will teach Harry a thing or two."

"Oh, no, no, my lord," Sir Gerald assured him with a shake of his powdered wig. "I am hopeful Jack's unpleasant overexuberance will be subdued while under this exalted roof. And in Lord Henri-Antoine's superior companionship his manners cannot but improve. My nephew has had a rather *provincial* upbringing," he apologized, showing his distaste. "I cannot bring myself to say more for fear of offending your lordship. If you knew the circumstances your lordship could only agree with me."

"I do not agree with you."

Sir Gerald blinked. "I beg your lordship's pardon?"

"I am delighted Jack has befriended my brother. His influence has considerably improved Harry's somber outlook on life. In fact, their divergent personalities complement one another very well."

"Do—do they indeed?" Sir Gerald stuttered with incomprehension.

"Your nephew is a fine young man."

"He is? Well, yes, I suppose he must be. Yes, I'm sure he is!"

"A credit to his aunt, who has had the rearing of him since he was—six? Yes, six years old. But I'm sure you aren't keeping me from my bath for the express purpose of discussing the merits of your esteemed nephew."

"I—I—No! No, indeed, my lord! No. I besought this interview to make it known to you that Lady Mary—Lady Mary and myself—we—you—have our unconditional support regarding this—um—unpleasant and most tiresome business. To think it has gone as far as the publication of slanderous pamphlets shows that these French tax collectors are indeed opportunistic little swine. That they dare think they can bring down a member of the nobility defies the imagination," Sir Gerald blustered on, a glance up at the Marquis whose face remained infuriatingly inscrutable. "This tax collector deserves to be locked up! His daughter put in the stocks for her wanton and outrageous behavior. Of course, those of us who know you—"

"But you do not know me."

"—would never seriously entertain the notion of the Marquis of Alston dangling after a mere tax collector's daughter," Sir Gerald concluded with a snort of bombastic self-consequence. "And I told my sister, as the Marchioness of Alston she is obliged to ignore such inconsequential chatter, whether there be truth in it or not."

"Told your sister?" Julian repeated.

He spoke so quietly Sir Gerald wondered if he had spoken at all and continued on as if he had not, oblivious to the cold hard light that dulled the Marquis's normally friendly and expressive eyes.

"Before Lady Mary and I embarked on the voyage to Paris, I made a point of calling on Deborah in Bath."

"And how did you find my wife upon that visit?"

Sir Gerald blinked again. "Find her, my lord?"

Julian came a little closer.

"Her health. Her person. How did she appear to you?"

"To tell you a truth, my lord, she was not keen to see me. She sent down some lame excuse with her maid about being too ill," Sir Gerald said confidentially. "But as I know she has not been ill a day in her life, I thought the maid's pronouncement my sister was too ill to see anyone save her quack doctor a bit rich to swallow. My persistence finally paid off. But of course, Deborah will play her tricks on her brother! When I was shown up to her boudoir, I found her lying upon the chaise under a coverlet with a basin at the ready!" He forced a laugh, but when the Marquis did not join in, he quickly banished the smile and added gravely, "Upon reflection, I must own she did look quite green, and listened to my advice without one word of dissent, which is most unlike her."

"Advice?"

"I made it clear to her that it was absurd to make more of a situation than was merited," Sir Gerald stated confidently. "That when a nobleman seeks the—um—favors of a French whore, it should be of no consequence, in truth a mere nothingness, to a nobleman's wife. I stressed to Deborah that it was beneath her dignity to even acknowledge the existence of such females. I told her it was time she stopped her pretense of outrage by remaining in Bath, and that feigning illness was merely delaying the inevitable. I let it be known that she could not expect a grain of sympathy or support from me. That it was her duty to be here in Paris at your side." He smiled with satisfaction. "And I am most happy to report Deborah took my advice, for she arrived in Paris only last night."

"You miserable worm," Julian muttered, surveying his wife's pompous prig of a brother with such an ugly pull to his mouth that he was the image of his ancient parent. "You have the barefaced audacity to tell me you took it upon yourself to lecture Deborah on her duty as my wife, and that you spoke to her about a piece of trumped-up filth you know not the first thing about?"

"My lord? It was not my intention to offend you," Sir Gerald apologized, completely misreading the direction of the Marquis's anger. "Indeed, if you only knew to what lengths I have gone on your behalf to support you in this matter."

"Your sister is no longer your concern. She is mine. Do you understand? Stay away from her!" Julian growled, and strode off through to the dressing room.

The inviting sweet smell of the heated water caused him to breathe in deeply as he removed the diamond-headed pin from the folds of his lace cravat, then tugged restlessly at the intricate knot.

"Frew? Frew!"

The valet came scurrying from one of the inner rooms carrying a pair of new high-heeled shoes just sent from the shoemaker. His master's black mood did not surprise him. It was Frew's considered opinion that the Marquis's frequent black moods and restless nights could be blamed on the strained relations with his bride, and that the sooner the couple resolved their differences and once again shared the marital bed, the sooner life could return to placid normality. But Frew kept these thoughts to himself and showed his master a perfectly neutral expression.

Julian fixed his scowl on the shoes.

"For the ball this evening, my lord," the valet explained.

"Send those ridiculous affectations back where they came from!" Julian ordered, kicking off the shoes he was wearing. He tugged again at the tightly-bound cravat as if it were choking him. "Get me a shoe fit for an *Englishman's* foot. Not some effeminate steepled creation only a Tom-thumb should wear!"

"An Englishman's shoe," repeated Frew. "Very good, my lord."

"In fact, toss out any shoe with a heel higher than the width of *my* thumb."

"No higher than the width of your thumb. Very wise, my lord."

The Marquis strode over to the cluttered dressing table and sat on the padded velvet stool in his stockinged feet.

"And, Frew, I won't be wearing powder this evening."

"No powder, my lord?" said the valet in horrified accents, outraged at the thought of such a social solecism. "But the b-b-ball..."

"What of it? I've had enough of this wretched grease and powder itching my scalp! No more powder! *Ever.*"

"No more powder—*ever*?"

Julian looked up sharply. "For God's sake, Charles, are you a parrot?"

"No, my lord. Not a parrot," Frew murmured, turned to scurry away and came face-to-face with Sir Gerald, standing as a statue by the hipbath.

If the valet was reeling from his master's orders to banish the powder cone from the dressing room, he was goggle-eyed to discover a trespasser in this inner sanctum. But not as goggle-eyed as the time he had walked in on the Marquis sharing his bath with his bride. Since accompanying his master on his bridal trip to Cumbria, Frew determined that nothing or no one could ever again ruffle his valet's feathers. So he took Sir Gerald's presence in his stride, bowed to him and departed, leaving the round-faced gentleman to front the wrath of the Marquis alone.

Anger made Julian speechless. He was incredulous that Sir Gerald had the stupidity to continue the discussion and worse, the social ineptitude to follow him into the inner sanctum of his dressing room. Sir Gerald took the silence as permission to speak—such was his overwhelming panic and selfish concern.

"My lord, I must tell you that no amount of cajolery on my part has persuaded Deborah to change her mind from a course of action that will be the ruin of her family name!" Sir Gerald declared on a nervous snort, inexplicably hot under the Marquis's steady gaze. "It will shock you to learn she had the effrontery to ask for my assistance in seeking an annulment to your marriage!" When this dramatic pronouncement was met with icy silence he added, "When she expressed this wish, I was as revolted into silence as you are now."

"Liar," Julian muttered, up off the dressing stool. "You put the idea of annulment into her head."

"No—no, my lord! It-it was my lawyers! My lawyers advised that there was no other way out of an arranged marriage," Sir Gerald said in a thin voice, backing across the deep rug as Julian came towards him. "I had no idea, no idea whatsoever, of the existence of the Act of '42 until informed by my attorney. You must believe me, my lord!"

He stumbled over the side of a wingchair and scrambled to pick himself up, adjusted his lopsided wig and immediately tripped over the carpet as he was backed against the door.

"Deborah will attempt to use the Act to persuade a judge to grant her an annulment. That is why I came to warn you, to assure you of my undivided support. I warned Deborah that there is not a judge in the kingdom who would go up against your family to grant her an annulment."

"You despicable piece of filth!" Julian seethed with white-lipped fury. He gripped Sir Gerald by the narrow lapels of his velvet frock coat. "God knows what unnecessary distress you've caused her with your pompous self-important lecturing and interference!" He let him go with a shove and opened the door that led to the passageway, saying flatly, "Tomorrow you will return, not to London, but to your estate, and stay there."

Sir Gerald's eyes widened in disbelief as he stepped out into the servant passageway, little realizing he had been relegated to lackey status.

There came a distant rumble like thunder from somewhere further along the warren of narrow corridors. Far off a bell began tolling. Sir Gerald recognized that distant rumble. It wasn't thunder at all but the scampering of a hundred soft-footed servants belonging to the Duke's household. The tolling bell signaled that the Duke's carriage and entourage had turned in through the black and gold gates of the Hôtel Roxton.

Sir Gerald blinked, distraction with the household goings-on evaporating as he realized the enormity of the Marquis's order.

"*Tomorrow*, my lord? To my-my estate? I am to be—*banished*?"

"I never want to see your lily-livered face again. Frew? Frew!" Julian called out as he slammed the door on Sir Gerald, and so hard a small watercolor of Constantinople in a large ornate gold frame jumped off the wall and crashed to the parquetry.

TWENTY-FIVE

A DOUR-FACED footman in livery escorted Deborah to a large anteroom and politely requested she remain until summoned to enter the library. She felt wretched and shivered with nerves. Although she had rehearsed what she intended to say to the Duke and Duchess over and over while confined to her bed in Bath, she dreaded forgetting her carefully crafted speech now she was to come face-to-face with her husband's parents. She kept telling herself she held the trump card. Whatever they said or threatened her with, news of her pregnancy was surely so momentous they would have to listen to her demands, and ultimately agree to her request for a formal separation from their son. His behavior in Evelyn's apartment merely confirmed he cared nothing for her personally, only for what she could give him. So be it, but his dearest wish would come at a price.

As she paced, she caught sight of her reflection in an ornate gilded looking glass over a fireplace and noted with a frown that her hair, despite time spent arranging it herself, appeared to be in an imminent state of unraveling. She hastily rearranged a number of pearl-headed pins before turning her attention to the sit of the square neckline of a new velvet bodice trimmed with tiny bows that was already growing too tight across her breasts. She really should have remained in the sacque-back muslin gown she'd changed into in Evelyn's apartment. But perhaps it would not do to be too comfortable in the presence of the Duke and Duchess. After all, she needed to keep her wits about her.

Such was her nervous preoccupation with looking presentable that when the library doors opened and a footman appeared to quietly usher her within, it was the servant's reflection at her shoulder that caused Deb to jump away from the looking glass. She went at his bidding, her slippered feet taking a moment to respond, hands clasped tightly in front of her.

The long book-lined room, with its heavy velvet curtains pulled across the windows, blazed with light despite it being the middle of the day. Every sconce held lighted candles, and as the footman took her deeper into the room, Deb peered nervously about at the gilded furniture and the three walls covered from parquetry flooring to painted ceiling with bookshelves crammed with leather-bound volumes. She passed by a wide heavy mahogany desk and glanced at its surface. Several opened picture books displayed maps and colored sketches of exotic lands. In the large ornate fireplace central to the room, an inviting fire blazed. On the mantelshelf were propped gilt-edged cards of invitation.

Pride of place over this carved mahogany mantel was a family portrait of the Duke and Duchess with their two sons and four faithful hounds. It was a recent portrait, for Lord Henri-Antoine appeared close to his nine years of age, yet the Duchess was painted as a young woman, closer in age to her eldest son and that could not be. Deb supposed the artist to be a flatterer, for the Duchess was surely closer in age to the Duke?

Two wing chairs, a deep cushioned sofa and a large tapestry-covered ottoman were arranged on an Aubusson carpet near the warmth of the fireplace. On the ottoman was an ancient backgammon board with its ivory pieces still in play, a small leather-bound volume with a silk riband between two pages to hold a place, and several opened letters tucked in under a corner of the backgammon board. Nervousness gave way to curiosity as Deb took in this quaint domestic scene, at odds with the masculine magnificence of the library, and it was only with the swish of stiff silk petticoats from the sofa that she realized she was not alone.

In fact, the footman had formally announced her and departed before Deb came to her senses and dropped into a respectful curtsy to the two persons who had risen as one from the sofa. She felt a hand on her elbow as she straightened, and a perfumed kiss lightly brushed one cheek and then the other, while words of welcome were uttered in French by a pleasing feminine voice. Deb caught the flash and sparkle of diamonds and emeralds about a slender white throat before space was put between her and the exquisitely embroidered silk petticoats of Antonia, Duchess of Roxton.

A masculine drawling voice offered her the wingchair opposite the sofa and when she declined to sit the Duke and Duchess remained standing. There was a moment of awkward silence that brought the heat up into Deb's throat, though her gaze remained firmly lowered to the carpet. It was only when she reluctantly sat where requested that her illustrious hosts did likewise.

"Under the—er—*circumstances*, I won't insult your intelligence with inane words of welcome into the family fold," drawled the Duke. "You have come to us in your own good time, so perhaps you would do the Duchess and me the courtesy of knowing how we may be of service?"

Deb's gaze flashed up angrily at the Duke's face.

He was regarding her with a thin smile of sympathetic insolence, and yet his dark eyes held a spark of mischief, as if he were enjoying her discomfort. He looked just as Deb remembered him. He had a shock of snowy white hair, coal black eyes, and a long face etched with the deep lines of dissipation. It was impossible to guess his age, only that he was ancient. And frail. It was as if breathing was an effort for him now. She looked away, lest she appear bad-mannered and more importantly, lost her train of thought.

"I sincerely hope you may be of service to me, M'sieur le Duc," she answered with a slight clearing of the throat, then continued forthrightly. "I am in this predicament through no fault of my own. My marriage to your son was for your political and dynastic preservation, and although such cold-hearted reasons for marriage are commonplace amongst the nobility, it is not the sort of marriage I had envisioned for myself."

The Duchess leaned forward; hands clasped in the lap of her billowing petticoats.

"*Ma belle-fille*, what kind of marriage did you have in mind?" she asked gently.

Deborah did not raise her gaze above the Duchess's slender arms where, encircled about both wrists, half a dozen diamond and gold bracelets sparkled.

"Mme la Duchesse, it is very difficult to explain to someone who cannot possibly understand that I find the idea and practice of arranged marriages abhorrent. Forgive me if my blunt speech offends you, for that is not my intention, but I had hoped to marry for reasons that would appear foolhardy and incomprehensible to you."

"You hoped to marry for love, *ma petite*."

It was not a question, and the sadness in the soft pleasant voice made Deb swallow and clench her hands in her lap. *I must remain strong*, she told herself. *Emotion must not get the better of me*.

Yet her conviction could not stop her curiosity, and she stole a glance at the face that owned such a sweet, sad voice. Her shock was evident in the way she was unable to resist staring openly, until the Duchess smiled at her kindly. Only then did Deb blink and quickly avert her gaze. Deb had thought the

Duchess beautiful in the family portrait over the fireplace, but in the flesh the word *beautiful* seemed a rather inadequate and inane description for this elfin creature. The Duchess of Roxton was so breathtakingly beautiful, she dazzled.

But surely she could not possibly be the Marquis of Alston's mother? She was far too young. Yet, Julian had those same emerald-green eyes. She must have been a child bride, reasoned Deb, and was revolted by the thought of the Duchess as a beautiful young girl forced into an arranged marriage—resigning herself to a life of titled privilege as wife and devoted mother and suffering in silence her husband's excesses and infidelities.

No doubt the Duke expected her to act accordingly with his son. How wrong he was!

"I trust you are recovered from the illness that kept you bedridden and a—er—*prisoner* in your own home for an astonishing twelve weeks?" inquired the Duke with that hint of insolent disbelief Deb found annoying.

It served to shatter Deb's mental musings and further inflame her anger.

"Illness or not, M'sieur le Duc, I was a prisoner in my own home until such time as I agreed to come to Paris," Deb replied in a steady voice. "The only visitors I was permitted were my brother and M'sieur Ellicott. The latter, no doubt, sent to confirm that I was indeed as ill as reported."

The Duke inclined his white head, saying with a smirk,

"Sir Gerald's visit was a regrettable oversight. As for Martin, I—er—*presumed* you would not object to his company. He is very fond of you."

"And I of him," Deb answered quietly and met the Duke's look squarely. "But that does not explain why my house was spied upon by your thuggish servants, M'sieur le Duc. It was not as if I were about to run off. Not that I could, had I wanted to. Those buffoons would have found me soon enough."

The Duke put up his white brows in mild surprise.

"I gave you credit for more brain, Madam. It was my son who requested that your house be watched for your own protection. There are those who could seek to do you a harm now that you are intimately connected with my family."

"Lord Alston's concern is gratifying, but I doubt a worse fate exists than being connected by marriage with your family!" Deb retorted in English before she could help herself.

"Flippant sarcasm does not become you!" the Duke rasped, and in such an icy voice that Deb involuntarily swallowed and dropped her gaze to her clenched hands.

The Duke took a few moments to recover, and in the ensuing silence, as his breathing became less labored, the Duchess asked Deb gently,

"The physician Medlow he assured us you are restored to full health, *ma petite*?"

Deb nodded. "Yes, Mme la Duchesse, I am well." She glanced at the Duke. "I trust Medlow's assurances were in response to your inquiry, M'sieur le Duc, and not the other way round?"

"If you are concerned Medlow broke his Hippocratic oath, you may rest easy," the Duke answered with a ghost of a laugh. "That is one physician who is—er—*incorruptible*. However, I regret to inform you Sir Gerald's lawyers are not."

Deb breathed in quickly, but instantly regained her composure.

"My brother is not to blame, M'sieur le Duc. He contacted his lawyers at my request, and most reluctantly too."

"Your honesty is to be commended. Perhaps you would care to inform the Duchess why you had Sir Gerald approach his lawyers?"

Deb frowned and bit back a retort. So he was going to humiliate her in front of his wife. Not if she could help it!

"As you are well aware of my reasons for doing so, Your Grace, I am surprised you did not tell the Duchess yourself," she enunciated calmly in English, eyes bravely focused on the Duke.

"Then again, you did not consult your wife on your son's marriage, did you? Was that because you consider females little better than children and thus incapable of rational thought and understanding? Or because you do not wish to upset her with the news her son's marriage is to be dissolved using the Act of '42 that grants annulment on the grounds of lunacy?"

The Duke's dark eyes sparked with anger and his thin lips parted in reply, but something made him pause, and in that small moment of hesitation Deb's gaze dropped from his lined face to his silken knee where two hands rested, fingers entwined.

The Duke and Duchess were holding hands! It was such a small affectionate gesture, and yet it spoke volumes about the true nature of the ducal couple's relationship. It surprised Deb. Even more so realizing that the mere movement of the Duchess's fingers had the power to silence the Duke. But what shocked her more was the fact the Duchess must understand the English tongue for her to give such an instant response to a speech she knew would anger her husband.

"Forgive me, Mme la Duchesse," Deb apologized quickly, reverting to French. "Had I known you understood the English tongue I would not have been so blunt."

The Duchess's green eyes twinkled.

"I understand that you did not wish to upset me, yes? That is very considerate of you, *ma belle-fille*. But me I am not one of these females who wishes to be treated as a child. You understand?" When Deb nodded and looked suitably chastened, she added, "And I must tell you, *ma petite*, that my son Julian he has a quick stubborn temper like his Maman, and a little of Monseigneur's great arrogance—yet that is not such a bad thing for a man in his position—but one thing he is *not* is a lunatic."

"Your son is not a lunatic, Mme la Duchesse," Deb agreed, bravely keeping her gaze on the Duchess's beautiful face. "But as I understand it, for a marriage to be annulled it need only be proved that one of the parties was of unbalanced mind *at the time the marriage took place*. The night we were forcibly married off, he was very drunk. I believe he had drunk himself into a stupor in order to forget his quite shocking behavior towards you, Mme la Duchesse."

She glanced at the Duke. His eyes were all for his wife and he had raised her hand to his lips. Deb swallowed.

"I do not know why he did what he did, but he did and that's all that matters to a judge. Such action goes a long way to proving his mind was unhinged at the time. According to my brother's lawyers, that one act of lunacy is enough to have my marriage declared null and void."

When the Duchess looked down and away, green eyes glittering with tears, it was the Duke's turn to squeeze his wife's fingers. Deb stumbled on, eager to bring this painful interview to a close, willing herself not to be overcome with emotion, to let the tears run down her cheeks.

"I am so very sorry to speak of events which are still painfully raw for you both, but surely you cannot blame me for wanting to end a marriage based on deceit and false promises? I was robbed of the choice to marry for love and companionship. Yet," she said on a deep sigh of resignation, "matters have conspired against me. I have requested Sir Gerald's lawyers to halt the annulment proceedings..."

There was a long silence before the Duke spoke in his peculiar insolent drawl.

"That begs the question, Madam: Have Sir Gerald's lawyers been instructed to pursue such proceedings at a later date? A time, perhaps, when you can again inflict cruelty on Mme la Duchesse—"

The Duchess interrupted her husband.

"*Ma belle-fille*," Antonia said earnestly, "tell me honestly you do not love my son, and me I will see to it that he Julian never bothers you again."

Deb gave a laugh that broke in the middle, a shaking hand to her trembling mouth.

"Mme la Duchesse, I'm afraid your assurances cannot help me now. I am five and a half months with child."

There was an audible intake of breath from the Duchess, and she spoke in rapid French to the Duke something Deb did not catch. The Duke's silence brought Deb's eyes up to his face. She was startled by the smile of tenderness he bestowed upon the Duchess, one he must keep exclusively for her. It transformed his harsh aquiline features, turning him into someone quite human and approachable. The Marquis had that same smile. His father was made of flesh and blood after all...

This intimate scene was all too much for Deb, and she was on her feet to pace the space between the sofa and the wingchair, her thoughts tumbling forth into speech as tears spilled onto her cheeks. The sooner she managed to say all that was on her mind, and they agreed to her wishes, the sooner she could flee their presence for the solitude of the rooms assigned her.

That they were overjoyed by her news only made her more wretched because in every other circumstance she too would have shared their joy at her pregnancy. It made her unconsciously put a hand to her growing belly, as if shielding her unborn child from the harshness of the terms she was about to force from her noble parents-in-law.

"I will keep up the pretense of an amicable marriage until the birth. But after the child is born, I want a formal separation and ultimately a divorce."

"And if I do not agree?" asked the Duke.

"If you do not give me your word that I may go my own road once the child is born then I will have no alternative but to force your hand, M'sieur le Duc."

"What method of—er—*spiteful* coercion do you intend to employ, Madam?"

Deb continued her pacing, not looking at the couple on the sofa.

"It would be an easy thing for doubt to be cast on the

child's paternity, given that our marriage is yet to be publicly announced. Nor are the circumstances surrounding your son's deception in legalizing our union universally known."

The Duke's upper lip curled in distaste.

"You would do that to your own child? Put his future in jeopardy, make his life an uncertainty, all to exact revenge?"

"*Revenge*? I do not seek revenge, M'sieur le Duc," Deb said simply. "I desire to have my freedom returned to me. With all due respect, it was you who forced your son and me into this intolerable union, and thus it is you who must concede to my wishes if your grandson is to be born in unexceptional circumstances."

"If I sanction a formal separation, you relinquish all rights to your son."

Deb stood with her back to the fire and faced them, both hands now to her belly, as if again shielding her unborn child. Her actions were in marked contrast to her words.

"Yes, M'sieur le Duc. That would be for the best."

The Duchess looked anxiously from the Duke to Deb. Her eyes widened in horror at such an outcome.

"*Quoi*? A child needs its maman, *n'est-ce pas*?"

"A child needs loving parents, Mme la Duchesse," Deb argued sadly. "If I continue in this loveless marriage, I will become a hateful, resentful wife and as such, I cannot be the kind of mother my son deserves. Besides," she shrugged, hands falling to her sides, and gaze dropping to the carpet where the shadows from the crackling fire played upon the woven oriental patterns, "once our marriage is at an end I am very sure Lord Alston will do everything in his power to keep our son from me."

The Duchess stood and the Duke did likewise. Antonia came across to Deb and took hold of her hands.

"If you think that he Julian would do such a monstrous thing to the mother of his son, you are greatly mistaken in my son's character, *ma petite*."

"I thought I knew your son very well," Deb replied softly, a sob in her throat, tearful gaze on the small hands that held hers. "But, yes, you are quite right, Mme la Duchesse. I find that I do not know Lord Alston at all."

A polite cough had all three occupants of the library turning to the double doors. The butler had quietly trod the length of the room and had been waiting to be noticed. At the Duke's nod he announced that nuncheon was ready and that family and guests had assembled. Deb was all for making her excuses to decline nuncheon when the butler departed, leaving the door wide open.

TWENTY-SIX

I NTO THE LIBRARY strolled a tall, thin boy with coal-black
curls tied back with a large white ribbon, dressed in a waistcoat and breeches of exquisite embroidered richness. His skin
was so pale it was translucent, and his black eyes were ringed
with dark shadows. There was no mistaking his parent. He was
the image of the Duke and had the beginnings of his father's
strong nose. At his heels pranced four whippets with diamond
collars, that upon seeing their master scampered up to the Duke
to receive his adoration.

And lastly came Jack. He bounded into the room, copper
curls falling into his eyes, clothes slightly crumpled and with his
shoes scuffed, which is what Deb expected of a rough-and-
tumble boy almost nine years of age. Not at all like Lord Henri-
Antoine, who was precise to a pin and carried himself with a
languid upright insolence, the antithesis of Jack's easy gait and
friendly open look.

At sight of her nephew, all Deb's pent up emotion spilled
forth and she rushed forward to enfold Jack in a tight embrace.
Through her tears she told him how much she had missed him,

and that if it had been in her power to come to Paris earlier to be with him, she would have done so. Did Jack forgive his aunt's neglect?

Jack suffered Deb's tears and hugs with good grace, for he had genuinely missed her very much, but was embarrassed by such overtly female carryings-on in front of his best friend. But Lord Henri-Antoine did not seem to care. After being introduced to Deb as his brother's wife, he bowed politely, showed mild interest in the fact this tall female was also Jack's aunt, and then promptly returned to the problem uppermost in his mind.

"Bailey says I'm to have an afternoon nap," Lord Henri-Antoine grumbled, tucking his hand in that of his ancient parent. "I don't want to, Papa. He had the impertinence to tell me he will bar me from attending my own brother's marriage ball tonight if I don't. It's most unfair!"

"But nonetheless a necessary evil," the Duke answered and brought the whippets to heel with a snap of his long fingers. He kissed his son's thin hand. "If you want to stay awake for the ball, you will take Bailey's advice and have a nap. Versailles made you overly tired."

"I think it's the most tremendous news you and Alston are married!" Jack was saying eagerly to Deb. "He lets me call him Alston, Aunt Deb. He says that it's only proper I should, now that he's my uncle. Alston says I'm to live with you both and that Harry can stay with us whenever he wishes. Can he, Aunt Deb?"

He looked at the Duke and Duchess as if for confirmation and felt heartened when the Duchess smiled. It made him add in a rush, forgetting his French, because his aunt looked as if she was about to burst into tears again,

"Harry and I had the most uncommon fun at Versailles! There's a great hall of mirrors, and *everything* is covered in gold! There are fountains that spring up everywhere along *l'Majesty's* walk, and we saw the King! He's *always* surrounded by hundreds of gentlemen in truly outrageous skirts and very tall-heeled shoes! And he has a great hooked nose just like on the coins and—"

"Oh Jack, I am very pleased King Louis did not disappoint you! And I cannot tell you how happy it makes me to see you so well and enjoying yourself. But perhaps it would be best to tell me the rest after nuncheon?" Deb said with a watery smile, aware that Lord Henri-Antoine was very pale and had slumped against the Duke's arm. "You must be hungry after your visit to Versailles?"

"But Harry and I aren't the least bit hungry. Alston's set up a row of archery boards on the courtyard lawn. There's to be a tournament for us and our friends this afternoon before the ball. Did he tell you about it? Did he show you the marquees? There are to be circus performers, and Alston's promised us a bear! Also ribbons and cake and—" Jack stopped at his aunt's knowing look and, suitably chastened, shut his mouth. With a bow, he apologized to the Duke and Duchess, then said with a smile, "Come on, Harry. We'd best eat something. If we don't, Bailey will—"

Lord Henri-Antoine scowled. "A curse on Bailey! What does he have to say to anything?"

The Duchess looked up from the dogs, at Jack and then at her son, who was paler than usual, his skin almost gray in hue and his eyes dull and sunken. He was completely worn out.

"He has a great deal of say, if it is your health which is of concern, *mon chou*," the Duchess said quietly. When Lord Henri-Antoine shot Jack an angry look she added gently, "Jack you must not blame. He is only concerned like us all for your well-being."

"But, Maman," Lord Henri-Antoine sulked. "Bailey would have me *forever* indoors if he had his way! You can't imagine what it's like to be *always* resting and being *forced* to eat pap when I don't want to in the least! It's insulting to be saddled with a jailer physician who won't even let me *pee* in private!"

At this final outburst the Duchess couldn't help an indulgent giggle, but the Duke raised his white brows in displeasure, which was enough to make Lord Henri-Antoine drop his head in penance.

"Forgive me, Papa, but it makes me madder than anything."

"Yes, it must," the Duke sympathized.

"Alston! Tell Papa what a Job's comforter Bailey was at Versailles," Lord Henri-Antoine pleaded with his brother. "Tell Papa how Bailey followed me *everywhere* like a beggar! It was most embarrassing."

He went up to his elder brother, who had just wandered into the room, and slipped his hand in his.

"You'll keep an eye on me this afternoon, won't you?" he asked earnestly, looking up at the Marquis. "I need not have a nap, or I might miss the start of the tournament. I don't *want* Bailey behind me. Not this afternoon and tonight, with Henriette and Paul and Rene here. *Please*, Alston, *tell* Papa!"

The Marquis was dressed in a simple linen frockcoat, tight buff breeches, white shirt with a plain linen stock and polished jockey boots. His black hair was freshly washed and simply dressed, and he was clean-shaven. He was as far removed from the pomaded and powdered courtier as was possible, and looked so much like her handsome wounded duelist Julian Hesham that the breath caught in Deb's throat and her heart gave the oddest flutter.

Julian pulled Lord Henri-Antoine into an affectionate embrace, an arm about his brother's thin shoulders, and came up to his parents. He acknowledged Deb with a slight bow, but that was the extent of his attention. After kissing his mother's hand and nodding to his father, he ruffled Jack's hair, before saying,

"Come, Harry, you can't expect me to spend my afternoon in Bailey's shoes, following you about like a beggar." He winked at Jack. "I have better things to do with my time than watch over a couple of scapegrace boys—"

"But, Alston," Lord Henri-Antoine whined, "You promised..."

"He's roasting you, Harry!" Jack said with a grin. "Of course Alston will keep an eye on us. The tournament was his idea after all. And if you want, I'll pick up all your spent arrows so you need not get tired."

Lord Henri-Antoine rolled his eyes, leaning against his brother's tall frame.

"Don't be an ass, Jack," he drawled in very much the manner of his father. "We keep dozens of lackeys to do such menial tasks—"

"Thank you, Jack, for your kind offer," interrupted the Duchess with a smile, a reproachful glance at her younger son as she slipped her arm over the Duke's velvet sleeve. "With a house full of guests and tonight the ball, I am sure not one servant can I spare to run after my son's whims. Is that not so, *mon chou*?"

"Yes, maman," Lord Henri-Antoine agreed reluctantly.

When the Marquis gave him a friendly nudge he apologized to Jack, who good-naturedly said there was nothing in it, and the two boys fell in behind the Duke and Duchess as they went into nuncheon.

Deb turned to follow the little procession, watching the Duke who, she noticed for the first time, leaned on a Malacca stick whenever he was upright, and who now used his wife's arm for support as they left the library.

"The walking stick is a recent addition," Julian commented, coming up to her, also watching his father. He offered her the crook of his arm. "Only eight months ago he was astride his horse every morning. Now... His breathing becomes labored taking the main stairs."

"His Grace seems little altered since that night nine years ago," Deb mused, walking with Julian through to the dining room. She looked up at him pensively. "Is he very ill?"

"Yes."

"I am truly sorry. The Duchess your mother is—is—"

"—much younger than he," Julian interrupted, finishing the sentence for her. "Therein lies the greater tragedy." And added in a whisper at her ear, before stepping back to allow Deb to be introduced to family and friends, who were all gathered in the anteroom, "Today is his birthday. Your news is by far the most precious gift..."

TWENTY-SEVEN

C RYSTAL, SILVER, and gold all winked in the blaze of light from two chandeliers suspended over the long mahogany dining table. Deb was sure that there was enough silver cutlery laid out at each place to confuse even the most fastidious of diners. Elaborate arrangements of fruits of the season were displayed in worked bowls of finest porcelain, and crystal vases were filled to overflowing with large heavily-scented roses. A roaring fire in the marble grate of the fireplace, over which hung a portrait of the Duchess by the fashionable painter Fragonard, kept the company warm, as did the many and varied courses laid on the table by the army of soft-footed and attentive liveried footmen under the direction of the po-faced butler.

Only immediate family were in attendance. Sir Gerald had excused himself with a head cold. But everyone knew his French was so poor he could not sit through a dinner without his wife as interpreter, and Lady Mary was visiting friends at a nearby hôtel. Julian's godfather arrived a few minutes late, and in time to hear Lord Vallentine declare loudly that he had yet to meet a musician whose delicate sensibilities permitted more than the ingestion of a thin broth. He conveniently ignored his son

Evelyn's plate, which was piled with capon, a wedge of pigeon pie and enough vegetables to fill a small garden plot. But the Duchess did not ignore this fact and she defended her nephew at the expense of his parent—their usual playful banter easing the formality of sitting through a nuncheon with an illustrious host who rarely joined in the conversation. And when he did, it was to make an acute observation designed to turn the topic to one he considered more worthy of discussion, and which usually left family and friends alike floundering until the Duchess steered the conversation in the right direction.

The laughter had barely died away from one of the Duchess's sallies at Lord Vallentine's expense when his wife, a fascinating gray-haired lady, blue eyes very large and resembling her elder brother the Duke, was heard to complain loudly about the rigid formalities observed at the Court at Versailles.

"It is quite unbelievable to me," Estée Vallentine said with a sniff of annoyance, "why an old lady is made to stand for hours and hours in the presence of the King until her bones seize up, and yet dearest Antonia is permitted to sit on her tabouret. I tell you, I do not see the fairness in it."

"Fairness has nothin' to do with it," Lord Vallentine stuck in, gnawing on the bone of a fowl soaked in garlic. "You ain't a duchess, and only duchesses get to sit in the presence of Louis. I told you how it would be, but you insisted we go. Never more bored of a place in all my days!"

"You did not enjoy the spectacle of the Court then, my lord?" Martin Ellicott inquired politely.

"Spectacle?" Lord Vallentine snorted. "A gentleman'd need glass bottle spectacles to get a glimpse of His French Majesty! Forced to stand around kickin' m'heels for most of the day watching His French Majesty surrounded by an entourage of perfumed fools, is not my idea of entertainment, I can tell you, Ellicott."

"We did not ask you to come with us," the Duchess said loftily. "It was you who would not be left behind by

Monseigneur. What was it you said...? Ah, yes! *To rattle around alone in this haunted mausoleum.*"

Lord Vallentine grinned and looked about at the other diners for confirmation of his own cleverness. "Did I say that? Well, I'll own to it!"

The Duchess opened her green eyes very wide. "But, Lucian, I do not like at all for you to call our home such a thing, especially when it was the childhood home of Monseigneur and of your wife, too. If this hôtel *is* haunted by ghosts, I should think they are of the living-dead variety only."

There was a hint of a smile about her lovely mouth as she exchanged a glance with the Duke and Martin Ellicott, the Marquis's godfather hiding his mirth behind his napkin.

Estée Vallentine glared across the table through the roses at her husband. "Lucian! Me you owe an apology!"

"Eh? An apology?" blustered Lord Vallentine. "But I didn't mean anythin' by it. She's teasin' again, you can see that, can't you? And I'll tell you all somethin' for naught: This place *is* full of ghosts." He shot the Duchess a dark look, caught her smile, and blinked. "Eh? Now, now, *Mme la Duchesse*, who are you callin' the livin'-dead?"

Deb laughed along with the rest of the family, very much at ease for the first time in a long while. She took an instant liking to Evelyn's father, Lord Vallentine. He reminded her of a stick insect with his long, loose-limbed frame and square-cut jaw. His saffron yellow silk frock coat she presumed to be all the rage amongst the dandy set of the aging nobility. And the Duchess she liked very much. Her youth and beauty were truly startling. Watching her now, as she held court at the dining table, Deb was surprised and delighted to discover that her beauty was matched in kind by a loving personality. There was an aura about her tiny person, of vitality and joy, and an eternal optimism, and it infected all those about her. Deb had never met a couple so dissimilar. The Duke certainly lived up to his reputation of being a phlegmatic and arrogant nobleman. Yet when he spoke with the Duchess or either of his sons he became a wholly different being.

It was obvious the Duke and Duchess were devoted to one another, and whatever the Duke's previous life as an unconscionable rake, Deb was certain he had mended his wicked ways upon marriage. She wondered how such cruel lies about the Roxtons' private life had continued to circulate, and was of the opinion that the Duke's reputation as a debauchee must have been very bad indeed. But she could not now imagine him being anything but a kind and loving husband and father, and thinking back on the baseless remarks she had hurled at her husband about his parents, she felt shame and wretchedness.

Suddenly the delicious food on her plate became unpalatable and she lost the thread of the chatter going on about her. But in her abstraction of self-castigation, she became aware of another, quite separate, conversation between devoted retainer and master. Martin Ellicott and the Duke chose to converse in English at a table overflowing with French repartee. It was the first time Deb had heard the Duke speak his country's native tongue, and if his tone in French was haughty, in English he sounded positively chilly.

"May I inquire if you gained your objective with his French Majesty, Your Grace?" asked Martin Ellicott.

The Duke looked away from the Duchess.

"The private audience went well. Louis, like I, is most concerned Antonia should not suffer any undue—er—*distress.*"

"Then one can presume the trial...?" Martin began, letting the sentence hang because he found the topic of his godson's upcoming trial a difficult one to broach with his father.

The Duke spooned oysters onto his plate from a silver dish lying on a bed of ice and held by a blank-faced footman wearing white gloves.

"It is most lamentable, but I fear not only has the trial judge fallen victim to an undisclosed—er—*contagion,* which has delayed proceedings now for some months, but the entire fraternity of judges has succumbed to the same illness. An early recess was called—cases are postponed for several more months." He speared an oyster with a small silver fork. "The precise nature of the illness remains a mystery…"

Martin Ellicott grinned and waved away the gloved footman. "I'm sure it will, Your Grace." He sipped his wine thoughtfully, a sidelong glance down the crowded table at the Marquis, who was heaping garlic-drenched quail onto Jack Cavendish's plate. "Yet, I believe your son was looking forward to his day in court. He will be disappointed."

"Yes," came the flat reply.

"After all, he is blessed with that rare quality amongst his kind—a strong moral code, if you will."

"Yes. He is his mother's son."

Martin patted his mouth with a corner of a linen napkin to hide a knowing smile. "Yes, Your Grace, he is. That must please you?"

The Duke put up his white brows in mock hauteur. "Are you daring to suggest I would not want my son and heir to follow in my—er—*rakish* footsteps?"

"Pardon, Your Grace, but even if you did desire it, which I know you do not, he could not do so. It is not in his nature."

"Ah, my declining prestige…" The Duke finished his oysters, pushing aside the plate to take up his wine glass. "Defending his honor in a French court of law against an upstart merchant prince and his cunning daughter serves no worthwhile purpose," he said acidly. "If my son has a taste for speeches let him satisfy it in the Lords where his—er—*values* can be put to good purpose. He'll be Duke soon enough." He signaled to his butler to refill the Duchess's wine glass and raised his own to her with a smile. "Yet, my dear Martin, this infirm old satyr is determined, God willing, to remain for as long as possible upon this earth—for her sake, you understand."

"Yes, Your Grace, I understand perhaps better than any other."

Deb followed the Duke's gaze down the length of the table to the Duchess and was witness to the look and the private smile they exchanged. For one moment it was as if the ducal couple were dining alone together at the long table and not amongst their chattering, happy family. The Duchess returned the Duke's toast with one of her own, and with the spell broken, the couple's attention came back to the dinner table. It was then that Deb sensed that she, too, was under scrutiny.

She looked across the cluttered surface of the mahogany table between two bowls overflowing with white roses and found Julian's gaze upon her. It was obvious he had been regarding her for some time, also with an ear to the conversation between his father and godfather, for he quickly looked away, pretending to adjust the silver knife and fork on his empty plate. Yet not before Deb glimpsed the abject sorrow reflected in his lovely eyes.

It was too much for her and she shot to her feet, none of the silent, liveried footmen lining one wall able to catch her chair in time before the ornately carved back clattered to the parquetry floor.

Instantly, Julian was on his feet. The rest of the gentlemen, with a lady out of her chair, politely rose, but at a more leisurely pace. The Duke, however, remained seated, regarding his son and daughter-in-law over the rim of his glass, and with an expression that remained unfathomable.

All conversation and laughter came to a halt.

"I—The heat—This gown—I-I should rest before the ball," Deb heard herself babble in the deafening silence. She dropped a curtsy, first to the Duchess and then to the Duke. "Please. Excuse me..."

Without waiting to be excused, she scurried from the room with a shaking hand to her mouth.

Evelyn threw down his napkin to follow her but two sharp words from his cousin and he remained where he was.

Julian cast a smoldering eye over the table as the gentlemen sank back slowly onto their chairs, Evelyn included.

"Deborah has had enough of this family's good intentions for one morning. Harry? Jack? If you've finished eating, we will inspect those archery boards before the guests arrive."

And with a bow to his parents, Julian left the room with the two boys in tow.

"What's that?" Lord Vallentine was heard to comment loudly. "*With child*? Alston's bride? Well, stamp me! The chit's only been here five minutes!"

TWENTY-EIGHT

Lady Mary found Deb seated at a cluttered boudoir table, a cotton dressing gown thrown over her flimsy chemise and frothy under-petticoats. She was staring, not at her reflection, but out the window, chin cupped in her hand, her mass of dark red hair tumbling freely down her back.

Draped over a spindle-legged chair by the ornate Oriental dressing screen was Deb's ball gown of heavy silk, embroidered with gold thread and pearls, and a matching pair of silk-covered shoes with diamond buckles. Deb's maid Brigitte, who held a silver-backed hairbrush, lifted her shoulders at Lady Mary's look of inquiry, as if to say she had done all she could to hurry her mistress along to finish her toilette in time for the ball. She then curtsied and stepped away to allow Lady Mary to draw up a chair. Such was Deb's distraction with the view that it was only when she rose half off the padded stool to take a better look at what was going on beneath her window, and then turned to comment to Brigitte that she saw her sister-in-law.

"Mary? What a pleasant surprise. But how formal you look with your hair so tall and powdered and feathered and—Is that truly a sailing ship atop a small straw hat?"

"It's all the rage. Do you truly like it?" Lady Mary asked anxiously, a tentative hand to her steepled coiffure. She failed to notice the quick look which passed between Deb and Brigitte, Deb biting her lower lip to stop a smile. "I told my hairdresser, Bernard, I did not want my hair so outrageously tall I would suffer a crick in the neck before the first dance—which is what happened to the little Countess Lowenbrue, and she had to sit out an entire ball with a bag of ice at her shoulder!"

"Is that so?" commented Deb, returning to stare out the window. "I am in two minds: Wear my hair down my back in the manner of a medieval princess, or let Brigitte work her magic. If I had my way, I would simply braid it and be done, but Brigitte says I must wear it up and so I shall. Oh, well done, Jack!" she announced, and this time did get to her stockinged feet. "Come look, Mary. Jack and Harry are having the most wonderful time with their archery bows."

Lady Mary came to the window with its view of the courtyard.

Gaily-colored tents festooned with ribbons and flags were erected at the far end of the rolling green lawn, and under their shade lounged the crème de la crème of Parisian aristocracy, their every whim attended to by an army of liveried servants, who came and went with heavy silver trays laden with food and drink. At some distance from these marquees a row of large bullseyes had been nailed to the chestnut trees lining the cobble-stone walk, and it was at these bullseyes Deb drew Mary's attention. Nurses and tutors watched over a cluster of children, dressed in rich fabrics and diamond-buckled shoes that mimicked those worn by their fashionable parents. Each possessed a bow and a quiver full of arrows. They stood a desig-nated distance from the bullseyes, ranked according to age, and fired off their colored arrows at the targets. When their supply of arrows was exhausted, liveried servants ran about gathering up the spent arrows and returning them to the quivers of their rightful owners.

Lord Henri-Antoine and Jack stood shoulder-to-shoulder amongst this excited group of laughing, happy children, and fired off their arrows in turn. Standing off to one side were the Marquis of Alston and Martin Ellicott, who looked to be keeping score with quill and blotter. Both were offering collective encouragement to the children in their efforts to strike the bullseyes. As Deb and Mary continued to watch, the Duchess came up to her son in a whirl of silk embroidered petticoats and stood between them, holding Martin Ellicott's arm, and barely reaching her eldest son's shoulder. When her younger son waved, she blew him a kiss. At that, Lady Mary turned away from the window with a frown and sat heavily with her back to the view.

"I've never understood why that old servant is treated better than any relative!" Mary commented with annoyance. "Sir Gerald says it's because Ellicott knows too many of the Duke's secrets and so can't be easily fobbed off. And if he weren't as ancient as his master, we would all be left to wonder at the true nature of his relationship with Cousin Duchess."

Deb swiveled about on the padded stool, mouth agape.

"Mary! How appalling to hear you, of all people, repeat such horrid and quite malicious gossip, particularly about a woman who, I suspect, hasn't a malicious bone in her body."

"When you've been a member of this family for as long as I have you—"

"While I am a member of this family, I never want to hear any of the untruths spread about the Duke and Duchess and Martin Ellicott or, for that matter, my husband."

"So you intend to remain Marchioness of Alston?" Lady Mary asked archly.

Deb glanced at her own reflection. "I... The baby—"

"The baby will at least be a consolation."

"How's that, Mary?"

"You'll have something to love and someone who loves you. All the ugliness of your marriage will disappear, and if you are truly blessed, you'll have a son and then, well..." Mary looked down at her white hands. "You won't have to submit to any further-further—*unpleasantness*."

"Unpleasantness?" Deb gave an involuntary laugh. "Mary, you goose! This baby wasn't conceived in unpleasantness. Far from it. That first night... It was the beginning of quite the most wonderful experience of my life," she said wistfully and inexplicably burst into tears. "Damn! What is wrong with me these days?"

Lady Mary offered Deb her handkerchief. "Females in your delicate condition often cry for any reason. I did, and at the oddest of moments."

"Well I can't bear it! First I'm bedridden with nausea and now I'm a weeping pot. How Medlow can tell me pregnancy is a perfectly normal condition... And how you can honestly sit there and say a child can make up for a loveless marriage is beyond me." She patted her eyes dry and disappeared behind the ornate dressing screen, calling for Brigitte, then saying through gritted teeth, the wet handkerchief twisted in her hands, "How dare he do this to me so soon!"

"Don't you want this child?"

"Want it?" Deb said with bewilderment, as if the question had never occurred to her. "Of course I want this baby," she called out. "I wanted a brood. But now... Brigitte? Good. Let's see if I can fit into that wretchedly heavy gown. And then perhaps I will have a stroll in the garden, for I need some fresh air before I enter a ballroom full of strangers."

"I know you've only just arrived, and I'd hoped to spend some time with you," Lady Mary called out, watching the maid come and go from behind the screen, first with the heavy silk gown and then returning for the shoes, "but Sir Gerald and I are leaving for England tomorrow morning. Sir Gerald says I've been away from Theodora long enough, which I quite agree, and there are pressing estate matters which require Sir Gerald's immediate attention." She stood close on the other side of the screen. "And what with the baby, you will have enough to do without worrying about an eight-year-old boy. Sir Gerald insists Jack return to England with us—"

"No!"

"Sir Gerald said you'd take the news badly, but you must be reasonable, dearest," Lady Mary continued patiently and in a voice that was beginning to grate on Deb's nerves. "Jack can't impose on the Duke and Duchess forever."

Deb came out from behind the screen and stood before the full-length looking glass, side-on at first to see if her expanding waistline was at all noticeable under so many layers of petticoats and a heavy silk over gown, and then face-on to inspect the sit of the bodice and in the reflection she caught her sister-in-law's frown of disapproval. Sitting before the looking glass so Brigitte could dress her hair, she said flatly,

"Jack belongs with me,"

"You're in no condition to look after him, dearest," Mary argued. "Indeed, in your present condition, I'm very sure you'll be expected to spend your days resting quietly—"

"Really, Mary, you make out I'm an invalid! I assure you I am healthier now than I've ever been. It's just that I find myself unexpectedly bursting into tears.

"—because you are carrying Alston's heir, after all," Lady Mary continued in that same patronizing tone, "So you can't afford to do anything silly that might jeopardize the baby, such as running after a particularly boisterous boy who gets himself into all sorts of scrapes. Did you know that not only does he take viola lessons from Cousin Evelyn—which is against Sir Gerald's express wishes—but that these lessons are conducted amongst Evelyn's pack of drunkard, good-for-nothing musician friends? Sad company for a boy. And after one considers what a horrid mess Otto made of his life, consorting with such musical riffraff, is it any wonder Sir Gerald is concerned that Jack may go the way of his father?"

"For pity's sake, Mary, Jack is only a boy!"

"Be that as it may, Sir Gerald feels Jack is imposing himself on Cousin Alston, and has become a nuisance—pestering Alston with all sorts of nonsensical requests, not to mention leading Henri-Antoine astray with games of hide-and-go-seek, and late night mischief. Sir Gerald is of the opinion that Jack's boisterousness will cause Henri-Antoine's next fit of falling sickness."

"Does he indeed, Mary?" Deb replied in a deceptively mild voice. Her large brown eyes narrowed. "Then pray tell me why Julian gives so much of his time to those boys, if Jack is being such a nuisance? Why do Jack and Harry seek him out so readily, if not encouraged to do so?"

Absently, she handed Brigitte the last of the pearl-headed pins, her long hair now expertly upswept with tortoiseshell combs, pins, and interwoven with a number of silk ribands threaded with pearls.

"How does Gerry—how do *you*—account for Julian's involvement in the archery tournament below my window?" she continued, trying to rein in her impatience. "You think he was pestered into it against his will? For the best part of two hours he has been with those children, applauding their efforts, offering encouragement to the little ones, and most particularly to his brother and Jack—"

"Oh, that's only because he has his mother's mild temperament," Mary said dismissively. "Cousin Duchess sees the good in everyone. She is exceedingly patient and caring—qualities that aren't particularly praise-worthy in a duchess surrounded by fawning sycophants."

"Possessing a kind nature does not exclude a sense of discrimination, nor does it assume the person is simple-minded."

Lady Mary's violet eyes widened at Deb's acute observation.

"That may be true, Deborah," she conceded. "Yet the fact remains: Alston has also inherited a bucketful of his father's most unsavory traits. They far outweigh the noble characteristics gained from his mother. His outlandish behavior caused Cousin Duchess to go into an early labor and Henri-Antoine to be born with the falling sickness—no coincidence that. His early birth and Alston's banishment certainly ruined both their lives thereafter."

"And you would now be Marchioness of Alston save for Julian's one bout of youthful imprudence?" Deb inquired, taking a leap of faith with her intuition, and not surprised when her sister-in-law blanched. "Poor Mary," she added with genuine sympathy. "Your heart was broken all those years ago by a fifteen-year-old boy. You thought yourself very much in love with Julian when you were fourteen, didn't you? Not that he had any idea as to your feelings. How could he at his age? That's why you, the daughter of an earl, rejected all suitors season after season, in the hopes that when Julian returned from his travels he would finally offer for you. I suppose his marriage to another was easier to accept if you convinced yourself his character was beyond saving. Was it when you discovered Julian was already married that you accepted Gerry's offer? Yet like the rest of your suitors, he will never measure up to Cousin Alston, will he, Mary?"

Lady Mary opened her mouth to refute Deb's assertions, face bright pink with embarrassment. She was saved from replying by a soft rap on the paneling, grateful for the interruption, even if the pleasant drawling voice at her back subjected her to playful ridicule.

"What a fetching coiffure, Mary. It reminds me of a church steeple. But I'm not entirely convinced about the boat motif. Perhaps a church steeple after a receding flood...?"

It was the Marquis, and Deb practically jumped off the stool, sending the last curl to be pinned up under Brigitte's deft fingers tumbling forward over her bare shoulder.

"You enjoy sneaking up on me, don't you?" Deb said with asperity to his looking glass reflection.

Julian grinned. "Naturally. Men are merely large boys after

all." He made her a bow and retreated to stand by the ornate dressing screen.

"I was just telling Deb that Sir Gerald and I are returning to England in the morning," Lady Mary announced in a clipped voice, smoothing a hand over her shell-pink damask petticoats. "Jack is to accompany us."

Julian glanced at Deb with a raised eyebrow before looking directly at Lady Mary. He sat with a deliberate slowness on the lattice-backed chair by the dressing screen, flicking out the stiff skirts of his black velvet frock coat with gold lacings, and crossing his long stockinged legs at the ankles so as not to overly crease a pair of thigh-tight silk breeches. His black hair was dressed but unpowdered, and his only jewelry was the familiar heavy gold signet ring on the pinkie of his left hand. He took out his gold snuffbox and tapped the lid.

"You have been singularly misinformed, Madam. Jack remains here with Lady Alston. It is for her ladyship to decide when her nephew will return to England. But I certainly won't release him into the care of your husband—ever."

Lady Mary noted the Marquis's use of his wife's title and she knew when to submit to an implacable higher authority. She curtsied.

"Naturally I will inform Sir Gerald of your lordship's wishes."

The Marquis swept a lace-ruffled wrist carelessly into the air. "Inform whomever you like, Mary," adding with a wink at Deb, "but Gerry certainly knows my wishes. As you said, you are returning to England tomorrow..."

Lady Mary gaped at him, but as the Marquis continued to regard her with an air of insolent amusement, she shut her mouth tight. She shot a suspicious look at Deb. But she was hiding her grin behind an unfurled fan of carved ivory, quickly snatched up from amongst the clutter in front of her. With a mutinous expression, Mary grabbed up a handful of her silk petticoats, and with a swish, stomped out of the bedchamber—the little sailing ship atop her towering headdress bobbing from side to side as if caught in gale force winds.

TWENTY-NINE

"I THOUGHT you would like to take a walk in the courtyard gardens before we get caught up in all the nonsense of this wretched ball," Julian suggested in that conversational tone he had used the day he'd walked into Deb's Milsom Street sitting room in Bath.

"Yes, I'd like that," Deb replied with a shy smile, adding in a tone she hoped sounded offhand, "Will it be nonsense?"

Julian remained silent at the window, an eye to the activity down on the velvet-green lawns. In front of the marquees, the children were all sitting in a row, adults standing behind their chairs, all rapt attention as a troupe of circus performers in brightly-colored outfits, funny hats and exaggerated shoes went through their routines. One juggler in particular was causing gasps and giggles as he tossed three colored balls high in the air while he swallowed fire from a lighted baton.

Finally, the Marquis tore his gaze from the view, and looked over his shoulder at Deb's reflection in the looking glass and held her gaze.

"Not if you are there beside me..."

THE AFTERNOON sun was still bright and warm, but the air was crisp, and a light breeze stirred the tops of the avenue of chestnut trees. The couple strolled down one length of the cobblestone walk, neither saying a word, Deb with her hand comfortably in the crook of her husband's velvet sleeve.

Where the avenue ended and the sweep of lawn began, a game of bowls was in progress, watched on by several spectators. lounging on chairs drinking champagne, and hovered over by attentive footmen. The Marquis stopped a little way off from this group so as not to disturb the game, but close enough to hear the banter between the players. He grinned. Deb understood why, for the repartee between Lord Vallentine and the Duchess of Roxton was constant and unflagging, and very entertaining.

"Me? I do not believe it!" stated the Duchess. "Lucian, you do not have the *eyes* to see the ball, so how is it you *think* you can hit it?"

"Now you listen to me, *Mme la Duchesse*. I ain't finished with you yet. I know gamesmanship when I hear it," grumbled Lord Vallentine, standing at the end of the bowling green with knees bent, ball in hand, sizing up his shot with a practice swing before making his drive. "Be on the ready to lose ten pounds! There! What a shot! See, Estée? What did I tell you, aye?"

From her chair beside Martin Ellicott, Estée Vallentine sighed her exasperation. "You will never win against Antonia, Lucian."

Vallentine straightened his thin frame, and with a dark look at his wife, stomped off down the green. "Loyalty! Ha!"

Antonia went after him, passed him, and blew him a kiss as she skipped on ahead, the many layers of her embroidered silk petticoats swishing about her. At the end of the green, where Lord Vallentine's bowling ball had come to rest, she clapped her hands and called to his lordship to see for himself her triumph.

After many minutes sizing up the state of play, his lordship finally conceded defeat, and with a flourish, bowed to the Duchess before turning on a heel and stomping back up to where his wife sat.

"Estée!? I need ten pounds," grumbled Lord Vallentine, and fell into the chair on her other side. He accepted a tumbler of wine from a footman and pointed it at the Duchess as she came to join them. "I still say if it hadn't been for a dip in the grass, I'd have beaten you, minx!"

The Duchess, who had spied Julian and Deb standing a little way off on the cobblestone walk, waved and smiled at them before turning on Lord Vallentine with a twinkle in her green eyes.

"No, Lucian," she told him bluntly, "that is a great piece of nonsense. Martin! Tell him: He Lucian is a very bad bowler and me I am a very good bowler."

"You are indeed a very good bowler, *Mme la Duchesse*," Martin Ellicott agreed demurely, and received such a thunderous look from Lord Vallentine, who had sprung half out of his chair, that he was forced to put up his shoulders in a gesture of total capitulation.

"You will support me, won't you, Estée?" Vallentine growled at his wife.

"But it would be a lie, Lucian," his wife answered matter-of-factly. "I do not know why it is you never listen to me. Antonia has always been, and will always be, by far the better bowler."

"Then why did you allow me to waste ten pounds if you knew I couldn't win, damme?" he complained. "I could've saved m'self a pain in the back and just handed over the ten, blast it!"

"Yes, you could," agreed his wife.

This sent the whole company sitting about the bowling green into whoops of laughter. Even Julian and Deb could not help having a laugh at Uncle Lucian's expense, and quickly turned away to hide their smiles lest his lordship turn a hostile eye in their direction, realizing his loss had provided entertainment for an extended audience.

Julian led Deb away from the lawn, and away from the striped marquees beyond the bowling green that were now overflowing with guests, with the smaller children being scooped up by their nurses to be taken home.

From this activity Julian realized there was little time left to him before he and Deb would be called to join the guests for supper indoors, and the formalities of a long evening would begin. But he wanted Deb to himself a little longer, and so, just as they passed a group of gardeners busy tilling flowerbeds and Deb turned to admire one of the many Greek and Roman statues dotting the walk, Julian pulled her sideways into a shady grotto of tall trees.

"Deb! I'm not a monster," he burst out, letting go of her arm. "You have every right to think me a-a bestial *fiend* given the lurid gossip about my past. And when I think of what I said to you in Martin's bookroom..." He dropped his hand heavily to his side and let out a breath. "God, I've made such a damned muddle of this speech already and I've barely begun!"

Deb blinked at him as he paced in front of her, the light-heartedness that lingered after watching the antics of the bowlers evaporating. Yet she remained remarkably calm despite the quickening thud of her heart as she sank onto a low marble bench and placed her closed fan in the lap of her billowing petticoats.

"If you're referring to that incident which occurred when you were fifteen years old, I know a little of that sad story..."

"Sad story? Ha! My actions were reprehensible. So much so that it is still gossiped about in drawing rooms to this day. Let me recount it for you, then you tell me if a judge will agree with you, that I was mad on the night we were wed."

Deb gave a start, opened her mouth to tell him it was unnecessary for him to recount such painful details, but then just as quickly realized she very much wanted to hear what he had to say, so she pressed her lips together and waited.

"I burst into my parents' Hanover Square residence demanding to see my mother," he said matter-of-factly. "My father was still at White's. Several of their friends had arrived for a dinner party. I'd come down from Oxford with Robert and Evelyn for term break. Yes, Robert Thesiger. He, Evelyn and I drank all the way to London. It was on the journey that Robert asked me how I felt about sharing my mother with another brat. I had no idea what he meant. Evelyn did. I could see it written all over his face. Robert had already confided in him to the last salacious drop, by the look on his face.

"So Robert told me. He gave a Covent Garden performance. At first I refused to believe it—that my mother was pregnant with her lover's child. And that my father, for the sake of the family name and because his arrogance would not allow for any other outcome, let the world believe he was its sire. But Robert and Evelyn convinced me to open my eyes. A beautiful young duchess, sweet-natured and full of life, married to a white-haired old noble who showed as much emotion as an iceberg. Why wouldn't such a vital creature look elsewhere for love and affection? It made perfect sense. I swallowed the bait whole, as it were."

"Oh, Julian, how could you? Five minutes in your parents' company is enough to convince a blind man they are so very much in love!"

"Well, I wasn't blind, I was a fifteen-year-old prig eaten up with my own self-consequence! I did not try to understand my parents' marriage. At that age, a boy wishes his parents to conform to the society to which they belong so he is acceptable to his friends. At Eton I was taunted mercilessly because my parents have an unconventional marriage by any standards. Theirs wasn't an arranged marriage, a bloodless union for the transfer of property and wealth. My parents thumbed their noses at convention and eloped."

Deb looked abashed, remembering the hurtful and totally unsubstantiated remarks about the Duke and Duchess she had hurled at her husband.

"I admit to being astonished by your parents. I do not know of another exalted couple that have married for anything but dynastic self-preservation, certainly none who married for love. The last Cavendish to do so was Otto, and he was banished from the family. My parents, Gerry, indeed most people I know, have had their marriages arranged for them. But I have interrupted you..."

Julian stopped his pacing and stood before her, clenching and unclenching his hands. He took a few moments before he spoke, cleared his dry throat and swallowed and looked at anywhere first but at her, before he found the courage to meet her steady gaze, color deepening in his cheeks—indication enough that he still found it difficult to speak of that night without emotion getting the better of him.

"My mother was in her boudoir. The physician was with her. The scene that presented itself to me in my drunken state was such that I... God, I didn't even see that they were not alone, that my mother's ladies-in-waiting were in attendance! After what Robert and Evelyn had told me, I let myself believe the physician was my mother's lover. I went into a rage. I overpowered the physician and dragged my mother, who was dressed only in her chemise and nightgown, out of the house and into the cold night..."

He sat on the bench beside Deb, elbows on his silken knees and stared at the hedgerow, as if seeing the events as he retold them.

"I remember there was a great deal of noise. People scurrying about with tapers. And there was shouting. There was lots of shouting. A gathering had formed at one end of the Square. They were held back from coming closer by our servants. The only person who wasn't shouting was my mother. She hardly made a sound. She was crying, but she never once shouted at me."

He turned his head into his shoulder and looked at Deb with a glaze of tears to his eyes.

"I called her a whore. I said she was a witch. I called her a *putain* and other foul names that I won't sully your ears with. You get the idea. I denounced her to the world as an adulteress. I proclaimed to the mob that the child she was carrying was not my father's but the ill-begotten progeny of a bastard whoreson. And then it all went very quiet. No shouting. No one talking. No one daring to move. There was only the sound of my mother whimpering in pain. She had gone into early labor. It was then that I saw the-the blood on her chemise and I came to my senses...

"And my father... He came home to a nightmare, a nightmare of my making. I may have been insensible with a rage fuelled by claret, but it was my father who was sent to the brink of madness. He punished me the only way he saw fit, and for that I do not blame him." He smiled sadly. "One brief moment of madness should not consign a man's entire life to Bedlam— should it?"

Deb took the hand he held out to her and rose up to be enveloped in his embrace. Instinctively, she rested her head against his chest and was comforted by the strong beat of his heart. Her voice was barely audible.

"No. No, it should not."

THEY STOOD IN the grotto, silent in each other's arms, listening to the sounds of celebration, and beyond the high brick walls that surrounded the Hôtel Roxton, the continuous rumble of carriage wheels and hooves on the cobbles of the Rue Saint-Honoré. And when Deb finally looked up at Julian, wondering how best to respond to his heartfelt confession, to assure him she understood, that she did not condemn him for his youthful folly, he bent and kissed her gently.

"Do you believe in fate?" he asked, smiling down into her upturned face. "I never did, despite my mother's belief she and my father were fated to be together from the very first day they met. But that day on Martin's terrace, when you splashed wine on your petticoats and I realized you were my fiddler from the forest, I knew our marriage was destined. *I knew*." He touched his nose to hers and looked into her eyes. "Since we parted on that most hideous of days, I've spent every day wishing you were at my side. I'm lonely without you. I need you to make me laugh, to make me forget my cares and responsibilities, to just be there for me—*Julian*."

Deb so wanted to believe him, and she wanted *Julian* to kiss her again more than anything, but the specter of Mademoiselle Lefebvre and the upcoming trial made her hesitate and doubt his sincerity. She thought of the lewd pamphlet she had seen in Evelyn's apartment, and he a stranger dressed as a French courtier just returned from Versailles. She reasoned there had to be a grain of truth to the scandal or why else would the Farmer-General insist on a very public trial? But even a grain of truth was one grain too many for her. She did not want to share her days, least of all her nights, with such a creature as the Marquis of Alston.

She pulled out of his arms and brushed down her petticoats with an agitated hand.

"And while Julian spends his days with his wife, forgetting his cares and responsibilities, with whom does the Marquis of Alston spend his nights?"

"What?"

He looked as if he had no idea to what she was alluding and had her almost convinced. Yet, his bewilderment was not enough.

"I forgive you your youthful folly," she said gently. "You were only a boy and misguided by others. I understand your parents have a marriage that is not in the common way, and I applaud them for that. But," she added flatly, "I cannot forgive the Marquis of Alston for deceiving me into his bed, just as I cannot forgive the Marquis of Alston for deceiving Mademoiselle Lefebvre in the same way!"

He balked and was incredulous.

"You dare to make such a comparison? You are my wife. She is nothing more than a harebrained demi-rep who will do anything to catch herself a titled husband."

"Which gave you permission to seduce her with impunity?"

Julian did not blink.

"I have maintained all along that I did not seduce her. I will say again: I did not seduce Mademoiselle Lefebvre. My word should be good enough for you to believe me—for *my wife* to believe me."

His arrogant self-assurance made her blurt out recklessly,

"You are vastly mistaken if you believe I am the sort of wife who will meekly sit in a big house by a lake, waiting for the occasional visit from her philandering husband so he can impregnate her. I will not be used as a-a—*vessel* to beget your children!"

"For pity's sake, Deb! Stop this self-torture at once!" he demanded. He sighed as if she were making a scene about a trifle of a thing. It was the handkerchief he held out to her that was the last straw. "Here. Take it. Dry your face. We are expected at the ball any moment. Take it!"

"I saw the pamphlet distributed by M'sieur Lefebvre. Have you? It boasts a cartoon of the Marquis of Alston with the biggest organ not housed in a church. Imagine!" she said on a note that was half hysterical laugh, half sob. "You and your French cronies must find such notoriety vastly entertaining, my lord."

Julian's face fired red and he scowled. "Don't be absurd, Deborah."

"Oh? Don't tell me you're *embarrassed*? Most men would be flattered."

"Now you are being unreasonable and hysterical."

She was being slightly hysterical but she could not help herself. She blamed her pregnancy for this newfound desire to self-castigate, and plunged deeper into recrimination.

"I dare say you must feel some sort of male pride knowing your wife derives just as much satisfaction from your body as any harlot of your acquaintance?"

Julian's jaw locked hard and he turned his head away, as if she had slapped his face. Deb interpreted this action as the mute obstinacy of a noble husband's right to keep his private life to himself. So be it. She had had enough of the Marquis of Alston. She picked up her petticoats and turned to depart, but he grabbed her elbow and spun her back to face him.

"If it's a confession you want, if nothing else will convince you, then you shall have a full and frank declaration of your husband's sordid past. But, by Jove, you will say not one word until I'm done!"

"Beggin' your lordship's pardon," Joseph interrupted with a loud cough into his hand and a bow. He came further into the grotto with a sheepish half-smile. "Wouldn't have interrupted you for the world but—Lord Henri-Antoine is missing."

"Missing?" Deb and Julian said in unison.

"No one's seen him since the circus folk left half an hour ago. Master Jack says his little lordship wanted to see a bear, and when the circus folk didn't bring one with them he went off in a bit of a huff to—"

"—to sulk? Yes, that sounds like Harry," Julian agreed, concern for his brother masking any embarrassment at the old retainer's interruption.

"The house and grounds are being searched," Joseph

continued, a sidelong glance at Deb. "The guests have all been ushered into supper none the wiser. Her Grace remains on the lawn, but says she can't do so for much longer without raising the Duke's suspicions. She sent me to find you."

With a quick nod to Deb, Julian disappeared through the trees.

THIRTY

A HANDFUL OF liveried servants were combing the avenues of chestnut trees when Deb and Joseph followed Julian out of the grotto. Jack was darting in and out amongst these servants, and when he saw Julian, his aunt and Joseph, he waved a hand high above his head and ran to them as fast as his long thin legs would carry him.

"Alston!" Jack called out as he finally ran up to them, out of breath and dry in the mouth. "You've got to come *now*! Harry *needs* you!"

"Thank God," murmured Deb, as her nephew fell into her arms. She cuddled him to her, saying with a smile, "That's good news, Jack. I knew Harry wouldn't be far away."

Julian squatted beside the boy, realizing he was crying into his aunt's petticoats. "Where is Harry, Jack?" he asked gently, and when the boy flung an arm out in the direction of the lawn added, "In one of the tents with his mother?"

"He's by the walled gate," said Jack with a sniff, turning his head out of his aunt's silk petticoats and dashing a sleeve across his eyes. "He'd followed the circus, wanting to know about the bear. I'm sorry I'm not being a man about it but he gave me a fright, y'see. He was on the ground. He'd had one of his attacks. But he's all right now, I think…"

"Shall we go and see how he is?" Julian suggested with a smile, though he felt anything but calm. He held his hand. "Don't worry about Harry. Bailey always knows what to do."

Jack looked up at his aunt and then at Joseph before moving out of Deb's embrace altogether to take the Marquis's hand and speak to him in a confidential tone.

"There's a gentleman… He came in the street gate just as Harry fell down. He said he'd keep an eye on him while I fetched Bailey. But I remembered what you said about strangers outside the gates, and so I wouldn't leave Harry until Bailey was fetched."

"What gentleman, Jack?" asked Deb.

The boy looked up at his aunt as if she should know the answer.

"The one who was always calling at our house in Bath and Saunders was always sending him away with some lame excuse. Well," he glanced at Joseph, "we thought it was lame, didn't we, Joe?"

When Deb looked none the wiser, the boy added, "You must remember him, Aunt Deb. He has a scar down his cheek—"

"*Parbleu. Non*," Julian muttered in French, and in two strides was off running up the avenue of chestnut trees towards the lawn.

He did not have to run far. At the entrance to the furthest marquee, the Duchess stood in silent vigil, a lady-in-waiting pacing at her back, while, striding across the cobbled courtyard from the direction of the tradesmen's entrance gate, and carrying Lord Henri-Antoine to his chest, was Robert Thesiger. At his side, Dr. Bailey and five liveried footmen tried to keep step. The Marquis was at his mother's side by the time Robert Thesiger entered the tent and placed the limp little figure on the divan.

The attack had passed and had not been as severe as the previous one some months before. That was Bailey's opinion as he felt the boy's pulse, and it received a collective sigh of relief from those surrounding the divan. The physician's diagnosis was borne out by the patient himself, who managed a weak smile when the Duchess sat on an edge of the divan and put a cool hand to her son's bloodless cheek.

"They promised me a bear," Lord Henri-Antoine complained weakly. He turned his head and blinked at Robert Thesiger. "He says there'll be a bear at the Tuileries tomorrow."

"I do not doubt it, *mon chou*. There are many wondrous sights throughout the capital to honor the Dauphin's marriage. But we cannot see them all," the Duchess said with a smile, and kissed Henri-Antoine's forehead, her heartbeat slowing knowing her young son was out of danger.

She stepped back to allow the physician to apply lavender drops to her son's temples.

"Now you must rest and I will thank this gentleman on your behalf for bringing you back to me, yes?" And in a move Julian found admirable, she turned and bravely looked up into the blue eyes of the son whose mother the Duke had discarded in order to marry her. "Thank you for restoring to me my son, M'sieur."

Robert Thesiger met her gaze, face devoid of emotion, and rudely turned his back and left the tent without comment and without according her the low formal bow her status demanded.

"You're damned impudent showing yourself here!" Julian snarled at his back.

Robert Thesiger looked up from brushing down the creased sleeves of his sapphire blue embroidered silk frock coat. Over the Marquis's shoulder, he saw Deborah coming across the lawn with her groom in tow.

"Show some proper gratitude. After all, I did restore the little pup to his bitch—Steady!" he added with a nervous laugh as he jumped away from the Marquis, who took a stride toward him, fists clenched. "You wouldn't dare bruise your own flesh in the house of our father, now would you, *Juju*?"

Julian mentally winced at the use of a long discarded nursery nickname saying in a perfectly controlled voice, "Can't bruise what is already rotten to the core—Steady!" he mimicked and grinned as he ducked a wild swing then caught Robert Thesiger's closed fist in his hand, and held it in a vise-like grip. "Mustn't be impolite in the house of our father, *Bob*."

Robert Thesiger tried to pull his hand free, but his inability to break Julian's iron grip melted his cool façade and he swore under his breath before saying through gritted teeth, "And if it is rotten, whose fault is that? Not my mother's, to be sure!"

The Marquis gave a bark of harsh laughter as he opened his hand and let go of Robert Thesiger with a contemptuous little push.

"Are you still using that pathetic twaddle to gain *entrée* to society's salons? For shame! Isn't it about time you freshened your calling card?"

Robert Thesiger seethed at his inability to match the Marquis in strength and agility, nursing bruised knuckles as he waited for Deb and Joseph to come within earshot.

"And what pathetic twaddle did you use on Mademoiselle Lefebvre? The same line of seduction the Duke used on my mother—the false promise of marriage?"

"Lord, no! That technique is as stale as last week's bread," Julian said with disdain. "Oh? Did *you* offer *her* that induce-ment? Dear me, I presumed you better practiced at the art of seduction than that."

"You sneer, but my pursuit of Mademoiselle Lefebvre was wholly honorable," Robert Thesiger replied stiffly, a glance at Deb who was now at her husband's elbow.

Julian was genuinely surprised. "She refused you? Why?"

"You know perfectly why!" Robert Thesiger said savagely.

"You dangled a dukedom on the end of your *telum* and she obliged you because she thought you meant marriage!"

"If she told you so then she is not only a whore but a liar."

"If Mademoiselle Lefebvre is either, it is your doing!"

Julian threw up a hand. "Robert, show some wit. Whether I was the girl's lover or not is quite inconsequential to the fact she rejected your suit. So if you're done, leave via the tradesmen's entrance from whence you came."

Robert Thesiger could hardly contain his anger and frustration at the Marquis's cavalier dismissal of his predicament, and it made him say recklessly, knowing he had an audience in the Marchioness, "This is not over! I will have my revenge, for the wrongs done my mother and for your cold-blooded seduction of the woman I hoped to marry! Even if it takes five, ten, twenty years—"

"Yes. Yes. I've heard all your melodramatic nonsense before," Julian said with a languid wave of one hand. But the light in his green eyes was hard. "Or perhaps you've forgotten how you came by that scar—that you would not now be alive if it weren't for your sordid claim to the dregs of my father's blood."

Robert Thesiger pretended offense. "Is it my fault I am your father's son?"

To everyone's surprise and bemusement, the Marquis gave a bark of unrestrained laughter as if told a good joke. "Now *that* is a winning performance and a much better calling card!" And almost in the same breath, the laughter died. "You are a thorn in my side, to be sure, Robert, but I shall live. Your bitter, petty attempts to disrupt my life are merely that, and are not worthy of my thought or time. But harm any member of my family, and I won't show you the same courtesy I did in Athens."

He then dismissed Robert Thesiger with a contemptuous wave as he turned his back to enter the tent to see how his brother was faring. That he had no idea he had an audience was evident by his startled expression when he came face-to-face with his wife. But she wasn't looking at him. She was staring at Robert Thesiger and Joseph had a hand on her upper arm, as if to restrain her.

"Beggin' your ladyship's pardon, but his lordship wouldn't want you to—"

"Damn you, I must know!" Deb hissed under her breath as she stepped past him and the Marquis to extend her hand to her husband's mortal enemy.

"Mr. Thesiger? Oh, how remiss of me! *Lord* Thesiger," she said with a smile, as if it were only yesterday they had parted in the Assembly Rooms in Bath, and was relieved when he bowed over her hand. "So much has happened these past few months," she said conversationally. "To both of us..."

"Just so, my lady," Robert Thesiger replied, a triumphant glance at the mute Marquis who, unable to hide his bitter disapproval of his wife's actions, walked away and disappeared inside the tent. He smiled crookedly and tugged at the white ruffles covering his hands, a sweeping look at the mansard-roofed palace that dominated the skyline. "I have acquired a title and wealth, while you, my lady, have sacrificed your independence of spirit to live in a gilded cage."

Deb continued to smile, ignored the slight and said with practiced calm, "Once we had a discussion at the Assembly Rooms about business in Paris keeping you away—"

"Business with blue eyes? Yes, intriguing that you should remember."

"Because you were adamant the adorable Dominique was more beautiful than I."

"Ha! You remembered her name. So you were piqued after all!"

"Is there a point to this, m'lady?" Joseph muttered in Deb's ear.

"May I know if the blue-eyed Dominique is Mademoiselle Lefebvre?" Deb inquired calmly, ignoring her groom, but with the blood drumming in her ears as she anticipated Robert Thesiger's reply

Robert Thesiger was bemused as to where the conversation was leading, but happy to oblige. He inclined his powdered head. "Just so."

"Dominique Lefebvre…"

Deb whispered the name as if it were reverential, and in that same breath a thick fog of uncertainty that had enveloped her for months suddenly dissolved, and everything was given clarity and meaning. Now she knew what she must do to secure her future. Decided, she flicked open her fan and held out her hand in farewell to Robert Thesiger, barely giving him a second glance. Although, when he bowed over her hand she was not so distracted that she did not hear his invitation.

"At the Tuileries tomorrow," he said in an under voice, "Mademoiselle Lefebvre arrives at noon. If you desire the truth, be there."

Deb watched him saunter off across the cobbled drive towards the tradesmen's entrance gate before turning away to find her husband waiting for her by the tent. She was so caught up in her mental strategies—on how best to escape the hôtel for the Tuileries tomorrow, without alerting Brigitte, the Duke's army of servants or her husband—that she was oblivious to the Marquis's stiff-necked silence. Nor did she see Joseph's jaw-swinging look. She kept her thoughts to herself as her husband escorted her indoors to present her to the hundreds of guests waiting to be introduced to his English bride.

THIRTY-ONE

I T WAS FOUR in the morning when the last of the guests straggled out of the Hôtel Roxton to be helped into their carriages by liveried footmen who were also doing their best to keep from yawning. Half an hour later, Julian padded through in his stockinged feet to his wife's apartment via the secret door concealed behind an enormous floor-to-ceiling tapestry. Deb had been put to bed well before midnight, and he wished he could have followed her, such was his aversion for large public gatherings where he and his family were the main attraction.

He really would have to tell her about the secret door, if Brigitte hadn't already. But he suspected he was right about the very discreet Brigitte—a gem amongst paste. And how did Deb think he had arrived in her boudoir via her bedchamber earlier that day—by conjury?

He found his wife curled up amongst the pillows, an arm caught in the tumble of her long dark red hair that had escaped her night cap. He set aside his taper, to pull the coverlet up over her, and to draw the curtains about the bed to keep in the warmth, when she woke and blinked in the muted candlelight.

"I'm not asleep," she said drowsily.

"No, you're not," he replied gently, and propped himself on the edge of the bed.

Deb sat up on an elbow and frowned under heavy lids. He was still dressed. He had removed his velvet frock coat and matching gold thread waistcoat, and thrown a silk banyan loosely over his open-neck shirt and breeches.

"You're not dressed for bed."

He laughed at her blunt disappointment.

"I didn't come here to be a nuisance. I just wanted to see how you fared after such an exhausting evening... And I couldn't sleep," he confessed. "Our conversation today was interrupted by Joseph."

Deb was suddenly wide-awake.

"Would you like to tell me now?"

He glanced at her fleetingly and pretended an interest in a pulled thread on the embroidered coverlet.

"I've been meaning to tell you something about myself that you should've known from the very beginning..."

"May I ask you one question before you tell me?" she asked, filling his silence. And when he nodded, said frankly, "Do you know Mademoiselle Lefebvre's Christian name, Julian?" When he gave a start, she grabbed at his hand and smiled. "Please. It is important."

He shrugged and frowned. "I have no idea."

"And the color of her eyes?"

"That makes two questions."

Her smile brightened. "I promise it will be the last time I mention Mademoiselle Lefebvre."

Again, he shrugged his ignorance. "Why does her Christian name and the color of her eyes interest you?"

She bit her lip to hide a grin. "Oh, they don't interest me at all. But no more. I promised. Tomorrow. First I must speak with Eve. Now what is it you want to tell me?"

He shook his head at her mischievous twinkle and swiftly kissed her hand. "Tomorrow then." And stopped, not knowing how to go on with his confession. Finally, he took a deep breath and said softly, "Perhaps it would be for the best if I begin at the beginning... The night of our hasty midnight marriage, I made a vow."

"A vow?" Deb clutched at the word, intrigued and she scrambled to sit up amongst the feather pillows.

"This vow was in the form of a promise to the children that would one day eventuate from our marriage. I have always wanted a large family..." He looked into Deb's eyes, the frown between his black brows a little deeper than before. "Very few noblemen take responsibility for the corollary of their immoral behavior. After all, it is arrogantly assumed any children that result from such a base coupling are a female's responsibility. But it was this appalling consequence—that there was a real possibility somewhere out there I had bastard brothers and sisters struggling through life, forgotten and in poverty, while I had every advantage, all my wants and needs, *my whims*, attended to without question—that had a profound effect on me.

"You can then well imagine my feelings when I discovered Robert was my natural brother. To come face-to-face with a boy who was my father's son... He blamed my mother for his base birth. Yet he was proud of his ignoble connection with my father... The shock... The idea that one day my son could be approached and his innocence of the world—the image he had of his loving parents and all that he held dear—could be shattered and corrupted by the existence of a bastard half-brother—it so appalled me that I vowed there and then such a hideous prospect would never befall my children."

Deb blanched. "What I said to you that horrid day in Martin's house—"

"But I goaded you to it, my darling," Julian interrupted her with a sad smile. "You have no need to apologize; but I do. What I hurled at you that day was unforgivable. In my defense, I was bewildered, and more than a little hurt, that after spending more than two months in my company and in the most intimate of settings and situations, you could think me capable of what I have been accused by a Farmer General. I only did what I did—carried out an elaborate subterfuge—so that you would get to know me, Julian, as a-a—*gentleman* and-and a —*husband*." He smiled self-consciously. "I hoped that if you got to know me you would fall in love with *me*. Just as I—as I— fell in love with *you*... You are my wife, Deb, but more than that, you are the love of my life. Of that I am convinced. And I—and I love—*love you*—with my whole heart."

Through a mist of tears, Deb threw herself into her husband's arms, laughing and crying at one and the same time. He dropped his head into the tumble of red hair at her shoulder and they stayed that way for a long time, silently revelling in the warmth of each other, until Julian sat up. He needed to tell her about the vow he had made long ago, before he lost his resolve.

Instinctively, Deb understood his embarrassment, and so she remained silent, propped against the pillows, her hand in his as he played with her fingers, and waited for him to tell her the exact nature of his vow.

After a hard swallow, and with a heightened color to his cheeks, he finally lifted his green eyes to her face and said resolutely,

"I was delightfully surprised to discover our views on the subject of fidelity and the bringing up of children are attuned... Honesty is also very important to us both, so I want you to know, while I was living in Constantinople, I had a lover—"

"I'd really rather not know."

"She was ten years my senior," he continued in a measured tone. "She was from a minor branch of the Russian royal family and wife of the Russian Ambassador. She taught me many valuable lessons about life and love—" He gave a huff of laughter. "—and in at least four languages. More importantly, she offered me the reassurance I needed that I'd no reason to be apologetic or feel ashamed of my convictions."

Deb kept her gaze lowered to where their intertwined fingers rested on the coverlet.

"You talk of a vow to ensure your own children are never plagued by children fathered out of wedlock, and in the next breath you are fondly reminiscing about this older woman who was your mistress."

"Darling, listen to me. She and I—we—we were never lovers in the *strict* sense of the word. In fact, I have never—that is, I have *experience* in certain particulars of lovemaking but I—I —*Damn it*!" he growled in frustration, a hot flush burning his stubbled cheeks. He pushed a hand through his thick black hair. "Why can't I just come out and say it?"

"I think I know what it is you want to tell me," Deb whispered, and sat up to put her arms about his neck. She leaned forward to brush her lips against his mouth and murmured, "Abstinence is nothing of which to be ashamed."

He held her against him, kissing her mouth, wanting to fulfil the promise in her brief alluring kiss, then pulled back saying candidly,

"A bride expects her husband to be a consummate lover, to initiate her into love-making—not an overeager virgin armed with raw instinct and expert lessons in foreplay!" He frowned, cheeks burning hotter than ever. "Forgive me, Deborah. I am a fraud."

"Fraud?"

"The vow I made was far more important than any momentary tawdry satisfaction to be gained from a casual liaison. Yet I never corrected the assumptions Society made about me, in particular about my love life. That's nobody's business but my own—and now, yours." He smiled shyly. "The Marquis of Alston is nothing like the man portrayed in the newssheets, or pamphlets, or the gossip circulating Society."

"So what is the Marquis of Alston truly like, Julian?" she asked softly.

His smile was bashful. "I'm afraid the Marquis of Alston—

your noble husband—is exceedingly strait-laced and conventional."

"Oh? You aren't one of those noblemen who are a sad rake and a profligate, with a string of discarded mistresses left in your wake?" she asked, feigning disappointment. But at his embarrassed scowl she laughed and said with an encouraging smile, "That is as well, because this wife expects nothing less from her noble husband. She also intends to keep to herself she has a husband who is a wondrously inventive lover."

"Am I?" he said with a self-conscious smile, brow clearing of uncertainty and embarrassment. Her simple sincerity vanquished any discomfort he felt at being so brutally honest. "Do you have any notion how much I love you, Deborah? How-how—*necessary*—you are to my health and happiness?"

"Tell me."

He kissed her, first gently and then ardently.

"No, my darling. Let me show you..."

<h1 style="text-align:center">THIRTY-TWO</h1>

JULIAN WENT TO sleep smiling, with his wife in his arms. It was the most contented sleep the couple had had for many months. They would've been greatly surprised to know that not only did they enjoy an unbroken slumber, but so did the Marquis's valet and her ladyship's maid. Julian was not smiling, however, when Brigitte woke him five hours later with the news he was to present himself in the south wing at once. She was asked to repeat the command. He had not been in that part of the hôtel since a boy. The south wing was his parents' private domain, off-limits to family and guests alike, and serviced by a half dozen of the Duke's most discreet and trusted servants.

There could be only one explanation for his summons by the Duchess, so he quickly returned to his apartment, telling Brigitte to let her mistress sleep for as long as possible.

He bathed quickly in tepid water and dressed in haste. Frew was lost for words when his master refused to be shaved and went off with the beginnings of a beard and in his shirtsleeves, throwing on a dark-blue damask frock coat as he went up the wide main staircase two steps at a time. Before he had reached the top step, where two sentries stood guard at the entrance to the private rooms the Duke and Duchess had shared for over a quarter of a century, the news had whipped through the myriad of servant passages like a blast of cold November air: The Duke of Roxton was on his deathbed.

THE DUCHESS was seated at a black lacquered breakfast table, dressed in marked contrast to the rich oriental magnificence of her surroundings. Her simple gown was of printed Indian muslin, her luminous skin devoid of cosmetics and jewelry, and her thick honey curls were braided into plaits and caught up at her nape in a silver net. She was reading a letter while a soft-footed footman cleared the table of the remnants of breakfast. A curl of steam rose from the coffee pot and two clean porcelain coffee dishes had been placed on the table.

Julian took all this in with one hurried glance as he buttoned his frock coat and strode across the wide room, unannounced.

"Maman!?"

Antonia looked up, startled. "Oh! I did not expect you so soon."

"I came at once." He glanced at the footman. "Where's Father? What's happened?"

She slowly folded the letter but did not return it to the pile of correspondence and invitations stacked on a silver salver at her elbow. Instead, she propped it against the porcelain milk jug and stared at it as if able to read the scrawled sloping handwriting on the reverse, then turned away to look up at her son.

"Monseigneur is in his library."

"In his library?" Julian repeated in a whisper and let his wide shoulders drop. The tightness in his limbs eased knowing his father was no better or worse than the day before. Anxiety was replaced with annoyance. "Maman, do you have any idea what your summons has done to your household? If Father is well, and he did not request to see me, then I will return to my apartment to shave. I should not linger here."

The Duchess waved away the footman, put her hands in her lap, and studied her eldest son. She was well aware her ambiguous summons would produce immediate results, and that she had been deceitful in its execution. She knew Julian would come at once because he suspected something had happened to his father. But she needed to talk to him and on a subject that had remained unspoken between them. But how to do this with a son who chose to remain aloof because it was easier than dealing with the past? She sighed and decided the best approach was to appear stronger than she was.

She put out a hand to pick up the silver coffee urn off its pedestal, but Julian was quick to do this for her. He poured out only into one dish.

"You will please sit, Julian," she commanded. "I do not care in the least if you have a full beard upon your face, or if you do not drink my coffee, but me I mean to speak with you."

The Marquis remained standing.

"There is little we can have to say to one another within these four walls that could not be said elsewhere."

The Duchess sat up straight and raised her arched brows.

"Is that so? Perhaps you would prefer to talk with your maman in the middle of the open field surrounded by animals of the barn, *hein*? That I could easily have arranged, but me I do not want to get my silk slippers muddied."

Julian's jaw set hard.

"I would gladly have you sacrifice one pair of slippers, Maman, than flame speculative gossip by having me summoned here to your private apartments."

She regarded him sadly and sighed. "An open field would do you more harm, *mon fils*."

When he threw up a hand but did not contradict her, she knew he understood. She watched him go to the window to stare out at the rose garden with its rows of fragrant white blooms the Duke had planted for her, and which were carefully tended by a team of gardeners. After what seemed a silence of minutes she said,

"I have never questioned your father's judgment. But when he sent you away on the Grand Tour at such a young age... I thought my heart it would break. And then later, much later, when he finally told me he had married you off in such a cold-hearted way... I was furious with him. I have never been so angry with him before or since. You understand, Julian, yes?"

"He did what he considered necessary."

"But... An arranged marriage... It was not what I wanted for my son."

That brought him back to the table. For want of something to fill the awkward silence between them he poured out a dish of coffee and stirred in a spoonful of sugar. His eyes locked on hers.

"But what choice did my father have? Allow me to make an imprudent match on the Continent just to spite him? Or secure his dynastic future by arranging my marriage with a Cavendish heiress in the hopes that in the future there would be children of the match before his death? It is no worse than the situation he finds himself in—old enough to be a grandfather to his own children and married to a woman who will outlive him by thirty years or more. I know which I prefer."

When his mother looked away swiftly, emerald-green eyes awash with tears, he wished he could have cut out his tongue than have wounded her by such unthinking truths. He drew up a chair.

"Lord, Maman, I didn't mean... I just wanted to reassure you—"

The Duchess cleared her throat.

"I am perfectly well aware your father... He and I we will not grow old together," she interrupted in thickly accented English—the first time he had heard her speak his native tongue in many years. "I realize this concerns you. That one day soon your father he will—that he will no longer be with us—and I will have to live—live without him..."

"There really is no need—"

"Yes. There is a very great need!" she said in a rush. "This opportunity I may never have again. You think it is easy for me to talk of Monseigneur leaving me? That we will soon be parted on this earth? It is a thing that is the most horrid imaginable and I never dwell on it. It is only that I must tell you how it is so you will stop worrying about me. And you do worry, do you not, Julian? That is the truth of the matter." She stared at the opposite wall with its patterned wallpaper of lotus flowers and cranes. "I do not know why it is so, but it is easier to explain these things to you in the English tongue, it makes it less real to me. So you will please excuse my pronunciation. I am out of practice."

She was trying desperately to be strong, but it only served to make her appear even younger, more fragile and more vulnerable. And her eyes were so full of sorrow that Julian could not look at her.

"We understand one another, Julian. Yes?" she asked. When he nodded his bowed head, she rallied herself. "I count each day with your father as a blessing, and I do not care what those fools, those idiot physicians say! I intend that your father live a great many years yet."

"Of course he will, Maman, a great many years," Julian assured her gently. But he was lying. Privately, he did not hold to such a conviction.

"You think because your father he is in frail health, he does not *see*? Never forget, Julian: Monseigneur is as omniscient as ever. He knows you frown on the consequences his dissipated past has brought to his family, and that you conduct your life very differently from what his was like when he first became Duke."

"But I have never judged him, Maman!"

Antonia covered her son's fingers with her small hand and smiled.

"That is very true, *mon fils*," she said, unconsciously reverting to her native French tongue. "But he sees that you view your future as Duke with trepidation and reluctance."

"Of course I am reluctant! To inherit my birthright he must be dead. You think that is a prospect I relish? That in order for me to strut the world stage as Duke, my father, a man I love and respect, must be cold in his grave? Lord, Maman, you above all others must see that I dread the coming of the day when I am saluted as His Grace the Most Noble Duke of Roxton."

"Yes, I see it, Julian," the Duchess replied sadly, tears glistening on her cheeks, "but I ask that you not *show* it. He wants to leave this world knowing you embrace his exalted position with all the enthusiasm and energy in which he inherited the title from his grandfather. What he needs now, at this the end of his long tenure as M'sieur le Duc, is the reassurance that your future it is secure—and to be at peace. Deborah's pregnancy has given him reassurance, but only you can give him peace."

Julian sat back in his chair, momentarily uncomfortable, and rubbed the tips of his long fingers across his stubbled cheek. "If he is concerned the annulment will go forward..."

Antonia dried her eyes on her lace-bordered handkerchief and shook her head with a smile.

"I am not talking about that great piece of nonsense at all! A one-eyed idiot can see that you and Deborah are very much in love. That pleases us both more than I can tell you."

In spite of himself, Julian felt his face flood with heat. "Strange," he muttered. "Deb knew instantly the same about you and Father..."

"Because she has a pure heart and thus sees the truth," the Duchess stated. She sat forward in the lattice-backed chair, as if fearing to be overheard. "Listen to me, Julian. What I want to tell you, your father and I have never told a living soul. So you must promise it will go no further, *mon fils, hein*?" Julian's nod of assent made her continue. "I tell you this without your father knowing I do so. It bruises my heart to go behind his back in this way because me I have never done so before, but... It is important for your future and the future of your sons that the past it is finally laid to rest.

"You see, Julian," she said in a halting voice, gaze lowered to where her hand rested on her son's embroidered upturned cuff, "The Comtesse Duras-Valfons has always maintained that her son is Monseigneur's son also. She says her child was conceived at Fontainebleau, when Monseigneur was hunting with the King. The parish records bear this out, for the boy was indeed born nine months after the King's Hunt, around the time of your own birth..." Her gaze flickered to Julian's immobile face and then lowered again with a small sigh. "Your father and I we were married two months after this Hunt, and you were born just seven months later. Before your time, we said. But that was a convenient lie. You were a small baby and that made it easier to convince others. But you had not quickened early."

Julian frowned. He wanted to stand to stretch his legs, for the conversation had taken an intimate turn that he was not convinced he needed to hear. It made him shift restlessly on his chair.

"What is the point of this, Maman? Given the Duke's past, I am not at all shocked to learn he bedded his mistress then turned around and married you out of hand. What's important to me is that he reformed his wicked ways for you."

Antonia squeezed his arm.

"Listen to me, Julian," she demanded imperiously. "Do you not understand that if Mme Duras-Valfons and I conceived around the same time, that your father he was not bedding that woman at all? I may have fallen in love with a great rake, but your father he knew very well what was expected of him before I would give myself to him."

Julian cocked an eyebrow at her.

"And you think I don't know who rules this noble roost?"

The Duchess waved her hands at him.

"Please do not interrupt again or I may not be able to tell you all of it before Monseigneur he returns. Particularly when this is the most difficult part to explain." She sighed again. "I tell you the rest bluntly. Your father he did reform his ways for me. From the moment he became my guardian around the time of my eighteenth birthday—while I was living here in this house— which was many months before we were married, he rejected all other females, and this while I was still engaged to another. It is true I tell you, Julian!"

"I believe you, Maman," he reassured her, hiding his astonishment and his spreading smile at her scowl.

"The day Monseigneur relinquished his guardianship of me I was to go to London to stay with my grandmother. Your father he went off to Fontainebleau, and your Aunt Estée she went with Vallentine to visit her Tante Victoire in Saint-Germain, and so the hôtel it was shut up. But I did not go to England straight away and Monseigneur he did not go to Fontainebleau. He returned at nightfall—to be with me. Martin he is the only one who knows this. We spent a week here alone in this apartment. That is when you were conceived." Her gaze flickered to her son's face. "You understand now, Julian, yes, why your father he will not speak of this time. Why it must remain between us?"

Julian could no longer sit still and he wandered to the windows and back again and looked down at his mother, at the heightened color in her porcelain cheeks and the hesitation in her eyes. He thrust his hands in his frock coat pockets.

"Because if the world discovered that the dissolute Duke of Roxton had taken advantage of a young innocent girl in his care, under his very roof, it would forever blacken his honor?"

Antonia hung her head and then bravely looked up at him.

"*Mon fils*, you know as well as I that Society it is indulgent of the degenerate ways of a great rake, but a nobleman who seduces a-a maiden who is under his protection... If this girl she is of the same social standing and betrothed in marriage to another, then this nobleman he has broken the unwritten code of his peers."

"And his peers will no longer consider him a gentleman," Julian continued when she could not. "They will turn their noble backs on him. He is condemned forever as an abhorrent monster."

"It wasn't like that, Julian. *He* isn't like that! Monseigneur and I we were so in love that we did not think through the consequences of our actions. All that mattered was having those few days alone together before we were to be forever parted. The future—living without each other—it was inconceivable." When Julian gave a grunt she added in a rush, "You are not to think of your father in that way, *mon fils*. If you must think badly of one of us, then it is I you should condemn. He would not have crossed the great divide that separates guardian from ward had I not enticed him to it!"

Julian shook his head solemnly and took a turn about the room, but when he came back to her he was smiling.

"Maman! As if I could think worse of you or Papa knowing what you have just told me. So I was conceived out of wedlock. What of that? Who am I to judge when I deceived my own wife into thinking me a common man so that she could get to know me as Julian, not the Marquis of Alston. I gave no thought to the consequences of my actions. Who thinks beyond the immediate when the heart rules the head?"

He pulled her out of the chair and hugged her to him, a great shudder of relief coursing through his body.

"*Merci, ma mère*. Your secret it is safe with me. And it has lifted a great burden from my shoulders."

Antonia stepped back and looked up at him. "Because that man he is not your brother, yes?"

Julian bowed over her hand and kissed it. "Yes."

Their moment of intimacy was abruptly ended when the breakfast room door opened and the Duchess's lady-in-waiting came into the room, bobbed a curtsy and whispered near Antonia's ear before departing, leaving the door wide.

"Mme le Duchesse, please excuse the intrusion. I wouldn't have disturbed you for the world, but Alston is not in his apartments and his valet—*Julian*?" Martin said with considerable surprise, suddenly spying his godson by the undraped window as he bowed low over the Duchess's outstretched hand.

"What is it, Martin?" asked the Duchess with alarm—her first thought always with the Duke.

The old man looked from mother to son. Julian came away from the window to stand by his mother. Both were ashen faced.

"Not the Duke," he assured them, though he still looked very worried. "It's Henri-Antoine. He's disappeared. Bailey thinks he's gone to the Tuileries with Master Cavendish." He smiled crookedly at the Marquis, eyes widening imperceptibly at the day-old growth on his godson's face. "It seems he's determined to see that wretched bear."

Julian put an arm about his mother's shoulders. "Don't worry, Maman. I know exactly where to find them." He rubbed a hand over his stubbled chin and grinned at his godfather. He had seen the flash of disapproval cross the old man's face. "I suppose a shave will have to wait until my return from the Tuileries."

Antonia touched Martin's arm. "Thank you for not telling Monseigneur. He has enough to worry him, what with that oaf Sartine daring to bother him."

Julian's head snapped round at his mother. "The lieutenant of police is *here* annoying Father? Why?"

"That it is unimportant," the Duchess said dismissively, propelling him towards the door. "Your brother he is what is important. So please you will now go fetch him home so that I may scold him severely and before Mon—Monseigneur!" she declared with a bright smile, not missing a beat in her speech and going forward to greet the Duke, who stood in the doorway, leaning lightly on his cane, and surveying his wife through his quizzing glass. "You have sent those horrid policemen away, Renard, yes?" she asked eagerly.

"What's this, Antonia?" the Duke drawled, twirling his quizzing glass on its black silk riband. He was frowning, but there was a decided twinkle of mischief in his black eyes. "Twenty-five years of marriage of—er—*uninterrupted* privacy in our own chambers, yet in one morning I am gone less than an hour and return to find my wife entertaining our son and his godfather without me?"

Antonia went up on tiptoe and kissed him. Her smile was impish.

"But, in those twenty-five years, you have never left me to breakfast alone, and so me I was lonely."

The Duke returned her kiss and playfully chucked her under the chin.

"Dear me, I see I must never leave you alone again."

"Sir, if Sartine was here, why wasn't I told of it?" Julian asked with annoyance, interrupting his parents' playful banter.

"Because, my son, he came to see *me*," the Duke replied simply. "There has been an interesting—er—*development* in the Lefebvre case."

"Such as?"

The Duke regarded his son with an inscrutable gaze.

"Correct my grand presumption, but I believe you know well enough already."

"That is exceedingly interesting, sir," Julian replied with a lift of an eyebrow. "So my cousin has finally done the honorable thing and confessed?"

"The words *honorable* and—er—*confess* do not readily spring to mind."

Julian's lip curled. Martin Ellicott was nonplussed. The Duke took out his snuffbox and tapped the lid. Antonia looked at all three and said bluntly,

"Me I do not understand at all! What is this development of which you speak, Renard?"

"I'm only too willing to allow Julian to tell you, my love. I find the whole Lefebvre imbroglio fatiguing in the extreme."

The Marquis opened his mouth to speak when unannounced into the breakfast room rushed the Duke's sister. Estée Vallentine crossed the room in a whirl of voluminous hooped petticoats and a mass of disordered gray hair festooned with curling ribbons, as if she had left off in the middle of having her hair dressed and powdered. She clutched a crumpled letter to her heaving bosom and spying her brother she flourished this at the Duke. Roxton rolled his eyes to the ornate ceiling and sat in the nearest chair as his sister launched herself, sobbing, into the Duchess's arms.

"Antonia! He's eloped! My son! My *darling* boy. *Evelyn.* He's run off with a filthy *bourgeois*!"

THIRTY-THREE

DEB WOULD HAVE preferred to make the short trip to the Tuileries on foot. It was a lovely day. But Brigitte, Joseph and two of the Duke's burly footmen had other ideas, and they arrived at the formal gardens by carriage. So much for slipping quietly away without anyone knowing her whereabouts! Yet she realized it was better to have her entourage with her than leave them behind to alert her husband and his father that she had absconded. The carriage was met at the terraced steps leading down to a broad central avenue by Evelyn Ffolkes, who had with him Jack, an odd assortment of musicians, and a small band of servants carrying musical instruments and chairs.

While the musicians and their retinue of hangers-on went off to ready themselves for their performance by one of the large fountains, Deb took the opportunity to stroll with Joseph and Brigitte amongst the crowded stalls that lined the walks. The two beefy footmen who had accompanied the carriage fell in behind the Marchioness and her party, keeping a discreet distance, yet ever watchful of the crowds.

The noise of carriages and barrows plying along the streets was not so deafening within the expanse of the Tuileries, where promenaded groups of pleasure-seekers out to enjoy a spring day of entertainment. News reporters huddled under the trees, old men played at chess in the shade, some enjoyed skittles, and groups of men and women partook of *cafe au lait* from one the many gaily-colored stalls. Stilt walkers, puppeteers, mime artists and even the quack doctors provided endless amusement for the passers-by.

There was such a carnival atmosphere within these walled gardens, with everyone intent on enjoying the festivities staged by the Parisian city officials to celebrate the Dauphin's marriage, that Deb almost forgot her dual purpose for coming to the gardens. To hear Jack play in Evelyn's string ensemble was paramount, but she also hoped Mademoiselle Lefebvre would be in attendance, as promised by Robert Thesiger.

A chance glance over her shoulder and she saw the Duke's burly footmen not far from her, jostling with a boisterous group of street performers. Their presence gave her an odd sense of comfort. So did the small pearl-handled twin-barrel pistol she carried in the pouch sewn to the side of her boot. It was a gift from Otto on her arrival in Paris, who had her carry it whenever she went onto the streets.

Just as she was beginning to wonder how she was supposed to recognize Mademoiselle Lefebvre or find Robert Thesiger in such a festive crowd, the gentleman himself materialized before her. He had broken away from a group of powdered and patched young men and came strolling towards her. He had a decided twinkle in his eye when he bowed low over her outstretched hand.

"Will the bride take a stroll with an old friend?" he asked smoothly, a glance over her shoulder at the stony faces of Joseph and her lady-in-waiting. Boldly, he offered Deb his silken arm and his smile widened when Joseph gave a start. "Yesterday I failed to wish you happy on your marriage. Are you happy, my lady?"

Deb met his gaze openly. "Yes. Very happy."

He smiled as if he did not believe her, and they strolled in silence amongst the fashionable Parisians who were enjoying the sideshows and entertainments. A few powdered heads turned to admire this handsome couple being shadowed by two sour-faced servants and a couple of ape-sized brutes in distinctive silver and red livery.

Did anyone know to whom the livery belonged? A Duke you say? Which one?

Three stilt-walkers and their entourage of tumblers and small band of musicians were making slow progress up the broad avenue towards them, scattering the promenading Parisians either side of the walk, teasing some and surrounding others with their antics. Deb and Robert Thesiger took refuge by a refreshment tent serving *café au lait*, to wait until this band of merry performers passed by. The commotion gave Thesiger the opportunity to face Deb, saying with a concerned frown,

"I cannot help wondering: Had I confided in you from the very beginning Mademoiselle Lefebvre's sorry predicament, would you now be Alston's wife in more than name only?"

"Tell me, sir: Did you pursue me in Bath to exact revenge on my husband because of Mademoiselle Lefebvre's ruin?"

"My dear, you are quite beautiful and I very much wanted to bed you, for its own sake as well as to cuckold your husband." He grinned, puckering up the scar indenting his left cheek. "Unfortunately, this absurd tenacity of yours to engage your feelings before tumbling into bed proved my undoing. It necessitated I rethink how best to secure my future."

He scanned the sea of faces moving along the avenue, and then looked at her again, saying with a sad shake of his powdered head, "It pains me to involve you in this matter between the Roxtons and myself. But father and son must be brought to account for their actions."

"I fail to see how my involvement in the matter will make an ounce of difference to father or son."

"Don't you? Strange you should be so naïve," he pondered.

"Tell me: Is it right that the Duke's legitimate son has all his needs, wants and desires—indeed the world—placed at his feet, while I, the Duke's natural son, am not recognized as of the same flesh?"

"And that's my husband's fault? You conveniently neglect the part played by your mother. The Comtesse raised you in resentment and bitterness, all because of her unreasonable and spiteful jealousy of a girl with whom the Duke fell in love and who never did her a harm." Deb's smile was sad. "No, you are not to blame for the actions of your parents, but your mother is just as blameworthy as the Duke."

For the first time in her company, Robert Thesiger's calm veneer fell away.

"Marchioness five minutes and you're persuaded by that family's arrogant line of argument? You simpleton! My mother was enticed with the same false promise that led to Mademoiselle Lefebvre's seduction—the promise of marriage!"

"I have not the least interest in your opinions, of me or of the noble family into which I am married!" Deb retorted.

She glanced about to find the most convenient path back to Evelyn and her nephew, who were at the large fountain. But all exits were blocked by the contingent of circus performers and their appreciative audience. She came as close to Robert Thesiger as her damask petticoats would allow.

"Be reasonable, sir. Surely it has occurred to you that perhaps Mademoiselle Lefebvre pursued my husband for his rank and fortune. That when he rejected her advances she turned her attentions to another who could offer her a pale imitation of the same, a gentleman who has a close association with the Roxton family?"

Robert Thesiger stared at her as if she were raving.

"Good God, Madam! Why the devil would she name Alston if he wasn't her seducer?"

Deb shrugged a bare shoulder. "Because rejection cut her to the quick. Because she did not want to reveal the identity of her real lover for fear of the consequences from her father, who had encouraged her to pursue the Marquis of Alston. They are but two reasons. You must admit, to the vast majority of females it is one thing to be seduced by a future Duke, quite another to allow a mere commoner between the sheets."

Robert Thesiger opened his mouth to refute this, had second thoughts, and said with a crooked smile, "Is that what persuaded you? That you will soon be Duchess of Roxton?"

"Why do you persist with this futile quest for retribution from the Duke of Roxton, a nobleman whose pride and arrogance will never permit him to acknowledge you as his son?" Deb asked calmly, ignoring Joseph's loud clearing of his throat. "Why do you assume my husband is cast from the same die? Is it because you cling to the absurd notion that, to fill the Duke's shoes, his son and heir must also be an arrogant and depraved debauchee as the Duke once was? Can't you see that my husband has always been the man his father became upon his marriage to the Duchess?"

"Madam, your husband doesn't deserve the rank thrust upon him by luck of birth. Who can respect a nobleman who'd prefer to live in the obscurity of his estate, surrounded by his peasants, his pigs and his sheep, rather than take his rightful place at the helm of society? At Eton he never put himself forward, and yet his peers, those idiotic fawning brats who now make up Society, thrust him center stage as they do now, all because one day he'll be Duke of Roxton!"

"You ridicule him only because you do not understand him," Deb answered with exasperated patience. "Would you care to go through life never knowing who are your true friends, if you are chosen on merit, fawned over and praised, not because of who you are but because of what you will one day become? Just because he doesn't strut about society like an overblown peacock, full of his own consequence, lording it over all who are cast under his shadow, but has a natural deference for his social position and the huge responsibilities that will one day be his, you judge him as-as—*weak*? Nothing could be further from the truth!"

Thesiger shoved his enamel snuffbox in a frock coat pocket, Deb's line of argument dismissed as credulous sincerity.

"Had the Duke done the honorable thing by my mother I'd be heir to a dukedom!" he seethed. "And I tell you this, Madam: I'm no social cripple. I'd know how to use such an exalted position to best possible advantage!"

Yes, for your own self-serving ends and with no regard for others, Deb thought sadly.

Her husband and this man were so dissimilar in every way that it was pointless to continue the discussion. Robert Thesiger was so twisted with jealousy and resentment that her arguments were incomprehensible and unheard. Nothing she could say would make an ounce of difference to his distorted view of life. It was time she ended this circular discussion before she missed Jack's performance altogether.

She signaled to Brigitte and Joseph she was ready to leave, and in a gesture of goodwill, put out her gloved hand in farewell to Robert Thesiger.

"Good day, my lord. I hope that in time Baron Thesiger's inheritance brings you some comfort and joy. Now, if you will excuse me, I must return to my nephew, where I hope Mademoiselle Lefebvre may be found amongst the audience for Mr. Ffolkes performance…?"

"I wouldn't know, Madam," he said softly, taking a step closer, searching the view over her head. "She has refused to see me these past three months or more."

"But… Did you not say she would be here today at noon?" Deb asked with a confused frown, a look out over the sea of faces. "And I am very sure she will be because—"

"I don't care one way or the other," Robert Thesiger purred, and before Deb could step away, his hand shot out to grip her wrist. "It's time to end this charade."

He pulled her against him, and in one deft maneuver had

her back hard up against his torso, her arm twisted tightly into the small of her back. Bound together, he shuffled them along the walk toward the closest group of circus performers, her capture accomplished before Brigitte and Joseph knew what was happening.

Deb tried in vain to free herself, but she was pinned against his torso, his hand that pressed against hers now uncomfortably tight on her abdomen.

"Let me go before you find yourself swinging from the end of a rope!"

"A grandchild will give the Roxton Dukedom a future—"

"You won't force the Duke's hand by taking me and my child hostage!"

"Don't take me for a fool, Madam," he growled, forcing her deep within a group of acrobats who closed ranks about them, dancing and twirling and tumbling, and making an unholy racket. "It's not a hostage I want. It's *revenge*."

A tumbler backflipped, came face-to-face with Deb and winked with a tobacco stained, almost toothless grin. She knew then, heartbeat rapidly increasing, these performers were in Thesiger's pay for the specific purpose of aiding her abduction. The appreciative crowd of onlookers, oblivious to the crime being committed under their very noses, applauded the tumblers' antics, as they swept Thesiger and his captive along the avenue in a processional that was heading towards the river.

"Look straight ahead," Thesiger commanded when Deb tried to catch a glimpse of Joseph and Brigitte.

The closeness of the performers surrounding her, Thesiger's arm about her waist, and the fact she had only picked at her breakfast, contributed to the nausea rising within her, and which was fast beginning to overwhelm her.

And that's when it came to her to pretend to faint.

Surely Thesiger would be forced to stop and revive her if he hoped to get her to the riverbank? So without another thought she let her knees buckle. As her legs collapsed under her, she expected Robert Thesiger to catch her in his arms. The reality was far more frightening.

As she crumpled into the dust of the graveled walk, Robert Thesiger's hold on her slackened and he stepped away. Unable to right herself in time, she fell towards the ground expecting to be trampled by the performers, who continued to tumble and make merry while their band of players crashed cymbals together and played their tin pipes a little louder than before. Her cry for help went unheard and unheeded. She wondered if this wasn't how Thesiger had planned for her to lose the baby all along, with no blame attached to him—just as blame hadn't been apportioned to him all those years ago, when he had whispered such horrid, foul lies in Julian's ear about the Duchess and her unborn child.

Yet just as her feet became entangled in the yards of silk of her crumpling petticoats, she grabbed for the nearest billowing shirt of a sinewy acrobat. His split-second reflexes reacted to pull Deb to him before she was trampled underfoot by his companions, and he picked her up in his strong arms and carried her the short distance along an avenue that led to the river.

Her stockinged feet in mid-air, Deb felt a hard object knock against the ankle of her old kid boot. It was Otto's pistol. How foolish of her not to remember before now that she had worn her boots specifically because she could carry Otto's pistol on her person! She was so relieved knowing she had her pistol, and grateful to the swarthy-faced acrobat for saving her that she made no attempt to struggle or cry out. She merely awaited her opportunity to reach down and remove the pistol from its holster. Her chance came soon enough.

The procession halted at the end of the avenue at the edge of the gardens. Beyond was the Seine, where a boat awaited them. Overconfident of their success, one of the kidnappers performed a victory tumble, back flipped, overbalanced and fell on his buttocks into a hedge. His fellows laughed and did nothing to help him up.

The acrobat holding fast to Deb finally set her on her feet, now they were away from the main avenue. Her moment had arrived. As she was put to firm ground, she carefully lifted her boot and slipped the pistol from its holster. She half-cocked both hammers, then hid it amongst the folds of her disordered petticoats. Her captors were none the wiser, as they continued to laugh at the expense of their fellow's embarrassing fall in the shrubbery.

One of the tumblers exclaimed that before they departed for the river they should have a little fun with their hostage. His suggestion was laughed away as the emotive talk of a drunkard, not to be taken seriously. Yet when the observation was made that none of them had ever been so close to a titled lady before, and that this was a once-in-a-lifetime opportunity to discover if a noblewoman's porcelain skin was indeed as soft as the fine silks she wore, more than one of their number turned a lascivious eye on Deb.

The tumbler who had fallen into the hedge grabbed a handful of Deb's petticoats and began to tug up the yards of an exquisite fabric he had never before touched, much to the delight and appreciative hoots of his fellows. They urged him on, to lift the gossamer layers above the girl's knees so they could see the garters that held up her fine white silk stockings.

A cheer went up followed by the explosive discharge of a pistol.

The report from Deb's pistol was deafening. It instantly silenced the musicians surrounding her, and then one of their number let out a bloodcurdling scream. The drunken tumbler who had dared to lift Deb's petticoats had been shot. The ball had pierced the leather of his jackboot. He fell to the ground, writhing in agony, clutching his ankle with both hands while his fellows stared at Deb in horrified silence. She was unharmed and had the great presence of mind to keep the smoking pistol leveled at her abductors—one bullet remained to be fired.

Shock gave way to anger tinged with wariness at such outrageous behavior from a female, a lady at that! There was collective unspoken consensus amongst the performers to abandon the girl and flee. They had already committed a hanging offense by abducting her. That she had the courage to fire upon them was enough to put paid to their plans. Tumblers and musicians scattered, most running back into the gardens, their escape route to the river blocked by the two burly liveried footmen who had accompanied Deb to the Tuileries. Even the acrobat she had shot managed to hobble away, supported by two of his fellows, heaping curses upon her head between his continued whimpers of agony.

The Duke's servants did not give chase. They had their orders. The safety of the Marchioness was paramount—everything and everyone else was of no consequence. To this end, one of the footmen mutely removed the pistol from Deb's hand and uncocked the barrel. His fellow scooped her up, despite her objections that she was quite capable of walking, and carried her to the steps where he set her gently down. His twin with the pistol then made Deb a formal bow of recognition and boldly offered her the contents of his hip flask to calm her nerves. Deb was about to tell him she was perfectly calm when she realized she was trembling. So she gratefully drank of the fiery liquid.

She was remarkably serene, helped by the gulp of brandy, given she had just foiled an attempt to kidnap her. Unharmed, she did not let herself dwell on possibilities. Yet, despite foiling the kidnapping and the protection of two footmen the size of Russian bears, she knew her baby would not be completely safe until she had returned to Julian and the protection of the Hôtel Roxton. Her concern was justified when she chanced to glance up the stairs, and there on the top step was Robert Thesiger. She gave a start, and one of the footmen took a step toward him, ready to meet any challenge. His fellow cocked her pistol and levelled it at Thesiger.

Robert Thesiger came lightly down the stairs, ignoring the footman standing over Deb as if he did not exist, not a glance in Deb's direction, or at the footman with the pistol. She watched him follow the line of the ancient stone wall and wondered what held his attention. He did not look left or right but out across the gardens at the fleeing hordes as he stripped off his frock coat, tossed it and his ruffles aside, and unsheathed his sword. And then she saw the reason for his preoccupation.

Coming along the gravel path was her husband.

THIRTY-FOUR

It was while striding the avenues in search of his brother, a head taller than those around him, that Julian had caught sight of Deb in company with Robert Thesiger. It brought him up short. He had left her safely tucked up in bed, and that's where he supposed she had remained, sleeping peacefully. And then he remembered something about Jack being involved in a musical performance and he should've realized Deb would do all in her power to ensure she did not miss her nephew's first public appearance. That she was strolling the Tuileries gardens in conversation with his nemesis not only angered him, but also brought with it an unwanted sense of trepidation for her safety. He was in no doubts that it was Thesiger who had sought out his wife, and he wondered what mischief the man meant.

He stood in the middle of the crowded avenue as stone, watching them, for how long, he had no idea. He stared at Robert Thesiger, willing him to look up, and when he finally did, their eyes met and Thesiger's face split into a grin. It was only then that Julian found his legs and he strode towards them, anger and fear extinguishing all thought of finding his younger brother. His eyes did not leave his wife, and when Thesiger grabbed Deb to him, back up against the man's chest and his arm about her waist, she struggling in vain to break free of him, Julian felt a gut-wrenching sense of helplessness for the first time in his life.

Frantically, he tried to push his way through the immoveable crowd that seemed to swell in number by the minute. Swarthy faces, toothless and unshaven, began to replace those of the gentlemen and women come to the gardens for a leisurely stroll. Tumblers, stilt walkers and a band of rowdy musicians clogged the avenue, and when he tried to break through their ranks he was rudely and unceremoniously shoved backwards and told that this section of the gardens was now closed to the public.

His second attempt saw him knocked off his feet, the promise of gold extinguishing all deference to rank. Although the acrobats who wrestled Julian to the ground took in the fineness of his clothes and the ornate hilt of his sword, and rightly concluded that here was a gentleman, if not a nobleman. But they had their orders, and what could one nobleman do against a gang of muscular circus performers?

What they failed to assess was that the nobleman's fine lace ruffles and exquisite coat of superfine disguised a well-exercised physique, whose strength was fuelled by a furious anxiety in his need to rescue his wife and unborn child from danger. He refused to stay down and had knocked out cold two tumblers and was all for taking on the third when Joseph materialized beside him. The man's nose was bloody and he had the beginnings of a black eye, but his grin was enough to convince Julian he was enjoying the fray hugely and obviously looked worse than he felt.

Joseph jumped in to assist the Marquis, who was beating off a particularly hard-set gypsy, and shouted out for his lordship to go after the Marchioness. He, Joseph, would take care of this ugly customer.

Julian nodded his understanding and took off running down the avenue.

Not a minute later there came the deafening report of a pistol discharge. The explosion rang out across the expanse of gardens, and visitors scattered to every quarter of the terraced gardens. Wild-eyed parents scooped up crying children, agitated shopkeepers and their customers dived under chairs and into the backs of stalls, seeking refuge from the unknown assailant and the stampeding hordes. Puppeteers, mime artists and street performers, animal handlers with their screeching monkeys and barking little dogs, all leapt out of the way or were pushed aside as hundreds of people trampled over carefully-tended flower beds, dived into ornamental ponds to hide with the fish, or raced with frenzied determination for the nearest exit.

Shouts went up for the militia.

At the sound of pistol fire, Julian's heart missed a beat and the blood rushed up into his ears. He had a nauseous presentiment that it was connected to Deb's abduction and it fuelled a furious determination to get to her as quickly as possible. He elbowed his way through the fleeing hordes, withstanding the mindless jostling and knocks from the onslaught of a frenzied mob. Size and height saved him from being trampled, but it also meant he stood out in a crowd seeking help to escape from a phantom madman. More than once he was appealed to, but he ignored all requests for assistance. He ran on.

And then he saw her, his beautiful, courageous wife. She was being watched over by the two liveried servants he had instructed to be her shadow whenever she ventured outside the protective high walls surrounding the Hôtel Roxton. She was sitting calmly on the steps that led up to the river, clothes and hair disheveled, but very much alive. The noise and madness surrounding him ceased to be important. The shouts and the screams barely registered. It mattered little that somewhere in the Tuileries there might be a madman with a pistol. Deb was unharmed and no one and nothing else mattered. He breathed deeply, as if for the first time since he saw her together with Robert Thesiger. A great stone weight lifted off his chest.

He strode towards her, a hand above his head to let her know he had seen her. When she waved back, he smiled for the first time since entering the Tuileries. Yet she did not look happy, and when she averted her face, his happiness evaporated and in its place was a heaviness of heart that made each step closer to her as if he were wading through thick mud. He felt empty and hollow, thinking that some harm must have come to her or the baby, for what else would make Deb look so stricken? He then chanced to follow her tearful gaze, and there, standing at the end of the avenue, sword drawn and awaiting him, was Robert Thesiger.

THIRTY-FIVE

I T HAD COME to this: A duel in the Tuileries in the broad light of day, with the formalities ignored and his pregnant wife watching on. The ludicrous reality brought a crooked smile to Julian's mouth as he watched Robert Thesiger make an elaborate display of flexing his rapier. The man's intentions couldn't be cruder, nor his methods more dishonorable. Julian was in no doubt Thesiger meant a duel to the death. So be it.

Julian stripped off his frock coat, tugged the ruffles free of his shirtsleeves, then rolled his sleeves to his elbows. He then scraped back the hair fallen into his eyes during the fight with the acrobats, and retied the ribbon at the nape. Preparations concluded (he would not allow himself even one brief glance at Deb), he approached Thesiger with sword drawn. They briefly saluted one another in the formal manner, and then blade hissed against blade.

The duel commenced.

From the moment the swords crossed, Thesiger went in for the attack, his frenzied swordplay instantly putting Julian on the back foot. Time and again Thesiger lunged, employing every trick of the fencing master's art, forcing his opponent back across the gravel at a furious pace in the hopes of wrong-footing him. He saw an opening in Julian's defense and delivered a lightning thrust. At the last moment, it was expertly deflected. But the tip of Thesiger's rapier caught inside Julian's rolled sleeve, flexed the shaft of the sword bow-like and then it sprang forward and upwards. The sleeve of Julian's shirt ripped, the needlepoint tip of Thesiger's blade glanced up along his bared upper arm and split the taut flesh of hardened muscle. Blood instantly flowed from the stinging wound and trickled down Julian's arm, and the blades disengaged.

But Thesiger wasn't about to give Julian any respite. He snarled *en garde*, and the fight went on. Far from giving Thesiger any advantage, the wound made little difference to Julian's ability with the sword, the stinging flesh and the trickle of blood ignored as he met Thesiger's every thrust and parry with a strong-wristed foil of his own.

Repeatedly the blades clashed with a sing of metal, neither achieving supremacy. Each man was able to counter every move of the other. Yet Thesiger was beginning to tire, evidence in the sweat that soaked his shirt and beaded his forehead. At one point he leapt back and wiped the moisture from his brow and Julian gave him the moment, lowering his blade to wipe the sticky blood from his forearm onto his damp shirt. Thesiger's blade came up again and the fight resumed, a little less frenzied than before.

They came in close, blades sliding off one another, Thesiger scrambling backwards and fending off a powerful lunge. He fell hard up against the stair wall, where just above his powdered head Deb sat on the step, watched over by a footman wielding her pistol.

He pushed his shoulders off the wall and righted himself, Julian awaiting his pleasure. It was Thesiger who called *en garde*. With a smile and a sideways glance up at the Marchioness, he taunted Julian, hoping to whip him into such a white-hot rage of unguarded passion that he would let down his defences.

Panting air into his deprived lungs, Thesiger said with a sneer as their swords disengaged, "Your wife—Your cousin—When she was in Paris last—They were lovers—He had her first."

"Liar!" Julian growled savagely.

White-lipped fury, and not the cool-headedness of time honored tactics drummed into him by his fencing master, caused Julian's lunge to go awry and it gave Thesiger the tactical advantage he was seeking.

It was Thesiger who now forced Julian against the wall, flexing the nobleman's wrist sideways and twisting his grip so that the rapier came down at an angle, enabling Thesiger to get under his guard. He made a final thrust for the nobleman's heart, but Julian's reflexes were the quicker and his sword came up to thwart the thrust. He managed to push himself off the wall, and using his superior strength and stronger wrist forced Thesiger back again, Thesiger's sword wide of its mark, the point stabbing the air between Julian's arm and torso.

Unable to halt the momentum of his final lunge, Thesiger stumbled forward, and as Julian leaped out of the way, he fell hard against the wall and then to his knees in the gravel. He scrambled to pick himself up and put out a hand for his rapier that had spun out of his grip. But the Marquis was there, looming large over him. He grabbed Thesiger by the collar of his wet shirt and hauled him to his feet. Righting him, he scooped up Thesiger's sword and this he tossed to him, stepping back and calling *en garde*.

But Thesiger knew he was spent, and that if he put up his sword, Julian would surely kill him in the short encounter to follow. He marveled at the nobleman's reserves of strength and wondered how best to extricate himself from a no-win situation. Wiping the sweat from his eyes, he glanced first at the Marchioness sitting as a marble statue, an unblinking gaze on her husband. He then regarded the large figure of the Marquis of Alston, standing tall, damp black hair falling into his eyes, green eyes ablaze and so resembling those belonging to his mother the Duchess that it brought a sneer full of hatred to Thesiger's lips, the scar puckered and pulsating with heat. He made a half-hearted effort to raise his sword and then did the unthinkable. Tossing his sword at Julian's feet, he rushed towards the stairs leading up to the river.

In two steps he was standing over Deb.

DEB HAD WATCHED the duel as if it were something of a blurred bad dream. When Thesiger's blade flashed up and split the muscle in her husband's arm she muffled a cry behind shaking hands, wanting to put a stop to the encounter there and then. Yet she sat calmly on the step as if she were attending an Assembly Ball, and she watching a couple dancing a minuet. As if it were the most natural thing in the world for Julian to be fighting a duel with this fiend who had sought to destroy her.

When the Marquis finally had the better of his opponent, her sigh of relief was audible and the tension eased in her limbs. Thesiger's last desperate lunge at Julian's heart had her eyes tightly closed for the briefest of moments, only for her to open them wide to discover Julian standing over Thesiger, he prostrate on the ground.

When the man scrambled to his feet then leapt up on the step beside her, she was startled into wondering what he was about, for the duel looked for all the world as if it would end in Thesiger's death. Behind her she heard the cock of her pistol and was about to order the footman to hold his fire when the Marquis shouted out for the servant to lower his weapon. Yet before the footman had a chance to obey the command, Thesiger made a grab for the pistol.

There was a brief, close struggle between the two men.

The pistol discharged.

The shot rang out across the eerily deserted Tuileries.

The footman and Robert Thesiger stood very still and then fell apart. For a brief moment it was unclear which man was shot. Then the footman took a step back, the pistol still in his hand and blood splattered across the front of his liveried uniform. Thesiger turned slowly and came face-to-face with Deb, who had risen to her feet, and his blue eyes were wide and blank. He had both hands to his belly and blood was flowing from between his splayed fingers. He took a step, pitched forward and fell off the stairs.

In three strides Julian was at his side and went down on a knee to cradle the dying man's head. Thesiger's eyes flickered open, and recognizing the blurred frowning face high above him, he grimaced, showing blood-covered teeth.

"Couldn't give you the—the—satisfaction..." he muttered with great effort, expelled a last breath and died.

Julian fetched Thesiger's frock coat and laid it across his upper body, covering his head and torso, before reaching into his own breeches pocket for his handkerchief to bind up his own wound. Deb came down the steps, took the handkerchief from him and did the deed, fingers shaking as she deftly tied a knot in the material to staunch the bleeding. He thanked her, and there followed a moment's awkward silence in which neither was able to form the words to express their feelings. All they could do was stare at one another until Deb fell into her husband's arms to be enveloped in a warm and protective embrace, relief bringing tears and fear of what might have been.

"My darling," Julian finally whispered in her hair, voice low and unsteady, holding her more tightly against him, "what—*hell* have I put you through?"

"We're alive and we have each other. That's all that has ever mattered."

He smiled and cradled her, face buried in her mussed hair, shudders of relief coursing through his exhausted body. The sound of approaching voices made him look up, with a kiss to Deb's bowed head.

Coming along the deserted avenue was his cousin Evelyn Ffolkes and a rag tag bunch of disheveled musicians, two militia on horseback not far behind them, no doubt come to disperse the small crowd gathered to ghoulishly view the dead duelist. Out from behind this gawping group appeared a blue-eyed beauty dressed in a confection of white and lavender petticoats who, having spied the Marquis of Alston, immediately rushed up to him as if her life depended on his protection. Julian stepped forward, not to greet her, but to shield Deb from the prying eyes of the morbid mob. The blue-eyed beauty took his advancement as an invitation to throw herself against his broad chest in a fit of mild hysterics.

"Dominique! Desist with these theatrics at once!" Evelyn Ffolkes called out.

He tottered up to his startled cousin in his red heeled shoes, to pry the beauty from his chest, only for the girl to turn and throw her arms about his neck. He bore her suffocating embrace for ten seconds then demanded in a voice one used with a spoiled child that she release him at once or be responsible for the ruin of a perfectly good Brussels lace cravat and his favorite silk Chinoiserie waistcoat. He had endured enough this afternoon to fill three lifetimes and he wasn't about to add the ruination of his clothes to the list!

"You missed the performance, such as it was, and are extremely fortunate to find me in one piece," Evelyn grumbled, still so overcome with angry annoyance that his first open-air concert had turned into a musical fiasco when it was interrupted by gunfire and then a riot, that he was completely oblivious to the situation at hand—that not twenty feet away lay the covered, bloodied dead body of Robert Thesiger. "If it hadn't been for my quick thinking in overturning our chairs to form a Roman barricade of sorts, I doubt we would've survived our ordeal with the stampeding cattle!"

"Cattle?" The girl's blue eyes opened very wide as she looked about her. "But, Evelyn, there are no cows here, surely?"

"Cattle! Cows! *Canaille*! They are all one and the same! Philistines!" Evelyn argued, setting his wig to rights and shrugging his shoulders in a bad-tempered way.

It was then that out of the corner of his eye he caught sight of the state of the carnage. Two militia were inspecting the lifeless body sprawled out on the gravel, lifting a corner of Thesiger's embroidered frock coat as if needing to verify for certain that the man was indeed dead. More militia on horseback were dispersing a group of onlookers to this macabre scene.

The composer looked swiftly up at his cousin, took in his tousled hair and blood-soiled shirt, saw the makeshift bloodied bandage about his upper arm and drew an audible breath.

"What happened here, Alston?"

"I thought that obvious," Julian stated coldly. "Thesiger attempted to kidnap my wife and child, and now he is dead."

"*Mon Dieu*!" cried the composer and crossed himself, a shaking hand to his mouth. "Is Deborah—is she—safe?"

Deb stepped out from behind her husband then, gown brushed down but irreparably creased, and with her long dark red hair littered with pins and tumbling loosely about her shoulders. She glanced curiously at the blue-eyed beauty clinging possessively to the composer's silken arm and knew her identity at once.

"I am safe, Eve. I used Otto's pistol. I'm afraid that's what started the riot."

Julian viewed his wife anew, eyebrows raised. He was not pleased but was all admiration for her quick-thinking courage.

"Did you indeed. Shoot my pheasants by all means, Madam wife, but no more carrying pistols on your person. Do you hear?" When Deb nodded meekly, but couldn't hide the twinkle in her eye or the dimple in her cheek, Julian put his arm about her shoulders to whisper near her ear, "I shall deal with you in my own way later, vixen."

"*O là là*! So this one, she is Madame la Marquise d'Alston?" the beauty blurted out with something akin to awe. "Evelyn," she said accusingly, "you omitted to tell me how very beautiful she is!"

"It is Dominique, yes? But you prefer to be called Lisette?" Deb asked calmly as the girl dropped a respectful curtsy.

"*Oui*, Mme la Marquise," Lisette Lefebvre answered diffidently, a shy glance up at the Marquis who was staring fixedly at his cousin.

"Well, Cousin, this is your last opportunity to explain yourself," Julian stated coldly. "If not for my sake, then you owe it to my wife to tell her the truth."

Evelyn swallowed and looked from his noble cousin's expression of implacability to Deborah, who was smiling kindly upon him. But before he could offer a word of explanation, Lisette Lefebvre took a deep breath and decided it was time to be brave.

"M'sieur le Marquis, Evelyn you cannot blame for the—the —*predicament* in which you find yourself with the Lieutenant of Police! The blame it rests entirely with me. I had no idea that one little lie, told so long ago, would fester into an even bigger more horrible lie." She glanced at the composer and confessed with guilty downcast eyes, "I was most offended, M'sieur le Marquis, when you ignored me at the Opera, and at the Duc d'Orleans' ball when you would not stand up with me. Which was most cruel of you, so I told a-a lie—"

"Ah! Dominique!" Evelyn burst out in despair. "I told you over and over but you refused to listen! Alston loathes being the center of attention."

"But, Evelyn, that is inconceivable to me. Why would the

son of a duke not want to be the focus of everyone's adoration? It is most natural and expected that a nobleman—"

"Dominique, for God's sake, get on with it before my mother has the Duke send out the militia for me, and then we will never be able to marry," pleaded the composer, a shaking hand to his throbbing temple.

The girl flushed scarlet and continued, a fearful glance up at the handsome nobleman whom she had failed to ensnare with her sweet voice and great beauty.

"When M'sieur le Marquis you would not dance with me, my friend Beatrice she laughed that I should be so cruelly ignored. I was angry at Beatrice for making fun of me so I told her a lie in the strictest confidence, knowing she would tell the other girls: That M'sieur le Marquis you were only feigning to ignore me and that in truth we were lovers."

A groan escaped from the composer and he hung his head.

"Evelyn! If you look at me in that horrid way again I will cry and not be able to go on. I admit I did not see the harm in adding myself to the string of beauties M'sieur le Marquis has seduced. What was one more name when it is rumored—"

"*Rumor*? A rumor has no more substance to it than a meringue, you little fool! Rumor is mere speculative nonsense! It is not fact," Evelyn argued angrily, adding with no regard for the presence of his stony-faced cousin, "If you want fact, my love, then let me disappoint you and all those scheming, doe-eyed creatures who have ever thrown themselves at my cousin's noble chest, by telling you that M'sieur le Marquis is the greatest stiff-necked moralist I have ever met. He would no more tumble into bed with you as willingly step on a dog turd!"

Lisette Lefebvre sniffed back tears and said pettishly, "Evelyn, you are merely envious because these females they did not throw themselves at your chest too! But as I have told you before today, M'sieur le Marquis he is to be a duke one day. Besides, what I said to Beatrice was not so very far from the truth, because you and I we were lovers by the time of the Duc d'Orleans' ball and as M'sieur le Marquis's cousin you—"

"And that makes it acceptable to—"

"Allow Mademoiselle Lefebvre to get on with her story," Julian interrupted coldly.

"Thank you, M'sieur le Marquis," Lisette answered in a small voice, the quarrelling lovers coming to a sense of their surroundings. "When I was telling this little lie to Beatrice, we were sitting in the Duc D'Orleans' beautiful gardens, with Chinese lanterns in all the trees and floating candles on all the ponds, but it was too dark for us to notice that our conversation it was overheard by M'sieur Thesiger, who was in the shadows. Me he must have followed out into the gardens. When Beatrice returned inside, M'sieur Thesiger revealed himself to me and wanted to know if what I said was indeed the truth." Lisette shuddered and appealed to the Marquis with big blue eyes swimming with tears. "You know Robert Thesiger, do you not, M'sieur le Marquis? He wanted to marry me. Many, many times did he ask, and me I said no, no and no! I could not marry a man who boasted of being a bastard son of a Duke! That is a thing most abhorrent to my family. And so I thought if I confirmed the truth of my lie to M'sieur Thesiger he would hate me and leave me in peace."

She glanced at Deb and hung her head, the heat of shame in her cheeks, and continued.

"Robert Thesiger did indeed believe me and he did indeed hate me after that. He told my Papa and it broke my Papa's heart. I did not think such a little lie would turn into one big scandal. After all, what could Papa do against a nobleman? I never dreamed Papa he would lock me away and have his lawyers question me. That horrid Lieutenant of Police he had me sign a paper condemning you, M'sieur le Marquis. I did not want to sign it, but Papa he would not let me out of my rooms until I had done so. And how could Evelyn elope with me if I remained locked away? Please, M'sieur le Marquis, I beg of you, if you cannot forgive me, please forgive Evelyn. Evelyn he loves you like a brother, but he could not tell you the truth until our elopement it was all arranged, and my Papa he was not to find out the truth before we were on our way to Italy. None of this is Evelyn's fault. It is mine entirely!"

She burst into tears and clung to the composer, who took her in a comforting embrace and whispered soothing words in her ear until she took a great shuddering breath and was quiet. A heavy silence followed this confession, broken only when Julian addressed his cousin.

"I gave you ample time and opportunity to make a clean breast of it, and still you hesitated to do the honorable thing and tell the Duke and your mother the truth," he said bitterly. "And, by God, when you finally drummed up the courage to set matters to rights, you left it damnably close! What would it have taken before you claimed responsibility for the consequences of your despicable actions?"

"Julian! I'd never have let you enter that courtroom, my word on it!"

"Your word became worthless the instant you bought into Mademoiselle Lefebvre's lie. If you've a shred of decency left, find a priest and marry her without delay!"

Evelyn glanced pleadingly at Deborah. "I did not mean for this business to drag out as long as it has. It's just that I didn't want Thesiger to know about us until I could safely get Dominique away without him—"

"—challenging you to a duel?" Julian interrupted contemptuously. "Heaven forbid you should risk your precious life for the woman you love!"

Evelyn lowered his gaze, unable to refute his cousin's inference because it was true. He was only too glad it was his cousin and not himself who had fought a duel with Thesiger.

"Dominique and I are eloping to the Italian States," he said quietly. "Who knows when we will see each other again—if the Duke will ever allow me back into the family fold... Julian, you and I, we were once the best of friends, as close as brothers. I need—no I *beg*—your forgiveness."

The Marquis met his cousin's impassioned gaze, features implacable as ever, but it was Deborah's hand in his and the faint scent of perfume in her tumble of hair that softened his features. It made him say on a more conciliatory note,

"Not yet. When you return from your bridal trip—perhaps. That's the best I can offer you."

With that he turned on a heel and walked away to greet two happy laughing boys coming along the avenue. Beside them Joseph, black-eyed and bloodied, but looking none the worse for fighting a bunch of sinister acrobats with his bare hands, and Brigitte, hair mussed and gown crumpled. Both servants looked relieved and pleased to see Deborah and Julian unharmed.

Deborah put out her hands to Evelyn and kissed his cheeks.

"I wish you happy, Eve. I truly do. If you ever return to England, please come and see us. I am sure, given time, Julian will forgive..."

Evelyn embraced her.

"*Ma chérie*, he may forgive but, like his father before him, he will be a most obdurate Duke. But I shall come, if only to visit your brood and to see how Jack progresses with his viola. I expect great things of that boy."

Lisette Lefebvre bobbed another curtsy, and then with Evelyn's hand in hers, they walked off up the avenue, neither one looking back.

THIRTY-SIX

W ITH THE DEPARTING couple disappearing behind a row of abandoned stalls, Deb finally turned away, and to discover the body of Robert Thesiger being loaded onto a cart by a couple of men under the direction of the militia. She averted her gaze and walked over to where Julian had carefully herded Harry and Jack to the other side of the steps, out of the line of sight of such a macabre scene.

Jack and Lord Henri-Antoine were regaling the Marquis with a vivid account of their adventures, considering it a great lark that people had panicked and begun running everywhere at the sound of a single shot. And they had enjoyed themselves immensely, helping to build a barricade of chairs with the musicians from behind which they had front row seats—particularly to the futile attempts of the animal handlers to regain control of their stampeding, squealing and rearing charges. Lord Henri-Antoine magnanimously conceded it was a pity the concert had been interrupted at the precise moment of Jack's solo performance, but both boys exclaimed that never in their wildest imaginings had they dreamed a dull garden concert would turn out to be the best day's entertainment they had ever seen. What did Alston think?

The boys were so bright-eyed and keen for the Marquis to enter into the spirit of their adventures that Julian hadn't the heart to deflate their exuberance with recriminations about his brother's truancy. And he was so relieved both boys were unharmed and unaffected by the day's traumatic events that he merely ruffled their hair with a grin and sent them off with Joseph to await him at the carriage. He then returned to Deb, whom he found sitting on the bottom step of the stairs, with her face in her hands.

He immediately went down on one knee beside her.

"Darling, what is it?"

"'Tis nothing," she replied with a watery smile as she lifted her chin. "Just a thought. I'm sure my condition is making me exceedingly missish."

He frowned. "Thought? You are well? You aren't hurt?"

"No. That is... I don't think so," she said quietly, looking with concern at his unshaven face. "But what if later—What if... Julian, what if the events of this day make me lose this baby?"

"Nonsense!" he said with false bravado.

"But... The exertions of today could bring on the child too early. Then Thesiger, he-he gained his objective..."

Julian sat on the step beside her, pulled her into his embrace and kissed her.

"If, for argument's sake, the baby did not make it to term," he said patiently, entering into the discussion, not because he believed that such a consequence was likely to occur, but to allay her fears, "then it would be a tragic loss to both of us. No one can deny that but... Thesiger can never win because we will always have each other." When she turned her head into his shoulder he lifted her chin to look into her eyes. "Deborah, our being together is not about this child. I admit that before I knew you I was intent on consummating my marriage to provide my father with an heir. But then I met you, and from that moment I wanted our marriage to be first and foremost about us. Since you stumbled upon me in the forest all I've ever cared about is being with you. I want this child as much as you do, but if it is not to be, then we shall both come through the tragedy and try for another. Darling, I hope we have six children, God willing. But more than anything, I want to spend the rest of my life with you and no other."

Deb smiled through her tears. "Then won't you please tell me here, what you told me last night in bed. What I've been waiting to hear you say in the cold daylight since I fell in love with you in the forest?"

He laughed, understanding immediately her request, and went down on one knee beside the stone steps. He took hold of her hands.

"My dear Lady Alston—Deb—My *only* love," he said, as he leaned in to gently kiss one hand and then the other. "I love you. I pledge my love to you and no other. I love you so very much that I intend to go on saying those three little words for the rest of our lives."

EPILOGUE

TREAT: THE ROXTON DUCAL SEAT
HAMPSHIRE, ENGLAND

THE DUCHESS threw down her hand of cards and smiled mischievously at his lordship.

"That is our rubber and, I think, the game, Vallentine. Monseigneur and I, we have beaten you for a third time!"

"When don't you, minx," Lord Vallentine grumbled good-naturedly and slowly rose from the walnut card table to stretch the aching joints in his bony knees. "Damme! I can't take much more of this waiting! They should've been here by now."

"You've been saying the same thing for three days, Lucian. It is most annoying of you," Estée Vallentine complained. "Is it not, Roxton?"

The Duke, who sat in his favorite wingchair by the fireplace, a coverlet over his knees, looked over at his sister.

"Four days, my dear. And yes, annoying in the extreme."

"Two, three or four days! What of it?" Lord Vallentine

demanded, beginning to pace the Duke's private drawing room with its view of the ornamental gardens. He took out his gold pocket watch and stared at the pearl face without noting the time. "Six days and still no word. A man could die from waiting!"

"I do not see at all why it is you who are so put out," argued the Duchess, sweeping up to his lordship in a froth of lace and muslin petticoats to tap a finger on the gold case of his pocket watch. "And this, you look at it to tell you that they will be here in what? An hour, perhaps two?' she teased. "Or does this watch count days as well as hours?"

There was laughter at his lordship's back that caused him to snap shut the pocket watch and shove it in a deep pocket of his saffron yellow frock coat.

"You can all laugh, but I'll be laughing the loudest when I win the wager! Heed my words!"

Antonia's emerald green eyes widened with mock surprise.

"But, Vallentine, I have wagered against you and so it is not possible that you will win. When have I been wrong in this? Renard?"

Lord Vallentine turned on a heel to wag an accusatory finger at the Duke before he could comment.

"I don't need you to tell me m'losses, Your Grace! Nor do I see what the two of you find to laugh at! It's a nerve-wracking business. Tell 'em, Estée!"

"As you did not give birth to our son, I do not see at all why you think you are suddenly an expert," Estée Vallentine lectured. "Furthermore, Lucian, you are making a big fool of yourself. After all, it is not you who are about to become a grandfather."

"Thank you for your wifely support, my dear," Vallentine muttered with annoyance, and eased himself into the wingchair opposite his host. When the Duchess handed him a glass of claret, he eyed her with loving hostility.

"Never will be able to get it into my head you're already

grandmother thrice over, minx." He raised his glass. "Your health!"

Antonia perched herself on the rounded arm of the Duke's chair. "So, Vallentine, you will please stop this nonsense and concede that Julian and Deborah they are to have a daughter."

"And why would I do that?" his lordship asked belligerently. "D'you know for certain the outcome?" When Antonia raised her arched brows, he sat up with a start. "Hey! What's this? You know! Those two rascals, they sent you a letter!"

The Duchess appeared to be offended.

"Monseigneur and I we have not had word from Henri-Antoine and Jack since before Michaelmas. Nor do I expect word until the boys they return here in person. Today, tomorrow or the next day!"

"So why are you so confident you'll win the wager?" his lordship asked silkily. "The odds at White's are fifteen-to-one it'll be a girl; three-to-one for a boy. Those are mighty strong odds, Your Grace. Besides which, you have the family history of boys against you."

Antonia shrugged.

"What of that? I told Deborah that please you will give me a little granddaughter and she said she would do her best, and so the *bébé* she will be a girl, I know it."

Vallentine stared open-mouthed at this explanation, and then fell into such whoops of laughter that he slapped his silken knee and almost spilled his wine. He dried the tears from his eyes with a scrap of lace and shook his powdered head, saying, slightly out of breath,

"Well, that's the best argument I've heard for stickin' to me original wager! What say you, Roxton?"

"My dear Vallentine, in these matters I leave it entirely to those who are most expert."

When the Duchess and Estée Vallentine exchanged a look of triumph, his lordship mumbled something about a female conspiracy, but he had to have a final say.

"You can't tell me, Roxton, that it don't mean a whit to the odds when Alston has already given you three healthy grandsons in as many years. Stands to reason this fourth child will be a boy."

"Lucian, I do wonder at your brain sometimes," his wife sighed impatiently. "Deborah she has given Alston three fine sons, so it is reasonable her fourth little one will be a girl because Antonia she would like a granddaughter."

Vallentine opened his mouth to refute this illogical argument when sounds of arrival in the anteroom closed his mouth and had him on his feet.

All eyes were on the door. There were voices and then the door burst open and in strode two long-legged and travel-worn youths, shoulder to shoulder. Antonia ran up to them and was embraced by both boys. Lord Henri-Antoine then crossed the room to stoop and kiss his father's cheek, then his aunt's, and shook hands with his uncle, Jack shaking hands all round. Henri-Antoine turned to his mother, and this time he kissed her hand and smiled into the light of expectation in her emerald-green eyes.

"All's well with the Alstons, Maman," he assured her. "I have letters and much news. Mother and child are well and the babe is thriving. Deb sends her love and looks forward to visiting you and Papa at the end of the month. The boys can't wait to visit. Jack and I had a devil of a time getting them out of the coach! We had to bribe them, didn't we, Jack?"

Jack grinned. "Frederick says that being *almost* four years of age, he is man enough to own a real pistol. And the twins— well, Louis and Augustus would be satisfied with a whirly top each, but—"

"—Frederick, as their elder brother and leader of the push, demands that we take all three of them fishing on the lake," added Henri-Antoine, a knowing look at his best friend. "Those're our days filled."

A discussion on the exceptional talents of all three Roxton

grandsons was cut off by Lord Vallentine before it had a chance to take hold, startling the butler and two footmen who came into the drawing room carrying a jug of weak ale and trays of food for the two young travelers.

"Hey! You two rascals! That's enough of your blather! Damme," his lordship demanded rudely. "You haven't told us what's important. What's had us pacing the boards this past month or more."

Henri-Antoine and Jack merely blinked at the old man. Accustomed to his eccentricities and knowing all about the wager between his lordship and the Duchess, neither boy could suppress a grin.

"Uncle Vallentine?" Henri-Antoine drawled in surprise, much in the manner of his ancient parent, and as if the answer was self-evident. "Maman requested a granddaughter, and Lady Alston has obliged her with Juliana Antonia."

"But we are to call her Julia," Jack proudly informed them all.

Vallentine stuck out his hand to his wife.

"Estée! I need ten pounds."

~ THE END ~

AUTHOR NOTE

The inspiration for Julian and Deb's unusual marriage came from the real life marriage of Charles Lennox, 2nd Duke of Richmond, and his wife Lady Sarah Cadogan in 1720. The noble couple met for the first time on their wedding day, when Sarah was thirteen and Charles nineteen. Reportedly, Sarah just stared at her future husband when brought out of the nursery for the marriage ceremony, while he, gazing with all the sophistication of his 19 years at the plain 13-year-old, burst out in horror, "Surely they are not going to marry me to that dowdy?"

After the ceremony the young husband set off on the Grand Tour, spending three years on the Continent. Upon his return to London he went to the theater and there spotted a beautiful young woman. When he inquired who she was, he discovered to his surprise and delight she was in fact his wife! The couple went on to have a happy marriage and 12 children. You can read more about the real-life Lennox family in *The Aristocrats* by Stella Tillyard.

Explore the real places, objects, and history on Pinterest:
www.pinterest.com/lucindabrant/falling-series

@ Pinterest

Lucinda Brant Author
lucindabrant
22.6k followers   596 following

Falling Trilogy
Falling OUT: Book 3

Miss Deborah Cavendish

Deb's nephew Jack Cavendish

Henri-Antoine & Jack

Julian's Court court costume

The Forrest of Avon

Hôtel Roxton Drawing Room

Deb's maternity dress

Lady Mary's sedan chair

Viola from 1760

Shopping on Milsom St. Bath

Julian's red heel shoes

Jardin des Tuileries

Deb's flintlock pistol

Martin Ellicott's House

Lady Mary's odd wig

View of Hôtel Roxton

Hôtel Roxton opulence

Deb's riding coat

Midnight Marriage Cover Reveal

FALL BACK

...to where it all began.

www.ingramcontent.com/pod-product-compliance
Lightning Source LLC
Chambersburg PA
CBHW011923190726
48283CB00009BA/2880